Leonardo Padura was born in Havana in 1955 and lives in Cuba. He has published a number of novels, short-story collections and literary essays. International fame came with the Havana Quartet, all featuring Inspector Mario Conde. The Quartet has won a number of literary prizes including the Spanish Premio Hammett. *Havana Fever* also features Mario Conde, now retired from the police force but drawn into a new investigation. The novel has sold widely in Spain, France, Italy and Germany.

HAVANA FEVER

Leonardo Padura

Translated from the Spanish
by Peter Bush

BITTER LEMON PRESS
LONDON

BITTER LEMON PRESS

First published in the United Kingdom in 2009 by
Bitter Lemon Press, 37 Arundel Gardens, London W11 2LW

www.bitterlemonpress.com

First published in Spanish as *La neblina del ayer* by
Tusquets Editores, S.A.,Barcelona, 2005

Bitter Lemon Press gratefully acknowledges the financial
assistance of the Arts Council of England

A CIP record for this book is available from the British
Library ISBN 978–1–904738–36-7

Typeset by Alma Books Limited
Printed and bound by
CPI Group (UK) Ltd, Croydon, CR0 4YY

Contents

Havana Fever

Once more and quite rightly:
for Lucía, with love and …

HAVANA, SUMMER 2003

There is only one vital time to wake up:
and that is now.

Buddha

The future is God's, but the past belongs
to history. God can't have any more
influence on history, but man can still
write and transfigure it.

Just Dion

The A side:

Be gone from me

. . .In your life I'll be the best
from the mists of yesterday
when you've forgotten me,
like the best poem's always
the one we can't remember.

Virgilio y Homero Expósito,
Be gone from me

The symptoms hit him suddenly, like a voracious wave sweeping a child off a quiet shore and dragging him into the depths of the sea: a lethal double blow to the stomach, numbness that turned his legs to jelly, a cold sweat on his palms and, above all, the searing pain, under his left nipple, which accompanied every single hunch he'd ever had.

As soon as the doors to the library slid open, the smell of old paper and hallowed places floating in that mind-blowing room overwhelmed him. In his far-off years as a police detective, Mario Conde had learnt to recognize the physical signs of his situation-saving hunches: he must have been wondering if he'd ever experienced such a powerful flood of sensations.

Initially he was all set to be ruthlessly logical, and tried to persuade himself that it was pure chance he'd come across that shadowy, decaying mansion in El Vedado: an unusual stroke of good fortune for once had deigned to come his way. But a few days later, when corpses old and new stirred in their graves, the Count began to think that no margin for coincidence existed, that it had all been dramatically prepared, like a stage set up for a performance that only his disruptive entrance could trigger.

Ever since he'd left his job as a criminal investigator, more than thirteen years ago, and devoted himself body and soul – at least as much as his battered body and increasingly enfeebled soul allowed – to the dicey business of buying and selling books, the Count had developed an almost canine ability to track down prey that would guarantee, sometimes in surprisingly generous quantities, his supply of food and alcohol. Whether for good or for evil – he couldn't decide which – his departure from the police and forced entry into the world of commerce had coincided with the official declaration that Crisis had hit the island – a galloping Crisis that would soon dwarf all previous versions. The perennial, interminable periods of austerity the Count and his contemporaries had faced for decades now started to seem, in the course of inevitable comparisons and tricks of memory, like days of plenty or nameless mini-crises, with no right to awe-inspiring personification by capital letter.

As if the result of a malevolent wave of a wand, the shortage of everything imaginable quickly became a permanent state, attacking the most disparate of human needs. The value and nature of every object or service was artfully transmuted by insecurity into something different from what it used to be: be it a match or an aspirin, a pair of shoes or an avocado, sex, hopes or dreams. Meanwhile church confessionals and consultancies of voodoo priests, spiritualists, fortune-tellers, mediums and babalaos were crowded with new adepts, panting after a breath of spiritual consolation.

The shortages were so acute they even hit the venerable world of books. Within a year publishing went into freefall, and cobwebs covered the shelves in gloomy bookshops where sales assistants had stolen the last light bulbs with any life, that were next-to useless anyway, in those days of endless blackouts. Hundreds of private libraries ceased to be a source of enlightenment and bibliophilic pride, or a cornucopia of memories of possibly happy times, and swapped the scent of wisdom for the vulgar, acrid stench of a few life-saving banknotes. Priceless libraries created over generations and libraries knocked together by upstarts; libraries specializing in the most profound, unusual themes and libraries made from birthday presents and wedding anniversaries – were all cruelly sacrificed by their owners on the pagan altar of financial necessity suddenly felt by the inhabitants of a country where the shadow of death by starvation threatened almost every home.

That desperate act of offering a few, genuinely or would-be valuable volumes, or putting on sale boxes, yards, shelves, even entire collections assembled over one or more lifetimes, raised conflicting hopes in the dreams of buyers and sellers. The former always claimed they were offering bibliographical jewels and were eager to hear figures that might assuage the guilt the majority suffered when they off-loaded their closest travelling companions on the voyage through life. The latter revived a mercantile spirit they'd thought banned from their island, and tried to make a purchase they could later transform into a killing by arguing that the volumes in question had scant value or commercial potential.

In his early days in this new profession, Mario Conde had tried to turn a deaf ear to the stories behind the libraries that fell into his hands. His years as a detective had forced him to live surrounded by sordid files, but this hadn't made him immune to the sorrows of the soul and, when he got his way and left the police force, he discovered painfully that the dark side of life still pursued him. Every library for sale was a romantic novel with an unhappy ending, the drama of which didn't depend on the quantity or quality of books being sacrificed, but on the paths along which the volumes had reached that particular house and the terrible logic now sending them to be slaughtered in the marketplace. Nevertheless, the Count quickly learnt that listening was an essential part of the business, because the majority of owners felt the need to discuss the reasons behind their decisions, sometimes dolling them up, sometimes stripping them bare, as if that act of confession at least salvaged a shred of their dignity.

Once the scars had healed, Conde began to see the romantic side of his role as a listener – he liked to describe himself as such – and started to weigh up the literary potential in those stories, often taking them on board as material for his ever deferred aesthetic endeavours. As he sharpened his insights, so he felt able to distinguish when a narrator was genuine or a pathetic liar, spinning a yarn in order to be better reconciled with his conscience, or merely to showcase his merchandise.

The more he penetrated the mysteries of his trade, the more Mario Conde realized he preferred the exercise of buying to the subsequent selling of the tomes he acquired. The act of selling books in a doorway, on a park bench, on the bend of a promising pavement, fanned smouldering remains of ravaged pride but above all provoked frustration at having to get rid of an item he'd often have preferred to retain. Consequently, although his earnings plunged, he adopted the strategy of working only as a trawler, replenishing the stocks of other street-sellers. From then on, when prospecting for mines of books, like all his colleagues in the city, the Count employed three complimentary, occasionally conflicting techniques: firstly, the most traditional: visiting someone who'd asked him to pay a call, as a result of his well-established reputation as a fair buyer; then, the embarrassing, almost medieval procedure of hawking – "I buy old books", "I'm the man to take those old books off your hands"; or the most in-your-face, knocking optimistically on doors and asking whoever opened up if they were interested in selling a few well-worn books. The second of those commercial approaches was the most productive in outlying, perpetually impoverished districts that were generally quite unfruitful – though there was the occasional surprise – and where the art of buying and selling the impossible had for years been the survival system for hundreds of thousands of people. On the other hand, the "truffle" method of sniffing out houses was necessary in once aristocratic districts like El Vedado, Miramar and Kohly, and in parts of Santos Suárez, El Casino Deportivo and El Cerro, where people, in the teeth of the poverty spreading across the nation, struggled to preserve increasingly obsolete ways of life.

What was extraordinary was that he'd not chosen that shadowy mansion in El Vedado, with its neo-classical pretensions and debilitated structure, as a result of any odour and much less as a result of his shouting in the street. In fact, Mario Conde was almost convinced he was suffering from a progressive loss of smell, and had already spent three hours on that sultry Cuban September afternoon banging on doors and getting no for an answer, on several occasions because a colleague had passed that way before him. Sweating like a pig, fed up, and fearful of the storm heralded by the rapid accumulation of black clouds on the nearby coast, Conde was preparing to sign off for the day, totting up his losses in the time-wasted column when, for no particular reason, he opted to go down a street parallel to the avenue where he'd thought he'd be able track down a minicab. Had the tree-lined pavement appealed, did he think it was a shortcut or was he simply, quite unawares, responding to a call from fate? When he turned the corner, the decrepit mansion came into view, shuttered, barred and swathed in an air of profound abandonment. His immediate reaction was that someone must have already beaten him to it, because that

16

style of edifice was usually profitable: past grandeurs might include a library of leather-bound volumes; present penury would include hunger and despair, and that formula tended to be a winner for a buyer of second-hand goods. However, despite his bad run over recent weeks, the Count yielded to the almost irrational impulse driving him to open the wrought-iron gate, cross the subsistence plot of banana trees, rickety clumps of maize and rapacious sweet potato lianas and climb the five steps that led to the cool porch. Barely pausing to think, he lifted the greenish bronze knocker on the indestructible black mahogany door, that hadn't seen a coat of varnish since the discovery of penicillin.

"Hello," he greeted the person opening the door, and smiled politely, as etiquette dictated.

The woman, whom Mario Conde tried to place on a scale descending from seventy to sixty, didn't deign to reply and eyed him severely, imagining her "visitor" was quite the opposite: a salesman. She wore a grey housecoat blotched with prehistoric grease stains and her hair was discoloured and flaked with dandruff. Furrowed by pale veins, her skin was almost transparent and her eyes seemed appallingly desolate.

"I'm sorry to bother you . . . I buy and sell second-hand books," he went on, avoiding the word "old", "and was wondering if you might know someone . . ."

This was the golden rule: you madam are never so down and out that you need to sell your library, or your father's – once a doctor with a famous consultancy and a university chair – or your grandfather's, who was perhaps even a government senator if not a veteran from the wars of independence. But you might know of someone?. . .

As if deadened to emotion, the woman showed no sign of surprise at the mission of the man on her doorstep. She stared at him impassively for a few lengthy, expectant moments, and Mario Conde felt himself on a knife-edge: his training told him a huge decision was being reached by the parched brain of that translucent woman, in desperate need of fats and proteins.

"Well," she began, "the fact is I don't . . . I mean, I don't know if in the end . . . My brother and I *had* been thinking . . . Did Dionisio tell you to come?"

Conde glimpsed a ray of hope and tried to relate to the question, but felt he'd been left dangling in the air. Had he perhaps hit his target?

"No . . . who is Dionisio?"

"My brother," the enfeebled woman went on. "We have a library. A very valuable one . . . Do come in . . . Sit down. Wait a moment . . ." and the Count thought he detected a determination in her voice that could see off life's hardest knocks.

She vanished into the mansion, through a kind of portico erected on two Tuscan columns of shiny, green-striated black marble, and the Count regretted the poor state of his knowledge of the now scattered Creole aristocracy, an ignorance that meant he didn't know, couldn't even imagine, who'd originally owned that marmoreal edifice, and whether the present occupants were descendants or mere beneficiaries of a post-revolutionary stampede to safety. That reception room, with its damp patches, missing plaster and cracked walls, looked no better than the outside of the house, but retained an air of solemn elegance and vibrant memories of the huge wealth that had once slept between those now bereft walls. Flanked by dangerously crumbling cornices and faded coloured friezes, the high ceilings must have been the work of master craftsmen, as were the two large windows that preserved remarkably intact romantic stained-glass scenes of chivalry, no doubt designed in Europe and destined to attenuate and colour the strong light from a tropical summer. In eclectic rather than famous styles, and shabby rather than broken, the still sturdy furniture also exuded an odour of decrepitude, while the black-and-white marble tiled floors, patterned like an out-sized chessboard, gleamed cheerfully and looked freshly cleaned. On one side of the reception room, two very high doors mounted with square bevelled mirrors, set in dark wood marquetry, reflected the desolation between flowery quicksilver blotches. It was then that the Count grasped what was behind the oddness he'd experienced on entering the room: there wasn't a single adornment or painting, a single visual prop to break the grim void on walls, tables, shelves or ceilings. He assumed that the noble bone china dinner services, repoussé silver, chandeliers, cut-glass and canvases with dark or elaborate still lives that once brought harmony to that scene, had been sent packing in advance of the books, to address food shortages – a fate that the library, already flagged as a very valuable asset, might similarly meet, if he were in luck.

The moment mentioned by the woman turned into a wait of several minutes which the Count spent smoking, knocking the ash out of the window, through which he saw the first drops of an evening shower. When his hostess returned, an older, more ancient-looking man followed in her wake, in urgent need of a shave and, like his companion, of three square meals a day.

"My brother," she announced.

"Dionisio Ferrero," responded the man in a voice that was younger than his body, as he held out a calloused hand with grimy fingernails.

"Mario Conde. I . . ."

"My sister has already explained," he said in the curt tone of a man used to giving orders, rounding off his remarks with an order rather than a request: "Come this way."

Dionisio Ferrero walked towards the doors with bevelled mirrors and the Count noted that his own appearance, framed in the reflection between the dark stains, was no better than the skeletal Ferreros'. The exhaustion in his face after successive rum-sodden, sleepless nights, and his squalid skinniness gave the impression that his clothes had outgrown his body. Dionisio pushed the doors with unexpected vigour and Conde lost sight of himself and his physiological musings at the same time as he felt a violent searing pain in his chest, because there before his eyes stood a splendid array of glass-doored, wooden bookcases, where hundreds, thousands of dark volumes rested and ascended to the lofty ceiling, the gold letters of their identities still glinting, neither subdued by the island's insidious damp nor exhausted by the passage of time.

Paralysed by that vision, conscious of his breath's halting rhythms, Conde wondered whether he'd have the strength, then ventured three cautious steps forward. When he crossed the threshold, he realized, in state of total shock, that the quantity of shelves packed with volumes extended down every side of the room, covering the roughly thirty-six square yards of wall. It was at that precise moment of more than justifiable emotion and awe, that the tumultuous symptoms of his hunch hit him – a feeling quite distinct from any surprise prompted by books or business, with the power to suggest that something extraordinary was lurking there clamouring for his presence.

"What do you think?"

Paralysed by the physical impact of his hunch, Conde didn't hear Dionisio's question.

"Well, what do you make of it?" the man persisted, standing in the Count's field of vision.

"Simply fantastic," he muttered finally, as his excitement led him to suspect he was most certainly in the presence of an extraordinary vein, one of those you're always seeking and which you find once in a lifetime, if ever. Experience screamed to him that it must hold unimaginable surprises, for if only five per cent of those books turned out to have special worth, he was potentially looking at twenty or thirty bibliographical treasures, able on their own to kill – or at least fend off for a good while – the hunger now torturing the Ferreros and himself.

When he was sure he was fit to make another move, the Count went over to the shelf that was looking him in the eye and, without asking for permission, opened the glass doors. He reviewed at random some of the book spines, and spotted the ruddy leather jacket of Miró Argenter's *Chronicles of the War in Cuba*, in the 1911 *princeps* edition. After wiping the sweat from his hands, he took out the volume and found it was signed and dedicated by the warrior-writer "To my warm friend, my dear General Serafín Montes de Oca". Next to Miró's *Chronicles* lay the two imposing volumes of the much prized *Alphabetical Index of Demises in the Cuban Liberation Army*, by Major-General Carlos Roloff, from its rare 1901 single printing in Havana and, his hands shaking even more violently, Conde dared remove from the adjacent space the volumes of the *Notes Towards the History of Letters and Public Education on the Island of Cuba*, the classic by Antonio Bachiller y Morales, published in Havana between 1859 and 1861. Conde's finger caressed even more lingeringly the lightweight spine of *The Coffee Plantation*, Domingo Malpica de la Barca's novel, published by the Havana printers Los Niños Huérfanos in 1890, and the pleasantly muscular, soft leather covers of the five volumes of José Antonio Saco's *History of Slavery*, in the 1936 edition from the Alfa printing house, until, like a man possessed, he fished out the next book. The spine was

20

only engraved with the initials C.V., and opening it he felt his legs give way, for it really was a first edition of *The Young Woman with the Golden Arrow*, Cirilo Villaverde's novel, in that first, mythical edition printed by the famous Oliva print shop, in 1842 . . .

Conde felt that space was like a sanctuary lost in time, and for the first time wondered whether he wasn't committing an act of profanation. He gingerly returned each book to its respective place and inhaled the lovely scent emanating from the open bookcase. He took several deep breaths until he'd filled his lungs, and shut the doors only when he felt inebriated. He tried to hide his discomfort as he turned to the Ferreros, whose faces now burned with a flame of hope, that was determined to triumph over the only too conspicuous disasters life brings.

"Why do you want to sell these books?" he asked, against all his principles, already seeking out a path to the history of that exceptional library. Nobody consciously, so abruptly, got rid of treasure like that, (and he'd only glimpsed the first promising jewels), unless there was some other reason, apart from hunger, and the Count felt an urgent need to know what that might be.

"It's a long story and . . ." Dionisio hesitated for the first time since he'd encountered the Count, but immediately recovered an almost martial aplomb. "We still aren't sure we want to sell. That will depend on the offer you make. There are lots of bandits in the antiques trade as you well know . . . The other day two paid us a visit. They wanted to buy our stained-glass windows and the cheeky bastards offered three hundred dollars for each . . . They think one is either mad or starving to death . . ."

"Of course, lots of people are on the make. But I'd like to know why you've decided to sell the books *now* . . ."

Dionisio looked at his sister, as if he didn't understand: how could the fellow be stupid enough to ask such a question? The Count cottoned on and, smiling, tried to refocus his curiosity for a third time.

"Why did you wait *until now* to decide to sell them?"

The transparent woman, perhaps stirred by the urgency of her hunger, was the one who rushed to reply.

"It's Mummy. Our Mother," she explained. "She agreed to look after these books years ago . . ."

The Count felt he was treading on typically swampy ground, but with no choice but to press on.

"And your Mother?. . ."

"She's still alive. She'll be ninety-one this year. And the poor thing is . . ."

Conde didn't dare keep on: the first part of the confession was on its way and he waited in silence. The rest would come of its own accord.

"The old girl's past it . . . she's been a bundle of nerves for a long time. And the fact is we need some money," spat Dionisio waving at the books. "You know what things are like these days, the pension goes nowhere . . ."

Conde nodded: yes, he did know about that. His eyes followed the man's hand towards the shelves crammed with books and he felt the hunch that he was on the verge of something big, still there, rudely pricking him under the nipple, making his hands sweat. He wondered why it hadn't gone away. He knew he was surrounded by valuable books, so why should the alarm-call still sound so loudly? Could it be there was a book that was *too* much to hope for? That must be it, he told himself, and if that were true it would only stop when he'd inspected every shelf from top to bottom.

"I've no wish to pry, but . . . But when was the last time anyone touched this library?" he asked.

"Forty . . . Forty-three years ago," the woman answered and the Count shook his head incredulously.

"Hasn't a single book left here in all that time?"

"Not one," interjected Dionisio, confident he was upping the value of the library's contents by making such a statement. "Mummy asked us to air it once a month and clean it with a feather duster, just along the tops . . ."

"Look, I'll be frank with you," Mario Conde decided to issue a warning, aware he was about to betray the most hallowed rules of his profession: "I have a hunch, in a manner of speaking. I'm quite sure there are books here worth lots of money, and others so valuable that they can't or shouldn't be sold . . . If I might explain myself: there could be books, particularly Cuban books, that shouldn't leave Cuba and almost nobody in Cuba has the money to pay out what they're really worth. The National Library, for a start. And what I'm telling you now goes against my own business interests, but I believe it would be a crime to sell them to a foreigner who'd only take them out of the country . . . and I say a crime because it would be more than unforgivable, it would be a felony, and that's the least of it. If we can agree terms, we can do business with the saleable books, and if you then decide to sell the more valuable books, I'll get out of your way and . . ."

Dionisio stared at the Count with unexpected intensity.

"What did you say your name was? . . ."

"Mario Conde."

"Mario Conde," he chewed on the name slowly, as if extracting from the letters an injection of dignity his blood sorely needed. "Standing where you can see us now, my sister and I have really run ourselves into the ground over this country, in a big way. I risked my life here and even in Africa. And although I'm starving to death I won't do anything like that . . . Not for a thousand or ten thousand pesos," and he turned to look at his sister, as if seeking out a last refuge for his pride. "Will we, Amalia?"

"Of course we won't, Dionisio," she assured him.

"I'm glad that we understand each other," nodded the Count, moved by the naivety of the heroic Dionisio, who thought in pesos, whilst he calculated similar figures, but in dollars. "Let's do it this way. I'll choose twenty to thirty books that will sell well, although they're not particularly valuable. I'll separate them out now and come for them tomorrow with the money. After that I'd like to check the whole library, so I can tell you what I'd be interested in taking, what books would interest no buyer, and which books can't, or rather shouldn't, be sold, right? But first I'd like to hear the whole story, if you don't mind, that is . . . I'm sorry to insist, but a library that has books like those I've just fished out and that's been untouched for forty-three years . . ."

Dionisio Ferrero looked at his sister, and the colourless woman stared back at him, nibbling the skin on her fingers. Then she swung her head round towards the Count: "Which one? The story behind the library or the one explaining why we're selling now?"

"Isn't it the same one, with a beginning and an end?"

"When the Montes de Ocas left Cuba, Mummy and I stayed on in this house, one of the most elegant in El Vedado . . . as you can still see, after all this time. Mr Alcides Montes de Oca, who had initially supported the Revolution, realized that things were going to change more than he'd bargained for and in September 1969, when they started taking over US companies, he headed north with just his two children, as his wife had died four or five years earlier, in 1956, and he hadn't remarried. Although business hadn't gone well under Batista, Mr Alcides still had lots and lots of money; his own, and what he'd inherited from his deceased wife, Alba Margarita, who was a Méndez-Figueredo, the family that owned two sugar mills in Las Villas among countless other things . . . And it was then he suggested to Mummy and me that we could go with him, if we wished. Just imagine, Mummy was his right arm in all his business affairs and on top of that had been like a sister to him as well. She'd even been born in this household; that is, in the house the Montes de Ocas owned in El Cerro before they built this one, because Mummy was born in 1912 and this house was finished in 1922, after the war, which was when the Montes de Ocas were at their wealthiest. That was why they could afford to ship marble from Italy and Belgium, tiles from Coimbra, wood from Honduras, steel from Chicago, curtains from England, glass from Venice and interior designers from Paris . . . At the time my grandparents were gardener and laundry woman to the Montes de Oca family, and as Mummy had been born in the house she was brought up almost as a member of the family, as I said, like a sister to Mr Alcides, and that's how Mummy was able to study and even get her finishing certificate. But when she was about to enter Teacher Training College she made up her mind to stop studying and asked Mrs Ana, the wife of Don Tomás and Mr Alcides' mother, if they'd let her work in the house as housekeeper or administrator, because she fancied being here, surrounded by beautiful, pristine, expensive things rather than life as a school teacher in a state school struggling with snotty-nosed children for a hundred pesos a month. That was when Mummy was nineteen or twenty, and by that time the Montes de Ocas weren't as rich, because they lost a lot of money in the 1929 Depression and because Don Serafín, who'd fought in the War of Independence, and his son Don Tomás, a renowned lawyer, refused to play along with Machado, who was a dictator by then. Machado and his people made their lives impossible, and ruined lots of their business operations, just as Batista did with Mr Alcides, although before Batista's coup d'état Mr Alcides had made a fortune in deals he made during the Great War, so it didn't matter so much if he didn't get a share in that degenerate's big handouts . . . Ah, but I'm losing my thread as usual . . . Well, the truth is that Mummy helped Mr Alcides an awful lot. She dealt with all his papers, accounts, income tax declarations, was his private secretary, and when his wife, Mrs Alba Margarita, died, Mummy also took responsibility for their children. Consequently, when Mr Alcides decided to leave, he suggested to Mummy that we should go with him, but she wanted time to think it over. She wasn't immediately sure if we should go or stay, because Dionisio, who'd joined the clandestine movement to overthrow Batista when very young, and was a hundred per cent behind the Revolution, had gone to educate the illiterate in the hills of Oriente, and Mummy didn't want to abandon him. How old were you, Dionisio? Twenty-four? But by the same token Mummy didn't want to be separated from Jorgito and Anita, Mr Alcides' children; she'd practically brought them up and she knew that Mr Alcides would really need her when he started up other businesses in the US. It was a tremendous dilemma. Mr Alcides told her to take her time and that when she'd made her mind up, the doors to his house, whatever it was like and wherever it was, would always be open to us, and we could join him whenever we wanted. If we stayed in Cuba, we could live here and he only asked one favour: to look after the house, particularly the library and the two Sèvres porcelain vases his grandmother, Doña Marina Azcárate, had bought in Paris, as he couldn't take them, although he was always one who thought the Revolution would be short-lived and when it collapsed he'd be able to return to his possessions and business here. And if it didn't and we didn't leave, he asked the same favours of us, until he, his son Jorgito or daughter Anita could fetch the books and vases and they would be reunited with the family. Naturally, Mummy promised that if he stayed in Miami, Mr Alcides could be sure that when he returned everything would be in place, that was her pledge, and it was a sacred commitment as far as she was concerned . . .

"I've never been able to find out what Mummy's real intentions were, if she'd already decided to stay or was only marking time to see what happened to Dionisio here or to Mr Alcides when he established himself over there. I asked her two or three times and she always gave me the same answer: her mind was a fog, she wanted more time, and it was a very big decision . . . But a woman like her must have known, however thick the fog in her head. The crunch came seven months later, in March 1961, when Mr Alcides, driving while utterly drunk, had an accident and killed himself. The news reached us a week later. When Mummy – who was already quite depressed – put the phone down, she locked herself in her room for a week, didn't come out or let anyone go in, and when she did finally open the door to me, I found a different woman: she wasn't the Mummy we knew, and we saw how her grief and feelings of guilt at not leaving with Mr Alcides had unbalanced her mind.

"I think it was then that I understood exactly what the Montes de Ocas meant to her, apart from her working for Don Alcides and feeling so important at the side of that powerful man who no longer existed. After all those years she couldn't imagine Don Alcides wasn't on this island to give her orders and ask her advice . . . Poor Mummy had organized her whole life around that man and had lost out totally. She shut herself up in her room and turned into a fossil, because if she'd once thought of leaving with Mr Alcides, and of helping him with his children and business, that now made no sense, because Jorgito and Anita were living with their Aunt Eva, who'd also left Cuba, and Mr Alcides had taken his promise that we would be welcome in his house to the grave . . . While she closeted herself in her room, and brooded over her sorrow and confusion, Dionisio and I tried to start out in life. Just imagine, I was twenty-one and had begun working in a bank. I became a member of the Women's Federation, then a militia woman. Dionisio joined the army when he returned from the literacy campaign, was soon promoted to sergeant, and we both began to live, well, differently, on our own account, for ourselves, not thinking about the Montes de Ocas or depending on them, as our family had for almost a century, as my mother had ever since she could remember . . . Although Dionisio may not agree, this was self-delusion, because the ghosts of the Montes de Ocas were still alive in this house: my mother's sickening isolation finally turned into madness; the china, library, Sèvres vases, furniture, lots of decorations and two or three of the paintings Mr Alcides decided not to take, stayed in place here, waiting for a Mr Alcides, who'd now never return, and then for his children, who never came or took the slightest interest in what they'd abandoned. I entered into correspondence for several years with Miss Eva, who'd gone to live in New Jersey, if I remember rightly, to a town or city called Rutherford, and kept in contact, though it was only one or two letters a year. But Miss Eva moved house around 1968, a couple of my letters were returned to sender stamped 'addressee unknown', and we had no news of them for years. I began to fear the worst. I wrote to other people who lived over there, hoping they might perhaps know where the Montes de Ocas were, but we had no news of them for ten years, until a friend of the family visited Cuba and we finally found out that they'd gone to live in San Francisco and that Miss Eva had died of cancer three or four years earlier. But the children were still alive and, out of respect for Mummy's pledge, I waited and waited in case they expressed an interest in the vases and books, and decided to keep them just so. The oldest books almost all belonged to Don Serafín, Mr Tomás's father, who also bought a lot, because he was a very educated man, a solicitor and law professor at the. Like his father, he used to buy every book that appealed to him, never worrying about the price, and he'd only ever give his friends and grandchildren books as birthday presents. The Sèvres vases had belonged to the family since the nineteenth century, when the Azcárates and Montes de Ocas of old had been exiled in France, whilst they waited for the war against Spain to resume. Those books and vases, like the house itself, were the real history of the family, and as Mummy felt she was a Montes de Oca, because they'd always treated her as such, it all had a sentimental value for her and we had to respect her pledge . . . although the fact is nothing remained of the Montes de Ocas, nobody remembered them, and that library and those vases were their only connection with the past and this country . . . But the years went by and the books and vases lingered on. As I earned a good wage and Dionisio always gave me money for Mummy, we were comfortably off and

I never thought of selling anything, because we never went short. But things took a real turn for the worse in 1990 and 1991. To cap it all Dionisio had a heart attack, was demobbed from the army and then separated from his wife. Although the year he was demobbed Dionisio started to work on the same wage for a company that supplied the army, what we both earned soon went nowhere, because there was no food and you had to be as wealthy as the Montes de Ocas to buy any food that did appear. To make matters worse, Dionisio left that company and started eating lunch and dinner at home. I'm not ashamed to say this, because you must certainly have experienced something similar: it got so bad that some nights my brother and I went to bed on a glass of sugared water, and an infusion of orange or mint leaves, because we gave the little real food we had to Mummy, and sometimes there wasn't even enough for her . . . It was then I decided to do something with the decorations, paintings, vases and books – the only things of any value we had. I swear it was a matter of life or death. Even so I stalled for months until I decided that we were going to starve to death from lack of food if we carried on like that; you only had to see how skinny Dionisio was, who, after being a major and leading men in the war in Angola, was now forced to plant bananas and yuccas in our patio and get himself a job as a night watchman to earn a few extra pesos . . . One day we stopped debating and started to sell what was left of the dinner services, then the decorations and paintings, which were nothing special, although we practically had to give them away, because we couldn't find anybody who'd pay us what they were supposedly worth. Then we sold a few pieces of furniture, some lamps, and got a decent amount for them, believe me, but it ran through our fingers like water and four years ago we finally decided to sell the Sèvres vases to an upstanding Frenchman living in Cuba who does business with the government. He paid us well for the vases, just imagine, they were this high and hand-painted, and that saw us through up to now. Those vases saved our lives . . . But after so many years, and at present prices . . . Dionisio and I have been thinking for some time that we should sell the books. I mean, Dionisio started thinking that way, because I'd made my mind up long ago. Whenever I went to dust the library I'd always ask myself what did it matter if nobody read them and nobody was ever going to reclaim them . . . Besides, I'd always felt resentful towards those books, not the books themselves, but what they represent and represented: they are the living spirit of the Montes de Ocas, a reminder of what they and others of their type were like, the people who thought they owned the country, I find it upsetting just to go into the library, it's a place I feel rejecting me, and one in turn rejects it . . . So, that's the story. I know there are people who aren't having such a bad time as they did five or ten years ago, that there are even people who live very well, but you just add it up: on two pensions and with no one to send us dollars, we're still in the same plight, if not worse. In the end, life itself made it easier for us: we don't have any alternative now and my brother understands . . . we either sell the books or gradually starve to death, poor Mummy included, who luckily is completely detached from reality, because I expect she'd forgive us for selling everything else, but if she ever realized what we intend to do with the Montes de Ocas' library, I think she'd have it in her to kill us both and then starve to death . . ."

The Count swallowed Amalia's torrent of words sitting on the edge of their threadbare sofa, smoking and using his hand as an ashtray, until Dionisio returned with a chipped, gold-edged dessert dish which he apologetically handed to the smoker. But Dionisio's actions went unnoticed by the Count, entranced by that chronicle of irrational loyalty. His emotions hadn't, however, entirely stifled his critical powers: the automatic alarm developed by his time in the police was alerting him to the fact that it was only part of the story, perhaps the most pleasant or dramatic part, though for the time being he had to go along with what he'd heard.

"Well, if you've made your minds up . . . I'll come back tomorrow . . ."

"Won't you take any books now?" Amalia almost implored.

"I'm really not carrying enough money on me . . ."

Amalia looked at her brother and took the initiative: "Look, we can see you are a decent, honest fellow . . ."

"It's years since I've heard that phrase," the Count responded. "A decent, honest . . ."

"Yes, we can tell," the translucent woman assured him. "Can you imagine the number of bandits we've had to deal with to sell the vases and other adornments? And how often they offered a pittance for things that were really valuable? Look, just make us an offer, take a few books and . . . pay us what you can. How about it? You can come back, draw up whatever inventory you want and take the books you then decide to buy . . ."

Conde noticed that while Amalia was talking, Dionisio reacted almost defensively as if he wanted to shield himself from the words he was hearing. He discreetly averted his gaze in the direction of the library, whose mirrored doors remained open, as if inviting him to walk in and help himself to the royal banquet spread out there.

"I've got five hundred pesos on me . . . Four hundred and ninety, to be exact. If I'm going to take a few books with me now I'll need ten for a minicab."

"That will do . . ." she replied, unable to rein in her eagerness.

Conde preferred to walk into the library rather than return Amalia's look, let alone Dionisio's. Able to obliterate the remnants of pride and an old pledge, their despair was the last scrap of dignity to be destroyed by the calamities that had destroyed those lives. Yet again, he regretted the sordid side of his trade, but soon found relief from remorse in his quest for books that would easily sell on the market. Two volumes of population censuses prior to 1940 that an Italian was after, a client of his partner Yoyi Pigeon, were the first he put aside. He then picked out three first editions of works by Fernando Ortiz – that were always easy to place with readers keen on rumbling the mysteries of the world of Afro-Cubans; a first edition of *The Slave-trader*, by Lino Novás Calvo; and, after putting to one side several books printed in the nineteenth century whose value he needed to check out, he bagged several historical monographs published in Havana, Madrid and Barcelona in the twenties and thirties, that didn't have tremendous bibliographical value, but were coveted by the non-Cuban buyers who flitted from one second-hand bookseller's stall to another. He was about to shut his bag and tot up the total, when he saw before his eyes a book that practically screamed at him: it was an intact, sturdy, healthy, well-nourished copy of *My Pleasure?* with the secondary title of *An indispensable . . . culinary guide*, printed by Úcar y García in 1956, and illustrated by the great cartoonist, Conrado Massaguer. Ever since that remote afternoon when the Count had seen that book for the first time in the hands of a nouveau riche owner of several of those private restaurants that sprang up in the first days of dire shortages, as a compulsive buyer of gastronomic literature, he'd tried to track it down, thrilled by its wonderful recipes for Creole and international cuisine, compiled to satisfy the most aristocratic kitchens in an era when aristocratic kitchens still existed in Cuba. However, the Count's persistent search wasn't driven by bibliophilic or even commercial goals, but the grandiose, self-interested idea that he might present that wonder to old Josefina, the only person the Count knew with a magical ability to conjure up miracles – even in times of Crisis – and convert those dream dishes into edible realities.

With his bag of books over his shoulder and his stomach gurgling in joyful anticipation, Mario Conde returned to the reception room, where the Ferreros awaited him looking grave and anxious. He only then noticed how the fingers of Amalia, who was at that moment wiping the sweat from her hands, were atrophied and sore around the cuticle edges, like frog toes, no doubt because of her compulsive need to nibble her nails and the skin surrounding them.

"All right, I'll take these sixteen books. There's only one that's special, the one on Cuban cooking, though it doesn't have a high market value . . . I want it for myself. How about five hundred pesos for the lot?. . ."

Dionisio looked at his sister and they stared at each other. They both slowly turned to the Count who rather uneasily anticipated possible recriminations: 'You don't think it's enough?'

"No," Dionisio immediately replied. 'No . . . not at all. I mean, it's very fair.'

Conde smiled with relief.

"It's not very much, but it's fair. That price includes my earnings, and the bookseller's, after he's paid the space he rents and taxes . . . You get about thirty per cent of any final price tag. That's how we work out the earnings from books that sell easily, a three-way split."

31

"So little?" Amalia couldn't repress that complaint.

"It's not so little if you're convinced I'm not going to swindle you. I'm a decent fellow and, if we don't fall out, I will buy lots of books from you at a good price." He smiled, assuming he'd dealt with that quibble, and, before brother and sister could do their sums differently, he handed over the agreed amount.

When he walked out into the street, he was hit in the face by the afternoon humidity the sun had whipped up: a short-lived shower that had stood in for the anticipated storm had merely increased the mugginess of the air. The Count immediately noticed the contrast in temperature: the Ferreros' house, once the property of the filthy-rich Montes de Ocas, could cope with a Havana summer and for a moment he felt tempted to go back and take a second look at the cool mansion, but an intuition warned him against looking back. If he had, he'd most certainly have been astonished to see a Ferrero running out of the house to the nearest market, trying to arrive before five o'clock when they closed the meat, vegetable and grocery stalls that might spare them for once the obligatory diet of rice and black beans they shared with several million compatriots. But as he walked off in search of a road where he might flag down a passing mini-cab, Mario Conde noted that, although some symptoms had slackened off, his hunch was still alive and kicking, clinging to the skin of his left nipple like a bloodthirsty leech.

Yoyi Pigeon, who'd been civically registered and Catholically baptized with the resonant name of Jorge Reutilio Casamayor Riquelmes, was twenty-eight years old, slightly swollen-chested – hence his pigeonnish nickname – and had an irrepressible propensity for verbal wit. He was moreover a man who thought on his feet and was quick and efficient at complex calculations, as endorsed by the academic diploma in civil engineering, framed in a soberly elegant, wrought bronze frame, that hung on the wall of his living room in Víbora Park. He was patiently waiting, said the engineering laureate, for toilet paper to go into short supply so he could adapt the crackling piece of university parchment to such use, given it had brought him little success and no economic advantage. Although the Count was twenty years his senior, he recognized, with a touch of envy, that Yoyi possessed a cynicism and practical knowledge of life he had never and clearly would never possess, even though those qualities were increasingly necessary for survival in the jungle of Creole life in the third millennium.

Ever since the Count had become one of Pigeon's suppliers three or four years ago, his earnings from buying and selling second-hand books had rocketed most pleasingly. Out of his many business ventures – the purchase of jewels and antiques, works of art, two cars now ready for hire and the ownership of twenty-five per cent of the shares in a small, entirely illegal building firm – Yoyi's only official connection with the authorities was his licence to set up a stall for the sale of books in the plaza de Armas, which was in fact supervised by a maternal uncle he visited a couple of times a week in order to supply new goods and control the commercial well-being of the business that served him as a front. The Count had finally concluded that the young man's innate ability to trade, sell at a good price and cajole potential customers – who, according to his principles, you always tried to rip off – must be the result of a genetic legacy from his general-store-owning Spanish grandfather to whom he also owed the name of Reutilio, for the boy had grown up in a country where scarcity and shortages had banished the art of making a good sale several decades ago. People sold and bought from necessity; while some sold what they could, others bought what their bottomless pockets allowed, with no stock exchange complications and, in particular, without the stress that choice entailed: take it or leave it, it's this or nothing, hurry up or it will be gone, buy what's there although right now you don't need it . . . But not Yoyi Pigeon. He was a consummate artist, able to place luxury items at unbelievable prices, and the Count bet that even if he realized his dream of leaving the island – to go anywhere, Madagascar included – he'd end up a successful entrepreneur.

When they met, Conde felt he was reluctantly rejecting the youth because of his appearance, his love of the jewels he displayed on his hands and neck and his relentless cultivation of his own body. Nevertheless, the relationship between the two, born of purely commercial motives, had successfully surmounted the iron barrier of the Count's prejudices and started to turn into friendship, perhaps because their complementary qualities balanced out any

33

apparent shortcomings. The young man's pitilessly mercantile vision and the Count's outdated romanticism, the former's rash impetuosity and the latter's scrupulous calm, Pigeon's occasionally unthinking outspokenness and the Count's guile forged by years in the police gave them a strange equilibrium.

Their friendship had been definitively cemented one afternoon three years ago when the Count called in at his partner's house on the pretext that he had to tell him he'd be bringing a load of books the day after, although what he really wanted was a cup of the excellent coffee the lad's mother used to make. But that afternoon, Conde's presence had saved him – at the very least – from a scam that was proceeding undetected by Pigeon's beady eyes.

Conde had arrived at Yoyi's just as the latter, dazzled by a job-lot of jewels offered at an unbelievably reasonable price by two characters who'd come recommended by a jeweller, was about to fetch from his bedroom the 2,200 dollars they'd agreed as an overall amount. When he arrived, Conde had greeted Yoyi and the jewel-sellers and discreetly made for the lobby, driven by a hunch that not everything was as it should be. He'd squeezed his memory hard and prised out an image of one of the would-be sellers, implicated years ago in a case of violent robbery. He immediately concluded the deal was fraudulent: either the jewels came from a robbery that had yet to be rumbled or, more dangerously, were simply a ploy to strip Yoyi of his money. Conde had no time to intervene and abort that operation, so he made his way along the passage down the side of the house to the backyard where he picked up a piece of iron piping which he flourished like a baseball bat. He retraced his steps and by the time he'd reached the living room, the scene had reached climax point: one of the sellers was threatening Yoyi with a huge knife, and demanding the money, while the other collected up the jewels. Almost without thinking Conde brought the pipe down on the rib cage of the armed man, who dropped his knife and fell to his knees in front of Yoyi, who kicked him in the jaw and sent him flying on his back. Seeing all this happening, the other thief grabbed the jewels as best he could and ran between Yoyi and Conde to get to the street before the ex-policeman struck again with his makeshift weapon. Feeling his body shaking after he'd acted so violently, Conde handed the iron pipe to Yoyi, kicked the

34

knife away, and flopped down on the sofa, beseeching the young man: "Don't hit him again. Let him be. Don't complicate life . . ."

But this afternoon, as on other lucky ones, Yoyi smiled contentedly when he saw his partner approaching with a bag of books. After asking his mother to prepare the indispensable cups of coffee, Yoyi followed the Count onto the terrace, where several pots of ferns and *malangas* fought for space, favoured as they were by the protective shade of the fruit trees growing in the next-door yard. The Count emptied his bag on the table and told Pigeon that this little consignment was only a very light hors d'oeuvre compared to the banquet of books he'd just discovered. The young lad listened to him as impatiently as ever, caressing the jutting keel of his sternum.

"I swear, my partner's a silly bastard," he finally commented. "How the hell could you tell those famished creatures there are books you can't sell? What got into you, Conde?"

"I felt sorry for them. They're starving to death . . . And because you know I won't do that kind of . . ."

"Yes, you only have to take one look at you . . . Look at your shirt, man, it's about to fall apart. You could make money hand over fist but of course you have to bleat on about books you can't sell . . ."

"That's my problem," Conde tried to cut that conversation dead.

"Of course," agreed Pigeon, shaking his left hand, where two gold bracelets entwined. "What's the game-plan?"

"I agreed I'd call back at their place with more money and make an inventory of what they've got and take off another batch. So you pay me for this lot and advance me some money to buy more."

Asking no questions, with a business confidence he reserved solely for the Count, the lad put a hand in his pocket and took out a sheaf of notes that made the other turn pale. He used his impressively nimble fingers to count the bits of paper at a speed the Count's addition skills couldn't match.

'Here's a thousand, that's yours, and three thousand more to start the negotiations. Fair dues."

"If I flash all this at them all, it'll frighten them to death." He recalled Dionisio Ferrero's greedy eyes and his translucent sister's worm-eaten fingers grasping the money he'd given them. "Remember the two censuses will fetch a really good price."

'When I've sold them to Giovanni, I'll settle with you. That Italian bastard's got a thing about censuses. I'll take twenty-five greenbacks off him for each . . . And they're as good as new. You see what things are like? Just a couple of censuses bring in thirteen hundred pesos, because I've got the right customer lined up. Get me? If you really bring me good books, I'll make you rich, man, I swear . . ."

Pigeon smiled and waved contentedly at Conde. He went into the kitchen and returned with two cups of steaming coffee and a bottle of vintage rum, along with two small cut-glass tumblers, separated by a sheet of very fine sandpaper.

"Start cleaning the books," he instructed the Count giving him the sandpaper.

While savouring his coffee and watching with relish as Pigeon poured out the rum, Conde cut the sandpaper in half to make his job easier and pulled the heap of books towards him.

"What about that one?" asked Pigeon, pointing his glass of rum at the volume half hidden under his bag.

"It's a present for Skinny's mother. It's a cookbook I've been after for a while."

The youth swigged his rum and smiled again.

"A cookbook? To cook what? Hey, man, you and your friends are incredible: Skinny, Rabbit, black Candito who's crazy about Jehova and all that jazz . . . Fuck, they're like a bunch of men from Mars, I swear. I look at them and wonder what the fuck they stuffed in their heads to make them like that . . ."

Conde took a swig and lit up. He took one of the books and started sandpapering gently along the top edge, to remove any traces of damp or specks of dust.

"They made us believe we were all equal and that the world would be a better place. That it was already better . . ."

"They fooled you, I swear. Everywhere you go some people are less equal than others and the world is going to the dogs. Right here, if you don't have any green'uns you're out of the running, and there are people getting rich, and not exactly on the straight and narrow . . ."

Conde nodded, his eyes wandering dreamily in between the trees in the yard.

"It was nice while it lasted."

"That's why you're all so fucked now: too long spent dreaming. What the hell was the point of it all?"

Conde smiled, put the sandpapered book to one side and selected another. He recalled that Yoyi was an avid reader of the sports pages of the dailies, which always went on about winners and losers, the only valid division, he reckoned, for the Earth's inhabitants.

"So you think we wasted our time and there's no way out?"

"You wasted your time and half your lives, but there is a way out, Conde: the one you take on behalf of yourself, the people around you, your family and friends. And this isn't pure selfishness: with this business of mine, not stepping out of my house, sleeping at midday with air-conditioning, and stealing from no one, I earn more money than if I worked for a whole month as an engineer, getting up at six and struggling onto the bus (if the damned bus actually came), eating the slops on offer in the works canteen and putting up with a boss set on clearing up at the expense of everyone else, hoping he'll get a job that will take him abroad . . . and to score points he makes everyone's life a misery harping on about coming top of the league, voluntary work and production targets. The name of the game is clear enough, man."

"You may be right," allowed the Count, who was perfectly aware of the reality sketched by Pigeon, and blew along the top of the book, signalling he'd cleaned it up.

"The thing is you were a policeman so you believe what's legal is right. But if people didn't do business on the sly and wheel and deal, how would they survive? That's why even God and his next-door neighbour thieve here . . . And some, as you know, are dab hands at it."

"Yoyi, I left the police more than ten years ago, but I've always known how people lived . . . It's more likely I'm going soft inside because I'm getting old," Conde picked up the first edition of *The Slave Trader* and put it to one side; he needed to attend to the stitching on the spine. He reached for the next one on the pile, one of the censuses, and started sandpapering gently.

"Well, factor that in . . . you are knocking on," agreed Pigeon with a smile. "And old age slows you down. OK, I'm going to have a bath, I'm going out on the town tonight with a hot date. Hey, you want me to come with you tomorrow to give that place a look over?"

Conde put the book on the table and gulped down his rum. He thought his answer through.

"All right. There are a lot of books and the two of us can size it up much quicker . . . But get this straight: I found this library, and if you come, I'm the one in charge, get it? I don't want you double-dealing these poor people . . ."

"Ah, these poor people, is it?" Pigeon stripped off his T-shirt and the Count stared at the thick gold links of the chain, with an enormous medallion of Santa Bárbara, resting on the young lad's prominent pecs. "Wasn't the guy a big deal in the army and then in a corporation? Did they tell you why they booted him out and put him on the shit-heap? You really think they're 'poor people'? . . . Fine, you're calling the shots. I'll swear to that, man."

"I'll call you in the morning before I leave home," the Count stood up, a second cigarette between his lips.

"Say, Conde, what will you do with that money you earned today?" Pigeon asked, smiling as sarcastically as only he knew how.

"Up you get, folks, and put your ration books away. Get ready to live it up . . ." Conde shouted as he walked in the front porch and slapped the palm of his hand against the sturdy bulk of that fine food compendium the mere contents page of which had activated all his hunger-related organs, glands and ducts. As usual, Skinny Carlos's house was wide open to the world, and as usual, after shouting his welcome greeting, the Count walked in without further ceremony.

"We're out here," he heard his friend's voice when he was already across the dining room and emerging into the yard, shaded by mangos and avocado trees, their trunks swathed in pliant orchids, luxuriating after the recent rain. Carlos and his mother sat there in silence, hanging on the last glimmers of twilight, like shipwrecked survivors from a life that was also closing down on them before any small island could appear on the horizon to come to their rescue.

Conde went over to the old woman, kissed her forehead and was rewarded in kind.

"How are you, Jose?"

"Getting older by the day, Condecito."

Then he went over to Skinny Carlos's wheelchair, who hadn't been skinny for twenty years and whose sickly flab spilled over the sides of that chair he was now condemned to, and with his free hand he pulled his friend's sweaty mass to his chest.

"What's new, savage?"

"Nothing changes here, don't you know?" Carlos replied, twice slapping Conde's empty stomach which echoed like a drum that wasn't properly tensed.

Conde sat down in one of the cast-iron chairs, giving a sigh of relief as he did so. He looked at Josefina and Carlos and felt the peace of twilight and the flow of love prompted by those two irreplaceable individuals he'd shared almost all his life with, not to mention most of his dreams and frustrations. From that increasingly remote, unforgettable day when he'd asked Skinny for a penknife to sharpen the point of his pencil, in a classroom in the Víbora Pre-Uni, without making any extra effort, they realized they'd be friends and would start off as such. Since then, fate or destiny had bolted them into an unbreakable relationship when Carlos returned from his short stay in the war in Angola with his spine shattered by a bullet shot from a place and hatred he'd never understood. The irreversible injuries of his friend, who underwent numerous futile acts of surgery, had become a spiritual burden the Count assumed with a painful guilt – Why Carlos? Why him in particular? he'd wondered all those years. Giving his friend companionship and material support had subsequently become one of his missions in life, and during the bleakest years of the Crisis, in the early nineties, when blackouts and shortages dominated their lives, Conde invested every cent he earned in his new profession as a bookseller in the quest for little comforts to make Skinny's atrophied everyday life tolerable. But in the last three or four years, when immobility, obesity and insane orgies of eating and drinking had clearly begun to endanger Carlos's life – kidney failure, hardening of the liver and an irregular heartbeat – Conde faced the terrible dilemma of either refusing to collaborate in such self-punishment or, in full knowledge of the outcome, helping his old friend towards the finale he himself tirelessly seemed to be seeking: a dignified termination of a shitty life that had been destroyed forever at the age of twenty-eight. Conscious of the terrible burden he was taking on by embracing the option of militant solidarity, Mario Conde thought it was his duty to be at his friend's side in life and death, and tried to find the resources and motivation to accelerate as happily as possible, the onset of his longed for liberation, through the slow but sure method of poisoning his bloodstream and lining his arteries with the fat, nicotine and alcohol Carlos ingested in huge amounts.

"What were you going on about just now, Conde?" Skinny asked.

"Didn't you hear? That's why you look so out of it . . . I was telling you to sharpen up your incisors; we're dining out on the town tonight. I've booked a table at Contreras's *paladar* . . ."

"You gone mad?" Carlos looked at him, smiling sheepishly, as if he'd misunderstood yet another of his friend's bad jokes.

"I earned five hundred pesos today at a stroke. And get this: tomorrow I'll earn double, triple, quadruple and the day after even more . . . I'm going to be filthy rich, so Yoyi says."

"You're a big liar, that's what you are," Josefina retorted. "What are you up to now? Who's ever heard of old books being worth that much?"

"Jose, get your glad rags on, we'll get a cab . . . Fuck, I mean it! I'm rolling in it . . ." the Count insisted, tapping the top of his trouser pocket.

"Mum, there's no point trying to argue with this lunatic. Go and spruce yourself up and bring me a shirt," said Carlos. "I could eat a horse. Anyway, we only live once, so let's . . ."

"Too true, and, man, am I in the money!" Conde purred, standing up to help Josefina to her feet, who went into the house chuntering to herself.

"Skinny, how old's your mum?"

"I don't know . . . Gone seventy, not eighty yet."

"She's really getting old on us," lamented the Count, returning to his chair.

"Change the subject," insisted Carlos. "Hey, what's that?" he asked, pointing to the envelope the Count was still gripping.

"Oh, it's a present for your mother. A book of recipes. They say it's the best ever published in Cuba. She can't open it until we're sat at a table groaning with food, otherwise you'd die of hunger just reading the first recipe . . . That's why we're off to Contreras's *paladar*."

"Contreras?" Carlos replied thoughtfully. "The fat guy who used to be a policeman?"

"The one and only . . . They gave him six years, he served two, and when he came out he became an entrepreneur. That guy was so streetwise, he must be loaded by now."

"Conde, have you noticed how many people who used to be in the police or armed forces now do business on the side?"

"A whole heap of them. *C'est la vie*. Almost all of them have sorted out their little escape routes . . . Though today I bumped into a retired army major about to drop dead from hunger . . . You know, the one who sold me the books," and he added enthusiastically: "Skinny, you've got no idea. I've found a real gold mine. They've got books you can't put a price to . . . Look at this one: it's a little treasure, illustrated by Massaguer to boot. We're off to eat in a minute, so just listen to this."

Conde risked opening it at the first page and, trying to find the best angle to benefit from the light in the yard and the best distance for his rampant farsightedness, he read out aloud: "*My Pleasure? An indispensable . . . culinary guide*. Under the auspices of the Godmothers of the San Martín and Costales Wards in the General Calixto García University Hospital . . . What do you reckon? It's a book of delicious recipes, written from the guilty consciences of the Cuban bourgeoisie . . . It's full of impossible recipes . . ."

"I reckon it's a tad subversive," Carlos chimed in.

"If not terrorist."

The Count casually began to leaf through the book and read aloud, the names of some of the recipes, never going into enough detail to set off the gastric juices, but showing his friend the illustrations by Conrado Massaguer. Presently, between pages 561 and 562, he found a page of newsprint that had been folded in half and, with the care inculcated by his experience as a bookseller and policeman, he carefully extracted it to take a look.

"What have you got there?" enquired Carlos.

Because it had been kept out of the light and air, the magazine page, roughly fifteen by ten inches, had preserved its original light greenish colour. Conde found the name of the publication at the foot of the page: *Vanidades*, May 1960. The facing page advertised new General Electric washing machines on sale in Sears, El Encanto and Flogar. Convinced the paper carried another more substantial message, he opened it out and for the first time looked into the dark eyes of Violeta del Río.

"I'm not sure . . . 'Violeta del Río says farewell' . . . Fuck, Skinny, take a look at this woman."

They'd printed a full-page photograph of Violeta del Río, sheathed in gold lamé – the Count assumed, although he'd never touched lamé – that it fitted her like a snake's skin. While suggesting the presence of wild breasts, the material also revealed a pair of firm legs and cut back the evidence of forceful thighs opening out from a slim, tempting waistline. Her 1950s-style black, slightly wavy hair cascaded down to her shoulders, framing a smooth-skinned face that highlighted her thick, sensual mouth, and eyes that now stared magnetically and vigorously at him.

"Hell, what a specimen!" agreed Skinny. "Who was she?"

"Let me see . . ." and he read, jumping from line to line: " 'Violeta del Río . . . the greatest singer of boleros . . . the Lady of the Night . . . revealed at the end of a wonderful performance that it was her last . . . Owner and leading lady at the *Cabaret Parisién* . . . At the pinnacle of her career . . . She had just recorded the promotional single *Be gone from me*, as a taster for her LP *Havana Fever* . . .' You ever heard of her?"

"No, never," confessed Skinny. "But you know what those magazines were like. They probably wouldn't recognize her in her own bathtub but they make out she was the Queen of Sheba."

"Yeah, probably. But I *have* heard her name somewhere," responded the Count, not realizing his gaze was still transfixed by the dark eyes of that sultry, exultant woman in her early twenties, her frozen image from long ago still generating real, live heat.

Josefina strutted back sporting the dress dotted with tiny flowers that she kept for her most important outings: her periodic visits to the doctor. The old lady had gathered her hair up, painted her lips a faint but shiny colour and now smiled shyly.

"Well, meet the Lady of Hot Nights in Víbora," quipped the Count.

"You look great, Mum," came the compliment from Skinny, who immediately asked: "Hey, you ever heard of Violeta del Río, a bolero singer from the fifties?"

Josefina lifted a small handkerchief to her upper lip.

"No, I can't say . . ."

"What did I tell you, Conde? She was a complete unknown . . ."

"Yes, probably . . . But I've heard of her somewhere or other . . ." and added: "Let's go out the front, Tinguaro will be here any minute now."

"Tinguaro?" asked Carlos.

"Yeah, the guy who used to be in the police. He's set up as a cab driver and sells Montecristo, Cohiba and Rey del Mundo cigars, just the same or even better than those from the factory, and he hires out a bunch of painters who leave houses, blocks or mausolea gleaming like new pins. And he finds them their paint!"

2nd October

My dear:

My only hope is that when this letter reaches you it finds you well, so far from here and yet so near. So near to my heart and yet so far from my hands that can't reach you, although every heartbeat feels you, as if you were here, next to my bosom, which you should never have forsaken.

You cannot imagine what these days without sight of you have meant, made worse by my inability to calculate how long our separation will last. Every hour, every minute I think about you, because everything here brings you to mind, everything exists because you existed and gave your breath to everything, to everybody, but particularly to me.

When it's still hot, and I go into the garden in search of a cool breeze and see the foliage of the trees you planted over the years, I feel that that breath of air, filtered through the sharp rustling leaves of the mamey, the whispering custard apple and faintly tinkling leaves of the old ceiba (your ceiba, do you remember how joyfully you greeted its first flowers every summer?), is a part of you coming to me from distant parts, and I dream that perhaps a particle of that air was once inside you and, summoned by my solitude, flew across the sea to console and nourish me and keep me alive for you.

43

My love, how are you? How do you feel? How have you spent your first days over there? Have you seen friends and colleagues? I know that place never appealed, that you preferred life here, but if you can think of this absence as a parenthesis in your life, the distance may seem more tolerable, and you will connect better with me. (For I like to think this time I spend here will be just that: a parenthesis in a passionate love that has been painfully truncated, but which will emerge strengthened and go on to a better finale). Don't you agree?

There is little to report from here. Paralysed as I am, I feel I have become the enemy of time that refuses to pass, that prolongs every hour and forces me to look at my diary several times a day, as if I could find the answers I crave in its cold numbers. The feeling of immobility is even starker because I have not stepped outside the house since you left. What I need to remember you and feel you close is inside here, while the street is the realm of chaos, oblivion, haste, war on the past and, above all, of people jubilant at the changes, cheerful, ecstatic even at what they are confident will come to them in their naïve excitement, never thinking about the terrible demands the unquestioning faith they now profess will soon impose. My only hope is that, as your father would say, nothing lasts very long in this country: we are inconsistent by nature, and what now seems like a devastating earthquake, will break up tomorrow like a glittering carnival parade.

Worst of all, however, is feeling the emptiness that floats between the walls of this house, dominated by silence ever since the children stopped chattering and by the absence of your spirit that distinguished this space which seems huge, where I feel disoriented by so many absences.

I've had little recent news of your son. I know he's in some out-of-the-way corner of the island, making the most of his revolutionary exploits. I imagine him lean and happy, for he is forging his life and his desires with that character of steel he inherited from your blood. On the other hand, your daughter seems withdrawn, as if she were sad, and with good reason, because she always felt closer to the family (despite the respect your aloofness inspired in her) and your departure has snatched from her any hope of one day enjoying what should be hers by natural right. (Forgive me, I had to say this.) Luckily, she spends most of the day working, which makes me think that is how she tries to distance herself from her home: by losing herself in her own activities, as if she wanted to flee from something that was persecuting her, by surrendering herself (she too!) to the new life in a country where everything seems set on change, beginning with the people.

So, when will you ring me? I know that after the nationalization of the telephone company communications are going from bad to worse, but you ought to make the effort: you're not like your grandfather. I'll always remember him, the poor old man who always thought talking down a phone to a person who was far away was so unreal he refused to use the telephone to the day he died and forbad his friends from ringing him. I don't think it is such an effort for you. The main thing is that you should want to do so. As you know, there is no way I can call you, since I don't know which number to ring to get you. I so want to hear your voice!

That's enough for now. I only wanted to tell you a little about myself and my feelings . . . Give the children a kiss on my behalf and keep reminding them how much I love them. Also greetings to your sister and brother-in-law, tell them to be themselves, and that they should write to me some time. As for you, please don't forget me: write to me, ring me, or at least remember me, just a little . . . Because I shall always, always love you . . .

Your Nena

Mario Conde's stomach was out of training and had to make a special effort to accommodate and then digest the astonishing nutritional challenge its inconsiderate owner now inflicted on it. While Josefina settled for a grilled fish fillet, a bright and cheerful green salad and a dish of almond ice cream for dessert, Conde and Skinny began the assault on their physical and intellectual, historical and contemporary hungers, with a cocktail of oysters and prawns, destined to subvert their palate with fishy flavours long lost in the crevices of memory. The former then prepared to disappear down a juicy path of meat and potatoes in purest Cuban style, while the latter flung himself into a spicy well of broth with chickpeas that made him sweat from every single one of his multitude of pores. Then, as their bodies warmed to the task, like long-distance runners getting into their best stride, they competed to see who could eat the most rice and chicken, served in ridiculous portions – of both rice and chicken, a friendly gesture from the management – before finishing off with a shared ham pizza that Skinny insisted on ordering and stuffing into a remaining space, which proclaimed its hatred of a vacuum. For their epilogue they chose fritters, drenched in fruit juices, with a *parfum* of aniseed and lime peel, and neither could refuse, being such gentlemen in the circumstances, a taste of the rice and milk infused with cinnamon that Fatman Contreras himself prepared –a recipe of his great-grandmother's, an Andalusian whore who liked the good life and died at the ripe old age of eighty-eight, puffing on her cigar and sipping a shot of rum. They'd downed two bottles of Chilean Concha y Toro before getting to the desserts and then ordered two double shots of vintage rum to wipe their chops clean and accompany their coffees – doubles that quadrupled when the friends lit up the delicately layered cigars presented to them by the ex-policeman who'd converted to gourmet living and who flopped his voluminous mass of humanity down between them and Tinguaro at the end of the night, so they could toast one another with a glass of chilled Fra Angelico. The Count wasn't taken aback by the bill for seven hundred and eighty pesos, and when he'd paid Tinguaro his hundred pesos, he happily brought to a close what had been one of his most profitable days ever with a net loss of three hundred and eighty pesos and the soothing feeling that he might be able to pass through the eye of a needle, because he'd never be a rich man . . .

Tossing in his bed, unable to read, Conde only got to sleep around four, and in the meantime, as he belched and sweated uncomfortably, his retina was revisited time and again by the almost irritatingly persistent image of Violeta del Río, a recent revelation to him and news to Fatman Contreras too. Perhaps his stubborn detective instincts had also been aroused by the surfeit and had forced him to notice a few incongruities in his find. The first and most perturbing was the strange decision, apparently unmotivated, at least as far as *Vanidades* was concerned, which led that "beautiful and refined" woman, "at the pinnacle of her career" to abandon the stage and, by all accounts, vanish so definitively that nothing was ever heard of her again. Might she have left the island, like so many thousands of Cubans around that time? The Count reckoned it was the most likely explanation, although he didn't discount the possibility she might still be living in Cuba, under her real name – Lucía, Lourdes, or Teresa, because nobody could, in real life, be a Violeta del Río – as a private individual, stripped of the lamé, limelight and microphones. It wasn't a wild conclusion to draw: in years of such radical change in the lives of the country and its inhabitants, there'd been an infinite number of political, ethical, religious, professional, economic and even sporting transformations: Grandfather Rufino had suffered the banning of cockfights as if it were a prison sentence and the Count's own father didn't see another game of baseball to the day he died, because he couldn't imagine or accept that the blue Almendares club had ceased to exist, a club he'd fanatically supported for every minute of the first thirty-five years of his existence . . . But no artist can stop being an artist from one day to the next, just like that – just as no policeman could totally cease to be one, however long he'd been off duty – something Mario Conde knew for a fact. Maybe that was why he was so intrigued by that press-cutting, slumbering inside a cookbook nobody had opened in years, as witnessed by its state of preservation as well as the fact, endorsed by history, that its contents were of no use in a country that had been on food rationing for almost half a century. Hare stew with sultanas? Eggs in foie gras aspic? Foyot veal cutlets? . . . You must be joking! Conde conjectured that the book must have belonged to the wife of Alcides Montes de Oca, although he thought he remembered that she'd died around 1956, the year the book of recipes was published. If, as Amalia Ferrero asserted, her brother Dionisio stopped living with them when the revolution was victorious, it was unlikely he could have left a cutting there which was published in 1960. Five people remained on his list: the deceased Alcides Montes de Oca and his two adolescent children, the aged, now blank-minded Mummy Ferrero and Amalia herself. How could one of them have been involved with a '50s Havana cabaret singer? The Count couldn't imagine, but some link must have existed between one of those individuals and the vanished singer of boleros, the seductress who'd been dubbed the Lady of the Night and who beat faintly in some remote cranny of the Count's memory as a diffuse, almost extinct presence, still able to send out disruptive tremors.

It was gone three a.m. when the Count heard a rather authoritarian scratching on his kitchen door. He knew it was useless to try to ignore it, since stubbornness was the scratcher's most pronounced trait, so he got up to open the door.

"Hell, Rubbish, what kind of time is this to be coming home?"

On the brink of the advanced age of fourteen, Rubbish retained his streetwise ways intact, and would prowl the barrio every night in search of fresh air, frantic fleas and females on heat. Ever since the Count had brought him home to live with them on that stormy night in 1989, the quarrelsome Maltese had insisted on his freedom, which the Count accepted, seduced by the character of the animal who, alerted by the faint, lingering scent of the evening's feast on his clothes, now barked twice, demanding to be fed.

"All right, all right, grub's up."

Conde fetched a metal tray from the terrace. He opened the bag of leftovers from the *paladar* and tipped part of the contents onto the tray.

"But you eat it outside . . ." the Count warned, taking the tray out on the terrace. "We'll talk tomorrow, because this has got to stop . . ."

Rubbish barked twice again, and wagged his battered tail like a shuttlecock, urging him to get a move on.

Back in bed, Mario Conde smoked a cigarette. With the dark eyes of Violeta del Río floating in his mind, his memory slipping over her thick wavy hair and satin skin, he was finally blessed with sleep and, quite unexpectedly, slept soundly for five hours, feeling swindled when he woke up, because he couldn't recall a single dream about the beautiful woman sheathed in lamé.

What the fuck am I doing here?. . . Conde stood in the church entrance and took in a far too pleasurable lungful of the damp draught blowing down the aisle of the modest slate and brick building he'd entered for the first time on the day he was baptised. Forty-seven years ago, according to his calculations – a number that never got smaller. Once again he saw in the distance the rather modest high altar and its peaceful image of the clean, pink-cheeked archangel Raphael, a heavenly being immune to the pull of world. The rows of dark pews, empty at that time in the morning, contrasted with the bustle the Count had left behind in the street, populated by its motley crew of churro and pastry sellers, passers-by rushing or dawdling, grumpy morning drunkards propping up the bar on the corner and resigned pensioners waiting for the deferred opening of the cafeteria where they would comfort their groaning stomachs.

Over the last ten to twelve years, Conde had begun to visit the local church suspiciously frequently. Although he'd never been to another mass and never contemplated the possibility he might kneel by the confessional, the urge to sit for a few minutes in the deserted temple, freeing up the floodgates of his mind, repaid him with a feeling of calm he argued had nothing in common with mystical or extra-terrestrial spiritual longings apart from its basic function that the Count never used – he never prayed or asked for anything, because he'd forgotten all his prayers and didn't have anyone to include in them – the church had begun to provide a kind of shelter where time and life lost the savage rhythms of the struggle for daily survival. Nonetheless, his conscience warned that, despite his lack of belief in life after death, a diffuse feeling did exist he'd yet to pin down, that wasn't sapping his essential atheism but was beginning to entice him into that world and its persistent, magnetic appeal. Conde had come to suspect that the blend of aging and disillusion overwhelming his heart might finally cast him back, or just return him, to the fold of those who find consolation in faith. But the mere thought of that possibility irked him: the Count was a fundamentalist in his loyalties, and converts might be contemptible renegades and traitors, but re-conversion verged on the abominable.

That morning Conde felt full of expectation: he wasn't entering church in search of passing solace, but to find an unlikely response, quite unrelated to mysteries of transcendence, but rather connected to those of his own past, in the most earthbound of all possible worlds. Consequently, rather than sitting anonymously on one of the pews, he crossed over the central aisle and headed for the sacristy, where he found, as he'd hoped he would, the ever-stalwart figure of octogenarian Padre Mendoza, Bible open at a page of the Apocalypse, searching no doubt for the text for his next sermon.

"Good morning, Padre," he said, entering the precinct.

"Ready then?" asked the old man without looking up.

"Not yet."

"Don't leave it too long," the priest warned.

"What did we agree? Is or isn't the Lord's time infinite?"

"The Lord's is, your's isn't. Nor is mine," he retorted smiling at the Count.

"Why are you so keen to convert me?" asked the Count.

"Because you're crying out for it. You insist on not believing but you are somebody who can't live without belief. All you need is to dare to take the final step."

Conde had to smile. Could that be true or was the wily old priest merely exercising his sibylline logic?

"I'm not prepared to believe in certain words again. What's more, you will ask me to do things I can't and don't want to do."

"For example?"

"I'll tell you when you give me confession," wriggled the Count and, coming back to earth, he handed the priest a cigarette, as he put another to his own lips. He lit both with his lighter and they were soon enveloped in a cloud of smoke. "I came to see you because I need to find something out and you can perhaps help me . . . How long have you known my family?"

"For fifty-eight years, since the day I first came to this parish. You weren't even a twinkle in your father's eye . . . Your Grandfather Rufino, who was even more of an atheist than you, was my first friend around here."

Conde nodded and again worried about what had really driven him to Padre Mendoza's door. A skilled hand in these uncomfortable situations, the priest helped him make the next step.

"So what is it you need to know?"

Conde looked him in the eye and felt the trust-suffusing gaze of that old man who'd once placed in his mouth a flour wafer that, he claimed, was the very body of Christ.

"Have you ever heard of a woman called Violeta del Río?"

The priest looked up, perhaps surprised by that unexpected question. He took a couple of drags, then put out the cigarette in the ashtray and returned Conde's gaze.

"No," came his firm reply. "Why?"

"The name cropped up yesterday and, for some reason or other, it sounded familiar. I had the feeling that something sleeping had suddenly woken up. But I can't think where or why . . ."

"Who is this woman?" enquired the priest.

The Count explained, trying to fathom why Violeta del Río seemed both mysterious yet remotely familiar in this perplexing story that made no sense at all.

"How old were you in 1958?" asked the priest, staring at him.

"Three," the Count replied. "Why?"

The old man pondered for a few seconds. He seemed to be weighing up his responses and which words he should say or keep to himself.

"Your father fell in love with a singer around that time."

"My father?" rasped the Count. The parish priest's words clashed with the strict, home-loving image he cherished of his father. "With Violeta del Río?"

"I don't know what her name was, I never did, so it might have been her or somebody else . . . As far as I knew, it was a platonic affair. But he did fall in love. He heard her sing and became infatuated. I don't think it went any further. I think . . . She lived in one world and your father in another: she was beyond his grasp, which I think was something he realized from the start. Your mother never found out. What's more, I didn't think anyone was in the know, apart from your father and me . . ."

"So why does the name sound familiar?"

"Did he ever mention her to you?"

"I don't think so. I'm not sure. My father never spoke to me about what he did – you know what he was like."

Conde tried to reshape the monolithic image he had of his father, with whom he never succeeded in establishing the channels of communication he'd enjoyed with his mother or his grandfather, Rufino the Count. They'd loved each other, certainly, but neither had ever been able to express that affection verbally, and silence governed almost every aspect of their lives. Besides, the idea he might have been chasing after a beautiful singer in bars and cabarets didn't fit with the image of his father that he clung to.

"Well it must have been him . . . I expect he told you one day and you just forgot. Men in love do do crazy things."

"I know. Tell me about it. But not him."

"How can you be so sure? He wasn't that different."

"We didn't speak much."

"What about Grandfather Rufino? Might he have said something to you?"

"No."

"I expect he did, he told old Rufino everything and it got through to you and . . ."

"But what was this woman like my father fell for?"

"I haven't a clue," smiled the priest, "he just told me he couldn't get the singer, Violeta or whatever her name was, out of his head. Your father came to see me because he said he was going mad. He told me everything right here. Poor man."

Conde finally smiled. The image of his father infatuated with a singer of boleros seemed unreal, but it was so human he found it reassuring.

"So my father fell in love with a singer and watered at the mouth at the mere thought of her. And nobody ever found out . . ."

"I did," the priest corrected him.

"You're different," explained Conde.

"Why am I different?"

"Because you are. Otherwise, my father would never have told you."

"True enough."

"So why didn't you ask him what her name was?"

"It wasn't important. For either of us. It was as if desire had struck like lightening: it came and turned his life upside down. What's in a name? I just told him to take care, that some changes can't be reversed," answered the priest, standing up and grumbling, "Well, I must get ready for mass. Will you be staying? Look, the altar boy's not come yet . . ."

"I'd fancy myself as an altar boy . . . Keep your hopes up, but don't get too excited . . . Know what? If I discover my father did in fact fall in love with Violeta del Río I'll start believing in miracles."

It was inevitable: as soon as he saw their faces he recalled Rubbish's early morning jubilation at the feast of leftovers; recalled the worst nights during the Crisis, when his desolate larder forced him to toast old bread and drink glasses of sugared water; he even recalled the old man who several days ago had asked him for two pesos, one peso, anything, to buy something to eat. The now happy but still emaciated faces with which Amalia and Dionisio Ferrero welcomed him told the Count that both had got to the market the previous evening before it closed and, like himself, had feasted on an exceptional banquet that, because they were out of gastric training, had made sleep difficult. Such an irritation, though, would never mar their real satisfaction at feeling stuffed, and safe from the cruel, stabbing pain of hunger. They might well have had some milk with their breakfast that morning and restored a creamy bliss to their gruel, even luxuriated in bread and butter, and drunk proper strong coffee, like the coffee they now offered their buyers, perhaps over-sweetened, as the ex-policeman's expert palate detected, though it was no doubt genuine, and not the ersatz powder sold in minimal amounts according to a strict ration book.

On arrival, Conde had introduced them to his business partner: flustered by the proximity of the treasure, Yoyi Pigeon hurried through the polite chit-chat and asked to see the library, as if it were a warehouse full of hammers or a container of scissors.

Amalia gave her apologies, because she had to wash and feed her mother, go to the market – did she still have money left? – and do a thousand things in the house, but Dionisio stayed with them in the library, hovering mistrustfully by the door. At the Count's suggestion, the buyers began their prospecting among the bookshelves located on the right of the room, a less crowded area where the bookcases had been cut back to create space for the iron-barred window overlooking the garden now dedicated to growing vegetables necessary for survival. Following the Count's plan, they started to make three piles on the desk's generous surface: books that should never be sold on the market, books of less interest or no interest at all, and books for immediate sale. Conde placed in the first group nineteenth-century Cuban publications that seemed straightforwardly rare and very valuable and a number of European and North American books, including a first edition of Voltaire's *Candide* that made him sweat excitedly and, especially, exquisite, invaluable original printings of the *Most Short Account of the Destruction of the Indies*, by Fray Bartolomé de las Casas, dated 1552, and The Inca's *La Florida: the History of Hernando de Soto, Governor and Captain-General of the Realm of La Florida and Other Heroic Indian and Spanish Gentlemen*, printed in Lisbon in 1605. But the books that most disturbed the Count were unimaginable treasures from Creole publishing, some of which he now saw and touched for the first time, such as the four volumes of the *Collection of Political, Historical, Scientific and Other Aspects of Life on the Island of Cuba*, by José Antonio Saco, printed in Paris, in 1858; *The First Three Historians of the Island of Cuba: Arrate-Valdés-Urrutia*, printed in three volumes, in Havana, in 1876 and 1877; *The Annals of the Island of Cuba*, by Félix Erenchun, printed in Havana, in 1858, in five hefty tomes; *Land Surveying as Applied to the System of Measuring on the Island of Cuba*, by Don Desiderio Herrera, also printed in Havana, in 1835; the extremely rare 1813 edition of the *History of the Island of Cuba and Especially of Havana*, by Don Antonio José Valdés, one of the first books ever made on the island; and as if handling gold bars, he lifted out the thirteen volumes of the *Physical, Political and Natural History of the Island of Cuba*, by the controversial Ramón de la

54

Sagra, published in Paris between 1842 and 1861 and that, if it was as complete as it appeared to be, should have 281 plates, 150 coloured by hand, which meant they might fetch more than ten thousand dollars even in the most sluggish of markets.

But the mountain that grew most, as if powered by inner volcanic forces, was the one of books that could be sold, which, apart from calming a neurotic Yoyi, worried by the quantity of books the Count considered unsaleable, brought a metallic glint to the eyes of that young man, transformed momentarily into a scavenging hawk.

While they checked the books, constantly surprised by dates and places of publication, caressed gnarled leather or original board spines, lingered occasionally to admire engravings or hand-painted illustrations, Conde felt the sharp pain from the previous day's hunch return, warning he'd yet to uncover all the surprises that were undoubtedly awaiting him in some corner of that sanctuary. Nonetheless, he couldn't avoid the uncomfortable truth: that he was introducing chaos into a universe of paper that, for more than forty years, had safely orbited beyond the wrath of time and history, thanks to a simple pledge that had been honoured with iron determination.

When another set of coveted books passed through his hands – as he fingered like a delicate child the now fragile, profusely illustrated volumes of the *Picturesque Stroll Around the Island of Cuba*, printed in 1841 and 1842 – he tried to persuade himself they might herald other surprising encounters, and wondered if his hunch related to the palpable possibility he was going to scale the heights all specialists in the trade dreamed of: the discovery of the unimaginable. Perhaps among those volumes lurked one that pre-dated *The General Tariff for the Price of Medicines*, the flimsy pamphlet published by Carlos Habre in Havana in 1723 and considered to be the first-born child of Cuban typography; might he find slumbering there with one eye half open the original parchment manuscripts to prove that the Gaelic writings of the mythical Ossian were awesomely genuine?; or the gold plaques etched with hieroglyphics of the Book of the Mormons, never seen by anyone after Joseph Smith found and translated them – with indispensable divine help – only for an angel to pick them up and return them immediately to heaven, according to every account? Or *The Mirror of Patience* that had never been described, let alone touched, although it supposedly marked the birth of poetry on Cuban themes in 1608? Its appearance would end once and for all the debate raging over the clever forgery or authenticity of an epic poem peopled with satyrs, fauns, wood folk, pure, limpid, frolicking naiads and napeas, enjoying life between Cuban streams and forests despite the island's perennial heat waves.

Conde's emotional exhaustion got the better of Yoyi's entrepreneurial energies, and they called it a day at three p.m., after counting out two hundred and eighteen saleable books, some of which could fetch juicy prices, nearly all printed in Cuba, Mexico or Spain between the end of the nineteenth century and the first half of the twentieth.

"Those go back on the shelves," the Count told Dionisio, pointing to the most valuable volumes. "We'll take these. Is that all right by you?"

"I don't have a problem with any of that. What do we do with the ones you say shouldn't be sold?" he asked, gazing at the mountain of fantastic books the Count was returning to one corner of the empty shelves.

"You decide . . . It would make sense to try to sell them to the National Library. They all have a heritage value. The Library doesn't pay very much, but . . ."

"But, man, I think . . ." Pigeon couldn't repress a reaction his partner quickly nipped in the bud.

"It's not open to debate, Yoyi," and he added, for Dionisio's benefit, "I already told you, you must decide. Most of those books are worth $500, others over a thousand and some several thousand." He watched the sickly pallor spread over Dionisio's face and, pre-empting a heart attack, added, "If you like, when we finish today, talk to him," and he pointed at Yoyi. "But I won't be part of that deal. My only condition is that, if you're not going to do a deal with the National Library or a museum, do it with Yoyi. He'll pay you best. I can assure you of that."

Excited by these figures, Dionisio Ferrero coughed, sweated, reflected, trembled, hesitated and looked at Yoyi, who welcomed his look with an angelic, understanding smile.

"I knew they could be quite valuable, but really never imagined they might fetch those prices. Naturally, if I'd had any inkling, I'd have . . ." Dionisio smiled, happy at the dazzling prospect of a better future. "So how much will you give me for the ones you have separated out?"

"We'll have to do our sums," Pigeon interjected hastily. "Can you leave us alone for a few minutes so we can tot up?"

"Yes, of course . . . I'll go and make some coffee. Some cold water as well?"

When Dionisio went out, the Count looked at his colleague and received the murderous look he anticipated and deserved.

"I'll kill you one of these days. I swear I will. How the hell can you be such a bastard? And to cap it all you tell him there are books worth over a thousand dollars . . ."

"I erred on the conservative side, Yoyi. What do you reckon for the thirteen volumes of La Sagra? And the first editions of Las Casas and the Inca Garcilaso? Got any idea what they'd pay out in Miami for the *Picturesque Stroll*? . . ."

"That's piss low, man. It's not as if you live in Miami or there are any buyers around here who'd pay over a thousand dollars for one of those books."

"That's your problem."

"Well, it ought to be yours as well. You realize that with two or three of those little books you could buy a year's supply of whisky and not that gut-rotting local brew you buy from Blakamán and the Vikingo."

"If you want to get plastered, anything will do . . . Come on, let's do our sums . . ."

It took them half an hour to value the books, and that included drinking two coffees. At the Count's insistence, they agreed a price they deemed satisfactory for all concerned. While Conde sat back on the sofa, Yoyi Pigeon preferred to stand next to the stained-glass windows, like a boxer waiting in the neutral corner for the count to stop or for the go-ahead to resume the fight. The Ferreros flopped down on their armchairs and Conde noticed their pathetic nervous tics, and reflected that hunger and principles, poverty and dignity, scarcity and pride are difficult pairings to reconcile.

"Let's see then," he said. "Today we picked out two hundred and eighteen books . . . Some will sell for a very good price, but we'll have to work hard to get a good price for others. We're looking at twelve, fifteen dollars, although it won't be easy, and others might make two or three . . . If we go by the thirty percent rule, my colleague and I have decided to offer you a flat price: three dollars a book."

Amalia and Dionisio glanced at each other. Were they hoping for more? Had they got too fond of the good life? Yoyi Pigeon sensed they were suspicious and, armed with a calculator, walked over.

"Let's see then . . . 218 books, at three dollars apiece . . . makes 654 greenbacks . . . Six, five five, rounded up. At twenty-six pesos to the dollar . . ." he paused theatrically, knowing full well it would clear away any doubts, and underscoring the point, he pretended he too was surprised. "Hell! Seventeen thousand pesos! I can tell you, no buyer will give you that much, because selling books has got difficult recently . . . What's more: what you've got in there will sort your problems for the rest of your lives . . ."

Conde knew the undernourished legs, stomachs and brains of Amalia and Dionisio Ferrero must be quaking at the sound of such figures, as his own had quaked that afternoon when he'd imagined himself as the happy owner of ten or twelve thousand pesos, which would pay his bills for half a year if properly eked out . . . They'd only been through a seventh or eighth of the library, too, and his hunch still throbbed, telling him that something extraordinary, something beyond his grasp would happen in that room. Would this deal really leave him a rich man, thanks to the discovery of incunabula whose magnetic pull – in monetary terms – not even he and his moral sense could resist?

"How do you want your money, in pesos or dollars?" Pigeon tried to wrap the deal up. As ever, brother and sister consulted each other visually and the Count spotted a poison in those glances that hadn't previously shown itself: the poison of ambition.

"Four dollars a book," spat Dionisio, recovering the verbal power of command he must have deployed in his glory days as a military leader on the battlefield.

Yoyi smiled and looked at the Count, as if to say: "You see? they're bastards, not poor wretches. Who are you kidding . . ."

"Half in Cuban pesos and half in dollars," added Dionisio, fully in control of the situation. "It's a fair offer and no arguments . . ."

"OK," said Yoyi, not daring to contradict him, but showing he was none too happy. "That makes twenty-two thousand six hundred and seventy pesos. I'll pay you ten thousand now and the remainder and the dollars tomorrow."

And he held out a hand to the Count who put in it the wad of three thousand he'd given him the previous day and added the money he'd taken from the bumbag hanging under his stomach. He separated out the two bundles and gave them to Dionisio, tapping the notes against his open hand.

"5,000 per wad. Please count them. I still owe you 1,300 pesos and 436 dollars," he spelt out to the ex-soldier, whose cockiness had evaporated on sight of the banknotes.

While Dionisio concentrated on counting the money, Amalia didn't know where to point her watery gaze: it kept sliding over the money her brother was sorting into piles of hundreds and then thousands, on the table in the centre of the room. She couldn't stop herself, lifted a finger to her mouth and began biting the skin around the nail that was shredded beyond the edge of the finger, as a shadow of painful, cannibalistic satisfaction flitted across her face.

"By the way, Amalia," the Count had been resisting putting the question but decided to take advantage of her moment of ecstasy, "Have you ever heard of Violeta del Río?"

The Count thought Amalia's expression of bewilderment and incomprehension genuine enough as she reluctantly abandoned her ragged fingernail.

"I don't think so . . . Why?"

"What about you, Dionisio?"

Dionisio barely looked up from the money, but did interrupt his counting.

"Never heard of her," he said, then resumed his tallying.

The Count briefly told them about the cutting he'd found, and then spoke to Amalia.

"Perhaps your mother might remember her?"

"I told you she's lost it . . ."

"But old people sometimes remember things from the past. Might I at least ask her?"

"No . . . It would make no sense," Amalia responded as if it upset her to admit as much, and added: "Excuse me, I must go to the bathroom."

She walked off between the marble columns and Dionisio, his mind closed to everything but counting notes, concentrated even harder on his task.

"Why does that woman interest you so much, Conde?" enquired Yoyi, smiling ironically.

"I haven't a clue . . ." the Count lied, unable to admit what he'd found out that morning, and added, "Which bookseller knows the most about old records?"

"Pancho Carmona. You remember, he used to sell records."

"I need too see him today."

"You know," Pigeon shook his head, "you're madder than an old coot, I swear, man."

"All present and correct," Dionisio piped up.

"We can take all the books, can't we?" Conde asked, assuming his honest looks might have waned over the last twenty-four hours.

"Yes," replied Dionisio, after hesitating for a moment. "That's not a problem."

"Let's get on with it then. I'll get some boxes. My car's outside," announced Yoyi as he left.

Amalia emerged from the inner recesses of the house and sat next to her happy brother.

"So . . ." began Dionisio. "You'll bring the rest of the money, won't you?"

"Of course," the Count reassured him. "Don't worry. We've got to select more books . . . By the way, Dionisio, and do excuse my nosiness: why did you leave that corporation you worked for after you were demobbed from the army?"

Surprised by the question, Dionisio looked at the Count and then at his sister, who'd tipped the bookseller to that particular story.

"Because I saw things I didn't like. I'm a decent chap. A revolutionary too, and don't you forget it."

The early morning and late evenings were the most fruitful hours for the sellers of old books who'd set up shop in the plaza de Armas, in the shade of weeping figs, the statue of the Father of the Fatherland, and austere palaces that were once the seat of a colonial power that believed the island was one of the most precious jewels in its imperial crown. The tourist hordes, either eager or bored by their compulsory immersion in a bath of pre-packed history, usually began or ended their itineraries in the old city in the vicinity of what was once its central square. Although the booksellers always welcomed them as potential, if overly wary customers, experience had shown they could get them to pocket the odd book only with great difficulty and after much persuasive spiel, and then it was usually one that was generally of little historical or bibliographical value. That throng of civil servants, small businessmen, hard-saving pensioners, old militants shorn of their militancy, but determined to see with their own eyes this last outpost of the most real socialism, together with a motley band of night-owls, talked into Cuba, the low cost paradise, by scheming travel agents, and who tended to be addicted to other more primitive passions, that were sensual, climatic, even ideological but never book-loving.

In fact, the sample of books on display in the historic square represented only the more sightly leftovers from the real banquet. Valuable volumes, the ones that would unerringly find their way to auctions where they'd wear a three or four digit ticket, were banned from sale to the public and were never part of these modest offerings. Such delicacies were generally set aside for more or less well-established buyers: a few diplomatic bibliophiles; foreign correspondents and businessmen based in Cuba, with enough dollars to buy paper jewels; a small number of Cubans who'd got rich legally, semi-legally or entirely illegally, intent on investing in safe bets; and a few book lovers who were frequent visitors to the islands and had established preferences in matters of literature, cigars and women. However, the real recipients of the invisible bibliographical rarities were various professional dealers in valuable books, particularly Spaniards, Mexicans and a few Miami and New York based Cubans, who supplied auctions or owners of bookshops that were advertised on the internet. In the early nineties these specialists had detected the rich Havana vein, exposed in the harshest years of the Crisis, and

61

came ready to purchase whatever their desperate Cuban colleagues might generously offer. Then, when they'd made their connections and plumbed the mine's depths, they changed tactics and brought on each trip a list of exotic goodies already flagged by customers seeking a specific title by a well-known author, and in a particular edition. This underground trade was by far the most productive and most dangerous, and now the Cuban authorities had rumbled that some booksellers had conspired with library employees to take Cuban and universal treasures, bibliographical holdings, including manuscripts that could never be recovered, out of the country. It was almost impossible to eradicate this constant drain because on occasions the provider was a librarian on two hundred and fifty pesos a month who found it difficult to resist an offer of two hundred dollars – representing twenty months of his salary – for extracting a magazine or tome requested by a determined buyer. Such piracy on the sly had forced Cuban libraries to lock their most precious books in remote vaults, but nobody could put a stop to the leak from a tap beyond repair, thanks to which some found a temporary solution to material deprivation.

Pancho Carmona enjoyed a reputation as the provider of the bibliographical jewels most in demand. His business card pompously introduced him as a specialist in rare and valuable books, although his commercial tentacles reached into adjacent areas, including the plastic arts, furniture, Tiffany jewellery and the most eclectic of antiques. Three times a week Pancho provided a range of legal delights in the plaza de Armas, and on the other three days, in the reception room of his own home, on calle Amargura, he'd organize a kind of bookshop only open to trustworthy or highly recommended customers. One month he'd invite them to sit on Louis XVI furniture, another on Second Empire armchairs and the next on comfortable Liberty sofas, always in the shadow of classic Cuban painting or drawing, lit by restored art nouveau lamps and surrounded by Murano or Bohemian glassware, keen to voyage to foreign parts. All his trade colleagues knew that neither place exhibited his most sought-after books, although nobody knew for sure where Carmona, a man whose best contacts came straight to him, as soon they arrived from Madrid, Barcelona, Rome, Miami and New York, kept his secret hoard.

Pancho had lived for twenty-five years on his salary as an industrial designer and had begun to specialize in the book trade when it took off as a profitable line, and the sales of records, his business at the time, took a turn for the worse, coinciding with the start of a Crisis that soon resulted in a bountiful harvest as far as he was concerned. Unlike other booksellers, Carmona had had the foresight from the start to see that the real money would never be in the modest exercise of buying books for two pesos to sell them for ten. The real challenge, he believed, was to take a leap into the void of really serious investment. Consequently, soon after embarking on this trade, he risked taking out a loan, once he'd sold his all-Soviet television, refrigerator and air conditioning acquired thanks to his former status as a model worker, in order to assemble the necessary funds to purchase bibliographical rarities that had been hidden for years and were now being disinterred by desperate hunger. He paid good prices to dispel the doubts of skeletal owners and fend off rival competition. Within a few months Pancho had accumulated several dozen exquisite volumes, which he put on sale at fair but high prices and, endlessly patient, on the verge of starvation, he sat down and waited for the spark to ignite. Fate smiled on him on one day in 1994 when he was close to suicide: a buyer flew in from Madrid and handed over $12,000 for a small job-lot that included *A General and Natural History of the Indies*, by Fernández de Oviedo, published in Madrid in 1851; the *Picturesque Island of Cuba*, by Andueza, also from Madrid, but from 1841; the *Political Essay on the Island of Cuba*, by Baron Humboldt, in two 1826 Parisian tomes; the classic *Types and Customs from the Island of Cuba*, illustrated by Víctor Patricio de Landaluze, in its 1891 Havana edition; the extraordinary Cuban edition of *The Comedies of Don Pedro Calderón de la Barca*, published in Havana in 1839 and illustrated by Alejandro Moreau and Federico Mialhe; and the six beautiful, much sought after volumes of the *History of Cuban Families*, written by Francisco Javier de Santa Cruz y Mallén, the Count of Jaruco and Santa Cruz del Mopox, in the substantial 1940-43 edition.

From then on the omnipotent Carmona specialized in buying and selling books that could fetch healthy prices in European and North American auctions. He would be visited at home, almost daily, by desperate owners of family relics that had survived previous earthquakes, now eager, at the very least, to hear decent estimates for their books, furniture and adornments, and, along the path he'd cleared for them, by the most serious buyers who'd come to the island in search of the young girls in blossom only Carmona could confidently supply.

Years in the catacombs of business had turned Pancho Carmona into a vademecum colleagues consulted to get their bearings in terms of prices, and the possible existence, whereabouts and potential sources of supply or sale. As a genuine specialist, this bookseller only offered advice on the three days of the week he worked in the plaza de Armas, and charged his colleagues a modest, set fee: an invitation to a coffee on the terrace of La Mina restaurant, down a side street leading from the plaza de Armas.

"One coffee and two beers," Yoyi Pigeon ordered when they'd sat down at the table nearest the entrance. From there Pancho could keep a watchful eye on his stall that was being looked after by his nephew whose job it was to set up and to take the books back at the end of the day to his house on calle Amargura where belying that street name he at least had little reason to feel bitterness.

"The coffee's for me, Lento," Pancho told the waiter to avoid the torture of an over-watery infusion. "We've not seen you for a while, Conde," he said, lighting the cigarette he always started to smoke before drinking coffee.

"Trade's going downhill, Pancho. It's very hard to find the necessary —"

"Yes, it's getting hard. There's nowhere to mine any more. *Tutto è finito*," he agreed, but Pigeon euphorically interrupted his lamentation.

"Well, Conde's found a little gold mine."

"Really?" responded Pancho, long since immune to rushes of excitement.

"How do you fancy a first edition of Voltaire's *Candide*?" Pigeon exclaimed. "Or a Las Casas from 1552, or The Inca's *La Florida* from 1605, and Valdés's *History of the Island of Cuba*? And how about the thirteen volumes of Ramón de la Sagra's *History*, all shiny and new, with all the illustrations intact?. . .

The gleam in Pancho Carmona's eyes expanded at the mention of each title and he finally blurted out: "Fuck! When do I get a list of what you've got?"

"Nothing Pigeon just referred to is for sale," interjected the Count. "We've got other things to interest you —"

"Within the week," retorted Pigeon, ignoring his partner's murderous looks. "When I say it's a mine . . ."

"See if you can find a copy with illustrations intact of *The Book of Sugar Mills* and the 1832 edition of Heredia's poetry. I've got a buyer who's desperate for them and he'll pay the asking price without protesting . . . I'll seal the deal for ten percent."

"What might the Heredia fetch then?" enquired the Count.

"That edition, the most complete and set by Heredia himself, now fetches upwards of a $1,000 in Cuba. Abroad . . . 3,000 plus. And if it's signed . . . So, where the hell did you find this library?"

Pigeon smiled, glanced at the Count and then at Pancho.

"What's the look on my face telling you, Panchón?"

The other smiled as well.

"I get you. When among sharks . . ."

"The only problem is that this fellow doesn't want to get his fingers dirty." said Yoyi pointing at the Count.

"And never did want to," the Count retorted, pouring the ice-cold beer into his glass.

"Come on, Pancho, give him a reason to change his mind," pleaded Pigeon and the bookseller smiled.

"To change his mind or give himself a heart attack?. . . How about this then: guess what I flogged the other day?" he lowered his voice. "Both volumes of the 1851 and 1856 first edition of Felipe Poey's *Reminiscences on the Natural History of the Island of Cuba* . . . with the *ex libris* of Julián del Casal."

"You're kidding?" Yoyi reacted in shock. "How much?"

"Two thousand green ones, I didn't want any hassle . . ." and he smiled, lifting his coffee to his lips.

"So where did you fish that out from?" the Count enquired.

Pancho shook his head at the naivety of the question.

"Fine . . . fine . . . what goes around comes around."

"Anyway you bring your list, I'm sure we can do business."

"What do you do with all that cash, Pancho?" Yoyi continued, intrigued, and unable to hide his admiration.

"That's not for public consumption, my boy. But I dream: I dream I will have a real bookshop one day, with lots of books, lots of light, a café at the back, I see myself sitting there, like a pasha, with my coffee, my cigarette, recommending books . . . While I'm waiting for that dream to come true, I'll sell from my front room and that wooden stand you see over there."

"I want to be like you when I'm older, Panchón, I swear I do," Pigeon declared and the Count knew this they weren't empty words.

"OK, that's enough bullshit," the Count interjected. "Pancho, can you tell me anything about a single called *Be gone from me*. I think it's a 78 . . ."

"It's a 45, by one Violeta del Río. The Gema company recorded it in 1958 or at the beginning of 1959, I think. *Be gone from me* on one side, by the Expósito brothers, and on the other *You'll remember me*, by Frank Domínguez. I used to have a copy and it took a while to get rid of it."

As he listened to the description of a record that finally assumed some kind of physical reality, the Count felt unexpectedly jubilant, as if Pancho Carmona had breathed vital life into his strange quest for knowledge.

"Did you ever listen to it?" he asked.

"No, I never felt like listening . . ."

"Who did you sell it to?"

"I don't remember right now . . ."

"Of course you remember, think for a moment."

"Lento, another coffee," Yoyi anticipated. "And it's for Pancho. And two more lagers . . ."

Pancho lit up another cigarette.

"What about the singer? What was she like?" Conde asked anxiously, lifting his smoke to his lips.

"Not the faintest fucking idea. I never knew anything about her . . . I got my hands on the record about fifteen years ago . . . Let's see," and Pancho Carmona shut his eyes, so he could see, he claimed: perhaps he was reading the lists of purchases and sales engraved on his brain. Finally, he raised his eyelids. "Got it, I sold it in a job-lot to the blind guy who writes about music . . ."

"Rafael Giró?"

"That's your man . . ."

"What else do you know about the singer, Pancho?"

"Zilch. Or do you reckon I should know all there is to know about everything?"

"For two one-dollar coffees you might dredge a bit more up?" said Conde, slapping the shoulder of the oracle of calle Amargura, the man who dreamt of owning a fantastic bookshop where they'd also sell the best coffee in Havana.

That Chevrolet, the four-door, pillarless Bel Air model, manufactured in 1956 was considered by experts to be one of the most "macho" cars ever to roll along Havana's ravaged streets. Driving it, gently pushing the horizontal gear lever, listening to that melodious combination of speed and power, feeling it slide along, robust, confident and proud, welcoming the breeze blowing through windows broad as an ecstatic smile, represented for Yoyi Pigeon the sensation closest to an erotic climax he'd ever experienced.

When Yoyi bought it two years ago, that Bel Air 56 was already a striking automobile, thanks to its classically distinguished lines and immaculate chroming, as a result of always being kept in a garage. It came into the newly graduated engineer's possession, thanks to the $7,000 he'd earned from a sale of a Goya painting that easily changed hands and flew off to an unknown destination. His uncle, the most renowned mechanic specializing in that brand of car – about to be dubbed Paco Chevrolet in Havana – focused his much-prized wisdom on converting his nephew's car into a holy relic on wheels. He tuned the engine in an attempt to maximize its horse-power, fitted it out with genuine spare parts, and added filters, carburettors and sensors to enhance its mechanical refinement and purring efficiency as a perfect piece of engineering, created for eternity. Then, the body-work was sand-papered to the tinplate, giving it a dazzling sheen when the car was repainted with the special metallic glow paint recommended by Ferrari, in a combination of sky blue for bonnet, boot, mudguards and doors, and brilliant white for the roof and the wedge-shaped side panels. The final elegant touch was achieved by halogenous headlights from Miami and white Firestone tyres from Mexico, so that this 1956 Bel Air Chevrolet was probably more magnificent than the one that emerged long ago from the automotive plant in Detroit, when its manufacturers could never have imagined that fifty years later it would still be the most beautiful, well-balanced, glamorous car that had ever rolled over the Earth.

The Bel Air zipped along the avenue of the Malecón and, sitting back in the high-backed beige imitation pigskin seat, Conde divided his attentions between the Marc Anthony music – broadcast from the CD player hidden in the glove compartment and amplified through the quadraphonic audio system Pigeon had incorporated, without sacrificing the original Motorola radio, luxuriating in its privileged position on the dashboard – and the contemplation of a tranquil sea, gilded by the last rays of that summer evening's sun. The tropical sea would always remind him of his fading dream: of owning a small wood cabin, on the edge of a beach, where he could devote the mornings to his imagination and writing one of those novels he still planned, the evenings to fishing and strolling along the sand, and the nights to enjoying the company and moist heat of a woman, smelling of seaweed, sea breezes and the sweet scent of night-time secretions.

"Yoyi," his words exploded uncontrollably, "is there anything you'd really like and were never able to get?"

Pigeon smiled, keeping his eyes on the avenue.

"What's this about, man? Loads of things . . . I swear . . ."

"Of course, but doesn't anything stick out?"

The lad shook his head, as if denying something only he knew.

"Before I bought this car I'd have given my life to have a Bel Air. Now I've got one, I'm not sure . . . I think . . . Yes, got it, I'd love to see Queen play live. With Freddie Mercury, of course . . ."

"Great," conceded the Count, who'd expected a less spiritual reply.

Pigeon's frustrated dream spoke of a sensibility lost or atrophied by the struggle for survival, and went back to a state of innocence before he'd turned ferocious predator.

"And come to think of it," continued Pigeon after a silence, "I'd also have liked to know how to dance properly. I can swear to that. I love music but I'm a terrible dancer."

"Ditto," confessed the Count, probing further. "Have you ever thought about what you want from life?"

Yoyi looked at him for a moment.

"Don't go so deep into things, man. You know that here we've got to live the day-to-day and not think too much. That's where you get it wrong, you think too much . . . Take now for instance, why you got such a bee in your bonnet about what happened to Violeta del Río?"

Conde gave the sea a farewell glance, before they started their descent down the ramp of the tunnel under the river.

"It must be because I'm an obsessive-compulsive . . ."

"And what else, what else?" cried Yoyi.

"I still don't know," the Count allowed. "Maybe it's just curiosity, a leftover from when I was a policeman, or something I haven't yet worked out . . . You know what? Those stories and characters from the fifties are my Bel Air. I can't get enough of going back over what people remember about it. It fascinates me. But what most intrigues me about her story is the strange way she retired and disappeared at the height of her fame, and that no one now remembers her, you know . . . So why did you want to drive me to Rafael Giró's place?"

"I don't know . . . to keep you company, I suppose. You're the maddest, arsiest character I know, but I like your company. Know what, man? You're the only straightforward fellow I ever deal with in this and all my other businesses. You're like a bloody creature from Mars. As if you weren't for real, I mean."

"Is this praise, coming from you?" enquired the Count.

"More or less . . . You know, we live in a jungle. As soon as you leave your shell, you're surrounded by vultures, people set on fucking you up, stealing your money, getting laid with your woman, informing on you and making sure you get busted so they can make a buck . . . A bunch of people who don't want to complicate their lives, and most just want out, to cross the water, even if it's to fucking Madagascar. And fuck anyone else . . . And don't expect too much from life."

"That's not what the newspapers say," Conde egged him on, to see if he'd jump, but Yoyi only seethed.

"What newspapers? I bought one once, I wiped my butt on it, and it left it covered in shit, I swear . . ."

69

"You ever hear talk of Che's New Man?"

"What's that? Where can you buy one?"

When they reached the crossroads of 51 and 64 Streets Pigeon turned right and looked for the number Pancho Carmona had given them.

"That's where the blind guy lives. Look, he's in the doorway," he said as he parked the car next to the pavement. "Don't slam the door, man, this is a real car, not one of your Russian tin-cans on wheels . . ."

Conde let the car door go and watched it gently swing to, pulled by its own weight. He crossed the small garden and greeted Rafael Giró. He explained how they were friends of Pancho Carmona, and appealed to his vanity by saying he'd read his book on mambo and thought it excellent.

"So why this visit? Do you want to sell me a book?" asked Rafael, who didn't stop his wooden chair from rocking. His eyes were like two powerful, round lamps behind the thick concentric lenses of his cheap, poor imitation tortoiseshell spectacles.

"No, it's not that . . . Pancho told us he sold you a record by a bolero singer, Violeta del Río, about fifteen years ago . . ."

"The Lady of the Night," said Rafael just as Pigeon joined them.

"You heard of her then?' he asked cheekily, flopping on an arm-chair before he'd even been invited to sit down.

"Of course, I have. Or do you think I'm one of those musicologists – at least that's what they call themselves – who talk about music they've never listened to and haven't written an effing book in all their effing lives?. . . Please take a seat," he said finally, addressing the Count who sat down in one of the armchairs.

"Well, we've asked a number of people . . ."

"I know, hardly anyone remembers her. She only made one record and as she worked in clubs and cabarets . . . Just imagine, in Havana at the time there were more than sixty clubs and cabarets with two or three shows a night. Not counting restaurants and bars where trios, pianists and combos played . . ."

"Incredible," said a genuinely astonished Pigeon.

"Can you imagine the number of artists required to sustain that rhythm? Havana was a crazy place: it was the liveliest city on the

70

planet. You can forget fucking Paris and New York! Far too cold
. . . *the* Nightlife was right here! True, there were whores, there were
drugs and there was the mafia, but people enjoyed life and night-
time started at six p.m. and went on till dawn. Can you imagine
in a single night being able to drink beer, listen to the Anacaonas
in the Aires Libres on Prado, eat at nine listening to the music and
voice of Bola de Nieve, then in the Saint John and listening to
Elena Burke, after going to a cabaret and dancing to Benny Moré,
with the Aragón, Casino de la Playa, the Sonora Matancera, then
taking a break to swing to the boleros of Olga Guillot, Vicentico
Valdés, Ñico Membiela . . . or off to listen to the crooners, grainy-
voiced José Antonio Méndez, or César Portillo and, rounding off
the night, escaping to the beach to see Chori play his timbales, and
sitting there cool as anything, between Marlon Brando and Cab
Calloway, next to Errol Flynn and Josephine Baker. And, if you'd
any breath left, down to The Grotto, here on La Rampa, to see
the dawn in with a jazz session with Tata Güines, Barreto, Bebo
Valdés, Negro Vivar, Frank Emilio and all those lunatics who are
the best musicians Cuba has ever produced? They were here in
their thousands, music was in the air, you could cut it with a knife,
you had to push it aside to walk down the street . . . And Violeta
del Río was one of them . . ."

"Just one of the crowd?" hazarded the Count, apparently
heading for a big disappointment.

"She was no Elena Burke or Olguita Guillot, but she did have
a real voice of her own. And a style. And a body. I never saw her,
but Rogelito, the *timbalero*, once told me she was one of the most
fantastic women in Havana. A real traffic-stopper."

"And what happened?"

"One day she said she wasn't going to sing anymore and
disappeared."

"Disappeared?"

"In a manner of speaking. She didn't sing again and . . . vanished
like a hundred other *boleristas* who had their days of glory followed
by their years of oblivion . . ."

"Any idea why?"

"I heard things . . . That her voice failed her. She had a smallish
voice, it wasn't a torrent like Celia Cruz's or Omara Portuondo's,

although she performed well with what she had. But I never bothered to find out where she ended up . . . Katy Barqué did talk to me about her once. She said they had a row."

"A row?" the Count smiled. "I can't imagine a woman as spiritual as Katy Barqué getting into a row."

"Katy Barqué is a little she-devil, don't believe all they say about her being the gentle singer of love songs . . . But their row was just words. They didn't see eye to eye because they had similar styles. Truth be told several *boleristas* sang more or less the same way, with lots of feeling, lots of high drama, as if they held everything in contempt. It was a very fifties style. Did you never hear the recording they made of 'Freddy'? In the sixties, La Lupe changed that style into some thing else rather sorrowful, contempt turned to scorn, drama to tragedy: La Lupe marks another era . . . But when Violeta started out, Katy Barqué was the best known in her style, and apparently she thought the other woman was competition . . . Hence the row."

"But wasn't there room for everyone?" wondered Yoyi.

"Down at the base of the pyramid, there was. It wasn't the same at the top. These *boleristas* were very special ladies, full of character. A bolero isn't any old song, obviously: to sing one you really make it yours, don't just feel it. Boleros aren't about reality but a desire for reality you reach via an appearance of reality, if you follow me? No matter . . . That's the philosophy behind boleros, I wrote about that in my book . . . And that was its golden age, because the classic composers who'd been writing since the twenties and thirties came together with these young men with lots of feeling who read French poetry and knew what atonal music was. And that encounter created those boleros that now seem to speak of life . . . Real life. Even though it's all lies: pure theatre, as La Lupe said."

"What about Violeta's record?" asked the Count, clinging to the edge of the precipice.

"I've got it in there . . . but my record player's broken. I'm waiting for a friend to bring me one from Spain, because . . . Do you know how many LPs, 78s and 45s I've got in there?"

Rafael followed his question with such an abrupt silence the Count was forced to follow his cue.

"No, how many?"

"12,622. What do you reckon?"

"Fantastic," conceded Pigeon.

"They cost me a fortune, and now with CDs nobody's interested. Every day someone comes with a box of records and gives them me for nothing."

"What do we have to do to listen to Violeta's?" the Count implored.

Rafael took his glasses off and rubbed them on his shirt-flap and the Count was shocked to see he hardly had any eyes. The sockets were two deep round holes, like bullet holes, darkened by the circles from the bags obscuring his mulatto skin. When he put his glasses back on, the man restored his wakeful owlish eyes and the Count felt relieved.

"I never lend my records, books or press cuttings. As you can imagine, people have nicked things hundreds of times . . ."

The Count's brain began to spin in search of a solution. Come back with a record player? Bring a needle for Rafael's system?. . . Or leave something in lieu?

"How about this for a deal? We've got seven boxes of books in our car boot you won't find anywhere else. I'll swap you the book of your choice for Violeta del Río's record . . ."

Rafael's unreal eyes glinted wickedly.

"Good books?"

"They're something special, believe me. Take a look and chose the one you want. Come on."

The Count stood up and held a hand out to Pigeon, wanting the car keys. The look on the young man's face showed his disapproval: that whim could cost them dear and, as Yoyi swore, you shouldn't gamble your children's food away – though he had none and didn't intend having any. The suggestion brought Rafael to his feet and they went into the street.

Pigeon opened the boot and pressed a button to switch on the light. Like any bibliophile stricken by the bug, the musicologist didn't hide the desire aroused by boxes stuffed with books and, turning to the Count, he checked: "Whichever?"

"Uh-huh . . ."

The musicologist inspected the books one by one, slowly, lifting them up level with his face, just a few inches from his spectacles, as if he needed to smell rather than see them. He lingered over some of the tomes he greeted with sporadic cries of "How wonderful!", "Christ, look at this!", or a self-satisfied shout of "I've already got this one". Finally, when he'd spread all the copies over the car-boot, Rafael focused his desire on the original 1925 edition of *The Crisis of High Culture in Cuba*, by Jorge Mañach, and another first edition, from 1935, of *The Universal History of Infamy*. Borges or Mañach? he tried to make his mind up and, sorrowfully, stretched out a right hand and put Mañach's essay back in one of the boxes he'd just emptied, while he patted his newly acquired copy of the Borges classic.

"Right then," he declared, as he caressed the book's spine, seemingly more frustrated by his inability to have them all than satisfied at being the owner of a rarity half the world was after, "let's get that record."

28 October

My dear,

Dawn brought rain today. It was a gentle, persistent rain, as if the sky was weeping and had no intention of stopping, so profound was its grief. God must know I have not seen you or had any news for thirty-nine days. Did you realize that? I never thought this would happen, but I have learned over the years that we often grow in strength, and have a strange, hidden capacity to resist the hardest blows, which compels us to keep on.

Tell me, how do you feel? I hope you have fought off the migraines that tormented you so in those last months and have new worries to occupy you, which must be both a blessing and a risk: the blessing being that time will not drag so and the risk that you might welcome the relief resignation and oblivion bring . . .

The cyclone that appeared to be heading towards us swerved and thankfully passed us by, its gales never touched us, though it did leave this rain in its wake. I had prayed to the Virgin: you know how afraid I am of hurricanes (I must have inherited that from my father, poor man, who trembled at the mere sound of the word cyclone). And, I must say, we have quite enough to deal with, if not too much, with the other whirlwind that has hit the country. There is something new every day, a new law is passed or an old one repealed, someone talks for hours in front of a television camera while another silently departs (many of your old friends, your university colleagues have left), or somebody renounces what he once was (some of these were also friends of yours), wraps himself in the flag and swears he was always a patriot (though he had never done anything to show it), and publicly salutes the freedom and national dignity we've finally been given, or so they tell us. We're living pages of history that are too turbulent: everything is collapsing and new myths are being thrown up; heads roll and things are being renamed. As in any revolution. As a distant witness, with no need to leave the house, I think I have a better view of all that's happening outside and for the first time I fear the situation may take a really tragic turn and, above all, become irreversible. Is it the definitive end to our world?

If you had been able to read it, you would have noted in my previous letter how I decided not to mention things that were too sad. But I think so much, all alone, that I need this confession where I can empty out my soul, and you are the only possible destination. I still think that everything that happened, before your departure, was a cruel blow from fate whose hand you were trying to force and which rebelled, like a curse, to remind you of hallowed alliances. I know: horrible thoughts have passed through your mind and most blame me for what happened. But, knowing me as well as you do, you will not find in your brain (if you are fair) and much less in reality the slightest reason to persuade you I was in any way guilty. What is more, my love: I now believe that nobody is guilty. Life simply tried to correct a deviation and return things to their original place, from where they should never have moved. I know your grief and anger will last a long time, but when oblivion begins to erase those feelings, you will understand I am right and see how unfair you have been to think I was guilty of something which you know only too well, I couldn't even imagine: the act of causing the death of another person is an act I could never commit, whatever the humiliations and grief I have suffered, whatever the grief inflicted on me by that person's existence and her undesired presence.

You know that, because of you and your love, I agreed to play the saddest of roles and defer my desires and rights when you embarked on the most ridiculous affair in your whole life. To love her was to kill me. You knew that but didn't hold back. Often the heart sends out orders when the brain should exercise common sense (something I know only too well) and nothing can resist these orders, although there are times when one has to curb feelings to reach a truth that is just.

75

3 November

My dear:

Here I am, again.

I left the house yesterday, for the first time since you left. That outing has given me strength to resume this letter I broke off a few days ago, numbed by grief that brought tears and made my hands shake.

Can you imagine where I went? I hope you can, because I did it for you. It was All Saints Day and, as was our wont, I visited the graves of your parents and grandparents, and took them the flowers you liked to place in their pantheon. It was a strange experience because it was the first time I'd done this without you. It was even more difficult because your son came with me. I was afraid to go alone, to go out into a world I feel is increasingly hostile, and, once in the cemetery, the poor boy didn't understand why his mother cried as if we were attending the burial of a loved one who had recently died. Happily, he doesn't know and doesn't suffer. He just thinks I am going mad because I weep over the graves of people who died so many years ago.

This outing helped me to realize how much the country has changed in very few months. From my taxi, I could see how the streets and especially the people still seemed overwhelmed and happy at what is happening, and live normally, without fear of the dangers that increasingly darken the firmament. I found their faces and their eyes expressed a joy that had been hidden too long and, above all, I thought I saw they had hopes and were enjoying a new dignity. How long will this state of collective grace last? . . . I must confess, my love, that I envied them: they have continued with their lives or rediscovered them (your son, in his fanatical enthusiasm, says they have been re-born) and are enjoying the time they will spend on this Earth with an intensity I could only have felt with you at my side, either here or there. As I watched I was persuaded that this time something important had happened, that nothing would ever be the same again. I suddenly understood that people like you and I belong to a time that has been played out. We are the dead from that past and perhaps that is why the cemetery is the place I saw most changes. You can't imagine how many graves where the people closest to the family used to gather on this day were quite solitary, without flowers, without the consolation of a beloved hand on the cold gravestone. It was then I had a real measure of what is occurring in a country where the living go far away, in search of happiness, or adapt as best they can and put on a smiling front, while their dead lie abandoned in the most unpleasant solitude.

I didn't seek to sadden you and make you feel guilty with news like this. You must have a thousand worries on your mind and, it is best for everyone if the dead are left where they are and in the peace they deserve. All the dead. And for life to go on, for those who may still possess such a thing.

My love, lots of kisses to the children and remind them how much I love them. And please, don't ever forget who most loved you,

Your Nena

He felt his hands sweat as he ever so gingerly lifted up the pick-up arm between two fingers, and moved it backwards so the turntable received its electric go-ahead and started to spin. Then he lowered it slowly, trying to find, though shaking slightly, the first groove on the small acetate. Conde rubbed his hands on his trouser legs and closed his eyes, about to embark on that voyage into the past.

Bitten by the curiosity bug, Yoyi Pigeon had driven him to Skinny Carlos's house, where the Count knew an old portable RCA Victor record player existed, that might still be coaxed into action. Thanks to that small machine, whose original speaker they once successfully swapped for a German democratic variety, Conde and his friends had listened hundreds of times to the plastic plaquettes on which Cuban engineers, helped by mysterious processes, pressed the music of Paul Anka, the Beatles and The Mamas and the Papas – now on the final strait to his fifties, Conde still got goose-pimply listening to "Dedicated to the One I Love". Those distant years, when only such quaint methods enabled you to hear groups on the island that were all the rage in the decadent, capitalist remainder of the planet, where they made and broadcast their petty bourgeois music, unsuitable for the ears of a young revolutionary, according to the wise, Marxist decision taken by the state's ideological apparatus that banned it from radio and etherized it from television. Only a few privileged children of what you'd hardly call groovy mamas and papas in government posts, who were occasionally allowed to set foot in Mexico, Canada or Spain, had access to the original records, which were so excessively used and abused that they often lost their grooves.

Like wizards before a mouth-watering brew, on unforgettable evenings and hot nights, Conde, Carlos, Andrés, Rabbit and Candito, all without the privilege of carrying a single drop of leadership blood in their plebeian veins, resigned themselves to those worn-out discs and, gathered round that same record player, dived in and soaked up the hot sounds and words outside their understanding that could leave no trace of ideology but which nevertheless touched sensitive nerve ends. Several years later, when Carlos finally got hold of a small cassette recorder, his friends ratcheted up their enjoyment of music, on copies no less tatty than the previous plaquettes, recorded on corrosive Orwo cassettes – German and democratic to boot. They entered the world of Blood, Sweat and Tears, Chicago and, above all, Credence Clearwater Revival, and turned "Proud Mary" and the gravely voice of Tom Fogerty into icons of the blood ties they had forged from those harsh times, plagued by material shortages and restrictions and slogans that had to be rigorously obeyed, socialist targets and mass-meetings to bolster political commitment. It was, nonetheless, a past that they'd think of as almost perfect, perhaps because of their romantic insistence on keeping it intact, as if hibernating in the favourable mists from the best years of their lives.

Conde and Yoyi had dropped by Carlos's place with pizzas they'd bought en route and two bottles of rum to clear their throats and brains. While Josefina improved the so-called pizzas by adding a few slices of onion, tomato purée and slivers of green pepper requested by her son, the Count delved into the cupboard on the terrace to unearth the record player, fearing all the while it would be unable to produce a single note. After dusting it inside and out, he cleaned the needle with a handkerchief soaked in a high octane, recently purchased rum, and finally connected it to the current, to see if the turntable at least spun round.

The first bottle uncorked was already on its third round when Conde started to lower the arm and put the needle in place, to allow the gravel-throated speaker to emit a few preliminary crackles. Then, like big drops of rain heralding the heavy downpours of summer, the almost violent chords of a piano, and only a piano, reached their ears, with no excessive flourishes or trills, quickly joined by the beat of a bongo, the deep sound of the double bass and, finally, a voice that spoke rather than sang, imbued with an almost male heaviness, first pleading, and then with an aggrieved, demanding resentment, making you feel you didn't need to see the woman to

78

know there was something different about her rich, husky voice, intent on speaking to the inner ear rather than singing:

You who fill everything with joy and youth
and see ghosts in the night's half light
and hear the perfumed song from the blue.
Be gone from me . . .

Don't stop and look at
the dead leaves on the rose
that fade and never flower,
look at the landscape of love
that is the reason to
dream . . . and love . . .

I've fought against all evil,
my hands, broken by clinging tight,
no longer cling to you.
Be gone from me . . .

In your life I'll be the best
from the mists of yesterday
when you've forgotten me,
like the best poem's always
the one we can't remember . . .
So now . . . be gone from me.

When the Count opened his eyes and silently lifted the needle from the virgin area of the acetate, he was absolutely confident that two days ago, when he'd been surprised by a hunch as he crossed the threshold of the library of the mighty Montes de Ocas, that it wasn't impelling him to discover a fabulous book, as he'd believed, but was marking out a path so he could confront that voice sleeping in his past, a voice that waited only for him. Could that be right? Not thinking or looking at the equally silent and moved Skinny or Pigeon, the Count put the arm back over the first groove on the record and let himself be transported by the melody and voice, like a lover overcoming the delights from a first touch, and embarking on a quest for the more recondite essences behind that punchy vocal. He tried to grasp the drama suggested by a voice directed at a you who might be anyone: him, or possibly his own father, perhaps bewitched by the same woman, voicing a feeling that was too much like true suffering and that, at the end of the first stanza, adopted a pleading tone when it asked: "Be gone from me". But then the voice ordered: "Don't stop and look", recalling distant echoes of the Bible, that made their full impact in the third stanza where the voice became slower, wearier, even more whispering, telling of its refusal to go on with that struggle to the death. The final act erupted with a fresh refrain where the voice anticipated a possible, if undesired, future, when its owner would vanish into the dense mists of yesterday. And concluded on an order that brooked no appeal, a last, heartbreaking "Be gone from me", intent on silencing the music that only returned, as the voice's last vibrations faded, hot and heavy, into a predicable total silence . . . but, a brief interlude opened before it reiterated its final wish beyond all appeal: "so, now . . . be gone from me", a visceral demand that convinced the Count her way of singing was involved in much more than a game of mirrors with reality: wasn't it in fact pure, genuine reality?

"What the fuck is all this about?" he asked, now out loud, and placed the pick-up arm on its stand, while the silent acetate continued to spin hypnotically. He raised his half empty glass and gulped down the rum trying to restore his composure. He slowly felt reunited with his anatomy and the place that had been blurred by emotions aroused by the music.

"You reckon that woman disappeared?" asked Skinny Carlos, his arms and hands exhausted by so much clinging, and now trying as best he could to sit comfortably in his wheel chair.

"Apparently . . . She never sang again," the Count confirmed. "I don't even know whether she's alive or dead . . ."

"I tell you, her voice is . . ." Yoyi sought in vain for an elusive adjective to capture that strange miracle.

"No one else sings like her, that's for sure," Skinny concluded, pouring round what was left in the bottle. "Put the other side on, savage."

"No," the Count rasped unthinkingly as he tapped the acetate. "No. Let me digest this first."

Conde reread the credits on the record, spotlighted by the glinting gem that was the recording company's logo, and finally put it back in the home-made grey-paper envelope Rafael Giró had made for it. He wondered whether now might be the moment to tell his friends he was sure his father had been in love with that singer, though he'd probably never spoken to her. But he decided it wasn't up to him to make such a confession and blurted out, almost unthinkingly, a desire that was burning inside him:

"Fuck me. I've got to find out who she was and what happened to her."

Mario Conde was now able to recall the twelve years he'd worked as a policeman without being attacked by an abrasive mixture of nostalgia and remorse. Reaping the benefits of the distancing process had been gradual, sometimes painful, like being cured of an addiction. The passage of time had exorcized the spell and removed the ballast his inevitably sordid police duties had lodged in the crevices of his soul. Relentlessly nostalgic or, as Skinny Carlos defined him, a bastard who was always remembering, he took a double pleasure from this distancing that finally allowed him to view his time spent as a police investigator as blurred and lethargic. Consequently, when circumstances forced him to recall his days as the representative of the forces of order he'd been for twelve years, he felt alienated from himself, like a stranger who'd lived too long among the supposedly strong and powerful, when he was naturally inclined to membership of the club for non-conformists.

Nonetheless, knowing he was too attached to his memory, Mario Conde was forced to recognize that the destruction of that fragment of his existence had simply been a survival strategy he'd clung to when deciding to give a new – or was it old? – meaning to his life. Perhaps what most helped exorcize the past, in that process of denial, was his belief that he'd never been unfair and, above all, the certainty he'd never acted arrogantly, unlike so many past and future colleagues. His allergic reaction to violence or the use of force, his rejection of the police's propensity to assault conscience and dignity, always spared him the usual excesses of his trade and, at the same time, other harmful secondary effects such as the corruption that blotted the copybooks of several colleagues, and destroyed many of the Count's illusions, enabling him to grasp more clearly than ever the all-conquering frailties of the human soul – even of souls who claimed they had the power and responsibility of justice on their side.

As he'd never found out for certain why he'd become a policeman – he was too young, needed work, was still being channelled through life by a gauche innocence – for a long time he'd put his decision to become a police investigator down to the simple fact that his youthful spirit couldn't stand the sight of the bastards doing things and not paying for them. Perhaps that was why he enjoyed so much exposing their supposedly whiter-than-white characters, knocking them off their pedestals and making them pay for their crimes and presumption, for the way they abused the power they'd abrogated to themselves, and thanks to which they screwed up the fates of others. In the course of such demolition jobs, Conde had felt immune and almost invigorated by the many looks of hatred he'd received from those once powerful individuals he'd defeated.

Luckily for the Count, this kind of reflection, conveniently hidden in his conscience, only dared surface in quite specific circumstances, such as that morning's, when, his hand gripping an early morning shot of rum, he felt an elemental need to seek out the truth stirring in him, and his brain tried to galvanize into action rusty old mechanisms that might still work.

"Hey, what the hell's getting at you now?"

The voice, from behind his back, came as no surprise. He'd summoned it himself, like a phantom floating in the mists from his own yesterdays, and felt how those familiar tones aroused deep-rooted joy. So he didn't turn round, but pushed his glass over the varnished wood of the bar, until it was opposite the next stool, then asked: "Now, tell me the truth, my friend, can one be a pansy for a while, and then opt out?"

"You must be joking. Once a pansy, always a pansy. Once you've swallowed the pill, there's no salvation . . . And the guy who was a policeman will always be one even though he burnt his bridges."

"Just as I'd thought," he answered, finally turning round to contemplate the eternally skeletal features, the irremediably squinting eyes and incredibly childish face of one Captain Manuel Palacios, his former detective colleague. "So even if I burnt all my bridges?. . ."

Manolo waited for the Count to get off his stool before giving him a hug. Then he raised his half-filled glass and gulped the whole lot down.

"Aghh . . . To your health."

"How's life treating you then, Manolo?"

When the Count left the police force, the youthful Manuel Palacios was barely a novice sergeant who'd worked as a plain-clothes detective only at the Count's insistence. Now a fully fledged captain, Manolo wouldn't allow himself to be separated from that uniform he so liked to show off, a uniform to which he'd certainly dedicate every possible year of his life.

"Lots of work, it's fucking madness. You can't imagine what things are like. Before it was child's play, now it's the hard men and no holds barred. Armed robbery's routine, drugs are booming, assault is a plague, corruption grows like wildfire, never dies however much you douse it . . . Not to mention pimping and pornography."

"I love pornography . . ."

"Child porn, Conde!"

"Hey, there are some fourteen-year old girls I've seen . . ."

"Fuck off, you never change."

"So, do you?"

Manolo smiled and put one of his hands on top of the hand Conde had placed on the bar.

"I'm trying to avoid it . . . How about a ciggy?"

"Another shot of rum?" asked the Count pushing the packet and lighter his way.

"No, what I just sank will do me for the moment . . ."

"Christ!" the Count called to the barman. "I'll have another . . . What's up then, Manolo? Is it true the end of the world is nigh? Why are people more buggered by the day?"

Manolo sighed and exhaled smoke.

"I keep asking myself that question. I don't know, too many people who don't want hard toil any more and take the easy way out. There are a lot, too many, who've grown up watching half the world steal, counterfeit and embezzle, and now it seems so normal they do it as if they weren't doing anything wrong. But the violence is the worst of all: they've no respect for anything and when they want something they'll do whatever it takes . . ."

The Count sipped his refill.

"I've got a partner in the book business. His theory is that people no longer believe in anything and that's why things are like this. Do you remember when we turned Havana upside down because three lads in Pre-Uni in La Víbora smoked the odd joint?"

"Happy days, Conde, I can tell you. Now they're on crack, coke, parkisonil with rum and amphetamines, when they can get them. If not, any anti-depressant with alcohol and even the stuff for anaesthetizing animals, will do . . . They used to inhale petrol, paint, varnish, industrial rubber . . . You know what the latest is? They set light to CDs and sniff them. And go to heaven but shed a load of neurones on the way . . . And don't think it's just a handful . . . If you drop by the Psychiatric Clinic, you'll see how many are tied to the stake like Hatuey the Indian. You know, whenever there's a public dance or dog fight, or they're bored, they get off on whatever they can find and start wanting to kill each other: really kill each other . . . And get money from all ends and sides, almost always by thieving, pimping or selling drugs to other people. Or by deciding to burgle, steal stuff, and kill two or three people while they're about it. *In Cold Blood*? Wasn't that the title of a book you gave me once? Well, I saw a case like that last week. Five murdered in one house, tortured, mutilated . . . and all for two thousand pesos and a television set."

"The newspapers never report these things . . . Doesn't anyone ask why it's all happening?" enquired the Count, alarmed by the panorama sketched by his former colleague and congratulating himself for being so far removed from that gloomy, ever expanding reality.

"I don't know, but someone, somewhere, should be. I'm a policeman, Conde, an ordinary cop: I pick up the shit, I don't dish out the grub . . ."

"So, we're done for, Manolo. I'd like to know when the test tube broke, as Yoyi says, and it all started to mess up."

"Yeah, it would, but enough philosophizing. I'm in a hell of a rush. Tell me what you're after."

"My request is less horrific but probably more difficult . . . I need to track down a person who was lost sight of forty-three years ago."

"Lost, disappeared, what's the story?"

"She vanished and nobody remembers her. I don't know if she's dead or alive, although she'd be sixty or so now, I really don't know . . ."

"Tell me her name and I'll look in the files."

"That's the first bloody problem: she was a singer and I only have her name as an artiste. No one was ever really called Violeta del Rio."

"Violeta del Río?"

"You heard of her?"

"No, no, and no again . . ."

Manolo stretched his arm out, grabbed the Count's glass and took a sip.

"Do you or don't you want another shot?"

Manolo shook his head and added: "Let me have a look anyway, she may come up under her alias . . . Why are you after her?"

"I don't know," the Count admitted. "At least I don't think I'll really know until I've found her. That's why it's so important."

Rogelito might well be the last of the dinosaurs, a kind of fossil who'd survived the natural extinction of his contemporaries and made it to the twenty-first century from a geological era only recorded in the old books shifted by the Count. His mythical beginnings belong to the year 1921, just after the end of an increasingly historic First World War, when as a mere seventeen-year old he joined the great Tata Alfonso's *danzón* orchestra and started to weave his very own legend as a brilliant *timbalero*, playing in all the remarkable orchestras and jazz bands that drifted through the crowded Cuban musical scene for over sixty years, the ones who pursued him for what he'd always been: the best.

It was said of Rogelito that back in 1920 he'd been lucky enough to be a pupil of Manengue the fantastic, eccentric, alcoholic *timbalero* who'd wanted novel resonances from his primitive instrument and had enriched it by incorporating a cowbell's metallic percussion and the rhythmic beat from the snare and a little Japanese wooden box, that with its sharp, torrid sounds became the basic percussive instrument for the *danzón*.

Despite this epic story, Conde wasn't shocked to find the eternal Rogelito living in one of those narrow, crammed "passageways" in the barrio of Buenavista, in a tiny flat with flaking, damp-oozing walls, with no view of the street, squeezed between two other tiny flats equally sentenced to stare at the wall separating them from next door's similarly dark, damp passage. As with all the musicians in his era, enough money must have passed through Rogelito's hands to have bought, rented or even built a luminous, airy house. Like most, however, Rogelito had dressed swankily, and drank, smoked and fucked every peso away – not a bad option, come to think of it, Conde told himself – while finally taking shelter, with a clear conscience, in one of those asthmatic flats where old age and oblivion had caught up with him. Might the once high-living Violeta del Río be holed up in one of those dismal rooms?

After asking the Count to wait for a few minutes, the great-granddaughter responsible for caring for Rogelito, a creamy-white mulatto with over thirty solid, steamy years behind her, owner of nipples intent on drilling through her flimsy blouse and jutting buttocks where a man could sit, led the old man to a sprung armchair with extra cushions that looked like a throne for a patriarch fallen on bad times. Rogelito tottered out of his bedroom on his great-granddaughter's arm, now unable to lift legs that had once danced in Havana's best venues and the Count had the impression he was watching a candle burning the last thread of its wick. Apart from his irrepressible ears, that had once belonged to a man of average build, and his false teeth, keen to lend him a permanent, grotesque leer, everything about the old man seemed about to vanish and turn to dust as a consequence of the implacable chemistry of time.

Sitting back in his armchair, eyes wide open, trying to reap benefit from the light, Rogelito looked like a chick prematurely hatched from a giant egg, and the Count concluded that excessive old age might be the worst punishment ever meted out to man.

"Why did you want to see me, young man?"

"First of all to greet a real maestro," replied the Count, thinking it would be rather indelicate to plunge straight into the reason for his visit.

"That's strange. Nobody ever remembers me now."

"Lots of books mention you. And there are old records . . ."

"That don't put no food on the table."

"True enough," agreed the Count now hit by the aroma from the coffee percolating in a kitchen mixed with a poverty-stricken smell of burnt kerosene. "When did you stop playing, maestro?"

"Agh . . . about fifteen years ago. Something odd happened to me: I couldn't read music any more, but was able to play any piece I'd played before. If you said, Rogelito, we're about to start, *El bombín de Barreto*, or *Almendra*, I'd start thinking and wouldn't remember a thing . . . But if I waited until the *paila*, and the piano or double bass played the first notes, I'd pick up the drumsticks and start to play, almost without knowing what I was doing, but never missing a beat. My hands were doing the thinking, not my head. But then I lost it," and he waved his huge hands at Conde, out of proportion in relation to the rest of his physique, "these sons of a bitch gave up on me."

His great-granddaughter emerged from the oppressive kitchen with a cup for the Count and a plastic beaker for the old man. The would-be coffee smelt of burnt split peas, and the Count waited for it to cool sufficiently to gulp down the unpleasant brew in one, and observed how Rogelito, helped by his great granddaughter, lifted his container with both hands and took small sips. Conde lit a cigarette, shifted his gaze from that depressing spectacle to those erect nipples marooned on a woman who was certainly tired of caring for an old man in the faint hope she'd inherit those four oozing walls and would, thus, be ready to grant herself a couple of hours of pleasuring without too much agonizing. Nervous, as he usually was in such circumstances, the Count focussed back on the image of the premature chick, with equine teeth and elephantine ears, and cut straight to the point. "Rogelito, someone told me you knew Violeta del Río . . ."

"One day we were having a few drinks in the Vista Alegre café before heading off to Sans Souci, where we were on at eleven. It was . . . hell, two thousand years ago, just imagine, you could order a coffee with milk on any street corner in this country. The point is that Barbarito Diez, the singer in the orchestra at that time, and I agreed a wager: as he didn't drink alcohol and ate well, and didn't go whoring but went to bed when he finished work, and I was quite the opposite, we laid a bet on who'd live the longest, a black guy who looked after himself as he did, or a mad black like me, and our witness was Isaac Oviedo. Isaac was my age, Barbarito a bit more of a kid, five or six years younger, but I gave him the advantage and, you know, I've buried poor Barbarito and poor Isaac, and both died at a ripe old age, and now there's not a brick of the Vista Alegre left standing, let alone any memories . . . but I'm still here, heavens know why or what for . . . More than sixty years playing in whatever orchestra came along, drinking in every bar in Havana, having a ball till daybreak seven days a week, you imagine all the people that I knew. From the twenties onwards Havana was the city of music, of pleasure on tap, with bars on every street corner, and that gave lots of people a living, not just maestros like me, for yours truly spent seven years in the Conservatoire and played in the Havana Philharmonic, but anyone who wanted to earn money from music and with the spunk to keep going . . . After that, the thirties and forties were the heyday of dance halls, social clubs and the first big cabarets with casinos attached, Tropicana, the Sans Souci, the Montmartre, the National, the Parisién, and the little cabarets on the beach, where my mate Chori ruled the roost. But in the fifties it all increased ten-fold: more hotels were opened, all had cabarets, and night clubs became the fashion, there were God knows how many in El Vedado, Miramar, Marianao, and they couldn't handle big orchestras, they only had room for a piano or a guitar, and a voice. That was the heyday of the people with feeling and heart-rending *boleristas*, as I called them. They were very special women, they sang because they wanted to and left their hearts on stage, lived the lyrics to their songs, and what they did was magic. Violeta del Río was one of them . . .

"I remember seeing Violeta three or four times, I think, I didn't have time to go and see other musicians. Once in the Las Vegas cabaret and another in The Vixen and the Crow, where they had a tiny little dance floor. That day she wasn't performing, I mean, wasn't on the programme there, but sang anyway because she really felt like singing and Frank Emilio was at the piano because he really felt like playing and as they were both so keen, what they came out with was something you'd never forget even if you lived to be a thousand. Did I say Violeta was a fantastic female? Well, she was eighteen or nineteen and at that age even Mother Teresa of Calcutta's a looker. She was olive-skinned, a dark tan, but not mulatta, with jet-black hair, and a big, beautiful mouth, with good teeth, that gave her lots of character even if they were a bit chipped here and there. But her eyes were her best asset: they could chill you to the bone if she pointed them at you, checked you inside and out, like an x-ray machine. She used to sing for the sake of singing all the time, so they said: she enjoyed singing boleros, always very quietly, always with a hint of scorn, half aggressively, as if letting you in on things from her own life. She had quite a husky voice, like an older woman who'd had to put up with a lot in life, and never raised her voice much, almost spoke rather than sang, but when she let rip with a bolero, people went quiet, forgot their drinks, as if she'd hypnotized the lot of them: men and women, pimps and whores, drunks and junkies. She turned out boleros that were dramas and not ordinary songs, as I said, as if they came from her own life and she was telling the whole world, there and then.

That night I was blown away. I even forgot Vivi Verdura, a big, fat whore, over six feet tall, who'd got her claws into me and was swigging my drinks. And the hour, hour and a bit, two hours, or whatever time Violeta was singing, was like being off the planet, or very close, so close you were right inside that woman, and you never wanted to leave . . . Fucking hell! That day a photographer who was always round the clubs and cabarets, because he earned his crust from taking photos of artists for newspapers and magazines, told me: 'Rogelito, Violeta's miracle isn't that she sings the best but that she can seduce anyone who walks in.' It was so true. So much so, that picking up gossip here and there one day, I discovered that a very rich fellow, one of the really rich who never went to clubs, had fallen in love with her, wanted to marry her, the whole lot, although he was thirty years older. It seems this big shot was the one paying for the record to launch her big time, get her on television and on the road to an LP with ten or twelve songs . . .

"But Violeta didn't need any such helping hand, because she was really good, I tell you, and that was why she began to make a name for herself with that kind of performance and, as always happens in this piss-pot of a country, people couldn't keep the lid on their envy. Other singers began to stick their knives in and some said if it weren't for the big shot she'd never get to sing, even in her own backyard. Katy Barqué was the most vicious. Katy was in her prime, but was always fucking venomous, and didn't want any competition. She knew that Violeta could beat her in that bolero style, as the hard, contemptuous woman, because it came more naturally to her, and because as a female she was much better equipped than Katy. That fracas led to a big row, I discovered, as was to be expected: one day Katy created a scene and called her every name under the sun, but Violeta didn't respond, just laughed a bit and said that if envy turned your hair yellow, Katy wouldn't need to dye hers every week . . .

"Everybody was talking about the cat fight between Katy and Violeta and the mysterious rich guy intent on marrying the girl when that same cabaret photographer, the one they called Salutaris, because he looked like the guy in the advert for Salutaris soft drinks, told me one night: 'Hey, Rogelito, Violeta's not going to sing any more.' He didn't really know why, and he was the one who knew the tricks everyone was up to, but the rumour was she was going to marry the rich guy, and that the rich guy, after paying for the record and all, now wanted her to give up the club and cabaret scene, not appear on television and become a proper lady. I believed what Salutaris said, because it had happened a thousand times before and Violeta's situation was nothing new: you bet, she was a girl from a poor background, even though she seemed gentle and good-mannered, and the fact was she lived by singing and if she could suddenly live like a princess, the songs, melodies, even the Parisién and the long, evil nights that do you in could go to fucking hell. Or do some people in, at least . . . Frankly, it surprised me, because I reckoned Violeta lived to sing rather than to earn a few pesos. She had so much passion, she wanted to sing so much, at any hour of the night, whether paid or not, unlike Katy Barqué and all the others, and that's why I was surprised she'd accepted the condition that she had to give up singing, although women sometimes fall in love – men too, for fuck's sake – and do what they have to do and especially what they shouldn't do. All the same, it smelt odd, *fishy*, as Vicentico Valdés would say . . . The fact is Violeta disappeared from the scene, like so many people in that period, Salutaris included, who went north and I never found out what happened to him . . . That was the last I heard of her, it must have been early 1960, because I went to work in Colombia that year, stayed almost three years, and, you know, I'd not heard her name mentioned until today . . .'

"Well, of course, apart from the photographer, as I remember it now, let's see . . . well, I told you Katy Barqué knew her. And she was a friend of Lotus Flower, that blonde who danced almost nude in the Shanghai and then set up her own whore-house. I know they were friends because that day in The Vixen and the Crow they sat at the same table and talked to each other for ages. Another guy who must have known her, because he knew everybody, is Silvano Quintero, the *El Mundo* journalist who wrote about the showbiz scene. But I never discovered who the guy with the big money was. It didn't make any difference to me . . . Although you bet he was from a well-heeled family and, if that was the case, flew the nest, probably with Violeta, for sure. If the man really was, say, fifty when that . . . if he was alive he'd be my age and not many of my generation are left, I don't think any . . . Hell, I once read, and have never forgotten it, that man's greatest misfortune is to survive all his friends. I don't know if the guy who wrote did so from personal experience, but I tell you he was right . . . Every morning, when I open my eyes at five o'clock and see I'm still here, I ask myself the same question: 'Rogelito, how long are you going to keep fucking around?' I've reckoned for quite a time that death's the only thing I've still to do in this life."

As soon as he got home that afternoon, Conde checked through the telephone directory and discovered, to his amazement, that Silvano Quintero the journalist still existed and lived in Havana, and after ringing him they agreed to meet in his flat on calle Rayo the following day. What time? "Any," Quintero replied, "I never go out." On the other hand, it was more complicated to set up a rendezvous with Katy Barqué, until he lied barefacedly and told her about a film a producer friend of his was planning and which would definitely use some of her songs and which, as she must know, would pay very well . . .

As if driven by a desire he couldn't put down, Conde opened the old portable record player he'd brought from Carlos's place the night before and listened to *Be gone from me* three or four times. He felt Violeta del Río's raunchy voice penetrating him, tearing his skin, scarred by the blunt needle running across the acetate, and understood the reasons why the other *boleristas* from Havana's nightlife in the fifties, especially Katy Barqué who'd never managed to sing that way, were so envious.

Intensely, even alarmingly entranced, more convinced than ever that her voice stirred him that way because it touched a sensitive fibre in his memory, Conde decided to turn the disc over and explore the unknown territory on the dark side of the moon. That side of the 45 promised strong emotions with its title *You'll remember me*, the Frank Domínguez song which, from what he knew already, would fit Violeta del Río's aggressive, despotic style like a lamé dress.

While the record settled after a few initial turns and spluttered plaintively on track to the recorded grooves, the Count shut his eyes and held his breath, allowing his ears to rule over the rest of his senses. As in *Be gone from me*, the piano introduced the melody and prepared the ground for the voice, as hot and husky as ever, its self-sufficient tone confirming her status as a conqueror refusing to grant the grace of forgiveness:

You'll remember me
when the sun dies at twilight.
You'll ring me
in the secret hours
of your sensibility.
You'll repent
you were so cruel to my love,
you'll be sorry,
but it'll be too late
to turn back.
Heavenly memories of yesterday,
will pursue you,
your unhappy conscience
will torment you . . .

You'll remember me
wherever you hear my song,
because I was the one
who taught you all . . . all . . .
you know about love.

Conde lifted the arm and then lowered the lid. Something morbid
was happening for that voice to stir him to the point of igniting
what was an unmistakeably hormonal fire. Can I be falling in
love with a voice? he wondered, with the ghost of a woman?, he
continued, afraid it might be his first step on the spiral to madness.
Refusing the masturbatory solution he frequently had recourse to
despite his now unseemly age, Conde opted to stand under the
water spurting from his shower and put his trust in its ability to
release him from adolescent obsessions and rushes of blood.

His refreshed brain could now review what he'd learnt so far,
hoping the encounters planned for the following day with the long-
lasting Katy Barqué and Silvano Quintero the journalist could clear
up the doubt most tormenting him: what did become of Violeta
del Río when she abandoned the stage? He'd above all try to find
out if the singer's rich lover had been Mr Alcides Montes de Oca,
the last owner and supplier of a stunning library that had put him
in such a sweat two days ago. The existence of that press cutting
in the entrails of a cookbook would then make sense and begin to
explain the possible relationship between those individuals from
such distant planets. However, a crucial piece refused to fit the links
the Count was making, because Alcides Montes de Oca apparently
only took his children with him from Cuba, and Amalia Ferrero
was adamant she'd never even heard of the *bolerista*'s name. Conde
realized he'd perhaps made a mistake: perhaps Amalia never knew
Violeta del Río, but a woman with another name who'd already
retired from a life of music, and he reproached himself for not
bringing the singer's photo along. But the possibility that the faceless
lover wasn't Montes de Oca, but some other man, still remained.
Was it possible that after leaving the cabaret Violeta had married,
given birth to three children, and lived more than forty years in
the deceitful shadow of domestic bliss, between her kitchen and
washing machine in a little house in Luyanó or Hialeah? Might

she now be a fat, flabby lady with wrinkled buttocks, poisonously embittered because she'd abandoned what she most liked in life? That devastating image killed the Count's latest feverish ramblings stone dead, although a truth hot from his wild imagination told him he was hallucinating: Violeta had always been the exciting woman in the photo, the unique singer who'd recorded the single, and had been forever and ever. Why did he think so? He didn't know, but was sure that was the case.

After shaving, he sprinkled on his best cologne. Right then he was confident the night would turn out as promising as he needed it to be. After checking the irrepressible Rubbish wasn't in the vicinity, he emptied some leftovers on his tray. He then stepped out into the street, and putting into practice his new status as a moneyed man, hailed a taxi and offered the driver thirty pesos to deviate from his route and take him to Santos Suárez.

Opposite Tamara's house, Conde said a quick prayer to Lady Luck, since of all the possible places known to him, it was *the* place where he could find the most telling relief for the restless sexual urges he'd been fobbing off for days. Cigarette between lips, sheltering behind a bunch of glowing sunflowers he'd bought on the way, he crossed the garden and greeted, as usual, the concrete sculptures that adorned the mansion, forms that were half human and half animal, between Picasso and Lam.

Tamara opened the door. Her eyes, limpid as ever, like two moist almonds, surveyed the newcomer and lingered on the bunch of flowers. Her sense of smell reacted first.

"You smell of whores. Not of flowers," she observed, smiling.

"We all smell of whatever we can . . ."

"And this miracle? Five days, no, a week ago . . ."

"I've been working like crazy to get rich."

"And?"

"I've made it. At least for a week. And a promising future as a businessman looms ahead. One must change with the times, Tamara. You know, it's not a sin to be a businessman . . . Quite the contrary in fact. Do you remember that Guillén poem that began 'I'm sorry for the bourgeois'?. . ."

"Of course . . . But what is one supposed to do when one is rich?"

"First one doesn't travel by bus. Secondly, one gives flowers to people," he handed the bouquet to Tamara, "and to round the day off one imagines one is Gatsby and puts on a fancy meal for one's friends, though before doing that one looks out one's girlfriend and asks her to accompany one."

"Oh yes? And who is Gatsby's impossible love?"

She took the flowers. He tried to smile and threw his cigarette butt into the street. He took aim carefully. If his next shot missed it could be fatal.

"The usual culprit, you know? The girl he met in the Pre-Uni in La Víbora in 1972 and . . ."

She smiled with a brief, unmistakable puff of sweetness, and the Count realized he'd won the match.

"Mario Conde, you've one hell of a nerve. Thanks for the flowers . . . Come in, I was about to put the coffee on. But what's that perfume you're wearing?. . ."

Conde followed her into the kitchen, relishing the rhythm of that first class piece of flesh he watched shimmy under her dressing gown, already imagining what he might soon elicit from that body he'd explored so often over so many years. Tamara's journey down the dangerous ravine of the forties had been pleasant and harmonious, although she'd helped herself with push ups and abdominal exercises, step-classes and creams destined to give her muscles more tone, her skin more sheen, and the Count appreciated such female cares of which he periodically was the direct beneficiary.

"What's all this about being rich then," she asked, putting the coffee on to boil.

"I've found a book-mine and am earning real money. It's that simple. That's why I asked old Jose to prepare a dream of a meal tonight, whatever the cost . . . Sometimes, you feel more than just hungry . . ."

"So you've come here for your apéritif?" She turned to see how the coffee was doing.

This tension always devastated the Count, who went for silence coupled with a frontal assault, though he began his attack on the mountainous rearguard: he went up close to Tamara, rammed his pelvis against her buttocks, and started to kiss her neck, sliding his hands from her stomach to her breasts, swinging free under the light material, and found them softer than fifteen years ago, when he'd caressed them for the first time, but still shapely. Conde sensed something preparing to take a rise between his legs, at once wary and bold. He greedily inhaled the smell of clean, female skin, not noticing how his hands, nose, and tongue were after one woman, while his frenzied brain was groping for yet another lost in the mists of yesterday.

15 November
My dear:

Tell me the truth: don't you ever miss me? Don't you think that squandering my love, and living far from me and from all I ever gave you, is quite unfair, even towards yourself? Don't you ever imagine, at some time in the day, that my hands are caressing your hair after I've placed before you a dish to nourish you and delight your taste buds? And wouldn't it be better to have me warming you in bed rather than to be lonely and distant? Without consulting you, (for the first time in all these years), I have dared take a decision: to move to your bedroom and occupy the side of the wedding bed I feel I have a right to. Every night, before going to bed, I fold back the bedspread, shake the sheet, as you liked me to do, slap your pillow to flatten it out, and give it the shape that is most comfortable for your bedtime reading. I switch on your night lamp and place by it the glass of water with a few drops of lemon juice and sweetened with honey that you used to drink to relieve your night-time coughing. Which book would you like me to get from the library for you to read as you move towards sleep and shake off life's worries? (I remember the last one you asked for was The Slave-trader, *by Novás Calvo . . . how often did you read it? What did you see in that book that you wanted to read it time and again?) Then I strip off, looking at that half of the bed where I can see you, lying there, waiting, and I usurp one of the many nightgowns you'd decided to keep as mementoes of your wife, and feel, at the touch of the loving silk, how my skin becomes that of a lady who owns that half of the bed, where she nightly welcomes strong, embracing arms, a male smell of cologne and tobacco, the tingle on my skin from the freshly shaved cheeks and moustache brushing against me. I turn over, my whole body sweats, set on fire by fever and craving that only has one cure, one you know well, for you often supplied it, the cure I must now seek myself in my solitude. I ask you, at my age . . .*

I sometimes toss and turn the whole night. And think: what can I do to convince you of my innocence? I think so hard, that in these exhausting bouts of restlessness, I sometimes fear lunacy is prowling, closing in, threatening to occupy the empty half of the bed, to marry and drag me into its world of darkness.

On such turbulent nights I have shuffled all the possibilities within my reach to explain what happened and find a reason for the tragedy that has inflicted this wretched separation upon us. All I can think is that we women have a surfeit of inner depths, we are too unfamiliar even to ourselves and are, consequently, capable of unimaginable acts. Who, apart from me, could benefit from an act as irreversible as her death? I am sure that is the question also echoing around your mind, but I swear: the truth is I don't know. She alone knows the reasons that led her to end her own life as she did or the reasons that she aroused in someone else who was intent on securing her disappearance and able to carry out that atrocious act. Think of it like this and be sincere: how much did you know about her, about her previous outside lives (I'm sure she had several) that you never even imagined whether they existed or not? Men's ingenuousness, even when they think they are so strong, makes them transparent and predictable, whereas women ... Who can know the infinite recesses of their souls, what they would do to save or ruin, revenge or humiliate, hide or expose themselves as they think fit? Do you really think she was that naïve girl who drove you mad with love?

Yesterday your daughter forced me to discuss what is happening to me, and what may happen in the future. As I listened to her I grasped the chilling reality of my own solitude. After learning the truth about us, she feels only indignation at the way you have behaved; to my horror, I think I have seen how that knowledge has turned into intense hatred of you. Now, like the people on the street, she talks of the past as of a time of infamy, servitude and humiliation, and is forcing me to refashion my life. I'm still young, I can still do it, she says, and repeats that the world has changed and holds a place for everybody. I've asked for time to adapt to that idea, to think of myself without you close by, and to be able to come to a decision.

If you could read these letters everything would be so much easier. To feel you on the other side of these words would be my salvation, to listen to your opinions as I always did, would end this life of deprivation. Ay, my love, if only we could talk ...

It will be your daughter Anita's birthday in a few days. From here I wish her all the happiness in the world at your side, and hope she is enjoying that

"Fuck, Jose, that smells good! Come on, tell me, tell me . . ."

Conde held his glass out towards Carlos and waited for his friend to dose him up to the brim. On a high from post-orgasmic fall-out, he'd gulped down the killer shot his spirit was demanding and focussed his attention on Josefina. Seated around the table, as if waiting for a mysterious will to be read out, Tamara, Red Candito, Rabbit, Yoyi Pigeon and Skinny Carlos imitated the Count and observed a silence, not daring at least for a few minutes to cast their hooks at one of the entrées, alive with exotic species they'd thought in danger of extinction, if not already eradicated from their collective and individual gastronomic maps: stuffed olives, cubes of Manchegan cheese, strips of mountain-cured ham, slices of Spanish chorizo, roasted peanuts and other nuts, foie gras, seafood brochettes, delicious wafers and asparagus bathed in mayonnaise . . .

"You know, the book you gave me has got so many recipes, I just opened it at the first page and I wanted to keep things simple so I selected a light dish to start with and a super heavy one to end on."

"OK by me," said the Count and the others nodded as if they were characters who'd been rehearsing that incredibly fantastic vaudeville, for once transformed into an edible reality. "No point going over the top . . ."

"We'll start with a Camagüey-style *jigote* . . ." Josefina announced.

"And what the hell is that, mum?" enquired Skinny.

"Don't be so thick, Carlos," interjected Rabbit. "It comes from the French gigot, and is a stew with minced meat fried lightly in lard . . ."

"How come you know that, Rabbit?" interrupted Candito.

"It's called being cultured . . . Although I've never eaten anything like —"

"Well, don't interrupt again," Conde shut them up. "Go on, Jose."

"It's a typical dish from Camagüey and the recipe is down to a Mrs Olga Nuñez de Argüelles . . ."

Conde pointed a finger at Rabbit, indicating he should keep quiet. Rabbit's eagerness to expound on any subject could spill over and sour the gourmet pleasures he'd summoned his friends to enjoy, after he'd handed Josefina a wad of notes that same morning to allow her to conjure up whatever fabulous supper her imagination dictated. After so many years of eating what was good enough to come her way – badly, in a word – and dreaming of succulent banquets, she could finally take revenge on objective reality, now the Count said he was rich and could accede – always accompanied by his old gang, since he could imagine no other way of enjoying his riches – to certain pleasures the doors to which only the crafty key of money or power can open.

"The ingredients for four people comprise: a big fat hen, three onions, three peppers, two sprigs of parsley, half a pound of almonds, a cup of dry wine and bread. As we're eight, I multiplied everything by two."

"You got that right," agreed Carlos. "When Manolo gets here, there'll be eight of us . . ."

"The recipe says you should chop the hen into pieces, put these in a pan with the onions, peppers, parsley, and fry lightly. Pour in water, enough to cover the hen, add salt to taste and cook until soft. When it's cold, de-bone and put it through the mincer. Crush a big onion in a mortar, another sprig of parsley and add the bits to the gravy and season it. Soak the almonds in water for a quarter of an hour so they'll peel easily. Then crush and wrap them in a small cloth to make a *horchata* paste, drop them in the gravy, put everything on the burner and keep stirring to stop it from sticking. When it's boiled for a while pour on the dry wine, and bring to the boil again . . ." she explained and then paused dramatically. "And serve with bits of fried bread"

Excited applause surged from the bottoms of hearts and stomachs astonished by a miracle made possible by Josefina's art and Conde's money.

"Well it sounds great," mused Yoyi Pigeon.

"You shut it, kid," the Count recriminated, tossing two olives into his mouth. "You've only been on rations for twenty-seven years, so

100

show some respect for us veterans here present who've experienced forty fucking Aprils of uninterrupted —"

"More than forty. We've each passed two boat-loads of split peas through our bellies," Candito reminded them, chomping on some cheese.

"Swear words not allowed, Red. Ugh . . . split peas?" recriminated Rabbit, hovering between mountain-cured ham and foie gras.

'And what's for second course, mum?' enquired Carlos, trying to ensure the audience wasn't distracted by that common diversion: a lament for the rationing worsened by all the years of Crisis, arduous times when more than one had tried to fool their stomach with banana-peel purée and orange-peel steak.

"For the second course I discovered stuffed turkey à la Rosa María. I know the second course shouldn't be flesh of a similar species, but I liked Rosa María's recipe and —"

"Who's that?" asked Rabbit, as irrepressible as ever.

"Rosa Mariá Barata de Barata."

"Oh . . ." he responded minimally under the Count's stern gaze.

"And how do you cook pullet?" asked Candito.

"It's turkey, Red, not pullet," the Count corrected him. "You know the rich eat turkey, not pullet . . ."

"First," rehearsed Josefina, "it's a ten-pound turkey . . ."

"This is looking good," commented Manolo, sticking his head into the dining room and waving a hand at those gathered there.

"Sit down and shut up. Or you might be left out for getting here so late," grunted the Count.

"And how do you cook that, Jose" interjected Tamara, fascinated by the gourmet circus to which she'd been invited.

"Mrs Barata de Barata's recipe says —"

"It cost me dear," quipped the Count.

"Says you must give the turkey a good wash in soap and water and rinse it well."

"When the pullet's alive?" asked Skinny. "What if it doesn't like being washed?"

"Piss off . . ." protested Rabbit.

"You cut the head off four inches above the breast —"

"Just as well," sighed Carlos.

"Clean its back side, as normal —"

"Fuck, Skinny, you were right," said the Count and raised his hand in order to slap his friend's proffered palm. "The pullet didn't like washing so his mum had to wipe his ass . . ."

"Shall I continue?" enquired Josefina, unable to repress a smile. "So, according to Rosa María, you wash the turkey, bone it, carefully, so as not to tear the skin. Then let it rest, basted in dry sherry and lemon, to which you add sliced onion, ground white pepper, salt and ground nutmeg. Before cooking it, stuff and sew it up."

"This is looking even better," commented Manolo.

"What's in the stuffing, Jose?" Tamara asked again.

"Five pounds of pork chunks, two and a half of ham, six or eight ground biscuits . . ."

"You added biscuits?" asked Carlos rather forlornly.

"Six raw eggs, an eighth of a pound of butter, a spoon and a half of salt and a quarter of a nutmeg, one apple, one melon pear, four stoned prunes, a quarter of a pound of roasted almonds and a small tin of truffles . . ."

"My God, truffles, I just love 'em . . ." the Count couldn't restrain himself. "I could spend my whole life eating white truffles from Alba . . ."

"What on earth are truffles?" enquired Yoyi Pigeon, astounded by the Count's *recherché* tastes.

"They're little, titchy animals, with feathers and a few hairs on their head . . . How the fuck should I know!" replied the Count. "I've not seen a truffle, dead or alive, in my whole damned life."

"We put all the ingredients together, stuff the turkey, put it on a tray and baste it with lemon, lard and crushed cloves of garlic. Put it in the oven at 350° for two hours, until it goes golden brown and dries completely," Josephine took a breath. "It can be served in its own gravy or with strawberry, apricot or apple jam."

"The Barata woman fucked up badly there," interjected Carlos. "Keep that sweet stuff off mine . . ."

"Hey, watch your language, young man," the Count complained, immediately adding: "Don't put it on mine either, Jose. Give me gravy . . ."

"There's enough for twenty people," concluded Josefina to a

fresh round of applause, and cries of "The days of plenty are upon us!" "Onwards and upwards", "Industriales for champions!" and "Viva Josefina!"

"And is it all ready?" asked Conde.

"Yup. Candito got all the ingredients, Rabbit and Carlos were my kitchen porters . . ."

More applause and exclamations followed, but Carlos raised his hands and tried to put a brake on the general jubilation. When silence was restored, Skinny looked solemnly at his mother.

"Mum . . . you forgot something."

"Oh, of course," the old lady remembered, "I made a pot of rice and black beans, and prepared a bunch of fried ripe plantains, a salad of tomato, lettuce, avocado and cucumber . . . And a simple sweet: chocolate ice cream sprinkled with ground coconut and nuts . . ."

"Is this all for real?" asked Manolo, historically, rationally and politically unable to surface from his state of stupefaction.

"And I brought along a crate of red Rioja," declared Yoyi, "plus four bottles of champagne . . ."

"The end of the world is nigh. Armageddon is upon us," commented Candito.

"You must have been toiling all day, Jose," Tamara sympathized.

"We've been on rice and beans for a week," recalled Carlos, "and we've not had any meat since our last ration of one ninth of a chicken . . . which was, in the last century, right, mum? She was in need of some exercise."

"How much did all that cost?" enquired Manolo and Conde jumped in: "Refuse to answer that, Jose. Let's eat, for fuck's sake. We rich guys don't worry over a few cents here and there."

"So how long will your wealth last you, Conde?" enquired Candito.

"At this rate . . ." Conde calculated, "eating out in *paladares*, using taxis, buying flowers, preparing banquets for a band of starving bastards . . . I'll return to a state of poverty the day after tomorrow. But it was worthwhile being a rich man for three days, wasn't it?"

"Of course it was, for hell's sake," Carlos agreed. Now we can probably face another forty years of imperialist blockades and ration books with greater strength and courage than ever before . . ."

When he opened his eyes, Mario Conde wearily felt as if his body was a sack of potatoes someone had dumped down on the middle of his bed. His accumulated experience – what the more philosophical Rabbit, with enough memory to recall the disquisitions in Marxist manuals, would call "praxis as the criterion for truth" – was again demonstrating to him with a sly dig that, after a night of gorging and tippling, he could expect a rough awakening.

"And what are you doing here?" he asked when he went to find the second pillow and it moved: "Who invited you into my bed?"

In reply, Rubbish lifted a paw, demanding that a hand scratch his belly, stuffed with the latest leftovers from his owner.

On mornings like these, the Count had the overpowering sensation he was hurtling, at breakneck speed, towards the dreadful figure of half a century's residence on earth. In that ascent – in effect one of his many descents, if not the most definitive – he had had to learn to coexist with his body, grow in awareness of its valves, axles, hinges and exhausts, in a way he'd not had to before his forty-fifth birthday. In his distant youth, after a boozy night, he might perhaps have suffered a headache, a rebellion in his stomach he resolved by expelling shit – in his case, generally, a lot of shit – and a shooting pain in his knee because of the way he'd knocked against the sharp edge of the bed, he'd curse as a son of a bitch after each collision: but it was all transitory, cured by a quick shower, a couple of pain-killers and an anti-diuretic. Not any more: he now knew, for example, that he had a heart where, as well as feelings and battle scars, there was a mechanism for pumping blood and, on certain post-orgy dawns, that pump galloped to the point he could feel it in his chest. He'd learnt he was the owner of kidneys which could hurt in the treacherous early hours; and he knew, sadly, that an ultra-alcoholic night required a whole day – this time he thought it would take two – to guarantee physical and moral recovery. For his body now refused to simply process the doses of rum it had received in a few hours, and instead wreaked its revenge in the most varied, cunning ways . . .

But the previous night could be etched in letters of gold among his memorable experiences, because not even Manolo's news that there was no trace in the police files of a person called or nicknamed Violeta del Río could dampen the Count's joy as he surveyed the turkey's bare rib cage, the bottles of rum, beer, wine and champagne that had been cheerfully emptied of their contents, and witnessed the obvious delight he'd given his friends, in particular Skinny Carlos.

With two painkillers in his stomach, a cigarette on his lip and a double espresso in his fist, he went out on his terrace and remembered that, when he'd arrived in the early hours, Rubbish had been waiting for him, as if he too had been expecting to partake in a banquet.

"Rubbish, don't get too used to this. When the party's over, we'll be back to the usual . . ."

As he watched the animal yawn, while a back leg tried to shake off a particularly annoying flea, Conde vaguely envied this dog that, despite its age, seemed ready to resume life every morning. For a moment he reflected that he should stop postponing the decision to take exercise and reduce his daily quota of cigarettes to a single packet, but shelved this thought immediately, as he realized that if he made the effort he might still have time to meet Katy Barqué before going to the rendezvous agreed with Silvano Quintero the journalist. Right then he was forced to recognize that the basic impulse fuelling this super human sacrifice was an unhealthy curiosity demanding to know – in a quite disproportionately violent fashion – more about Violeta del Río.

"I've always said this: you need two things if you want to sing boleros: a heart this size for all that feeling, and steel-plated, blockbuster ovaries. Your voice is the least of your worries . . . And it's a fact that, apart from this voice that God gave me and preserves for me as if I were a young fifteen year old, I've always had more heart and ovaries than all the other singers put together, starting with Violeta del Río."

Conde scrutinized the singer's mummified face. Katy Barqué was bordering on eighty though perhaps you could agree she was well preserved for her age. But her efforts to look twenty years younger, including surgery to give her face an artificial tautness, were rounded off with several layers of cream, swathes of re-energizing blusher, eyelashes like fans, lips stuffed with silicone and a foulard anchored in the middle of her forehead to pull back towards her skull the most rebellious folds of drooping skin.

"The bolero is feeling, pure feeling with lots of drama. It speaks about tragedies of the soul and in language that goes from poetry to reality. That's why you can sing just as well about a cloudy sky, say yours is a strange way to love, or shout 'be gone, the heat's gone from between your legs' . . . The important thing is for it all to come from your soul, making it seem credible, you know?. . . That's what I do, and I'm a big star; I've done films, musical theatre, operetta, lots of shows . . . Does your film producer know all this?"

She accompanied her harangue with florid gestures, would-be intense looks and melodic support from snatches of old boleros, as if she were facing the most critical of audiences.

"Europeans and Americans are very cold, that's why they don't understand what a good bolero is, and lately they've been going for records full of versions sung by pretty boys, versions that make you want to shit your pants. But really shit them. The bolero is from the Caribbean, that's why it was born in Cuba, and took root in Mexico, Puerto Rico and Colombia. It's the love poetry of the tropics, always telling the truth, rather thickly laid on at times, but then we are thickly laid on, nothing we can do about that. Listen to Arsenio Rodríguez's lyrics and tell me what you think:

> After you've lived
> twenty disappointments
> what does one more matter,
> after you've seen
> life in action

106

you shouldn't cry.
Just accept
everything is a lie,
nothing is true.
Just live for the moment,
learn to enjoy what's there,

(She shakes her head, endorsing Arsenio's deep truths. Her intense gaze devours Yoyi's exultant youthfulness.)

because all considered
life is a dream
and nothing sticks.
Only birth and death
are for real

(A second, more categorical affirmation. She gazes at Yoyi again, more suggestively.)

why get so anxious,
to live is to suffer eternally,
the world's a place . . . without joy.

"Hell, look at my hair standing on end . . . Do you know when poor Arsenio wrote that? When New York's best doctors said there was no cure for his blindness and he realized he was going to be blind forever . . ."

Conde looked at Yoyi and, as if by prior agreement, they both nodded. The old diva had more malice than voice, but there was something pathetic about how she sang Arsenio's memorable bolero, from behind that face mask, wrapped in a kimono covered in Chinese or Japanese characters.

"As I was saying . . . There was terrific rivalry at the time, you had to be really good to get a slice of the action. You couldn't imitate anybody, you had to find the best composers, get the arrangers to work to your style, and be lucky enough to put on a good show and then shift to television, which was already in colour here when in Spain they had one television set for Madrid and another for

Barcelona . . . I got it all, purely on the strength of my lungs and talent, because I was the best and everybody knew I was the best. By the way, did you read the last interview I gave to *Bohemia*?"

Right then Conde had a flash of insight as to why he'd always spontaneously rejected Katy Barqué: it wasn't, as he'd previously thought, down to the almost masculine timbre of her voice, the ridiculously aggressive, at times filthy lyrics she often wrote herself in her self-appointed role as self-sufficient-woman-able-to-scorn men, or even the opportunist versions of revolutionary anthems and political eulogies she'd slotted into her repertoire at different stages, or the facile poses she adopted on stage – and not only on stage, as he now saw. In fact, his rejection was altogether more visceral, down to the singer's patent disregard for any sense of historical boundaries and her attempt to cling, against the wind, tide, logic, time and fear of the grotesque, to a pre-eminence that was no longer hers and that for the last twenty years or more had turned her into a singing caricature of herself, a kind of circus act. Unlike others Conde knew, Katy Barqué would never get off her high horse: you'd have to unsaddle her or be resigned to watching her die, disastrously, holding the reins, leaving no heirs and playing the worst of roles in the theatre of life: that of the buffoon.

"Then Violeta appeared from nowhere all ready to snatch what was mine by right. She was young, with a good body and heart on her, I think, but lacked ovaries . . . and a maestro to teach her how to sing. Poor woman, at times she sounded like she was about to choke . . . But she was a cunning bitch! She landed herself a lover who was mad about her and gave her a push up to get her name in lights. Just imagine an upstart like her as the star on the second bill at the Parisién, when that cabaret was *the* place to meet those who decided who was or wasn't any good in Havana, in Cuba . . ."

From the moment they reached the well-lit penthouse in that big house on Línea, Conde and Pigeon felt that they'd visually entered a kind of museum of bolero kitsch. An evidently amateur portrait in oils, of Katy Barqué at the height of her physical splendour, occupied the premier spot on the wall in a reception room crammed with china and glassware – the height of bad taste was a metal flower, now rusting, on a plinth that declared: *Prize for the Most Popular* – awarded in recognition of her fifty plus years in the business.

"Besides that she had a nerve. Really quite shameless. One day I found out she was saying things behind my back and I just had to put her straight: I grabbed hold of her and even told her to go to hell. Because it's one thing to defend yourself as best you can, quite another to clamber over the heads of others to get some of the limelight. I wasn't having any of that. We had some good singers here, Celia Cruz, Olguita Guillot, Elena Burke, a good number, but each trod her own path and nobody ever trespassed on somebody else's terrain. It was like an unwritten law. But that girl didn't understand a thing and was messing us all about. Do you know what singing all night in a club for no pay means? Excuse my honesty, but they were bad tactics and it was bad for business . . . Don't you think?"

Yoyi Pigeon nodded: his trading ethics appreciated Barqué's logic. But Conde pondered over the star's thoughts, and remembered how in her interviews he'd never heard her mention any of the great *boleristas*, the really great ones, the ones who might make it obvious that Barqué's rise had most to do with self-promotion and opportunism of every stripe, including the sexual and political varieties.

"I never found out who the man was behind her. There was a lot of gossip in Havana, but he never showed his face. He must have been a wealthy fellow and full of prejudices and he didn't want to be seen with a cabaret singer, who, what's more, certainly had a peculiar look about her: lovely hair and all that, but don't anyone try to fool me, she looked like a nigger."

The absence of a clinching name, however, confirmed the Count in his idea that the mysterious lover was none other than Alcides Montes de Oca. And that was reinforced by his suspicion that for some unknown reason Katy Barqué was avoiding identifying a person he was sure she knew, so intent was she on waging her individual war against Violeta del Río.

"After that row I never saw her again, fortunately . . . Five or six months later, she announced she was giving up singing and promptly disappeared from the scene. I was as happy as Larry: one less, another with no stamina for the fight, sleepless nights, and the struggle to get good performing and recording contracts. If she was going to marry that wealthy individual, she could put all that behind her and enjoy her good luck, because she wasn't like me, an artist devoted night and day to my art. She was a just a bed-hopper who'd struck lucky . . . Later on, when I barely remembered she'd ever existed, I found out she'd committed suicide. That's right: she killed herself . . . By the way, how the fuck did you come across her?"

The news of her suicide, right out of the blue, provoked a primitive response from Yoyi and sent the Count's mind and body into a whirl. The certainty that Violeta del Río was now just a press cutting and a voice heard dimly on an old crackling 45 killed at a stroke Mario Conde's high hopes, nourished over the two days he'd been dreaming, that he might find the mysterious, seductive woman alive: she whose image and way of singing had begun to obsess him as if were an infatuated adolescent. A wave of frustration hit him. He suddenly felt lost in the tragic final lines of a bolero: lines written to shatter expectations raised by a sultry love song.

"Where the fuck does that old man live?" enquired Yoyi when a bewildered, disappointed Count pointed him out of calle Zanja and into Rayo, in search of Silvano Quintero's residence.

Despite a few recent cosmetic touches, Havana's old Chinatown was still the same sordid, oppressive place. Over decades the Asians who'd come to the island had huddled together there, vainly hoping they'd find a better life, even dreaming they'd get rich, a dream that had been quickly flattened. These ancient, increasingly obsolete Chinese businesses had postponed their inevitable and natural demises, by changing into restaurants – their greasy offerings got pricier by the day – and had brought life and atmosphere to the area. But the district was still gripped by its rapid, apparently unstoppable, degeneration. It emerged from potholes in the streets brimming with stinking water, climbed over metal bins packed with detritus and scaled walls gnawing at them, and occasionally causing them to collapse. Those old buildings from the beginning of the twentieth century, many now turned into tenements where several families crammed in, had long ago shed any charm they might have once had, and unremitting decline now offered up vistas of horrific poverty. Blacks, whites, Chinese and mestizos of all bloods and beliefs lived in a poverty that didn't discriminate between skin tone or geographical origins, putting everyone on an equal footing in a struggle to survive that made everyone aggressive and cynical, like the hopeless beings they'd become.

"Go another two blocks in that direction," the Count instructed him, imagining Pigeon couldn't be well-pleased at having to navigate his shiny, white-stripe-tyred Bel Air between the puddles in the street and razor-sharp eyes giving them the once over.

"The other day the television said the worst of the crisis was over . . ." Yoyi talked as he steered round the potholes in the street. "The guy who said that hadn't been round here. It gets worse and worse . . ."

"It always was a barrio in a bad state," the Count recalled.

"Never like this. With all this restaurant mess and tourist riffraff this place is about to explode. And to cap all that now they're pushing drugs . . . And we're not talking opium . . . What should do I do?"

"Go on, it's the next corner . . . You ever tried drugs, Yoyi?"

"Where you going with that, man?" he replied jumpily.

'I'm not a policeman anymore. I was just interested to know . . ."

"The odd spiked rum, a party spliff, but nothing harder, I swear. Look at this body on me: it takes some looking after . . ."

"How'd you react if I told you I'd never done any drugs at all?"

"I'd not react any different, man: you and your friends are Martians. They put you lot into a test tube . . . And how did you come out? The New Man you mentioned the other day? No, they filled the tube with alcohol and you lot got off on that fix . . ."

"Why do you reckon so many people get hooked? Is it that easy to get drugs?"

"You have to be kidding. There's zero money here and zero money equals zero trade. Ten, twenty, say a hundred tourists, prepared to buy the odd drug? A hundred kids with enough dollars for a line? That's not enough to start trading . . ."

"So where do they get it? Because there are drugs out there . . ."

"Consignments float in from the sea and someone fishes them out. The cycle kicks off: the guy who gets it out of the ocean invests nothing and sells it cheap to the man who sells it in Havana. It's pure profit from day one, no big investments, that's how the trade started. But after the police cleanup it's got more difficult, though some lunatic will always take a risk and sell whatever washes up. The worst of it is that it's more expensive now and more diluted, so dealers earn more and junkies get into bigger messes trying to get money . . ."

"When we were fifteen or twenty, we'd not even seen a joint. I had to join the police to find out what one smelled like . . . And look at me now."

The lad smiled.

"I believe you . . ."

"Stop, it's here."

"Conde, you know that woman committed suicide years ago . . . so what are you after exactly?"

"I don't know," he confessed again. "Whatever I've yet to find out, I suppose."

Yoyi parked his car in front of the building. It was typical of the area, and in a state of decline the Count had anticipated. In the adjacent half ruin, a swarm of people busy cleaning century-old bricks, salvaging rusted metal bars and prehistoric tiles, ready to recycle rather than to patch up their houses, while others sniffed among the debris looking for the unexpected something they'd almost certainly never find. Several people were dragging fifty-five gallon tanks of water along the street, on trolleys cobbled together with old bearings, as if sentenced to hard labour, and the only two real Chinamen the Count could see – so old they might be millenarian – were sitting on a doorjamb selling small tins of the Chinese ointment the Count got through so quickly as balsam for his headaches. From windows open onto the street, small counters hawked pizzas made from dubious cheeses, pastries made from stolen flour, coffee blended with cat paw, and dubiously filled croquettes. Men chatted on each street corner, as if they owned time itself. The Count calculated that on that hundred-yard stretch of street more than sixty people were inventing ways to sort their lives or at least endure them with the least trauma possible. The feeling of decline in the air alarmed the ex-policeman, and his skin trembled with fear: it was a situation at explosion point, and nothing like the pleasant city he'd known for so many years.

Too many people without hopes or dreams. Too much heat and pressure under the lid of a pot that, sooner or later, would have to burst.

While Pigeon agreed a price for protecting his car with two black guys who looked like ex-convicts, the Count crossed the street, sidestepping a swollen rat floating in a puddle, and bought four tins of pomade at ten pesos apiece from the Chinamen. He surveyed the scene and was reminded of images of African cities he'd seen on television. A return to our origins, he thought, as he geared himself up for the bigger shocks in store.

Conde and Yoyi went into the building and up the stairs. A smell of rank damp and fermenting urine hit them, and despite feeling queasy, Conde didn't dare touch the grimy banister, and kept his distance from the wall and its hanging garden of dozens of frayed electric cables, constantly threatening to short circuit. On the first floor the stairs led to a narrow passage dotted with mostly open doors. Conde peered over the metal parapet and down at an inside yard, where several people sat around a domino table, seemingly immune to the fetid atmosphere, exacerbated by the contribution from a pen where two pigs slept and a cage where several spindly hens pecked. On each corner of the table, Conde registered bottles of beer and plates with leftover food.

"Obviously nobody here works," the Count said almost to himself.

"Everybody lives by his wits," Yoyi reminded him. Those guys are playing dominoes purely for cash, evidently. But one of them rents out the space; another sells beer; that guy does the food; yet another sells cigarettes; another breeds fighting dogs; another rents out his room; another keeps an eye out for the police . . ."

"How come we walk in and they don't budge?"

"Those big black guys looking after my car, man . . . they're the security and they gave us a safe-pass . . . They circulate the money among themselves and get by that way. At night, one of them changes hats and burgles houses, offers whores to tourists and, obviously, sell drugs , as you know . . ."

"What the fuck is this? Hell?"

"Yes . . . but only the surface. Like the first circle. But you can sink even lower, I swear. Been a while since you went around Prado at night? Go take a look and you'll really see fireworks, and all out in the open . . . Your ex-colleagues take their Alsatians with them when they go there."

The Count didn't look into the interiors of the flats he walked by and came to the door marked number seven, which was shut tight, and knocked.

Silvano Quintero turned out to be younger than the Count was expecting. He was in his seventies and his extreme – if not genetic – thinness might have flattered him, but the purple shade of his skin marked him out as card-carrying, diehard alcoholic. Silvano needed a shave, a haircut, and was crying out for a good bath. When he ushered them in, Conde noticed the man's right hand: it was like a stiff, half-closed claw, with a gaping hole in the smooth flesh at the top. The small room was in the same wretched state as its tenant. The foulest stench wafted across the threshold of the small doorless lavatory and the place didn't appear to have been cleaned since some remote date in the previous century. Under the wooden zinc-covered table supporting a kerosene stove, the Count's trained eye spotted an army of empty bottles that had certainly been drunk in honour of the man's leathery liver.

Silvano pointed them to two rickety chairs and settled himself on the edge of the bed on a steely grey sheet. Conde couldn't stop thinking about himself and his own alcoholic inclinations and was alarmed to think he might be watching a science-fiction film, perversely intent on showing him his future.

"Well, then?" asked Silvano.

The Count took out a packet of cigarettes and handed one to the man, who took it in his left hand, then placed it, as if in an ashtray, between the two fingers of his crippled right, while the other searched his shirt pocket for a cigarette holder where he slotted the cigarette, an operation entirely executed by his left hand.

"I explained yesterday . . . my friend and I are in the business of buying and selling books and old records . . ."

"And can you live on that?" asked a suspicious Silvano, drawing on his holder in a rather finicky, old-fashioned way.

"Sometimes we can, sometimes we can't . . . In one deal we came across a record of one Violeta del Río, and someone told us you definitely knew her."

114

"Who told you I did?" he rasped, wiping his snot away in the same sophisticated style he adopted when smoking.

"Rogelito the *timbalero*."

"Is he still alive?" he almost droned.

"He's about to hit a hundred," the Count assured him. "He reckons he doesn't know how to die."

Silvano took a few more drags, as if he were reckoning up his own options, which the Count had reduced to two: speak up or shut up. From then on the situation threatened to get complicated. The Count produced the page from *Vanidades* devoted to Violeta del Río's farewell. The old journalist took it in his left hand and rested the fold on his garrotted right.

"For Christ's fucking sake," he whispered, folding the page and returning it to a Count already intrigued by what might have prompted his outburst. "Why are you looking for her? Don't you know she died in 1960?"

Conde nodded.

"We'd like to find out more about her. Pure curiosity."

"Curiosity killed the cat," the other retorted. "It's a long story which I don't like telling . . ."

"Nobody seems to know anything about Violeta, not even that she committed suicide and —" the Count implored.

"Why do you say she committed suicide? As far as I know, that was never resolved . . ."

The Count half-closed his eyes, trying to process the old man's words.

"What are you implying?"

"As far as I know, it wasn't clear whether she took her own life or someone else saved her the bother."

Conde tried to make his buttocks comfortable before continuing.

"You mean she might have been killed?"

"I believe I am speaking Spanish."

"And how do you know?"

"It was what I heard. There were doubts; her death was never cleared up . . . But, wait a minute," Silvano changed his tone of voice, "what do I get for telling you all this?"

Conde didn't think he'd understood the question, but was then sure he'd heard right after Yoyi, quick as a flash, put a price on the conversation.

"A bottle and two packets of cigarettes. Give me that little bag . . ."

The Count couldn't get over the shock. It had to be the first time ever that someone had charged him for a conversation, and Pigeon was the one sorting it for him, to the extent of pointing out the straw basket tied to a piece of rope, that was most certainly what Silvano used to lower and raise goods in and out of the central yard.

"All right," he demurred and gave Yoyi the basket, after he'd put an empty bottle into it.

"How much, granpa?" enquired Yoyi.

"Twenty-five a litre and eight pesos a packet of cigarettes . . ."

The young man left and the Count looked at Silvano, who diverted his gaze to his mutilated right hand. He blew his cigarette out of its holder, and the Count was confirmed in his belief that he understood less and less by the day, because the codes and languages in current use were beyond him. He thought yet again that Yoyi was right: he was like a fucking Martian who'd just popped out of a test tube.

I was twenty-five and had everything: drive, intellect, a well-off, if not exactly rich family, a job on one of the country's best newspapers, no energy-sapping vices . . . That's why I think I might have had another life and still think I could have if Violeta hadn't crossed my path. Or if I'd not crossed hers . . . When I met her, it was all going her way too: that sculpted body and face which gave her power over men, the slightly husky, but utterly convincing voice, the spurs of a real fighting cock – ready to fight in whichever arena life might cast her.

I remember the first time I saw her, in the Las Vegas, on one of those crazy Havana nights at the end of the fifties, after the attack on the Palace, when Batista saw things were getting serious and the police got bloodthirsty. It was really dangerous being in the thick of it, but one was irresponsibly bohemian, going out on the town all night, as if going to bed were a sin. You started to knock around, a glass here, another there, your hook baited to catch a beautiful fish to justify the hours drinking, smoking and street-crawling.

I saw and heard her for the first time on one of those thrilling nights when sleep's not on the agenda, which suddenly turned into a magical night, because as soon as I heard her voice in that shadowy cabaret I was dazed, convinced after just two minutes that I was listening to something unique, and worse fucking still, I knew at once the experience was contagious, because her voice got under your skin and gave you the shakes, as if something had turned your insides upside down. Naturally, that night she sang several songs, but the one that really got to me was *Be gone from me*; it was her battle hymn, and she always sang it as if her life depended on it . . . The illness's complications surfaced several days later, when I began to realize something had lodged in me that night and was refusing to go away. Almost unawares I began to trail her, to try to befriend her, to see if I could take it any further, because her voice was embedded in my brain, and so were her face, hair and damned body . . . I wasn't a child, I was twenty-five, I'd covered a lot of the scene, particularly since I'd been writing for the entertainments page of *El Mundo*, and as all those singers, dancers and chorus girls wanted to see themselves in print, by publishing a story on one, or just promising to do so for most, I laid a good number of the sexiest females in Havana, back when women were really sexy, with good bums and busts on them . . . Have you noticed how women now don't have tits, and are even happy when they go hungry so their bum doesn't get fat?. . . Well, I laid a lot of them, especially singers who were my weakness, Katy Barqué, for example . . . who was more wrapping than goods, really. Anyway I started to throw some candy Violeta's way, but not coarsely, because I realized straight away she wasn't one who was desperate to get into the newspapers, so I approached her cautiously, elegantly, or at least so I thought, following her across the whole of Havana, two or three nights a week, inviting her for a drink, asking her for a song . . . And when it came to act I was already madly in love with her, or rather fucking stupidly in love, the only way you can be in love.

By the beginning of 1958 she'd stopped singing in second-rate cabarets. It was then they contracted her at the Parisién. I wrote about her show and christened her The Lady of the Night, and

117

it stuck, because what Violeta sung only made any sense if you heard it at night, and the later, the better. I'd written two or three short pieces on her, but decided to go on the offensive and did a half-page report that made a lot of singers loathe me, to publicize her new spot in the second show at the Parisién. By that time, we'd got to know each other, even become vaguely friends, lots of nights we were the last two drinking in the bar, but Violeta never raised my hopes, and that made it worse, I got more hooked, wanted to flirt more outlandishly with her, even get serious if she'd allow me too, although Violeta was a girl, well, a woman with lots of secrets, and I never did find out who she was or what she was like . . . She knew how to shield herself. Her name, for example: she once confessed to me her real name was Catalina, that at home they called her Lina, but she never told me her surname, and my only explanation for that mystery was that the story about her coming from a country village was pure hearsay and the truth was that she had a surname with too high a profile in Cuba which was why she wanted to hide it, because being a high-class lady and a singer in mafiosi-run cabarets didn't go together. I finally decided that she sang because it was what she most liked doing and not because she was trying to make a living. Perhaps that's why she didn't give me much rope and didn't ask me to write about her, unlike the others: it was as if she couldn't care less about anything provided she had a little stage to sing on and people ready to listen to her . . . All in all, Violeta was a strange one . . . What I couldn't get my head round was why that woman, who mixed up with other women of the Havana night, wasn't footloose and fancy-free like them and apparently didn't have a boyfriend or lover, although people were beginning to talk about a wealthy man who was with her or after her. But mystery was part of her charm, of her powers of seduction . . . And I was so desperate I consoled myself by thinking that Violeta's problem might be she preferred women – Katy Barqué said so, with that viperish tongue so typical of her – and that was why she didn't take any notice of me or the guys chasing her every night, wanting a fling with her. And as she was very friendly with strange women, that idea got stuck in my brain. One of those friends, the one she most seemed to like, was Lotus Flower, the blonde who made a name for herself dancing naked in the Shanghai Theatre and then started up as a Madame of exclusive whores . . . Lotus Flower always hung around the cabarets where Violeta was singing, and you could see she loved listening to her. The pair of them liked talking together, and would often sit together at the end of a show and chat endlessly, drinking cocktails – Violeta always asked for a Bacardí and ginger ale highball – and they never let other people in on their conversations, as if there was a secret between them . . . although I never saw anything that indicated anything sexual between them: it all made Violeta yet more enigmatic and desirable.

But a true journalist is like a bloodhound, and you know what a dog's like when it's after a devious bitch: that was me. I started sticking close, following her even during the day, until I finally discovered the reason for so much mystery. Violeta lived in a flat on Third Street, in one of the best parts of Miramar. It was a modest place compared with the palaces on Fifth Avenue, but the truth is, it was very nice and she had a little English car, a very chic Morris, shaped like a wedge twisted backwards. I started investigating whose name the car and flat were registered in, with the help of a couple of banknotes and my *El Mundo* card, and one Louis Mallet, resident in New Orleans, appeared as the legal owner. I first wondered whether this Mallet might be Violeta's father or lover, or even her husband, which would explain why the house and car were in his name, and, as he lived in New Orleans, he surely came to Cuba from time to time if he were her lover or husband, or never, if he were her father . . . But it struck me as strange that people in Violeta's walk of life could have a lover or husband, providing her with a home and car, and that she was being so faithful. In other words, my suspicion that she liked women held firm, particularly when I saw how, two or three nights later, she spent the evening talking to Lotus Flower and they then spent the night together in the Miramar flat. What's more, when I began trailing her during the day, I saw a woman in her forties going into Violeta's flat – I found that out when one day she looked over the balcony – she was good looking and spent hours there, God knows what she was up to; she didn't look like a maid or cook . . . I kept my chase up for several weeks, until one day I realized they'd been flying me a kite and, as I had my nose in the air, I'd not seen what I should have seen. A man seemed to be living in one of the flats, but wasn't there very often. He was in his fifties, an elegant dresser, and drove the latest Chrysler, the most expensive model, and although he only popped in for ten minutes, he'd park his Chrysler in the garage to the block. I always thought it strange that the guy went two or three days without showing up, but I didn't smell a rat until one afternoon I spotted Violeta with a potted plant, on his balcony. Then I realized he must be Violeta's lover and that for some reason he was taking precautions and pretended to live in the flat under Violeta's. It wasn't so hard to find out this gentleman's name and then I started to put two and two together: Alcides Montes de Oca was in big, big business in Cuba, belonged to an well-established family, society people, real top-hat high society, as people used to say, grandson of General Serafín Montes de Oca, son of Senator Tomás Montes de Oca. The icing on the cake was that he was married to a Méndez-Figueredo, that is, to a mountain of money. I thought I'd got to the bottom of Violeta's mystery, but I wish I'd obeyed my first inclination to disappear and forget the whole affair, knowing what I then knew and convinced that playing in the First Division wasn't for an amateur like me.

But when things start happening, they do just that. Three days after making these discoveries, I was out once again keeping an eye on Violeta's place, like an idiot, and saw Alcides Montes de Oca drive up in his Chrysler, but this time with a chauffeur, a big black guy who looked like a prize fighter. Ten minutes later who should appear but Lotus Flower with a man in his fifties, and a bit later another man in another chauffeured car, whom I recognized, although lots of people in Havana wouldn't have, because he didn't let people take photos and rarely appeared in the newspapers. I knew this guy was Meyer Lansky, Lucky Luciano's partner, who now ran the gambling and brothel trade in Havana. He had invested a lot of money in building new hotels with the say-so of Batista, who naturally got a healthy cut of the bacon. For anyone, especially a journalist, that blend of cabaret singer, respectably rich Cuban, brothel Madame and a Jewish Mafiosi was a strange, heady mix, and I got sucked into trying to find out what they were hatching, since it was too big a deal to be about sex and only sex, however *recherché* that might be. Violeta and Lotus Flower? Violeta and

Lotus Flower and Lansky? All together? Whatever one imagined it was clearly a man and woman thing and no one was going to get too excited, apart from the fact no newspaper would ever print this kind of story, because the combined brawn of Lansky and Montes de Oca was one hell of a lot of muscle power. My second mistake was to think that maybe Violeta del Rio was the victim in that strange business, perhaps it was even true she was a poor little country girl who'd got drawn in that murky scene because she wanted to sing. That night I went home, slept for a few hours and in the morning stocked my car up so I could keep watch for several days. By nine I was on the corner opposite the building on Third and Twenty-Sixth, my eyes glued to the flats on the second and third floor. Right now I couldn't tell you what the hell I was hoping to get out of my espionage, whether I did it because I was in love with Violeta or out of curiosity, or if I was just narked because the rich guy and mafiosi had what I couldn't get my hands on. Violeta came home alone that night, at two a.m., drove her car in and went to sleep. The following day she emerged around six p.m. and came back at two a.m., by herself again. The same the following day and the next . . . I'd spent four days in my car, shitting and pissing as best I could, eating the bits and pieces I'd brought with me, sleeping on and off, when I decided I was wasting my time. What I should have done was leave and forget what I'd seen, but as I wasn't thinking straight, I did the most stupid thing imaginable. I got out of my car, walked to the ground floor of that block and pissed right there, in a final act of revenge, and it was then I heard Violeta's voice: she was singing her song, *Be gone from me* . . . You just have to believe this: something took hold of me which I couldn't resist and which made me enter the building, climb the stairs to the third floor, and start kicking on the door that voice from hell was still singing through, like it was trying to drive me insane . . .

When I regained consciousness I was in my car, reeking of piss and shit, with an excruciating pain all down my right arm. I made an effort to lift my hand. When I saw it I realized why I was in such pain: the hole in my palm was so big you could see right to the other side and I don't know if it was the shock or pain but I fainted again. I don't know how long I was there. It was a wasteland, with no trace of human life as far as the eye could see. Somehow or other, I used my teeth to tie a handkerchief round my hand and started the car. I drove round and round until I met a man on horseback who indicated the way out and finally found a track, somewhere between Bauta and San Antonio. It was a real struggle to drive on to the highway, and eventually I had to get out of the car and get someone to bring me to Havana, because I could feel my life slipping away from me.

They kicked up a terrific fuss in the hospital, because they thought I was a revolutionary and that a bomb had exploded in my hand. They refused to look at me, but I screamed I was a journalist and had been assaulted, by God knows who, until they took me to the operating theatre. When I woke up a police lieutenant was in the room who asked me a thousand questions, and I trotted out my assault story a thousand times, but revealed nothing new, and although he didn't seem that convinced, he finally left me alone. The doctor who'd operated on me came to see me and explained it was very strange because I'd been shot in the hand, not once, but twice, with a big calibre revolver, maybe a 45, and that's why it was such a big wound. They'd done all they could, but what with the shattered bones and tendons, it probably wasn't enough and I'd lose the movement in that hand. The police interrogated me again. I suppose they were prepared to hunt down the people who'd assaulted me. I told them almost the whole truth: I said I'd been hit on the head and only regained consciousness when I was in the wasteland, with my hand smashed to smithereens . . . After a warning like that, who'd dare say any more?

When I left the hospital, I also left the newspaper: I wasn't my old self, I was even afraid to go out in the street, I didn't want to be involved in anything that might lead me to Violeta del Río and even less arouse the suspicion of the police, who still didn't believe my story and in those days the police didn't use kid gloves: they'd drop you on any street corner as your first stop to the cemetery. I shut myself in my flat and the truth is the next I heard of Violeta was when I read that article where she announced her decision to give up singing, just after she'd recorded her first record . . . I just had to go to a music shop and buy that single. When I heard it, I started to cry; for myself and her; for my crippled hand and her wasted voice; for the life we might have had together and that was

122

killed stone dead when someone put those shots through my hand, whether I was to blame or Violeta's voice was . . .

I had no further news of her until I heard of her death shortly afterwards. They said she'd used cyanide to commit suicide, although a journalist told me the police weren't at all sure and were still investigating. But the truth was Violeta was dead and what did anything else matter? The little that was left of my world collapsed, because when I heard that news I felt that her salvation could have been in my hands, in these hands . . . Because I knew right away that suicide explanation was a nonsense. The writing on the wall was clear enough: if they'd shot my hand twice just for knocking on a door, what wouldn't they do to her for knowing what she must have known?

1 December

My dear:

Today is the first day in the final month of this miserable year and I am full of hope, letting my mind wander and dream that in thirty-one days a new year will dawn that can bring us a really new and better life, the life we've had to defer so long: full of love, quiet and family peace, oblivious to everything around us. Don't we perhaps deserve that? Don't I deserve that?

If anyone understands my life, you are that person. You know only too well how I threw everything onto the bonfire of oblivion and denial to be near to you, to belong to you: I closed my eyes and ears to other possible loves; I renounced regular family contact with my poor, very naïve parents (I was ashamed of their poverty and naivety) so I would feel I was climbing to your heights; I abandoned my future as an individual, gave up study, a job that could have sustained me, so I could always be in your shadow, in that moisture where I felt I could grow, even blossom, as your wife. You also know how zealously I kept your most secret secrets, shared your riskiest plans, and always gave you the same support. And never asked for anything in return: only for you to give me opportunities to show you I was the woman who had the right to your love.

What did I receive in return? Oblivion, silence, distance . . . The years I lived with you sapped the strength I once had and now I am unable to make another life, because I can't imagine and don't want to live my life without you, because I am your creation. I have thought long about what to do with my future, and in the end always come up with the same response: I will continue to wait, like a cloistered nun awaiting definitive grace from her Lord upon death.

123

What I most miss now is the festive atmosphere we used to breathe in the house. The new month would begin and joy would be in the air, with dinners to prepare, wine cellars to restock, presents to buy, visitors to enjoy, to wish happiness and prosperity to. All that has disappeared today, at least from this household. What about your new household? Do your children see to the decoration of the Christmas tree and crèche in Bethlehem? What do you feel far away? What does a man like you think, suddenly shocked by his exiled status, living far away, just one more in the crowd? Do you feel sorry for yourself or hatred towards those who forced you to leave and abandon what was yours?

It is incredible how everything is so topsy-turvy, how so many things have been ruined. Politics and an absurd death ended that happiness, that was incomplete for me, but at the end of the day it was my happiness, one I enjoyed with you close by. Today I see how life and what has happened have shown you were right, my love; if only we had had the time to change our story and this history by simply killing the person who did deserve to die, for if I can see the guilty party in all this it is that man, dripping in medals, drunk on ambition, who refused to go when he should have and whom we so often wanted to see out of the way: better still in hell, which is where his crimes and sins should have sent him.

But history overtook us. Nothing from that past remains today: a few happy memories perhaps, regrettably blotted out by your suspicions about my guilt. For God's sake: how can I demonstrate my innocence to you? I think by the minute about what happened, look for some detail to release you from the doubt tormenting you, and in the end I can only think that some very secret reason must have led that accursed woman to take her fatal decision which we shall never explain without that missing clue. Or could it be true she had a second life you were unaware of? I know this will sound sacrilegious, but I have to think this if I am ever to reach truth and redemption. Could someone, in that other life, have been interested in seeing her dead? Did someone, seeing her so happy, with the world at her feet, decide to make her pay dramatically for her happiness and possession of things that weren't hers by right?. . . This is madness, but thinking and searching is all that is left to me, particularly on days like today, when so many people want to hold parties and I can only let the hours drag by to see if a new year, this time for real, will bring me a new life, and not put dead bodies in my path. And at your side, my love.

I love you always . . .

Your Nena

As long as he'd lived, Mario Conde had become adept at co-existing with the most diverse idealizations or demonizations of the past, with convenient rewritings, pure imaginings and impenetrable silences, sometimes perpetrated with dramatic finesse or the utmost arrogance. Such co-existence had taught him that, in spite of themselves, every individual, every generation, every country had to drag behind them, like a ball and chain, a past that is inevitably theirs, even with a glossy varnish or black spots conveniently highlighted. But he'd also learnt, slowly, even painfully, through experience that the truth about the past can be buried in the most hermetically sealed trunks and the keys cast out to sea, but that's no guarantee you'll be spared its frantic clawing to get out, because neither the deepest nor the angriest self-inflicted oblivion can silence forever the onslaught of memory, which naturally can only feed on the past.

Silvano Quintero's macabre story had swept away the last remnants of his hangover, sucked dry by a narrative able to crack the pleasant plinth where he'd been erecting a romantic statue of Violeta del Río, swathed in the Count's dreams of the colourful musical backcloth of dodgy Havana nights in the fifties, as full of glitter and gaiety as of death and terror. With all his alarm bells now ringing like mad, he felt the need to pursue the hunt, to search out the elusive clue to the hidden truth about the life of that woman who'd faded from almost all memory.

While Yoyi Pigeon, struck dumb by the story they'd just heard, drove his gleaming Bel Air Chevrolet to the Ferreros' house, a flood of unanswered questions began to torment the Count who had finally no option but to conclude that the hunch he'd had a few days before was just another dirty trick played on him by a destiny which seemed to like throwing him into bottomless pits of uncertainty. After all, Silvano was right: if they'd shot his hand up for daring to kick on a singer's door, what mightn't they have done if he'd got to the bottom of something dreadful. Something now tarnishing the murky image of Mr Alcides Montes de Oca and fate of Violeta del Río the *bolerista*, both parties to an obscure deal with *capo* Meyer Lansky and an elusive figure by the name of Louis Mallet? What might they have done to the singer if she'd become a potential threat simply because she knew things she should never have known? Could someone like Violeta del Río have been so cruel to herself or have felt so trapped she'd have committed suicide by swallowing cyanide?

Conde felt a real satisfaction when he saw how the Ferrero brother and sister welcomed them with the broadest smiles, as if they were real-life ambassadors from the Land of Milk and Honey. Their faces were visibly beginning to freshen up with the injection of protein they'd received thanks to the books sold, and even Amalia's sad, watery eyes had recovered a sparkle they'd thought buried forever. A tiny but significant detail alerted the Count to extent they were now welcome: they'd placed a small glass ashtray on the shabby table in the centre of the room, the cheapest, simplest variety, but quite ready to play its role.

Amalia disappeared between the marble columns, promising to be back in a minute with the coffee, and the men settled down on the rickety armchairs in the reception room.

"Isn't life full of coincidences?" asked Dionisio, almost smiling. "This morning a man knocked on our door asking if we had any books to sell . . ."

Conde and Yoyi's steely glances clashed.

"And?" asked the Count.

"I said we had, but we'd already got buyers, naturally . . ."

"How did he come to call by?"

"Like you, I expect?" responded Dionisio, confident his explanation sounded convincing, although he saw immediately where the Count was coming from. "Or do you think he knew?. . ."

"We've not said anything to anyone about where we got these books from," said Pigeon.

"Did the man leave any contact details?"

"No, he didn't, he didn't even tell me what his name was, which is odd, isn't it? But he did ask me if he could take a quick look at the library. As I wasn't going to sell him anything, I let him in."

"What did he look like, Dionisio?"

"Black, tall, thirty to thirty-five years old. He seemed to know something about books but they came as a real shock to him. You know? He was like one of those pastors who give sermons in Seven Day Adventist churches, the way he spoke, and his polite manner. Oh, and he had a slight limp."

126

Conde and Yoyi toyed with various possibilities.

"Perhaps he was one of Pancho Carmona's buyers?" the young man asked.

"Could be," agreed Conde, watching Amalia return triumphantly, carrying a tray with three cups, one of which had lost its handle. "Pancho could quite easily have got someone to trail us. Which was the guy's gammy leg, Dionisio?"

Dionisio selected the forlorn cup and looked at it thoughtfully.

"Don't you remember?" the Count persisted and got a reaction.

"His right one," Dionisio responded, looking quite sure, as he lifted the cup to his lips.

Conde sipped his coffee and felt pleased with himself – it was real coffee, *coffee* – and prepared to test drive the ashtray.

"Right then . . . shall we begin?" smiled Dionisio in a hurry.

"Yes, let's get to the library," nodded the Count, although he remained in his chair, "but before we do I want to ask you something, and I apologize for being so insistent . . . have you really never heard of a Violeta del Río? It seems her name was Catalina, and she might well have been called Lina, but that's not for sure . . .'

The siblings glanced at each other, as if wanting to agree a possible answer. They seemed surprised by the buyer's persistent interest, but the response from both was simple and to the point: no.

"It seems that this woman, apart from singing boleros," the Count continued, trying to open up channels of information and disturb a dormant cranny in the memories of their hosts, "had a relationship with Alcides Montes de Oca. An amorous relationship, that is. It's definite they knew each other, so that explains why this cutting turned up in one of the books . . ."

Conde showed them the page from *Vanidades*. Amalia needed only a few moments to repeat her negative, but Dionisio looked at it for a few drawn out seconds before confessing that even so he didn't recognize her.

"Do you think if your mother saw the photo?. . ." The Count was afraid he'd seem impertinent asking such a question, but took a chance, taking advantage of his current economic pre-eminence in that household. "If she was Alcides Montes de Oca's trusted confidante . . ."

"I told you Mummy can't . . ." whispered Amalia before Dionisio interrupted her.

"Look here, Conde, Amalia's problem is she always gives half the picture, uses euphemisms . . . right, euphemisms, because she finds it hard to spell things out: mummy has been completely mad for the last forty years. And when I say mad, I mean really mad, incurably so . . ."

"Well, forget it then . . ." the Count lamented. "Let's get on with the books."

Amalia apologized; she had to get back to work – off to the market again – and the men went into the library.

"Which books did that buyer look at?" the Count enquired.

"He started by looking at the ones you say are very valuable. Then he crouched down over there, by the bookcase, the lower shelves," pointed Dionisio. Yoyi went over to the area in the library he'd indicated, strangely enough, on the left-hand side they'd not yet inspected, and immediately called to his partner.

"Come here, Conde, come here . . . Look at this . . ."

Pigeon's index finger ran over the spines of several books and the Count crouched down to get a better view.

"God! No, that's not possible . . ."

The ex-policeman's exclamations and negatives alarmed Dionisio Ferrero, who walked over to the bookcase, from which the Count, who'd opened the glass doors, now extracted two very large, leather-bound tomes.

"What do you mean?" asked Dionisio.

"How could the guy know, man? . . . Did he walk straight towards these books? . . . I don't get it, man, I swear I don't," Yoyi confessed. "It can't be true . . ."

Conde felt his heart racing, opened the first of the books read the motto that advised "*Labore et Constantia*", ran his eyes over the hand-tinted etchings that reproduced the appearance of some fish so exactly it was as if they'd been photographed still dripping wet after they'd been fished from tropical seas. But anxiety spurred him on and he immediately began to leaf through the other volume, a heavy album, some seventeen by twelve inches. The buyers' dazzled eyes viewed a succession of lithographs: a port where several sailing boats were moored, a valley planted with sugar cane, a country landscape captured in all its detail and various views of sugar refineries in action. As delicately as he knew how, Conde caressed the heavy paper with the engraving of the proud, idyllic image of La Flor de Cuba sugar mill, then closed the volume, got up and leaned awkwardly against the shelves, pressing the two books against his chest, as if wanting to protect them against the endless dangers out there in the big, wide world.

"These are two jewels. They're priceless. They're unique," he muttered, feeling that his language was inadequate, wondering what adjectives he should use to describe those invaluable wonders of Cuban publishing . . . "Everybody calls this one 'The Book of Fishes', but its proper title is" – he opened the cover and read the frontispiece – "*Description of different items of natural history mostly from the maritime branch and illustrated with 75 plates*. It's the first important book printed in Cuba . . . in 1787 . . . And the other one, you can see, is *The Sugar Mills*, printed in 1857, that should have twenty-eight plates by Eduardo Laplante and is one of the most beautiful books ever made in the world. Needless to say they are two of the most valuable books ever published in Cuba."

"What do you mean by 'valuable'?" nerves betrayed Dionisio, his martial voice cracking as he asked the question.

"Well, I mean they're worth a fortune . . ." Conde's emotions didn't subside, his mouth got drier, as if he'd been struck down by a raging fever. "If all the engravings are in place, I think the National Library might even be capable of unearthing enough money to buy them . . . We're talking about more than ten thousand dollars a piece, more even . . ."

Dionisio Ferrero turned pale.

"That's impossible," he retorted, convinced Conde was hallucinating. "I'd never touched them before."

The Count had forgotten Dionisio and, keeping them close to his chest, caressed the books' leather. "If only Cristóbal could see them . . ."

'Cristóbal?' Dionisio seemed more and more in a dither, unable to understand what was unravelling so unexpectedly in front of his very eyes. "Who might Cristóbal be?"

"But how the fuck did that black guy, who limped out of his mother's fucking cunt, ever walk straight to these books?" an angry

Yoyi almost shouted, in a state of shock increasingly fanned by bad vibes about the future.

"Far too great a coincidence," allowed the Count, finally taking the books to the bookcase they'd chosen for the editions they were putting in the not-for-sale category. "Far too great," he repeated, caressing the awesome spines of the two volumes yet again, as if amorously bidding them farewell, and he tried to shake off the sensations gripping him. "Down to work, Yoyi, unless we want that man to beat us in a little fraternal socialist rivalry, right?"

Until he'd turned into a professional predator of books, intent on feeding from his profits, Mario Conde had enjoyed a respectful, almost mystical relationship with libraries. Although the over-heated, quarrelsome barrio where he'd been born wasn't home to a single library of more than twenty books, luck would have it that there were a dozen books in his own house – all belonging to his mother, for his father, like his Grandfather Rufino the Count, never opened a book in his life – that had got there along the most diverse paths, and were now arrayed proudly and prominently, and as if someone suspected those objects might be valuable, at one end of the sideboard top, next to his parents' wedding photo, a Viennese porcelain clock and a small art nouveau vase. Throughout his adolescence, Conde read those books in his odd moments – two volumes of Reader's Digest *Selections*, the tearful, as far as he was concerned abominable *Heart*, by Edmundo de Amicis, one of Sandokán's adventures and, above all, *Huckleberry Finn*, in a cheap edition that was falling to pieces – and felt timidly enthused at being attracted by an activity that was so uncommon in members of his family and inhabitants of his barrio, who were generally not very fond of such passive hobbies. Even when the Count preferred to spend his time playing ball-games, idling around the streets and stealing mangos, his innate curiosity led him to take his first step to becoming a bibliophile when, after reading *The Count of Montecristo* in a state of emotional ecstasy, he decided to find out about Edmund and Mercedes' final destinies. He'd hunted out the second act of that fabulous adventure, only to encounter a disappointing, almost cruel Dumas, who in *The Dead Man's Hand* destroyed the happiness over which generous-hearted Dantès and his beloved Mercedes had expended so much effort. A couple of years later, now enrolled at Pre-Uni, curiosity again came to his aid, this time conclusively, after reading a ridiculously abridged version of *The Iliad*, as an exercise in class. Conde visited the well-stocked library in the old La Víbora grammar school in search of a complete version of Homer's poem and, intrigued by the fates of its warriors, looked for answers in *The Odyssey* and naturally, without any effort on his part, fell into a trap with no way out as he tried to discover the fates of the remaining Greek heroes. It was Cristóbal, the old one-legged librarian, who first encouraged him to read the *Aeneid* and later other sagas of Achean heroes.

His relationship with Lame Cristóbal, as they all called him at the Pre-Uni, was an encounter that decisively shaped the life of Mario Conde, who soon became a voracious, compliant reader, able to finish any book he started – he got the better of *Les Misérables* and even *The Magic Mountain* – and began to love books and libraries the way believers worship their shrines: as sacred places only to be profaned at the risk of eternal perdition.

Apart from supplying him with books and guiding him in his reading, Cristóbal was the first to detect that the boy had latent sensitivities and to urge him to try his hand at writing. Mario Conde, who always possessed an acute sense of his many limitations, was terrified of looking like a fool and so discounted the idea, but the seed lodged in a hidden corner of his consciousness, ready to germinate. In the meantime, he deepened his relationship with books and, thanks to the old librarian, familiarized himself with the important books published in Cuba in the nineteenth century and first half of the twentieth, and began to value books not only for their content, but often for their frequently ignored continent, age and origin.

One of Cristóbal's most persistent challenges was to bring the young man closer to a part of Cuban literature that was being concealed by new political and aesthetic tendencies. Consequently, he made him read the innumerable writers damned and slandered in the arid decade of the seventies, writers who Conde wouldn't hear about in public until many years later. To open the door to that past world, Cristóbal selected Lino Novás Calvo and Carlos

Montenegro, with whom he intuited – quite rightly – the young man would soon easily connect, thanks to their tales of slave-traders, thugs and convicts. Then followed Labrador Ruiz, Lydia Cabrera and Enrique Serpa, and he was later thrust into the caustic worlds of Virgilio Piñera, who at the time was sentenced to the most crushing silence, where he met his death. As a result of all those writers he read at the age of sixteen and seventeen, Conde shaped a complex view of his past, of the past of all the island's inhabitants, and gleaned that the world could enjoy a variety of colours and truths infinitely more complex than those officially on offer.

In his wild youth Mario Conde committed various excesses – he stole food on sugar-cane encampments where they were sent off harvesting for several months, cheated in examinations when the questions were leaked by the management of the Pre-Uni to guarantee high rankings, was deceitful when it came to paying in the ice-cream shop next to the school, and filched books from The Woodworm bookshop – but he never dared take a single school library book for personal gain, even though Cristóbal made him an unthinkable exception and let him go into the store-cupboard to sniff around and choose books to read. The conviction that the world was a battlefield whereas a library could be an inviolably neutral, collective terrain, took root in his spirit as one of the most pleasant insights in life, a notion he'd have to revisit, when the Crisis came, in order to survive, as so many others had to with their memories and even dignity intact.

In spite of the years he'd invested in book buying and selling, Conde always felt quite uneasy when he worked as a library predator and, as a matter of principle, decided never to buy any book that was stamped as public property. However, in all the time he'd devoted to such commercial dealing, he'd never sensed he was so acutely engaged in an act of profanation as with the library of the Montes de Ocas. Perhaps the fact he knew the treasure had remained untouched during more than forty years of revolutionary hurricanes – until the moment he had entered the sanctuary – as a consequence of an unbending pledge, contributed to his feeling of unease. Knowing that three generations of a Cuban family had devoted money and effort to that wondrous array of close to 5,000 volumes, that had travelled half the globe in order to find a place in these bookcases which were immune to damp and dust, seemed like an act of love he was now mercilessly destroying. Most painful of all was the certainty that profanation would lead to chaos and that chaos often sparked off the collapse of the most solid of systems. Wasn't his presence helping to verify that equation? His hands and economic interests were violating something sacred, and the Count anticipated his deed would provoke a chain reaction he still couldn't imagine, but which was imminent.

It was on one of those lethargic afternoons when young Conde had taken shelter with a book in the coolest, most out-of-the-way corner of La Víbora Pre-Uni library, that Lame Cristóbal, leaning on his crutches, interrupted him on the pretext that he wanted to share a cigarette with his pupil. For the rest of his life, Mario Conde would never forget how that initially nondescript conversation suddenly changed tone when Cristóbal began to speak about the library's uncertain future. His retirement date was long past and, at some fast-approaching date, he'd have to take his crutches and love for books elsewhere, perhaps to the grave. The old man most fretted about what was going to happen to the books he'd preserved and defended for almost thirty years, books he was sure nobody would love and look after as he had.

"Each of the books back there," he pointed to the stacks, "has a soul, has a life of its own, and retains part of the lives and souls of boys, like you, who've passed through this library and read them over these thirty years . . . I've classified every one, put them in place, cleaned, refurbished and glued them whenever necessary . . . Condecito, I've seen so much lunacy in my lifetime. What on earth is going to happen to them? You're graduating this year and will leave. I'll retire or die, but will have to go as well. The books will be abandoned to their fate. I hope the next librarian will be like me. It will be a calamity if he or she isn't. Each book here is irreplaceable, each has a word, a sentence, an idea that's waiting for its reader." Cristóbal put his cigarette out, pulled himself up on the table, and stuck a crutch under an arm. "I'm going to have a bite to eat. Look after the library . . . Before I get back, go in and choose the books you need or like. Take them, save them, and above all, look after them."

133

Astonished by the very suggestion, the Count watched Cristóbal leave, swaying on his wooden supports. Half an hour later, when the old man returned, Conde was still in the same place, reading the same book.

"Why didn't you do what I told you to do?" enquired the librarian.

"I don't know, Cristóbal, I can't . . ."

"You'll be sorry . . ."

Fifteen years later, when Detective Lieutenant Mario Conde went back to the old Pre-Uni in La Víbora, to investigate the murder of a young chemistry teacher, one of the first places he visited was the once neat and tidy library, where Cristóbal had urged him to read Virgil, Sophocles, and Euripides, Novás Calvo, Piñera and Carpentier. To his eternal grief, the ex-student had had to acknowledge that Lame Cristóbal's fears had been surpassed. A few battered, moribund books were dozing among the empty spaces on the once packed shelves, whence Greek and Latin classics, tragic Englishmen and Italian poets, chroniclers of the Indies and Cuban novelists and historians had flown their nest. The plundering had been merciless and systematic, and apparently nobody had been held responsible for the vandalism. Conde thought how, in his grave, Lame Cristóbal must have felt that wilful profanation whiplashing his bones, destroying his poor life's finest work as a handicapped librarian who loved his precious books.

That afternoon's crop was worth the sacrifice that Yoyi and the Count made by missing out on their lunch break and stifling the cries of anguish from bellies that wanted more corn to grind. Spurred on by fear of other undesirable intrusions, they managed to inspect a third of the library and took 263 highly coveted books from the house of the Ferreros who, apart from receiving the $436 and 1,300 pesos the buyers owed them, shook all over when they heard they were now owed a total of 28,400 pesos, of which they received the 6,000 Yoyi was carrying on him. In the meantime, Conde and his business partner decided to create a third reserve from the books they'd originally discounted, volumes that were certainly sellable but at a modest price, forming a bulky emergency holding of almost 500 books, set aside for a second phase of buying and selling. At the same time, they put several tomes in the section of those "not for sale", including the two illustrated books that so aroused the Count's sensibility, plus an extraordinary 1716 Mexican edition of the poetry of Sor Juana Inés de la Cruz; the highly prized, much sought after *Island of Cuba*, illustrated by thirty luminous engravings by Federico Mialhe Grenier, printed in Havana in 1848; a copy of the *Birds of the Island of Cuba*, by Juan Lembelle, dated Havana 1850, the always much coveted 1891 New York first edition of Martí's *Simple Verse*, endorsed by the apostle's signature in a dedication to "the compatriot and brother Serafín Montes de Oca, the good man", and the two tomes – which the Count walked away from particularly sorrowfully – of the very rare, much sought after edition of the *Poetry of Citizen José María Heredia*, published in Toluca in 1832, which was presented as the corrected, extended second edition, though valued by connoisseurs as a first edition of the Cuban classic, because it removed inaccuracies and added important poems excluded from the 1825 New York original.

Their great pleasure at the incredible deal they'd just clinched couldn't, however, dispel Yoyi's distress at the alarming presence in that mine of books of a buyer equipped with dangerous radar able to lead him to the most coveted treasures of Cuban publishing. Nor could it silence the malevolent echoes of Silvano Quintero's story, still ringing in Mario Conde's ears, who, immediately after agreeing the financial deal with Pigeon – a deal loading him up with many thousands of pesos the like of which he'd never seen – preferred to take refuge in the solitude of his own home as he needed time and space to think things over.

After taking a shower, he swallowed the two pork sandwiches he'd bought in one of the barrio's pokey shops – although he only handed his money over after critically inspecting the protein content, for he wouldn't have been the first to eat roast dog or stewed cat at porky prices – and decided against hunting for rum or ringing Skinny to talk over recent events, or Tamara, to suggest a visit so he could tell her of the discovery of the Heredia poems she liked so much. The previous day's excesses, his exhaustion after an excitement-packed day on the streets and a desperate need to sort his own ideas out, all disposed him to enjoy an exemplary peaceful night. Armed with his cigarettes and half a cup of coffee, he went up to his house's terrace roof, followed by Rubbish, and settled down on a block of concrete, his feet on the edge of the eaves. Despite the daytime heat, night brought a pleasant breeze, heralding October, and the Count felt happy in himself at being able to occupy a vantage-point overlooking the old barrio of the Conde family, the territory of his nostalgia and ancestors. He looked at the hill with the quarries and, through the foliage of poplars, gum-bearing *ocuje* and weeping figs, he intuited, rather than saw, the castle with its English tiled roof, where his grandfather Rufino el Conde had laboured almost a hundred years ago. It was always a relief to know the haughty, larger-than-life castle was still there, as it made him feel there were things that never changed in this world, that could navigate unharmed the turbulence of time and history.

Rubbish nuzzled and nibbled in between his legs wanting a spot of affection, and the Count scratched him behind the ears, where his pet most appreciated it. Ignoring the swollen tick Rubbish must have picked up on one of his sallies into the street, Conde let his mind float freely and was visited by the grotesque image of Silvano Quintero's hooked hand. Something far too grim must have occurred in the vicinity of the late Violeta del Río for her so-called friends to give such a drastic warning to a nosy journalist. The presence in the apartment block on Third and Twenty-Sixth of a character like mafia capo Meyer Lansky might have simply been fortuitous, but what Silvano Quintero had suffered indicated the unfolding presence of a darker intrigue, a mystery the Count, with his usual fondness for prejudice, refused to admit might directly implicate Violeta, whatever the dark, hidden motivation was. The most visible factors pointed to a connection between Lansky and Alcides Montes de Oca, who, according to Amalia Ferrero, had amassed a fortune in that period, even though he didn't belong to the circle of those favoured by the bloodthirsty Fulgencio Batista. Had Don Alcides done profitable business thanks to his criminal connections? Possibly, since apart from the drug-trafficking which Lansky personally avoided, the Jewish mafioso had succeeded in laundering all his operations in Cuba thanks to the fact that gambling was legal on the island and to Batista's self-interested support of all his banking and real-estate speculation. Those deals fulfilled the former hoodlum's golden dream, transforming him into a respectable businessman at the epicentre of a great Cuban tourist project, conceived as a Gold Coast between Mariel and Varadero, stretching along more than one hundred and twenty-five miles of warm idyllic coastline, barely ninety miles from Florida and forty minute's flight from Miami, a blue strip on the edge of warm currents from the Gulf of Mexico, endowed with the best beaches in the world and especially suited to the construction of hotels, casinos, luxury residential estates, marinas, restaurants and countless other attractions, able to generate almost inconceivable millions of dollars in a very few years. If all that took off on a secure legal base backed by government support, Conde couldn't see any reason to risk a scandal by mutilating a lovesick showbiz reporter who'd banged on a door behind which a woman was singing. But why use a flat under the name of one Luis Mallet who'd still not put in an appearance? The fact that Alcides Montes de Oca belonged to the Creole aristocracy, and was the widower of a Méndez-Figueredo, might explain why he was so wary about his relationship with Violeta del Río and even more so about any he might have with Madame Lotus Flower. Nonetheless, the precautions surrounding those connections were excessive if it was just a matter of clandestine affairs, as Silvano Quintero had remarked. All the paths from the Count's logic led to a dark abyss, at the bottom of which must lie the convoluted reasoning that might be the real cause of all that secrecy and violence and, perhaps, the *bolerista*'s cyanide suicide.

But, come on, you tell me: what the fuck has this half-century old story got to do with you? What does it matter to you if she killed herself or was killed, if you're never going to find out the truth? Are you obsessing like this in homage to your father? Smoking a second cigarette and intent on crushing Rubbish's impertinent tick on the layers of adobe covering the roof, the Count decided the time had come to dampen his curiosity, forget his hunches and close the book on that story which belonged to someone else. He should be more than content to settle for his pleasing discovery of the recorded voice of Violeta del Río, the revelation of the impossible love that had tormented his father and, above all, to enjoy his dip in the most astounding private library any Cuban of his time had ever stepped into, thanks to which he could now enjoy an economic breathing space in the company of Tamara and his old friends. Insistence on exhuming that past, on searching for a female suicide's increasingly complicated ghost, brought a bitter taste like attempting to make love to a beautiful corpse, when what he needed right now was a living, breathing woman. The truth was beyond reach, he thought, and would have to remain locked in the stronghold where it had been locked away, for there were only two possible leads he could play with: mad Mummy Ferrero and Lotus Flower the singer, presuming that the latter was still alive, within reach and prepared, moreover, to tell what she knew.

His straightforward decision to apply the guillotine to his morbid curiosity revealed the extent of the exhaustion he'd built up over three long days of bibliographic, alcoholic and nutritional orgies: a yawn brought tears to his heavy-lidded eyes.

"Violeta del Río can go to hell," he muttered and was surprised to hear the sound of his own voice. He yawned again, adding, as he stroked his dog's head: "Well, buddy, don't know about you but I'm off to bed?"

Rubbish shook his tail strictly negatively, and the Count followed him downstairs. Back in his kitchen, holding the door open, he asked for one last time: "You coming or going?" Rubbish pranced backwards, and the Count understood he wanted to go out on the town, just like Silvano Quintero before he lost his way in life and half a hand.

"What kind of dog did I land myself?" he wondered, as he bid him farewell and closed the door. He scattered his clothes on his way to his bedroom, pressed the maximum button on his fan, fell on his bed, and didn't even consider opening a book. Ten minutes later he was asleep and deep in a pleasant dream, watching a beautiful young woman emerge from a golden sea, where the sun was beginning to sink and dim its fiery light behind the horizon. When the woman was close to him, he realized it was Tamara, but he identified her as Violeta, whispering, in her husky *bolerista* voice that she'd stay the night with him, looking out to sea, watching the day's miseries and splendours fade.

The B side:

You'll remember me

The knocks echoed around the house as if summoning him back from the past. Mario Conde opened his eyes but had a slippery grip on the world: he didn't know where he was or what the time was, and was surprised his head wasn't aching and that day was only just breaking, which was what the red numbers 6:47 flashing on his luminous watch informed him in the most obvious way possible. More bangs on the door and his brain cleared: Skinny, he thought immediately, something's happened to Skinny – his immediate response when he received unexpected calls in the night or early morning visits. Before he got up he shouted: "Coming", and walked towards the door, then almost collapsed when he saw the figure of Manuel Palacios looming large.

"Something happened to Skinny?" he asked, his heart thudding.

"No, don't worry, it's not that."

The relief brought by the knowledge his friend was still of this world immediately gave way to indignation.

"So what the fuck are you doing here at this fucking time of day?"

"I need a few words. Aren't you going to put the coffee on?" asked Manolo, stepping inside.

"It better be important. Go on then, come in."

The Count went into the bathroom, urinated the usual fetid, early morning quantities, washed out his mouth and wet his face. He dragged his feet into the kitchen and put the coffee on, an unlit cigarette between his lips. With or without a hangover, dawn was the worst moment of his day, and being forced to talk was the most excruciating of tortures.

"I came to see you because . . ." began Manolo, but Conde's hand cut him short.

"After a coffee," he insisted and pulled up the underpants that were threatening to slip off his lean waist.

Conde opened the door to his terrace and saw Rubbish curled up on his mat. His belly moved slowly in and out: he was breathing. He coughed and spat in the direction of his sink. Coming back in, he picked up the faded jeans he'd abandoned to their fate the previous night, and pulled them on, leaning on a wall where he scratched his back in the process.

He handed Manolo a coffee and sat down with his big cup sipping on a liquid able to power the re-establishing of contact with himself after waking. He lit his cigarette and peered into the vaguely squinting eyes of the uniformed captain of the detective squad.

"I've come to see you because we've got problems . . . Big ones."

"What's up?" asked the Count routinely, not prompted by any real curiosity. Manolo had sought his advice over the years in a wide range of cases and the Count wondered if he'd not gone too far this time waking him up at that ungodly hour.

"Dionisio Ferrero is dead. Murdered."

The blast hit Conde smack in the chest.

"What was that?" Conde asked, now completely awake and convinced he'd not heard him right.

"Amalia got up at three to go to the bathroom, and was surprised to see the light on in the reception room. She thought it was her brother and went to see if he was OK. She found him in the library, bleeding from the neck. He was already dead."

Mario Conde's brain started to process what he'd just heard at an unlikely rate of knots. The policeman he'd once been surfaced in every cell of his body, like a latent gene that had suddenly been activated.

"Did they take any books?"

"We don't know yet. That's why I've come to see you. His sister needed an injection and is quite groggy."

"We gave them loads of money yesterday."

"Amalia says none is missing, it was under her mattress."

"Let me have a quick wash and get dressed," replied the Count, picking up the shoes he'd worn the day before. He took a shirt from his wardrobe and, as it fell over his shoulders, the real reason for Captain Manuel Palacios's early morning call finally struck him. He padded back to the living room, where Manolo was smoking, deep in thought.

"Manolo . . . why did you come here?"

The detective stared at his former colleague his eyes more free-floating than ever. He looked at the cigarette he was puffing between his fingers and whispered: "Right now you and Yoyi are the main suspects. I hate to say it, but you do understand why, don't you, Conde?"

The first spurts of blood, pumped by his heart, had hit the bottom right corner of the mirrored door, and the stains ran into those created by leaking mercury, trailing down and drawing elusive abstract art shapes, that joined and extended the pool still being fed by the last secretions from the body that had fallen to the ground. A blackish puddle had coagulated, forming a narrow-mouthed bay on the chessboard tiles, its shores opening out to the interior of the library. The chalk line marked out Dionisio Ferrero's final position, and the first thing to catch the Count's eye was that he'd died with his hands splayed open. Or had someone prised something out of them?

While Manolo argued in one corner of the room with the forensic doctor who'd ordered the body to be moved without his authorization, Mario Conde, under the scrutiny of a sergeant who'd been introduced as Atilio Estévañez, began to think the situation through. Apparently, Dionisio had been stabbed from behind by someone still in the library. If that were the case, it must have been a person Dionisio wasn't expecting to attack him, otherwise he wouldn't have turned round so tamely, and left his rearguard unprotected, as any manual of war would point out. He clearly knew his aggressor, a right-handed one at that, judging by the slash on that side of his neck. Whoever the murderer was, he'd been intent on killing his man. If it had been a fight that had got out of hand, he might have stabbed him in the back first, but the killer had gone straight for his neck arteries, trying to murder him at a stroke and simultaneously choke and silence him with the flow of blood. The idea that the murderer was someone familiar to Dionisio was supported by the fact that no door into the house had been forced, which meant, the ex-policeman presumed, that the man had opened the door to his own executioner. The only feasible explanation, among those the Count ran through, was that Dionisio, enticed by figures he'd heard in recent days, had started negotiating with someone behind his sister's back, possibly the mysterious buyer who'd put in an appearance the previous day, as if out of the blue, or someone similar, who wasn't even known to Amalia. The probable absence of particular books might clarify the motivation for the crime, although that spelt danger for the murderer: the missing items would be clues that could be easily tracked down.

Manolo came over and the Count looked him in the eye. The captain gestured to Sergeant Estévañez to move away.

"It's the fucking last straw, these forensics have more power than us these days . . . They're the scientists . . . Wait, before we go in," he pointed to the library. "I wanted to say a couple of things so you understand . . ."

"A couple of things?" asked Conde, wanting to grab Manolo by the neck of his uniform.

"Conde, I know it's beyond you . . . but try . . . for Christ's sake."

"I don't understand . . ."

"Do you think if I really thought you were a suspect, you'd be here with me now? Don't take the piss . . . But remember the high-ups don't know you and you've been a renegade as far as they're concerned ever since you left the force . . ."

"Look, I don't give a shit what the high-ups think, or the low-downs for that matter . . . Anyway, go on, say what you —"

"The murderer took his knife with him, judging by the kind of gash inflicted the forensic says it's a normal kitchen knife, sharp-pointed but pretty blunt."

"Uh-huh."

"He was killed between twelve and two this morning. That'll be more precise after the autopsy. The murderer is right-handed —"

"Yes, I'd worked that out."

"He was attacked from behind, and the angle of entry indicates that the murderer is about four inches shorter than Dionisio."

144

Conde put the squeeze on his brain and recalled that the mysterious buyer described by Dionisio was a tall black man.

"About my height then," the Count acknowledged.

"Another important detail: they cleaned the door handle. So far we've only found fresh fingerprints of five people . . ."

"Dionisio, Amalia, Yoyi, the buyer who came yesterday and myself . . ."

"Maybe. The footprint in the blood was Amalia's doing, when she went to see if he was dead. They're going to check Dionisio's fingernails now, but I don't think there was any fight. And we'll take your prints, Yoyi's and those two, and see if the fifth person's on file."

"What else?"

"That's all . . . The high-ups want me to resolve this as soon as possible. Dionisio was in the military, part of the clandestine struggle against Batista and his friends are going to create a fuss any minute now."

"Something they didn't do when he was starving to death," Conde recalled. "Dionisio worked in a corporation for two or three years and was booted out when he started to notice things he didn't like. That was at the worst bloody moment of the Crisis . . . And nobody expressed any interest in him after that."

"I'll find out what happened in the corporation," agreed Manolo. "OK, now let's look at the books. See if any have gone astray . . ."

Manolo gave Conde a pair of nylon gloves and they went into the library, taking care not to step on the dried blood or the silhouette that had been marked out. Conde paused in the centre of the room to get an initial overall view: on the left, the section of shelves they'd yet to inspect; on the right, next to the door, the books Conde and Yoyi considered to be unsaleable, piled higgledy-piggledy on the bottom of the shelves; the books held back for a second phase in their deal, on the shelves either side of the window, also looking as if they'd been piled up in a rush; perching precariously on the shelves opposite, the three expanding piles where they'd put particularly valuable items the Count refused to let loose on the market. Almost unthinkingly he went over to the most coveted volumes, rubbed a finger twice over their spines and concluded that, if his memory wasn't playing tricks, they were all present and correct, even the most valuable Cuban editions, each of which he remembered perfectly.

He went back to the centre of the room, closed his eyes, and tried to chase any preconceived notions from his mind. He looked around again and, apart from a few strange spaces between the books on the bottom shelves of the area they hadn't yet inspected, he didn't think he noticed any changes, although he regretted not scrutinizing the room more carefully the previous afternoon. At that precise moment Conde had a feeling that Dionisio or Amalia, in one of their conversations, had mentioned something crucial about the library, an important revelation now floating in his memory that he couldn't pin down. What the hell was it? he wondered, before deciding to leave the self-interrogation until later.

Conde racked his memory as he moved towards the area they'd yet to explore, trying to recall whether at some moment Yoyi or Dionisio had taken a volume from that bookcase. Using the torch Manolo had given him he could see changes in dust levels indicating that six books had recently been removed and he noted that the remaining volumes concentrated in that section were old tomes to do with legislation, customs tariffs, trade regulations in the colonial era, and a long row of magazines specializing in business topics, all published between the thirties and fifties.

"I can't swear to it, but I don't think a single book is missing," he told Manolo as he pointed out the jewels in the library, "and there are books worth several thousand dollars —"

"Did you say several thousands? For an old book? How many thousands?"

"This one," he indicated the black spine of the *Book of Sugar Mills*, "could fetch ten or twelve thou in Cuba . . ."

"Twelve thousand dollars?" Manolo reacted in a state of shock.

"At least. And double that outside Cuba."

"Shit," exclaimed the Captain, shaken from head to toe by that statistic. "More or less what I'll earn in my lifetime on my wages . . . They'd kill anyone for a book like that."

"We hadn't touched that part of the library, but six books have gone missing from there. The most valuable are still here . . . I don't get it. It must be a sextet of very special books . . ."

"What about them? . . ."

146

"We'll ask Yoyi and Amalia, I certainly didn't take any from there. Perhaps Dionisio . . . They might be somewhere else in the library or perhaps were stolen."

"But could they be worth even more than the others?" Manolo ventured. "If there are books that could fetch twelve thousand dollars . . ."

"Could be, though I doubt it. The books on that side are legal and commercial, and I don't think any would be worth that much. I reckon that's the case because if anyone was in it to steal books and knew the trade, they'd have removed some of those we'd put aside. If you can carry six, you can carry ten . . . So if six *were* taken, it wasn't because they'll fetch a lot of money, but because they were valuable to someone in particular, and that could only be because of the story they told and not because they were antiques or very rare . . . Unless they weren't books but manuscripts that were important for other reasons," he concluded, thinking that cold logic threw out of court the idea that any items in the legal and commercial section should have been in a safe: although what about the extremely slim, much coveted *General Tariff for the Price of Medicines* believed to be the first text printed on the island?

"So what do you reckon?"

"I expect Dionisio was so excited by the cash flow from the books that he took six he thought were very valuable and put them somewhere else or sold them behind our back and his sister's . . . But that's pure supposition. If he did do something like that, the money can't be far away."

"Despite what you say, perhaps those six books were valuable and the murderer settled for them, knowing you hadn't looked at the books concerned?"

"All very plausible . . . Can I tell you something?" Conde observed the library silently. "When I entered this room four days ago, I had a hunch there was or is something very special here. Then when I started looking at the books, I thought it might just be that some were priceless items. I even thought there might be a manuscript or some missing piece to an unsolved puzzle . . . When I found the photo of the *bolerista*, I decided it must be that and her forgotten story . . . Now I'm sure it wasn't those books or manuscript or the photo. But something that's probably not here."

"And what the hell might that be?"

"If I had a sixth sense . . . What's more, Dionisio or his sister said something important about this library, but I can't for the goddamn life of me remember what . . ."

"I'll ask these genius scientists to tell me when those books disappeared yesterday. They can probably say if they went before or after you were working here."

"Right you are."

Manolo stretched his hand out and took the gloves the Count had just slipped off. The men looked each other in the eye until Manolo averted his gaze.

"It's not right so many valuable books are kicking around here, Conde . . . You realize you've got to come with me to Headquarters? For fingerprinting and —"

"Don't worry, Manolo. I'll only make one request: that you're not the one to interrogate me . . . Right now, as calm as I am, I'd like to take you by the neck and throttle you. You know what I'm like when I go crazy."

Mario Conde looked round, trying to escape from Yoyi Pigeon's imploring eyes. His temples were pounding at the degradation he was being professionally and efficiently subjected to: the forensic put each of his fingers on the inky pad in turn and lifted them, like inert fishes, on to the card set out with ten greedy spaces, where he imprinted those personal marks, prints of a man now on file, by the name of Mario Conde, alias "the Count", born in . . . son of . . . inhabitant of . . . Till that precise moment, the ex-policeman had never really grasped the levels of harassment a human being suffered when experiencing that humiliating treatment, which appeared painless but was in fact similar to what cattle must feel when metal tags are attached to their ears: now, despite his obvious innocence, he'd become one more name on the handy list of people registered in police files and, with each case, his details would be run through the cold memory of a computer, in the malign hope they'd coincide with some incriminating prints.

As he used a dirty cloth to bring the colour back to his fingers, Mario Conde tortured himself thinking about the hundreds of times he'd put other men, guilty and innocent, through that same humiliating process. He suddenly grasped the reasons behind the evil, hate-filled looks he received from men he'd subjected to that ritual, because his own discoloured skin had now suffered that degradation, and he thought how he'd plied a destructive trade for far too many years. Although he'd always known the police are a necessary social evil, charged to protect and to serve – as one motto said, one of the most euphemistic ever coined – more often to repress and so protect the rights of the powerful, was their real mission in life, though it was never stated so brutally. Working hard to get his fingers spotlessly clean, Mario Conde scanned the horizons of his conscience, hoping to find some comforting evidence there that he'd been an honest cop, unable to be violent towards other men, averse to arrogance, romantically sure he was performing tasks that would help the world to become a better place, however minimally. But no such assurance came to his rescue, and he was left to sink in the mire of evidence that he had been a policeman after all – perhaps a too cerebral, if not bland example of the species – and had formed part of that uncompromising fraternity now stripped naked before him and exposing its distinctive features.

With no strength to offer resistance, he let himself be led by Sergeant Atilio Estévañez down the corridors of Central Head-quarters, whose walls still echoed with stories of his miraculous solutions to complex cases he was always assigned by a mythical boss. A boss suspended for perpetuity in an underhand manner by the Internal Investigations Committee, and who went by the still unutterable name of Antonio Rangel. Had he really always been even-handed? He tried to persuade himself he had, to salvage some of his devastated self-esteem, because the Count knew they were heading to one of the rooms used for interrogations and that he was going to need massive amounts of that in there.

When he entered the oppressive cubicle, Sergeant Estévañez pointed him to a chair, behind a small formica table. Conde looked at his place, opposite where he sat when he was the interrogator, and at the mirror across the room. He imagined Manolo must have put off his conversation with Yoyi in order to sit, perhaps next to a big boss, behind that glass panel that separated the interrogation room from the room for officers and witnesses, drawing an iron line between the powerful and those stripped of all power.

"I'm sorry," said Sergeant Estévañez, as if that were really possible, "but we have . . . just a few questions, more routine than anything else . . . Captain Palacios told me to say you're making a statement rather than being questioned . . . You say that last night you were by yourself at home? Did anyone see you or ring you?. . ."

At that last word the sergeant was shocked to see Conde stand up, as if jet-propelled, knock his chair over, and walk towards the mirror, which he banged twice with the palm of his hand.

"Manolo, come in here."

Conde returned to his place but, before he got there, the door opened and his former colleague came in.

"Couldn't they talk to me elsewhere? Does it have to be in this interrogation room, like some fucking murderer?" his voice was angry and staccato. "Is he taking a statement? Don't try to mess me around . . ."

"Listen, Conde, it's different now from when we . . ."

"Different, my ass, my friend, my ass," a wave of indignation restored his lost energy, sent feelings of harassment packing, and he flopped down.

"Go out for a moment, Atilio," Manolo instructed Estévanez, then added, glancing at the mirror. "Leave me alone and switch the equipment off, right?"

Manolo waited a few seconds and rested one buttock on the edge of the table, as he used to in the old days.

"Calm down, for fuck's sake . . ."

"No, I won't. I've spent too much time in a state of calm. Now I'm going to defend myself."

Manolo sighed, clicked his tongue and shook his head.

"Will you let me say how much I regret this?"

'No," the Count answered, not looking at him. "You must be kidding."

"It's a formality, Conde. We have to find things out . . . Do you think I ever thought you?. . . Don't you realize I've got bosses who wouldn't believe their own mothers?"

"I've never felt so humiliated . . ."

"I can imagine."

"No, you can't, you can't. And if you can, it's worse, because you know what you've done to me."

150

"That's why I'm saying I'm sorry, for hell's sake," Manolo lamented.

"You've burnt your bridges, you've really fucked it up . . ."

"Hell, Conde, it's not that bad. Don't start playing the victim . . . Does all this mean you're not going to help me?" there was a familiar imploring tone to the captain's voice.

"Don't imagine I will for one minute," replied the Count, driven by indignation, and making the most of the advantage he'd just established. "I'm going to fuck you up good and proper . . . because I'm going to find out who killed Dionisio Ferrero before you do. And I'm going to show all the hotshots like you and your current bosses who's the best detective in town."

Manolo smiled, slightly relieved. The Count was fighting back, as was to be expected.

"All right, OK. Is that what you want? We'll see who gets there first . . . But I warn you: it will be a pleasure rubbing this who's best shit in your face. Because now we're playing hardball, I'll remind you of something: when we worked together, on the pretext that you were my boss and my friend, you always gave me the shit: you took over our cases, and got me to check the files, like an asshole, because you didn't think I —"

"That's a lie," the Count protested.

"It's true, and you know it. But we'll soon see who's really who when it comes to being a detective."

"Are you being serious?"

"What do you think? I'll tell you one thing: I'm a policeman and I'm going to do my job, whichever heads have to fall. I don't like bastards doing things and getting away with it . . . Remember that? . . . So if your partner Yoyi is involved in this . . ."

Conde lit a cigarette and looked at Manolo. He had a sudden thought: that they might work together again, but he gave the idea short shrift.

"You still think it's about stealing a few books?"

"I don't know," Manolo admitted. "I'm going to have to investigate. I'm going to find out who killed Dionisio Ferrero before you. That much I do know . . ."

The midday sun seemed about to melt the pavement when Yoyi Pigeon came out of Headquarters. Mario Conde threw his cigarette on the ground and bid farewell to the stone where he'd been sitting for more than two hours, in the shade of the weeping figs planted in the street that ran along one side of the building.

"What a bloody mess we've got ourselves into, man . . . These police are like crabs; they want to crawl into everything. Even the car, your gold chains . . . And your friend Manolo is the worst: when he gets his teeth in, he won't let go without a struggle. I thought they were going to keep me inside I swear."

"What's new: they don't have anything and are looking for scraps to help them," pronounced the Count as they walked up the avenue. "They're at their most dangerous when they're flailing around. If they let you go, it means they don't have a thing to go on."

"Oh yes they do," whispered Yoyi and the Count looked at him quizzically. "Dionisio had a piece of paper with my telephone number in one of his pockets. I'd written it down . . ."

"I don't get you," hissed the Count.

"I gave him my telephone number, just in case . . ."

"Were you going to do business behind my back?"

"No, Conde, I swear I wasn't . . . It was just in case."

"So it was just in case . . . You've fucked up, Yoyi."

"They say I've got to be reachable."

"Don't worry about that. So have I."

"Who might have done it, Conde?"

"So far there are four likely candidates . . . and you and I are two of them. Amalia and the man who paid them a visit are the others . . . But it might have been someone else . . . In any case it was someone Dionisio knew."

"But why the fuck should we want to kill him? It would only make doing business more difficult . . . You know that, don't you?"

"They know that too. They realize we didn't need to kill Dionisio for a few books we could buy for three or four dollars a time . . . But we police know odd things happen. For example, a future murderer and would-be corpse agree to do business and —"

"Don't fuck on about that: all I did was give him my telephone number . . . But I get you. And look what you just said: *we* police know . . ."

"Did I say that?"

Yoyi nodded.

"If there was a bit of policeman left in me, they killed it off today."

"I think they're really riled because we earn in one day what they get in a month, and we don't have bosses or union meetings . . ."

"That's true. But there are police who like to work properly. Like Manolo . . ."

"So what about the lame black guy who wanted to buy their books?"

"We're going to find out who he is," said the Count. "That's the only lead we have, because apparently six books were removed from the section we'd not checked out, and that's probably what Dionisio's murderer was after . . . What I can't get off my fucking brain is that hunch I've had from the moment I entered the Ferreros' library. It's one hell of a feeling. It's stuck right there," and he pointed to the exact spot in his chest where the hunch was burning him, "There was something strange in there and, I don't know why, but I still think it's all got to do with Violeta del Río . . ."

"That same old tune. What the hell's the connection between Violeta del Río and all this?"

"I don't know, but hunches are like that sometimes you can't make head nor tail of them, but when you try to dig deeper, all hell breaks loose."

"I told you you were crazy, man, didn't I?"

"You tell me three times a day," the Count calculated and pointed to a stall selling coffee. "Are you going to help me find out who killed Dionisio, and get to the bottom of what was in that library that we didn't see?"

Yoyi ordered two coffees and stared at the Count, feverishly stroking the bony protuberance on his chest.

"You mean we can play cops and robbers?"

"Stop pissing around, Yoyi. You're a fucking idiot sometimes. Don't you get it? You and I have been let out but there's still a guilty party out there. Don't you realize the bit of paper with your telephone number puts you in danger?"

"But I didn't do anything. Do I have to swear that to you?"

153

"Don't fucking swear anything: start helping me. You're going to find out where the tall black guy interested in buying books came from and I'm going to see Silvano. Isn't your talent getting good deals? Well, the best deal now is to play to our strengths, because we know things they don't. We two are going to find out what went on last night at the Ferreros' place. Fucking hell, this coffee tastes of shit . . ."

24 December
My love:
What else can I wish you, on such a day as this, than for you to be as happy as can be, and to enjoy being with your children, wherever you now live. What else could I desire (it is what I long for most) than for you to share that happiness with me, with all your children, unburdened by secrets that now weigh far too heavily, and with eyes on the future, that no longer stare into the past.

The Christmas and New Year holidays always make me more vulnerable, and this year I've felt more fragile than ever. Some thing strange is happening, I don't know if it is the time of year or a backlog of sorrow, but at night I hear voices that speak of guilt, sin, betrayal, sometimes so vividly that I am forced to switch on my reading lamp and look around me but then I only find the same loneliness.

I think all this began to stir after the visit from that persistent policeman, just over a week ago, do you remember? the one leading the investigation. The damned fellow came to see me to tell me exactly what you think: he is convinced something happened that he cannot get to the bottom of, but he is prepared to swear that she didn't commit suicide, even when he hasn't the slightest proof to back his idea. After saying that, he explained that in fact he had come to tell me the case was going to be closed on orders from his superiors, or, in other words, the investigation will not continue, in spite of his doubts. Nonetheless, while he was drinking his cup of coffee, he asked me ever so many questions, almost all the ones he'd asked before, about that woman's friendships, possible enemies, unfinished business, drug addiction and, naturally, possible suicide motives. I told him yet again what I know, as sincerely as I knew how but not mentioning other matters I still think are unrelated to her death: you know what I'm referring to.

But that man's suspicions, your doubts and the voices that speak of guilt, are undermining my convictions. Although there is something I am totally clear about (my innocence and, I hardly need to say this, yours as well), I have begun to think about what happened over that period of days, looking for a black spot, a detail that does not fit the usual patterns, to try to find, if one existed, an indication that her death might have been provoked by an individual who desired it.

I have thought, naturally, that someone like her, in spite of the unhappy past as an orphan girl she told you about, as a decent girl desperate to sing and be successful, must have left behind her enemies and hatred. So, the change you brought into her life might have sparked resentment in somebody determined to make her pay for a happiness she thought was undeserved.

What is terrible, given everything you and I know, is how the portrait of this individual keeps evoking my own face. The knowledge I am innocent allows me dismiss that false image, but does not help me find another, if one exists. Could one of her girlfriends have been the guilty one? Perhaps that good-for-nothing who used to visit her and even accompany her on her trips to spoil herself with your money, who even dared to pass herself off as a respectable lady when everyone knew what she did in life . . . But why should she want to? Was she really her friend? Could envy at your lover's good fortune be sufficient to push her into preparing that road to death? She had opportunities enough: she went in and out of that woman's house whenever she wanted, even used to spend afternoons at the flat with your friend Louis. But I don't think envy is motive enough, because if you work through it in logical fashion, by killing her, she would have killed the goose laying the golden eggs, since when that woman became your wife, as you had decided, the other ne'er-do-well could continue to profit from her old friendship, thanks to which she'd succeed in gaining God knows what benefits, apart from the ones she already enjoyed because you were grateful to her for introducing you to that woman in the first place.

28 December
My love:
The voices pursue me, obsessed as I am by finding out. I put this letter to one side a few days ago because a frightful headache prevented me from writing. Today, I feel calmer and I will try to finish it, but only to say that a voice woke me up last night and told me it's my fault because I don't know what I ought to, what I would never wish to have known. What was it referring to? I don't know, but I swear to you that, with or without those voices, with or without your agreement, I will continue to search for my only solution: the truth. Although it may be the most terrible of truths.

155

I hope you enjoy a lovely end to the year. We've experienced twelve wretched months, with all manner of misfortune, exacerbated by your being so far away for more than three months now. I hope these festivities and holy celebrations bring a little peace to your soul and that you have a happy respite. In my solitude, I console myself as ever with the idea that we will soon be into another year, and that it will be a year to favour us all.

I really hope you are very happy, as happy as one can be, because I love you . . .

Your Nena

One of the blessings Mario Conde never ceased to be thankful for was the fact he had three or four good friends. The almost fifty years spent in this world had taught him, sometimes perversely, that few states are as fragile as the state of friendship, and hence he fiercely protected his many layered camaraderie with Skinny Carlos, Candito and Rabbit, because he considered it to be one of his most precious gifts from life. Several years earlier, Andrés's departure to the United States had provoked a sense of desertion among the remaining friends, but, at the same time, it had had the beneficial secondary effect of bringing them closer together, welding their connections, making them more tolerant of each other and transforming them into life members of the party of eternal friendship.

The permanent threat represented by Carlos's physical deterioration meant the Count never failed to safeguard the time he spent near his old friend, dedicating all the hours he could to him, aware it was the best way to act in preparation for a future emptiness, the arrival of which drew nearer by the day.

In spite of Carlos's insistence that his friend should set time aside to write the stories he invented and frequently promised to put on paper, the Count felt strangely fulfilled when he spent his evenings and nights in lethargic conversations meandering through the unpredictable labyrinths of memory, obstinately chasing a no doubt imaginary state of grace they dredged up from a rose-tinted past, spurred on by dreams, projects and desires reality had crushed long ago. In these repetitive exchanges, refusing to discover anything new, they allowed themselves to be swept along by the illusion they'd once been really happy, and while they spoke, drank and reminisced, put despair to one side and resurrected the happiest moments from their sad lives.

That night the Count lamented Rabbit's absence, then started to tell Carlos and Candito about the recent events he'd been implicated in and his corrosive reflections on the duties of a policeman that had come to him when he was being put on file. He concluded by telling them of the decision he'd taken that afternoon after the conversation with Silvano Quintero: to start searching for the once famous Lotus Flower, real name Elsa Contreras, about whose existence the journalist had received some vague but reliable information about ten years ago.

"So, after all that, you're back to being a policeman, but on false pretences?" smiled Carlos as he poured himself a shot of the genuine rum they could now drink thanks to the Count's economic good health.

"Ironies of destiny, as a good bolero might say. Although you said it: on false pretences."

"Do you want me to help you look for her?" Candito ventured, and the Count shook his head.

"No, not now. I might need you to give me a hand later, but I'd rather start off by myself. I don't want to kick up any fuss and frighten her off."

"And do you really think that business is connected to what's just happened?" enquired Carlos.

"How the hell should I know, Skinny? I'd certainly like to find out what happened to Violeta del Río. Yesterday I promised to forget her, but now she won't budge from here . . ." and he hit his forehead with the palm of his hand, "at least until I know why the fuck she committed suicide. Or had it committed for her . . ."

"You've got it bad," said Candito and the Count nodded vigorously, weighing up if that was the moment to relate the strange story of his father's platonic love affair. But he opted to keep that under wraps.

"From the minute I first saw that picture something strange happened: it was as if I'd once known something about her and had forgotten whatever it was. I don't know where the idea came from, but if I find out what happened to her, I'll probably discover why I had that feeling . . . Later on, when I heard the record, she really did start to complicate things."

"I'd liked to have seen her sing as well. Nobody sings like that nowadays, do they?" asked Carlos.

"Maybe it's because we've spent the last twenty years listening to the same old singers?" asked Candito.

"Twenty?" reflected the Count. "You mean thirty plus . . . Fuck, you know, we're just a bunch of old farts."

"Do you remember, Conde, when they shut the clubs and cabarets because they said they were dens of vice and relics of the past?" recalled Carlos.

"And as a reward they sent us to cut cane in the harvest in 1970. All that sugar that was going to save us from underdevelopment at a stroke," Candito remembered. "I was cutting cane for four months, every single day God brought."

"I sometimes think . . . How many things did they take away, ban, refuse us for years in order to catapult us into the future and make us better?"

"A hell of a lot," declared Carlos.

"And are we any better for it?" enquired Red Candito.

"We're different: are we three-legged or one-legged? I'm not exactly sure . . . The worse thing was we weren't allowed the chance to live to the rhythms people were enjoying on the rest of the planet. To protect us . . ."

"Do you know what most pisses me off?" Rabbit interrupted, sticking his teeth round the door. "They killed dead our dream of going to Paris at the age of twenty, which is the right time to go to Paris . . . Now they can stick Paris up their asses and Brussels too, if there's room."

"What kept you, Rabbit?" the Count welcomed him, handing him the bottle of rum, after he'd helped himself.

"All the time, day in, day out we've been living out our responsibility for this moment in history. They were bent on forcing us to be better," said Rabbit, but the Count shook his head, hardly able to restrain himself.

"And why do so many young people now want to be rastas, rockers, rappers and even Muslims, and dress up like clowns, abuse themselves putting rings everywhere and even tattooing their

158

eyelids? Why do so many do the hardest drugs, why do so many become whores, pimps, and transvestites, and wear crucifixes and voodoo necklaces though they don't even believe in their own fucking mothers? Why do so many cynics swear one thing and believe another, and why do so many live by thinking up what they can steal to get money so they don't work themselves to death? Why do so many just want to leave the island?"

"I have a name for that," the group's historian picked up the baton: "historical exhaustion. After being so exceptional, so historical and so transcendent, people get tired and want a bit of normality. As they can't do that, they decide to be abnormal. They want to be like other people, not like themselves, that's why they are rastas, rappers or whatever, and drug themselves up to the eyeballs . . . They don't want to belong, don't want to be forced to be good. Above all they don't want to be like us, their fathers, a load of failed shits . . ."

"These aren't the ones that piss me off most," the Count reflected. "The ones who make me want to vomit are those who look perfect and trustworthy but are in fact a bunch of opportunists."

Rabbit nodded and sipped on his rum. Something prickly and sour refused to go down his throat.

"Have you ever considered what kind of place we were lucky enough to be born in? Have you or haven't you?" he waited for an answer that never came and spelt it out. "Well, you should. This is a country pre-destined to exaggeration. Christopher Columbus started the rot, when he said that this was the most beautiful land ever seen by man and all that jazz. Then we had the geographical, historical misfortune, to be where we were when we were, and the bliss or bad luck to be like we are. And you see, there was even a time when we produced more wealth than this island needed and we thought we were wealthy. Aside from that considerable misconception, we have produced more geniuses per inhabitant and square yard than we had a right to and long thought we were better, more intelligent, stronger . . . This exaggeration is also our greatest burden: it threw us into the midst of history. Remember how Martí wanted to put the whole world to rights from here, the whole world mind you, the entire planet as if he'd got his hands on the blasted lever Archimedes was after. And you can see the consequences . . . A decent sense of history and shocking memory, lethargy and predestination, grandeur and frivolity, idealism and pragmatism, as if balancing out virtues and defects, right? But exhaustion follows all that. Exhaustion at being so historic and so predestined."

"Historical exhaustion," the Count savoured Rabbit's definition, downed his rum and looked at his friends, model sufferers from acquired historical exhaustion syndrome: Skinny who was no longer skinny, his spine destroyed in a war, that was of course historic, but about which nobody now spoke; a gawky Rabbit, his increasingly long teeth sticking our from a skull much in evidence, still able to theorize on insular exaggeration but who'd never written any of the history books he'd dreamt of writing; Red Candito, historically anchored in the noisy tenement where he'd been born, going hungry ever since he gave up his countless illicit endeavours and insisted on looking for transcendental answers in a chronicle written 2,000 years ago, and which spoke of an apocalypse bristling with terrible punishments for all those who didn't deliver their soul up to the Saviour. And finally, how could the absent presence, Andrés, possibly have concluded that to erase his nostalgia and mock his historic fatigue, it was best never to return to the island? Or even see another baseball game in the Havana stadium? Or even come to a drinks, music and conversation session with those friends, who, in spite of their mutilations, frustrations, beliefs and disbeliefs, historic exhaustion and physical and intellectual hunger, never said no to a night of shared evocations, vaguely but latently aware that if they had given up that friendship they'd perhaps have forgotten what living was a long time ago?

"Life was passing us by on all sides," said Rabbit, "and to protect us they gave us blinkers. Like mules. We should only look ahead and stride towards the shining future awaiting us at the end of history and, obviously, we weren't allowed to get tired on that road. Our only problem was that the future was very far off and the path went uphill and was full of sacrifices, prohibitions, denials and privations. The more we advanced, the steeper the slope and more distant the shining future, which was fading quickly anyway. The bastard had run out of petrol. I sometimes think they dazzled us with all that glare and we walked past the future and didn't even

160

see it . . . Now we're halfway round the track and are going blind, as well as bald and cirrhotic, and there's not even all that much we want to see anymore."

Listening to Rabbit, the Count felt the bittersweet taste of immeasurable sadness congeal in his mouth.

"You can always seek out God," Candito pronounced.

"Nobody's up there looking after us, Red. We're completely on our own," the Count contradicted him.

"Don't you believe in miracles?"

"Not any more. But I do trust in my hunches. And that's why I won't fail to find out what happened to Violeta del Río," concluded the Count, whose mouth was then overwhelmed by the feeling he still lacked a really plausible motive, and so he spelt out the first that came to his lips. "I want to find out why history swallowed her up."

Not worried why he was doing so – and not really interested in finding out – perhaps driven by a mixture of alcohol and the persistent allure of certain phantoms and fascinations, Conde hailed a taxi going in the opposite direction to his house and asked the driver to take him to the corner of Twenty-Third and L, or any other street corner that might encompass the same evocative ciphers. He was pleased to see that even at that late, late hour of the night, the fast-beating heart of the city was still packed with spaced-out youths and adults trawling for illicit offerings. In the doorway and vicinity of the cinema, and on the other side of the street, next to the iron rails protecting the ice creamery, an insomniac crowd slipped past under the sleepy gaze of various pairs of policemen. Gays of every tendency and category, rockers with no stage or music, savage hunters and huntresses of foreigners and dollars, bored birds of the night with one, two and even three hidden agendas seemed anchored to that spot, not fearing the imminent dawn, as if hoping something out of the blue might drag them down the street, perhaps out to sea, or maybe up into the sky.

The new life re-surfacing in the city, after the deep lethargy it was plunged into by the Crisis's darkest years, had a pace and density the ex-policeman couldn't pin down. Rappers and rastas, prostitutes and drug addicts, the newly rich and newly poor were redrawing the geography of the city, now stratified according to the number of dollars possessed and which was beginning to seem more normal, although it always made him wonder which was for real, the life he'd known in his youth, or the one he was now contemplating in his mature, illusion-free years

Conde wasn't particularly looking for a right answer, and moved away from the night-time bustle, taking to the slope of La Rampa. The chronological boundaries of nostalgia were set way beyond his most distant memory, and so he tried to find the still visible traces of a dazzling, perverted city, a distant planet, familiar from hearsay, heard on forgotten records, discovered in infinite reading, always appearing, peopled with lights, clubs, cabarets, tunes and characters he now knew Violeta del Río must have been familiar with almost fifty years ago, her hopes soaring, in search of her place in the sun.

He walked non-stop past the revitalized luminous sign of The Vixen and the Crow, where she'd once sung, and which was now off limits to anyone not carrying the five US dollars necessary to guarantee a seat; he contemplated the barred and bolted entrance to The Grotto, which didn't betray the slightest echo of the late night chords that echoed in that musical cave when the sun was about to rise; he looked with no particular emotion at the charred ruins of the old Montmartre, proletarianly re-christened Moscow and prophetically devoured by fire years before that empire disintegrated; he passed by the soulless entrance to the Las Vegas cabaret, where a man, around his own age, caught his attention, looking distinctly nostalgically at the place that was now boarded up where for so many years you could drink your last cup of coffee in the early hours; he walked without a glimmer of hope past the garlanded mansion of the White Peak, no longer enticing passers-by with graceful guitar arpeggios; he walked up towards the now darkened Red Room at the Capri, its doors shut and chained, and finally entered the gardens at the National Hotel, under the gaze of grumpy security guards equipped with walkie-talkies, who let him off and through without asking a single question, although they visually arrested him on charges of being Cuban, not possessing dollars or belonging to that scene; he lingered for a few minutes in front of the luxurious, equally dollarized portico of the Parisién, the cabaret where the immortal Frank Sinatra once performed – to an audience of Luciano, Lansky and Trafficante –as well as a young, now forgotten woman who went by the name of Violeta del Río and sang for the supreme pleasure of singing.

In front of the door to this cabaret, reserved for the tropical pleasuring of ephemeral foreign visitors, accompanied by their willing, nationally produced and tariffed escorts, Conde felt, for the first time in his almost forty-eight years, that he was wandering through an unknown city, one that didn't belong to him, and one moving him on, shutting him out. That cabaret wasn't his; nothing about its visible decor enticed him or induced nostalgia. The night air, the long walk and feeling of alienation had freed him from the spell of alcohol, but an annoying lucidity had commandeered his battered feelings, set on making him understand that, except for the odd almost faded memory, Violeta del Río and her world of lights and shadows no longer lived at that address, and had departed leaving no other signs of life beyond the physical remains of those boarded up, burnt-out or inaccessible scenarios, even in the memory of a man stubbornly opposed to ultimate oblivion. The Count's fascination with that world had received the kiss of death, and he realized that the only way he could revive it was by giving himself the satisfaction of finding out the final truths about Violeta del Río and the reasons why she'd turned up inside a book of impossible recipes he'd found in an equally impossible library.

With sadness spreading through his soul, the Count returned to the street and contemplated the vista of buildings that were once pretentiously modern and were now bent double by premature senility. He observed, almost loathed the young woman with the permanent smile who, back to the wall, was letting an old, Nordic-looking guy whom she called "*mi amor*" slaver all over her. He listened to the din created by young lads coming up O Street as they let out cries of potentially drug-inspired glee and kicked at sacks of rubbish they encountered en route. He was alarmed by a gleaming Lada that sped past, its sound system blasting out at top volume, keen to show off its ostentatious, prefabricated happiness. He went down towards Twenty-Third and watched two well-equipped policemen walk by, as jumpy as their gigantic Alsatians. He looked around, not having the slightest idea and hadn't the slightest idea what direction he should take to exit the labyrinth his city had become and realized that he too was a ghost from the past, a member of a species galloping towards extinction, witnessing, on this night, lost in the city, the evidence for genetic failure as embodied by himself and his brutal dislocation between one world that had faded and another that was fast disintegrating. All in all, thought Mario Conde, Yoyi wasn't wrong, though he hadn't got it quite right: it wasn't that he seemed so incredible he was like a lie, but rather that he *was* a living lie, and his whole life had been one stubborn, if unsuccessful, manipulation of reality.

The Calzada de Monte and the only in name hopeful calle Esperanza form an inverted wedge, ready to gouge the most flaccid urban flesh, opening up the entrails of what was once the old walled town of Havana. The Calzada and calle Esperanza almost create a vortex in the barrio of the Single Market neighbourhood, until they peter out on the bustling calle del Egido, a perpetually run-down triangle that still throbs on the city map. Over the centuries its guts have accumulated the human, architectural and historic debris generated by a bullying capital always marching westwards, and moving away from that bastion of poorly paid proletarians, lumpens of every stripe, whores, drug traffickers and emigrants from other regions of the island and the world, all eager for a slice of the action that will almost always elude them. The Calzada, its shops run by Lebanese, Syrians and Polish Jews selling remnants, second-hand clothes and a selection of trinkets, marked out the frontier between the palaces, luxury-goods shops, parks, fountains, theatres, dance halls and hotels of Havana's splendid commercial centre, and that other down-at-heel area, the adjacent Atarés and Jesús María barrios, home to poor blacks and whites, in cheap buildings with no pretence of style, on narrow streets, their inhabitants crammed together and ground down by poverty and marginalization. In the memories of Havanans that neighbourhood of the city, frequently invaded by black exhalations from the Tallapiedra power station, poisoned by leaking butane gas and besieged by effluvia from the bay's most polluted streams, was like territory conceded to infidels they never expected or intended to reconquer. History seemed to have passed down its winding streets and never stopped, while generation after

165

generation hoarded pain, oblivion, rage and a spirit of resistance that expressed itself in illicit, sinful, violent acts, ruthlessly seeking to survive, at any cost and by any means.

In his years in the force, Mario Conde suffered immensely when an investigation led him to that Havana backwater where nobody had ever known, seen or heard anything, where people poured their hatred into scornful looks they directed at the representatives of a distant establishment that always repressed them. Violence, the means to vent chronic frustration, was the everyday currency used to repay debts or insults and lawlessness had long ruled that ravaged territory, where to be frail was the worst illness imaginable.

Since the day he'd entered the book trade, the Count hadn't been back to that rough corner of the city: he knew in advance he'd have been wasting his time – and would perhaps have lost his wallet, shoes and other bodily possessions – if he'd dared to meander down its streets, searching suspiciously for something as exotic as a book for sale. Consequently, although he'd assumed the darkest days of the Crisis must have decimated that Bermuda triangle, he hadn't imagined how hard the degeneration from the years of the worst shortages – bad times the country had now supposedly overcome – had hit.

Conde abandoned his taxi at the miserable, downtrodden cross-roads of Cuatro Caminos – that once mythical location, where a restaurant stood on each corner, competing in quality and prices with its equidistant colleagues – and walked down a couple of alleyways in search of calle Esperanza. He immediately began to understand Yoyi Pigeon's claim that Chinatown was only the first circle in the urban hell, because a first glance made it clear he was penetrating the heart of a world of darkness, a shadowy bottomless pit that was barely held in check by any wall. Breathing that atmosphere of hidden danger, he progressed through a labyrinth of impassable streets, like a city ravaged by war, strewn with potholes and debris, tottering buildings, cracked beyond repair, propped up by wooden supports rotted by sun and rain, containers overflowing with putrefying mountains of rubbish, where two men, still in their youth, sniffed after any recyclable bounty. Packs of mangy dogs wandered about, with nothing in their stomachs to shit on the street, alongside raucous sellers of avocados, brooms, clothes pegs, piles of torches, second-hand lavatories and wood for cooking; next to hard-faced women, sharp as knives, all geared up in lycra Bermudas that got tighter and tighter, ideal garments for emphasizing the quality of the nipples and sex on proud display. The feeling that he was crossing the borders a land of chaos warned him he was witnessing a world on the brink of an Apocalypse that it would be difficult to escape.

No sooner was he past those borders than Conde realized he'd set himself an almost impossible mission. None of the ploys he'd considered – introducing himself as a journalist, a distant relation of someone, a public health officer looking for an AIDS victim, or a desperate hunter after rented rooms – was going to help once he'd asked his initial questions and revealed his real concerns. So, his only chance of finding the faint trail of Elsa Contreras, Lotus Flower the dancer, resident in the area as Silvano Quintero had recalled – was the hope that his old informant Juan Serrano Ballester, alias Juan the African, was around in the barrio and not in prison – his normal location.

When he was in front of the tenement in the dead-end callejón Alambique where Juan the African had been born and lived the few years of freedom he'd enjoyed in his lamentable existence, Conde was pleased to see nobody in the entrance. He immediately wondered why that man had bothered to spend his life stealing, defrauding and looting if it'd never got him beyond that elemental state: it was a three-storey building from the beginning of the twentieth century and its sombre, balcony-less façade strongly resembled that of a prison. Where there'd once been a front door supposedly separating the street from the passage and stairs leading to the higher flats, only a gaping hole now remained, and the Count imagined how, in the direst days of the Crisis, the wooden frame and door must been sacrificed to a wood-burning stove. Steam from pig shit and urine rose from the floor, while equally fetid water dripped down the stairs, no doubt leaking from dilapidated sewage pipes.

Juan lived on the third floor of that phalanstery, in a half room he managed to retain after ceding the remainder of an already oppressive flat to the country girl from Guantanamo who'd borne him twins. As the room was at the back of the building, you had to negotiate a narrow door-lined passage, one part of which had collapsed in some remote prehistoric era and been replaced by two planks that gave access to the back rooms. The Count filled his lungs to avoid taking a breath on his journey across the planks, arms spread like an intrepid tightrope walker. When he was finally opposite the door the African had added to the passage, Conde wondered whether his stubborn quest for the truth about the fate of a lost songstress made any sense at all, and again logic said it didn't, though something inexplicable compelled him to knock on the door.

When Juan recognized him he almost fainted. He was only two months out from his last stay behind bars, after a three-year sentence for repeated fraud. Seeing that policeman from a dark corner of his past in his house could only signal impending disaster.

"Don't be scared, for fuck's sake, I'm not in the police any more," the Count quickly explained, while the other man shook a jet-black head profiled like a Dahomey sculpture. "I swear, man, I've been out more than ten years . . ."

"You swear on your mother?" the African said threateningly, sure nobody would take his mother's name in vain unless it was a very last resort.

"I swear on my mother," the Count replied, reminded of Yoyi and his oaths. "I need your help: I can pay cash," he added, tapping his pocket.

"Did they kick you out of the police?"

"No, I left because I wanted out."

The African half shut his eyes to process that information.

"I get it: now you work for foreigners and run one of those so-called corporations, right? You getting lots of the green'uns?"

"I don't run a thing. Can I come in?"

"Swear again you're not a policeman. Come on, swear on your children, who you'll find dead when you get home if you're lying . . ."

"I swear."

In his peculiar situation, the Count had decided it was better to tell the African the truth, or at least part of the truth related to his search for the lost past of Violeta del Río, however incredible it might seem to a rational ear. While he told the story, he tried to imagine how his ex-informant could help him, but he'd only just started to say why he was so interested, when the man dashed his hopes of a quick fix by stating he knew the names of every stray dog in the barrio, but had never heard of Elsa Contreras, let alone any Lotus Flower.

"You're fucked. I can't help you," Juan concluded, a happy smile in his bloodshot eyes, no doubt pleased to think that, now he could be no help, the Count would beat a quick retreat back the way he'd come.

"I need to be sure that woman doesn't live around here. I've got to talk to someone who really knows this barrio. Or don't you want to earn yourself a few pesos? Look, can't you introduce me as your ex's cousin who's going to spend a few days with you . . . I don't know, because I've just got out of the clink, OK?"

The African laughed, almost roared.

"You gone mad? Conde, everybody here's just out of the cage. What prison do I say you were in if nobody saw you, whichever one you were in?"

Conde agreed it wasn't a good idea, and then the African suggested: "I know, we'll say you're a cousin of the girl from Guantanamo, but have come from Matanzas . . . Your business was killing cows and the police were after you and you came here to let things cool down. What do you reckon?"

"I'd buy that."

"But you can't stay here. There's no room . . ." He opened his arms wide and almost touched the walls of the two and a half by four-yard hole.

"I can leave at night and come back in the morning."

"And as soon as you find the woman, you disappear . . ."

"I'll disappear," the Count agreed

"If that's it, then OK. Now down to the serious stuff: how much is the job worth?"

"A thousand pesos," said the Count, sure such a figure would clinch it.

"I don't put my life on the line for a thousand." The African yawned and stroked one of the three scars on his face, that were blacker and shinier than the rest of his skin. "Two thousand, and you pay for food and everything else."

"OK," replied the Count without flinching.

"Right then, to get a feel for the place, let's have a few drinks down the street, then we'll eat in Veneto's underground chop shop. He knows about everything that moves around here. I'll make sure he sits down with us and you find a way to find out about that woman without him realizing you're really after something else. But be warned: if they smell a rat, we'll both be done for . . ."

"It's not such a big deal," replied the Count, and the African shrugged his shoulders.

"Give me the money. I need it right now."

Conde looked at the ex-convict and shook his head.

"I might seem crazy or an asshole, but I'm not . . ."

"All right, give me half," the African almost pleaded. "Look, just so you know: people here want my guts. I did a bit of business, it went bad and I owe them. If I can give them something on account, they'll calm down a bit. If not, I can't set foot in the street . . . Those guys don't believe anything . . ."

Conde pondered for a moment and realized he didn't have much choice.

"All right, I'll give you half. And the rest when the woman puts in an appearance."

When they went out into the street, the raging midday sun had dispersed the crowds. Music now filled the spot once occupied by people, flooding the space, melodies criss-crossing, competing in volume to blast the minds of anyone who risked entering that atmosphere steeped in sones, boleros, meringues, ballads, mambos, guarachas, hard and soft rock, danzones, bachatas and rumbas. The houses with entrances onto the street, open windows and doors, tried to take in a little of the warm air, while men and women of all ages rocked on their chairs, enjoying the artificial breeze from fans and the deafening music, while, resigned to their lot, they watched dead midday hours pass by.

They walked into a tenement and in the inside yard several men were drinking beer, equally gripped by the music. A mulatta in her forties, with coloured beaded plaits and sheathed in lycra pants straining to contain the excessive poundage of her buttocks, seemed to own the establishment and she stared straight at the African when she saw him come in with a stranger.

"Two lagers and don't piss around. This guy's my buddy."

170

"I couldn't care fucking less if he's your buddy: I just don't like strangers around here . . ." the mulatta shouted, looking defiantly at the Count.

"Africa, let's go fucking elsewhere, she can stick her beers up her ass," reacted the Count, half-turning round to leave, when a voice from behind stopped him in his tracks.

"Hey, friend, not so fast." The Count looked round. Michael Jordan was now standing next to the African, or at least his double was: a huge, brawny black guy, with a shaved head, wearing the uniform of the Chicago Bulls. "This woman talks a lot of shit."

"Why all the secrecy, if the whole barrio knows you sell beer?" asked the Count, accepting the freezing beer on offer from Michael Jordan, whose other hand held one for the African.

"I'll have that lager please," Juan demanded, smiling.

"So you're safe to walk the streets?" enquired Michael Jordan, handing it over.

"Next stop is Veneno's. I'm getting there."

"Pleased to hear it," said Michael Jordan, smiling in turn, "you're ugly enough when alive, dead you'd scare the living daylights . . ." and he flashed the whitest of smiles at the Count.

Three beers on, Mario Conde had explained how rustling and slaughtering cattle worked in the increasingly scalped plains of Matanzas and was himself informed about the spots in the barrio where they sold basketball kit, baseball and football shirts, powdered milk, cooking oil and the site of the best supplied stock of electrical goods in the city, all sourced directly from nearby warehouses in the port. By his fifth he had a pretty accurate idea where and when in the barrio you could get marijuana or pills to pop, and discovered it was possible to buy crack and coke, and what the going rates were for: head-downers specializing in fellatio, slags, who came the cheapest but highly unrecommended, the Juanitas-of-all-trades, ready for anything and down-on-their-luck whores, easy goers who could be hunted down, in the late early hours, sometimes at very reasonable price (though always in dollars), if they were desperate after a night of wasted incursions into city hotels and tourist spots . . . They lived a life that was at once frantic and slow, with time to drift along and time to struggle by, in that ghetto, the streets of which were periodically visited by a couple of police on the beat or a patrol car, as a reminder that the cage doors were always open.

"Let's eat. I'm ravenous," suggested the African, and they went back into the noise and the sun.

They crossed filthy streets, each as filthy as the next, until they clambered through a hole in a ramshackle wood and zinc wall that barely hid the ruins of a three-storey building. It now had neither roof nor mezzanine, only a skeletal frame, where small zinc and canvas panels hung, held in place by wire and wooden props, attempting to shelter a few shapeless objects and some huge cardboard boxes.

"The people living there don't have homes. Most have just arrived from Oriente. They nearly all drive taxi-bikes. They sleep on their bikes, shit on bits of card they throw into the rubbish, and wash when they can," explained the African.

"And they're allowed to live there?" the Count ingenuously tried to bring a little logic to bear.

"Every now and then they pull their roofs down and chuck them out, but they're back within a week. Them or others . . . It's all about not starving to death . . ."

They walked through the ruins and the African pushed a wooden door and poked his head inside. A few minutes later a mulatto swathed in gold chains appeared astride the doorstep.

"This is my mate, Veneno," said Juan, turning towards the Count. "And this is my buddy, the Count," he told Veneno, who looked critically at the stranger and without uttering a word moved a few steps away to the back of the demolished building. Conde couldn't overhear the conversation between the two men, but he did see Juan take out the wad of banknotes he'd only just handed him and give it to Veneno, who took it but hardly jumped for joy.

Sitting in that clandestine open-air eatery ruled over by Veneno, bent on extracting from the Count every last cent he could, the African ordered the most expensive dishes on offer: lobster enchilado and steak in bread crumbs. When they were on their post-coffee beers, Juan invited Veneno to chat with them for a while and, casually, mentioned a cousin of the Count's mother who, according to his friend, lived in the barrio.

"Elsa Contreras?" asked Veneno, gulping his beer down. Veneno was a light-skinned, almost white mulatto, keen to show off his prosperity by displaying numerous teeth crowned in eighteen carat metal, three chains with medallions (living in harmony with a couple of coloured bead necklaces), bejewelled rings, two bracelets and a Rolex of similar golden purity that all told must have weighed in at a good four pounds. Such a load of precious metal couldn't be the fruit of earnings from the culinary delights of that down-at-heel eatery and the Count imagined that was only the most visible illicit business Veneno engaged in, intuitions he put to one side to light a cigarette and drink his beer.

"She was a real character. Nobody mentioned her much at home though, because she was a whore and danced naked at the Shanghai . . ."

"The girl must be older than an Egyptian mummy, right?" Veneno asked.

"Must be eighty, I reckon, if she's . . ."

"I really haven't a clue. If you're in the barrio a few days, I'll find out."

"Great. I'd like to pay her a visit . . ." said the Count, pointing a hand and three erect fingers at the waiter.

That night, while he scrubbed himself in the shower, trying to wash off the filth, infamy and sordidity in which he'd spent one of the strangest days of his life, Mario Conde again wondered how a perverted universe like that could possibly exist in the heart of Havana: a place where people lived who'd been born at the same time, in the same city, as he, but who seemed alien, almost unreal in their level of degeneracy. The experiences he'd suffered in a few hours surpassed his wildest predictions and he now wondered if he'd have it in him to continue his nauseating quest.

After eating and drinking several beers at Veneno's, the African demanded a second advance of 300 pesos that, so he said, were indispensable if the search was to go on. Trapped in a net of his own making, the Count separated out a couple of twenty notes and handed his material and spiritual guide the three hundred pesos he had left.

"Let me tell you something," he said, looking him in the eye, and flourishing the money in one hand. "I'm no longer police, but I've got lots of friends in the force. So I don't think it would be a good idea to try to trick me. I can still fry you alive, right?"

"Hell, Conde, I wouldn't ever . . ."

"So make sure you don't ever," he warned, handing over the notes. "Remember I'll always track you down."

Cheered up by the beers drunk and the sum received, Juan asked him to wait on a street corner and went into an even gloomier tenement than the one with Michael Jordan's clandestine bar. He emerged five minutes later, smiling cheerfully, and suggested the Count accompany him to the roof terrace, so he could show him a panoramic view of the barrio.

Between two uncovered water tanks and sad clotheslines full of patched up clothes, Conde peered out over the eaves to get a prime view of the twilight hustle and bustle in the barrio. He calculated the sea was in front, behind various dark concrete blocks, past the blackened towers of the power station, so near, yet so alien to that place. Lost in geographical and philosophical musings, he snapped back to reality summoned by the sweetish smell of burning grass, and turned round to find Juan the African, leaning back on one of the tanks inhaling from a spindly joint.

"Now I'll see if you really are police. Go one, have a drag," Juan threatened, holding out a roll of paper.

"I don't care a fuck what you think. I'm not going to smoke."

"And if I get in a mess, are you going to put the police on to me?"

"They already are, and have been from the day you were born. I'm the one they'll piss on if they see me with you . . ."

"You never smoked?" the African asked, looking happy, waving the joint, and broadening his smile when he saw the Count shake his head. "I've smoked from the age of thirteen. And whenever I can I smoke here, by myself, so I really enjoy my drag . . . Look, this is my little hidey hole. I've hid things here ever since I was a kid," he said, showing the Count how he put two other joints in a little nylon bag, that he lowered down an air vent protruding by the side of one of the water tanks.

"Who you hiding them from?" enquired the Count, flopping down against the other tank.

The African took a heavy drag.

"I owe five thousand pesos. I'm a loser, right? I always get bad luck. I got involved in a spot of business, took out an advance and gave it my best . . ."

"A five thou advance?" the Count thought aloud. "That was drugs or a contract killing . . . Right?"

"Don't get too nosy," and the African started smoking again, almost burning his fingers.

"Was the business with Veneno?"

Juan smiled and shook his head.

"No, Veneno was the middleman. The business was with other guys. Not from the barrio. Real hard guys who don't get their hands dirty for four pesos. They handle quantities of loot that would make you shit your pants."

"Did you meet them?"

"Negative. You can't get to see them just like that. They're people who've got it here," and he tapped his temple, indicating intelligence. "They're whites who are OK, well set up and only doing the big stuff."

"Sounds like mafia?"

"Well, what do you think?" Juan took a last drag and ditched his tiny fag end.

"Were you told to kill someone, Juan?" the Count asked again, afraid he'd say yes.

"I told you not to ask so many questions. End of interrogation . . . Now let me enjoy the moment, man."

Conde got up and looked for the best angle from which to survey calle Esperanza. On a neighbouring terrace he spotted a hut probably built for pigeon-rearing, behind which some fifteen-year olds were noisily taking turns with binoculars, masturbating all the time, watching a scene the Count also wanted an eyeful of.

When night started to fall, the African, now very high and uninhibited, suggested going for a walk, to see what was on, and the Count, not imagining what he was letting himself in for, accepted his invitation. They went up Esperanza, towards the edge of the barrio, and along one of the alleys that cut across, its name hidden under tons of historic grime, where his companion suggested they wait a minute, ostensibly, to test the temperature. Several people greeted the African, two stopped to have a chat, and walked off seemingly convinced the Count was an expert cattle slaughterer, a cousin of the African's ex from the countryside and a friend even of Veneno and Michael Jordan. Just after eight, the African bought a pack of cigarettes from a street-seller and offered the Count one.

"You'll smoke one of these, won't you? Now you see how I share my money around," he said, smiling, and added: "and I'll now invite you to lay some whores."

Taken aback, Conde was at a loss for what to reply. In an existence entirely spent between the island's four walls, he'd joined in the most diverse moral and physical adventures, some in, others out of the police, some drunk and others horribly sober. He'd never before been invited to have sex you paid for and he was shocked to feel doubt impishly coursing through his veins and wondered whether he might not like to try that for once.

"If you really want to be part of this scene, and nobody to suspect you, then you've got to go on, right to the bottom," said Juan, as he took the first step.

"No, forget it," he protested feebly.

"Hey," the African threatened him, "I can see you're a bit delicate. You won't smoke pot and don't want to shaft a little lady . . . You're not queer by any chance, my friend?"

The knocking-shop, as his ex-confidant described it, was half way along the block. An old married couple, owners of a three-bedroom house, rented them out by the hour to couples with nowhere to make love and to local whores and their customers. The best strategy to get a lay, according to the African, was to linger in the vicinity of the knocking shop and wait to be picked up by an available woman on the job. Suffering an attack of butterflies, the Count leaned expectantly on the wall, a virgin in terms of such experience. He lit a cigarette on his previous butt and looked at both sides of the street, where several people were wandering. Two women appeared ten minutes later. One was a mulatta, dyed blonde, and the other white, very thin, with bright red hair; the Count reckoned, with some difficulty, that they must be in their twenties, although they shifted from seeming older to

176

being almost adolescent. The African immediately chose the white woman, and, with a yellow smile, casually asked how much she charged for the works.

"A hundred pesos," came the reply, and Juan recoiled like a shocked punter. "You think that's dear? Look, you big black, it's twenty to be rubbed off, forty to be sucked off, sixty if you put it in but don't kiss, eighty with a kiss and for a hundred you can stick it up my ass . . . And that's not counting the fact you're a black monkey and are getting to shaft a white woman with a pink cunt . . ."

"Can I give your cunt a feel?"

"Five pesos," the girl responded, adroitly halting the advancing, simian hand.

The Count had begun to feel the first symptoms of asphyxia as he listened to the terms of the agreement between the African and this Juanita-of-all-trades and was about to faint when the mulatta flashed a smile that showed off two gold molars at the corner of her huge mouth, and whispered: "And does, *papi*, want general servicing?"

Conde did his best to smile, knowing he'd be unable to bed that woman, or even kiss her, and glanced at the African, who was relishing the situation. He then understood that all his moral openness was just a childish game in that insane world where sex acquired other values and uses, and became a source of sustenance, a way to put the miseries and tensions of life out of mind.

"No more arguing," said Juan. "In we go."

Conde felt the situation, so everyday for the African and the girls, was forcing him into his most stressful decisions ever: either he ran for it, found his way out of the barrio and salvation for his battered ethics, or followed the impulses of his morbid curiosity and participated in a purely commercial act, to the extent his stomach would allow. Refusing to think further, almost about to hurl himself into the pit of degradation, he got as far as the living room, where Juan was already caressing the small, firm buttocks of the white girl, agreeing terms with a respectable looking old man and paying the agreed amount, though hardly haggling over the hire terms: no drugs, no beating up, no shouting; only beer and rum sold by the establishment; paid for in advance; at an hourly rate . . .

Without looking at the house-owners – their eyes now glued back on the television, as if their lives depended on the news reports – the Count, in a kind of hypnotic trance, crossed the passage and followed the mulatta into the first bedroom, only to be rescued by an attack of nerves when he saw the African and his girl follow him in.

"But what?. . ."

"They've only got one free," replied the African who took his first swig of rum from the bottle and began to wildly shower his companion with kisses.

For the rest of his life, however much he tried, Mario Conde could never remember what the room was like or what was in it, apart from a bed and the washbasin attached to the wall. However, he could never forget the precise, rapid gesture with which, once inside, the mulatta for hire dropped a packet of condoms on the bed and lifted up her skimpy blouse to present him with two breasts and two black aureolas, which she pointed at his chest as if he'd been sentenced to execution by firing squad.

An expert of sorts, the girl saw the scared look on Conde's face and with a lascivious flourish of her tongue drew him near and bathed him in sickly-sweet breath.

"Don' wan' me titties, *papi*? Gimme a lickle suck and gimme the hots?"

Right then Conde realized he'd exhausted his curiosity and that if he went any further he wouldn't live long enough to cope with his repentance. He grasped the only dignified exit on offer.

"This isn't my way. I can't carry on with them in here," and turned round to point at the African and white girl, only to find them completely naked already, not the least inhibited by the presence of others, and going at it hell for leather. And though he'd have preferred not to, he did see it: Juan the African's knob, a huge black sausage, veins bulging, topped by a slavering, purple head, over bull's balls entwined by curly black hair. Rationality restored, his mind fleetingly considered the spatial issue of whether the girl with scant breasts and protruding ribs could host that piece of firm meat whose back and belly she'd begun to lick with great relish, before her mouth swallowed it whole. He felt an emptiness between his own legs and concluded that his decision had been made.

"Wat's the madder, *mi amor?*" the girl yelped, afraid she'd lose the money that was in her grasp.

"This isn't my way," the Count repeated, clinging to these words of salvation.

Conde stayed under the shower, trying to clean that mind-curdling scene from his brain: the African's cudgel-like prick, the white girl's ribs, the mulatta's nipples and reptilian tongue, her faked voice of passion and, above all, the sight of himself opening the door and taking a step backwards, the first in his noisy retreat into filthy streets where he finally recovered his ability to breathe.

The Count left his bathroom, wrapping a towel round his body, shaken by an awareness that he was upset by his own nakedness. Not sure why, he looked for his record player in a corner of the room. He placed it on the useless television stand, put Violeta del Río's record on the turntable and activated it by moving the arm. He carefully dropped the needle into the first groove and sat on the distant sofa, as if he required that space in between. Resting his elbows on his knees and his head between his hands, trapped in a feeling of vertigo, he tried to clean his mind of the fetid traces of the experiment he'd let himself be dragged into and just listened to Violeta del Río's voice, imploring, demanding, ordering: "Be gone from me". He soon felt the melody change his skin, his hair and his nails, and realized he was recovering his sense of urgency to find out the real fate of that woman whose ghost had apparently returned to end an artificial silence, who had spent too long in a precarious vacuum. Like a man possessed, and powerless to resist, Conde sensed the latent spirit of that woman reduced to her voice, to her voice alone, slowly becoming blood of his blood, flesh of his flesh, transforming him into a living extension of the dead, as if Violeta del Río herself was beating at his temples, unexpectedly convinced that her voice was summoning him to reveal more than a single truth.

"But, fuck, it can't? It can't," he told himself and ran to the old cupboard in his bedroom where he kept the souvenirs and flotsam from his previous lives. In the process he lost his towel and, stark naked, flung its doors wide open. On his knees, he extracted the wooden container in the bottom left-hand side, provoking an avalanche of objects he'd pushed out of his way.

There were things belonging to his father inside the box he'd decided to keep; things that he'd not revisited since the long distant day when his dad died. A pre-historic baseball glove, two photograph albums, an envelope containing merit certificates from work, a pair of black and white winkle-pickers, a dog-eared telephone book, two packets of rusted Gillette blades, and his bus-driver's hat and identification tag emerged from the trunk, and then Conde saw what his memory had finally dredged up from the depths of his murkiest reminiscences. The original sleeve seemed washed out by damp and old age, but it was unmistakable: he took out the small record, lit up by a yellow circle, the shiny gem of the recording company. Conde stroked the vinyl and saw it was warped and unusable. He finally remembered his father, sitting in the living room in that same house, wrapped in a gloom that seemed mysterious to his childish gaze, listening, enthralled, to that record, perhaps experiencing sensations similar to those that were now disturbing his son, forty years on. Retrieving the image of that solitary man, sat listening to a woman sing on an electric appliance, finally seemed to account for his visceral empathy with a voice he'd met for the first time so long ago and that had been slumbering, had not died, at the back of his mind. How much had his father really loved that woman he listened to in darkness? Why had he kept that record that had probably been unusable long before it made its way into the Count's junk? What had he said to his son on that night which had disappeared in a succession of yesterdays? Why had he, the man who remembered, forgotten that strange episode which should have floated quickly to the surface of his memories? Mario Conde again stroked the vinyl surface, as undulating as the night-time sea, and thought how his father had been just one more man to succumb to Violeta del Río's seductive powers and how, like Silvano Quintero, he must have wept when he heard the news of her death and realized that the only testimony to her voice was pressed into the grooves of that little record. Or were his memory and hitherto untarnished image of his own father playing yet more tricks on him, concealing truths that might be truly horrific?

8 January
Dear love:

I had decided to wait several days before writing to you again, to allow the spirit of Christmas that passed by without giving me a glance to vanish, but the events of the last few days changed my mind, because they have snatched away my few remaining hopes. What will become of our lives now? Will you ever come back? What will happen here? Although I have tried to shut my ears to the noise in the street, the decision to break off relations just announced by the United States fills me with new fears, because the doors to possible homecomings have now shut, and yours, the one you so longed for, now becomes practically impossible.

Hence, more than ever, these letters are my only consolation, and my greatest reward would be to receive a reply. You cannot imagine what I would give to know if you thought of me if only for a second at Christmas or New Year. I would give my life to know whether you remembered the years of love and prosperity we shared together (although they sometimes seem so distant) as the chimes of the clock reached the final second of the old year and we swallowed our grapes, in time-honoured tradition. How can I tell if this end to a year of separations and resentments was better than those when we shared an expectation of happiness, in necessary silence?

What I cannot understand in the slightest is why you've not even sent me a card with gleaming snow or the twinkling star of Bethlehem, pre-printed thoughts and space for a couple of personal words. Is my punishment to be eternal? I suppose it is, since I must sadly assume that your resentment is more than a passing irritation, a suspicion that may fade when other ideas and soothing thoughts . . . Your resentment is like a life-sentence, and my only salvation is to be able to persuade you of my innocence, with irrefutable proof. That's why I have decided to go in search of that proof. I intend to overcome

181

the terrible fear I feel when walking in a strange world, that is no longer mine, that I don't understand and that becomes daily more radical and dangerous. I will overcome the echoes from voices that pursue me in the night destroying the peace of solitude, and will reach out to the greater good of your forgiveness.

Today, when I decided to write to you and begin my search, I felt that I regained a different attitude of mind, an energy I thought lost, and I devoted almost all day to cleaning your library. It is the first time in months that I have returned to this sacred place in the family memory, because it is too painful, it recalls the happy times in our lives and the lives of the whole family. I have looked again at the books your grandfather bought in his youth, with that passion that made him never hesitate for a second when it was a choice between a book or a pair of shoes; those gathered by your father on the days he worked at the office, in the university, in the period he had political commitments; and above all those that you, driven by the family fervour, bought in every corner of the city and hoarded like treasure, books that aroused so much envy in those privileged to see them. I saw your private collection of books on legal matters and customs regulations and your business magazines and, I can't deny I felt my heart crushed by the thought that you will perhaps never again touch their leather covers, grainy pages or read the words that meant so much to you. Consequently, when I finished cleaning I reminded your daughter that whatever happens, whoever dies, everything in this sanctuary is absolutely and eternally sacred: not a page may leave, not a single volume put in a different place, so that the day you return – because against all the odds I know it will come – you will be able to walk with your eyes shut to the bookcase of your choice and take out, as was your habit, the book you want. I have arranged for the bookcase doors to be opened once a month, for a few hours and always on a hot day, when no rain threatens, to allow the books to breath and gather strength, as you would say. Once every six months, a cloth and feather duster will pass along the spines and tops of the books, which will never be moved, to avoid the slightest disorder entering your personal order. But above all I wanted these decisions to ensure that if anything should happen to me, that no hand, not even your children's, can penetrate the most hidden secrets of your life and mine, that from today await you between the pages of these books.

Dear love: I will say farewell for a time. I won't write until I have news from you or have my hands on the truth. And no matter if that truth, as the voices persecuting me say, is my worst punishment. Because I cannot stand you despising me and blaming me for a crime I have not committed. But rest assured that I will go on loving you as now, even more deeply, ever more longing for you to return . . .

Your Nena

23 January
Dear Love:
A few days ago I swore not to write again, at least not until I had news from you, or could tell you what we are desperate to know. I was so disappointed by your silence and blinded by my own situation and the accursed voices speaking to me in the night, intent on driving me crazy, that I forgot the importance of this date: happy birthday, my love!

As soon as I remembered your birthday I decided I should celebrate it, even without you. Sadly, because it will be like a party without a host, where I will be privileged to be the main guest, the only one in fact, because your children are ever busier and more remote, swept up in the whirlwind of changes being brought in from day to day. Then I made a mistake, another mistake. Exhilarated by feelings of joy, I went to the library and looked for that cookbook you were so fond of, do you remember?, the one you often used to select the dishes you suggested for our meals at home. As I leafed through, I remembered how you liked ox-tongue in sherry, cod in parsley sauce following Juanito Saizarbitoria's Basque recipe, those Creole-style prawns that were so tasty, or the stuffed turkey à la Rosa María that in recent years you preferred as the main dish for Christmas Eve dinner (forgetting, naturally, all those jams you thought a Yankee aberration . . .) How surprised I was as I flicked over a few pages looking for the recipe for your favourite dish (kidneys in red wine) to come face to face with a photo of the dead woman and the news that she had given up singing. Can you imagine what I felt? No, you cannot. Can you imagine how much I hated her, how pleased I was by her death? Yes, I am sure you can, because your silence tells me daily, ever more insistently, you think I provoked her death, though you know I would be unable to contemplate any such thing.

That was when my party ended. My solitary celebrations fell flat and I was strengthened in my conviction that my life will only regain meaning if I succeed in discovering the truth you demand to exonerate me from those unfounded accusations. And I will find a way to that truth, because I love you always,

Your Nena

The smell of recently watered soil, the morning scent of flowers, the blue sky untainted by a single cloud and the mockingbird's song from a fruit-laden avocado tree represented for Mario Conde extraordinary evidence of life, gifts of nature without which life was impossible. What if one had to pass through this world without the chance to enjoy those simple miracles? – if one awoke each dawn to a magma of ugliness and filth, trapped in quicksands dragging you into theft, violence, the daily *sauve-qui-peut* and most diverse forms of moral and physical prostitution? And does the mockingbird really trill alike for everyone, the same melody and harmonies? Mario Conde looked at his apparently clean hands, and then back up at the yard, certain that, despite the shortages and frustrations over the years, he could still think himself a fortunate human being, because neither he nor his nearest and dearest had ever been forced to cross the final frontiers of debasement in the struggle to survive.

The aroma of coffee hit home and, anticipating its delicious taste, he lifted a cigarette to his lips, preparing to perform the fusion of those two wonderful sensations so lambasted by medical hype. But the grief and doubt clawing at his brain almost stifled his smile when Pigeon, tray in hand, offered him a china cup threaded with gold.

"Go on then, how'd you get on?" he asked after drinking the infusion and lighting up.

"I started with Pancho Carmona, as always. While I was at it, I sold him fifteen books, at a much better price than we were expecting. I'll settle with you in a tick." As promised, Pigeon went on to tell him the results of his investigations which had thrown up a negative, if revealing result: nobody in the old book trade knew of the tall black man, with a lame right foot and an evangelical gift of the gab, who'd appeared in such untimely fashion at the Ferrero's.

"That man has some features you can't change," the Count thought aloud: "he's tall and black. But lameness can be faked and so can a particular way of speaking."

"I swear I'd never have thought of that," Yoyi had to admit.

"So you're not the brain-box you think you are . . . And the other thing you can't change is familiarity or unfamiliarity with the book trade. If that man homed in on six specific books it's because he's familiar . . ."

"Like the blind musicologist . . . Do you know what Pancho told me? They're selling the book Rafael Giró chose, the first edition of the book by Borges, dedicated to one Victoria Ocampo, for twenty thousand dollars in a bookshop in Boston . . . So the item you swapped for that poxy record is worth a fortune . . . So you're not the brain-box you think you are either, man."

"I've always said I've got a diploma and various postgrad certificates in shit stupidity. And yesterday I got my masters and tomorrow I'm up for my doctorate."

"Why? What happened?"

With a fresh cigarette between his lips and holding a second cup of coffee, Conde gave his business partner a short report on his walk in the valley of shadows, carefully leaving out his at best dubious escapades and confirmation of his father's murky loves.

"Didn't you know what that barrio was like?" smiled Pigeon as soon as he'd finished. "You only scratched the surface. There's worse underneath. I swear."

"I can imagine . . . You know what? I reckon this city is changing too quickly and I've lost my grip. Pretty soon I'll have to start taking a damned map with me . . . Well, I'm off to Police Headquarters. I want to find out if they've got anywhere. We could do with knowing if that mysterious black guy's fingerprints are on file and they know who he is. I'll also see if they can help me find something on Lotus Flower. I've got to think how to persuade Manolo to give up that information . . ."

"And what do I do?" enquired Yoyi, stroking the prow of his sternum.

"I'll ring and let you know whether I get anything on the black guy. If not, do what you did yesterday, but bear in mind the suspect is probably not lame and doesn't talk like a preacher."

"More of the same, man?" the young man protested.

"*C'est la vie,* Yoyi."

'Yes, but we're up shit creek what with not being able to get more of the Ferreros' books and wasting two days on this wild goose chase. Time is money, remember, and I've got business to attend to."

"But remember we've also got a corpse hanging over our heads . . . And as you know well enough, the police don't like people like you who make money they don't have any control over. They'd love to pin this murder on you —"

"A murder I didn't commit! That's obvious enough, man! I'm clean and finding the one who did him in is their problem, not mine. They get paid to do that and I fight for my bread on the street. But if you fancy playing the detective and wandering around in pursuit of an old whore and a singer of boleros, that's your call. I'm opting out of this drama, I swear."

Conde gazed anew at the yard, at its flowers, tried to hear the mockingbird's song and waited for the inevitable rebuff.

"Don't you see, Yoyi? The sooner we find Dionisio Ferrero's killer, the sooner we get our hands on the rest of the books . . . and I'm going to offer you a deal. Look: if six books that have already disappeared were probably very valuable, it makes no odds if another five, six, seven go . . . We'll buy the six you want . . ."

"The ones I want?" The expression on Yoyi's face changed.

"The ones you want," reiterated the Count.

"Like the *Book of Sugar Mills* or the Gothenburg Bible if a copy turns up?"

"The ones you want," repeated the Count.

"Don't worry, man, I'll find that black guy. I swear I will," and Yoyi kissed the cross he'd made with his fingers.

Elsa Contreras Villafaña, alias Lotus Flower, alias the Blonde, ceased being of interest to the police in the year 1965, when she underwent revolutionary regeneration from brothel-mongering to heading a shift in a seamstresses' workshop in El Cerro, and declared her abode to be 195, Apodaca, in Old Havana. Her police file, recovered by the new authorities created in 1959, had recorded its first entry in 1948, when she was put on file for practising prostitution in areas not authorized for such activities. Then, up to 1954, Elsa Contreras Villafaña, now known as Lotus Flower to the habitués of the Shanghai Theatre, was arrested twice on counts of causing a public outrage, once for a knife attack and once for possessing drugs – marijuana – and did a short spell inside the women's prison in Havana. However, from 1954 the woman apparently opted for an honest life, since no fresh criminal acts appeared on her police record. She resurfaced in 1962, when she was again arrested for procuring and pimping in a bar in the port of Nuevitas, in Camagüey, as the result of an uproar prompted by a peculiar attack launched by a local pimp and hard man, who bit off part of a breast that belonged to one of the whores from her knocking-shop. As a result, Elsa was confined to a re-education centre for eight months, at the end of which she began a new life as a seamstress in a workshop, where a year later she was given the position of head of shift.

"There's something fishy here," commented the Count, and Sergeant Atilio Estevánez, under orders from Captain Palacios to supervise the Count's searches, looked at him intrigued. To persuade his ex-colleague who was reluctant to open up the doors to the police files to him – "You're no longer police," Manolo had insisted, "You know the superiors don't like this kind of thing" – Conde had resorted to his subtlest arts of persuasion and to the obvious fact that finding out extra things about Elsa Contreras would in no way obstruct the official murder investigation. Manolo reluctantly agreed, repeating that he didn't like what he was doing, and only on condition that Sergeant Estévañez continued to supervise his searches.

The information he then found confirmed the police silence initiated in 1954, indicating that Lotus Flower must have made a qualitative leap around the time enabling her to immunize herself against –at least visible – harassment, that was the fate of defenceless street walkers who were always at the mercy of pimps and police alike. To make that leap, coveted by the hundreds of whores swarming through the streets of fifties Havana, she'd have needed a special boost, more so – according to Silvano Quintero – if the business she would soon head dealt in exclusive escorts and not bog-standard brothels in the barrios of Pajarito and Colón. And that kind of trade, in the Cuba of the time, usually had one visible face, the famous Madame known as Marina, who lorded it over twenty whorehouses, and an owner concealed in the shadows of his new respectability: the Jewish Meyer Lansky.

Driven by a hunch, Conde asked the sergeant to track down the file on Alcides Montes de Oca, and wasn't too surprised by the negative response he received: nobody with that name appeared on the police books. He wondered if it might be useful to check the Lansky dossier, but decided it would be a wasted effort, because the Jew didn't appear in Cuba as the legal owner of very many concerns, which he put in the care of his Cuban acolytes or rogues recently imported from the United States, where they were no longer smiled upon.

They telephoned the Office for the Registration of Addresses and requested the names of the occupants of the house at Apodaca 195, and the reply couldn't have been more final: the building had collapsed during a storm in 1971, and its occupants moved to temporary accommodation. But nobody by the name of Elsa Contreras Villafaña figured on the list of those who received compensation as a result of the demolition. His curiosity aroused, Estévañez, called the identification department at the Central Office for Identity Cards and Population Registration, and requested information on the woman. They gave her permanent address as being Apodaca, 195, flat 6, according to dàta obtained in 1972.

Conde smiled at the shocked expression on the face of Sergeant Estévañez who couldn't explain how Elsa Contreras had managed to perpetrate such a blatant deception. How could she have fooled the police and Registry for Addresses and Consumers, who constantly collaborated in respect of deaths, house-moves or any other physical shift made by the island's eleven million Cuban residents easily monitored by the beds they slept in and the food they received? For the Count this gave the mystery a more disturbing dimension: why had she done it?

"We must find out if she is dead first of all," said the Count. "Have you any men available to check cemetery records?"

"Every single cemetery?" asked the terrified sergeant.

'At least those in Havana. Two men could sort that in a day.'

"Let me see what I can do," agreed Estévañez, "but I still don't see how one thing relates to the other."

"Nor do I, but there may be a connection with the Catalina who was known as Violeta del Rio, and she's the person I'm really interested in . . . And what did you find out about this mysterious black guy?" the Count now enquired. Estévanez shook his head: "I can't say . . ."

"Hey, it's not that important. I only wanted to know whether you'd identified him."

The sergeant grumbled, too loudly.

"The prints found in the library aren't on file."

"And what did the autopsy reveal about Dionisio Ferrero?"

"He was killed around 1 a.m. There are no other signs of violence, nothing on his nails, so he was caught by surprise and killed by a single blow."

"And what about the books missing from that last bookcase?"

"They walked the same day as they killed Dionisio. The only other thing we know is that Amalia can't find the knife that Dionisio used in the garden. We think that may be the murder weapon . . ."

"Too many mysteries all told," whispered the Count. "It's like it's a put-up job."

"Just what Captain Palacios says. He thinks it was all set up by someone who knows only too well how to make life difficult for detectives."

Conde smiled, imagining what Manolo might be imagining.

"When you see your captain, remind him on my behalf that what's most hidden is always visible. And also tell him from me not to be such an asshole. If he starts hiding things from me, you can bet he's only making it harder for himself to get to the bottom of this heap of shit."

The Count tired of banging on Juan the African's door and quickly concluded he'd scarpered from callejón Alambique with net earnings of thirteen hundred pesos and a sarcastic smile of satisfaction on his yellow teeth. The risks implicit in the situation, that sooner or later the identity of that supposed cousin of his ex would get out, must have persuaded the African that his best option was to extract money from the former policeman – revenge is sweet – placate his creditors and disappear from the barrio or hide in its deepest catacombs.

To help weigh up his options, the Count walked the shaky planks again and reached the bright light and less fetid air on the roof terrace. The African's absence put him in a delicate situation, because it was more than likely that, before vanishing into thin air, his old informant had explained, in the appropriate quarters, how he'd acted under pressure from a policeman. If that were the case, the Count was completely exposed, in real physical danger, transformed into a pale-face in Apache territory, with all the connotations such intrusions brought. Leaning back on one of the water tanks, where the African had smoked his joint the previous evening, the Count decided the most rational option would be to leave the barrio immediately. He wouldn't be very welcome in Michael Jordan's beer shop or Veneno's chop shop, and it now seemed obvious that his stroll through the barrio and chats on various street corners might have been part of the African's plan to show him to all those who ought to register him in their mental files, in a more subtle, no less efficient way than the police grilling his former colleagues had subjected him to. If his speculations were at all on target, that venture had shut off any avenue to the possible whereabouts of the volatile Lotus Flower, and right now he couldn't see any practical way to make a breakthrough. His investigative foray had just set him up to be blatantly double-crossed.

"You fucking idiot . . ."

A cigarette on his lips, the Count smiled, laughing at himself and his incredible naivety that had included an invitation to beers and a lobster and beefsteak lunch. He gazed up at the cloudless sky and felt oppressed by the relentless midday sun: he'd been left empty-handed, devoid of hope, and even more burdened by the mysteries harassing him. He coughed, cleared his throat and spat to his right. He puffed twice on his butt and dropped it down the air vent next to him and only then recalled it was the African's little hidey hole. Kneeling down, taking care not to burn himself on his still-glowing cigarette butt, he put his arm down the cast-iron pipe and felt in a bend a smooth surface his touch recognized as a piece of plastic. A two-finger pincer-like movement enabled him to extract a small transparent envelope containing a poorly rolled joint and a scrap of paper, where round, unsteady writing, allergic to apostrophes and commas, informed him: Her names Carmen and she lives in the tenement at Factoria 58. Leave what you owe me and lets call it a day. Fella you don't know what you missed and I boned the mulatta on behalf of us both. Watch it.

Almost elated by the African's demonstration of ethics which restored his faith in the human race, the Count put his lighter on top of the note. A breach had been opened and a feeling of joy restored to his body. With no second thoughts he placed the remaining 700 pesos in the envelope as payment for information received. He shut the envelope and, as he was about to put it back in its hidey hole, realized that the presence of the joint was no coincidence either: it seemed like a gift or invitation from the African, intent on reducing the distance between an ex-cop and an ex-convict. Intrigued, Conde extracted the spliff and returned the plastic bag to its place. He took another look around and checked that he was completely alone. Did he dare? He then remembered his demeaning experience in the knocking-shop the night before, and muttered that some of his wholesome values were obviously being eroded if he'd got as far as the bedroom of a real whore on set rates. And now an open invitation to try out the wonders of marijuana pulsated there, another real temptation. What the fuck's got into me? He wondered whether it wouldn't be best to take the joint home and decide what to do with it in the privacy of his own home, though he was dissuaded by the risk entailed in walking the streets of that barrio with drugs on his person, particularly when he was under investigation for murder. As he went to put his hand in the vent and return the marijuana, he recalled his conversation with Yoyi on the subject of his one hundred per cent virginity in narcotics, and hesitantly put his lighter's flame to the end of the joint between his lips. He inhaled and held the sweet, light smoke from the mythical Indian cannabis leaf in his lungs. A force greater than any desire immediately rebounded across his brain, blocking off all other options and leaving him with no choice but to crush his smoke on the tiles of the terrace roof, frenziedly rubbing it into the scorched clay with his shoe. A sense of relief spread through his body and, giving himself no time to think, he stood up, determined to cross the barrio and find the answers only a reformed prostitute, in flight from her past, could supply.

After he left the building he took almost a minute to locate the whereabouts of calle Factoría, which he concluded must be several blocks to his left. As in his days as a policeman, he began to prepare for what might be a trying interview. He walked along the pavement, his mind in ferment, hardly hearing the music that switched and changed from house to house, or noticing the hectic activity in the barrio.

Stripped of his capacity to react, Mario Conde only realized something was amiss when they'd pushed him violently through the open door of a tenement. Propelled by a violent shove, his feet twisted like slack ropes and, in a free, seemingly endless fall downwards, Conde's retina registered electric cables dangling next to a staircase, plastic sacks full of rubbish, a bicycle's deflated tyre, and even a dirty, bare concrete floor inexorably approaching his face, as his nose was hit by the horrifically acidic stench of stale urine, and he felt them pull his head back and put out the light.

His throat felt on fire, as if he'd swallowed a cup of boiling sand . . . He would die for a drop of water, would give his kingdom for a mouthful of water . . . A remote instinct made him put his hand in his pocket and dig around, until his fingers touched a small metal pot and he thought: an oasis, I'm saved. Trying to keep his movements to a minimum to avoid setting off more pain, he forced open the tiny container and dabbed Chinese pomade on his forehead. It was a shock to find his head in its usual place, not entirely centred maybe, although it was clear the afflicted mass was not the same head he'd had that afternoon: it felt as if it had grown, overflowed its bone structure and that its swollen version was about to explode. With the edge of his nail he placed a dab of pomade on the tip of his tongue: the heat from the Asiatic ointment was soothing and reminded him vaguely but unmistakably, that in some murky, not too distant place and time, he'd talked to a pale, slow-moving man, who'd emerged from the deepest shadows in an absurd orange tunic that had almost made him roar with laughter. Why did the images from that hallucination seem so real? Could it be the memory of a real experience? He remembered how the man who was perhaps too tall to be true, had walked over to him, his silhouette swathed by a thick luminous halo – could he be God himself? he'd wondered at the time – and immediately, without even introducing himself, he'd begun to talk, in a deliberate, guttural tone, of noble truths and suffering. Although he still couldn't decide where he'd met him before, when he saw him close-up and heard him hold forth, he was quite sure he already knew who he was, even felt he was very familiar and struggled to follow his argument on pain as an intrinsic element of the human condition, from birth to death, because life is only a cycle that's renewed with each reincarnation. Reincarnation? So I'm dead, am I? wondered the Count, thinking that state would better explain the presence of the Enlightened One – I know this bastard – but the man shook his head and he told him: "You're wrong on every front, you are always wrong, you are wrong too often . . . And you're stubborn: you want to find an explanation for everything, that's your problem, and you refuse to understand that nature cannot be explained by any single or fixed system of definition," he embarked on a protracted pause. "The world, Conde, is as it is, independent of any specific thought one may have about it. And you're full of terribly specific thoughts, you even want your thoughts to change the world, and forget that all your mind can change is yourself. Get rid of your prejudices and meditate . . ." "Where do I know you from, how come you know me and are able to speak of my thoughts and prejudices" the Count remembered asking, and felt those words were sounding increasingly familiar when uttered by this spectre hovering between this world and another. "Suffering comes from the desire for possession. Our mind and feelings malfunction when they cling to the prejudices of experience. Don't prevaricate any more: meditate and ascend, meditate and set yourself free. You will then understand that nothing is random: everything that has happened wanted to happen . . ." These words suddenly assumed their full meaning in the Count's mind and unleashed tremors in his brain: "wanted to happen". "No, that's impossible," he told the Enlightened One, "is it really *you*? I don't believe it . . ." "Do you understand what I was saying?" his pale interlocutor reproached him: "You only dare believe in what you think you should believe in and never open your mind . . ." "Don't tell me it's *you*?" the Count persisted, overjoyed, ignoring his interlocutor's reproaches: of course, *wanted to happen*, and for many years the Count had wanted it, even when he knew it was impossible. The slow, pale man was one of his unmovable gods, right, an Enlightened Being, almost a *mukta*, a man who knows God – or at least someone who'd got very, very close to him, along the way to perfection – and to have him there, at his side, and hear him, was a priceless privilege. "I've always wanted to speak to you," he finally whispered, his voice overcome by emotion, "though not to speak of death and suffering, or even of reincarnation, which, if truth be told, I couldn't give a fig for. This shit life is hard enough to cope with, and I don't hanker after another. I want to talk to you about something much trickier, more intangible, as you say . . . Tell me please, what do you do to write stories that are really squalid and moving? What's the secret? Why does Seymour commit suicide on his honeymoon night? And what about Buddy, what happened to Buddy Glass after he moved to that cabin outside New York? And did Esmé ever find happiness? Did she get the story the soldier wrote for her? Tell me that and also tell me: is it true you wrote nothing in all these years?. . ." Reeling from this flood of questions, the Enlightened One looked uncomfortable in his orangey tunic, frowned severely, and shook his head refusing to spill forth, but was unable to repress a brief smile, when the Count renewed his onslaught: "I can't believe it's true you've not written again. You do know that's a crime? It's all very well meditating, enlightening yourself – you must see really well with all that light you radiate, to be sure – and distancing yourself from the world, hell, but you can't stop writing, you can't. I can't accept you've given up writing in order to meditate, *you* of all people. That's more than criminal . . . What's your name?" "Call me J.D.," conceded the man. "Uh-huh, J.D., J.D.,' the Count repeated, happy to have done the necessary reading and meditation to merit that trust that enabled him to call him J.D., and went on: "Yes, it's a crime, J.D., because you had lots more to write and we had lots more to read." "How do you know?" the Enlightened One interjected, and Conde began to feel several hidden sorrows surface again, as the light emanating from J.D. faded into the darkness, his pallor deepened, and his tunic melted away. But Conde shouted: "I know because when I read you I want to go on reading you. I love reading you . . . Do you know what else? Yes, you do: what I most cherish, when I'm feeling totally exhausted after I've read a book, is my wish to be the author's friend and be able to ring him at any time. I would have rung you lots of times. It's that simple, you see?" J.D. nodded and his blurred face reflected invincible pride in the fact someone could quote a character of his from memory. But he shook off the hint of earthly vanity and looked pitifully at his interrogator: "Never meet a writer if you like his book, *dixit* Chandler. And he was right: writers are a strange breed. Better read than meet them, that's for sure," and he straightened his orange tunic before fading into the Havana night, although the Count thought he heard, or at least thought he recalled hearing the increasingly ethereal voice of the Enlightened One telling him, before he vanished completely: I must leave myself things to do in my other lives . . . and besides, too many books have already been written. Remember what the Buddha taught: there is only one essential time to wake up; and that time is now. So wake up now, you bastard . . . Darkness returned, as if obeying an order, and, now totally conscious, Conde became painfully aware of his body and the thirst burning his throat. He quickly tasted a little more Chinese pomade, wondering if that was the magic formula to bring J.D. back, but J.D. didn't return and he felt sorrow rather than pain, because J.D. hadn't given him a little telephone number so he could ring him after he'd read one of his squalid and moving stories for the hundredth time.

Lying on the grass, wracked by the pain issuing from his battered anatomy, Mario Conde realized he couldn't pinpoint how long he'd needed before finally daring to open his eyes, because in spite of his wishes, only one eye raised its lid, the bare minimum necessary to see that night had fallen and he was alone. He closed his working eye and felt the other, only to find a moist, latent swelling extending from his eyebrow to his cheek. Had they knocked an eye out? he wondered, momentarily forgetting his conversation with the Enlightened One, because thirst and pain were pummelling him, and he felt a desperate desire to cry from his surviving eye. He fought off the pains shooting up his back, knee, stomach, face, the nape of his neck and, especially, from inside his head, pulled himself up and, hands against the ground, rode out a dizzy spell that was regrettably non-alcoholic. From the heart of darkness he saw he was on empty wasteland and a few minutes later glimpsed, 200 metres away, a poorly lit street along which the odd car sped.

He wondered if it would be best to crawl to the street, but was afraid he might cut his hands on the broken glass that was no doubt scattered among the grass. He summoned all his energy, pulled himself up on his knees and, holding his battered head, made the supreme effort necessary to totter to his feet as if in one of his most drunken moments. He then realized that he was barefoot and, when he touched his chest, that he was bare-chested too. And what about that eye? Had they really knocked it out?

Twelve falls later, burnt by the thirst searing his throat, with a new sharp pain in the sole of his left foot, the remnants of Mario Conde finally made it to the road, and he saw he was near the silent, rusting power station that cast its gloomy, geometrical shadows over the wasteland. He thought his best option would be to cross the street to the service station and try to locate Yoyi or Manolo from there, but doubted he had the strength to make it that far. Before attempting such a risky crossing he'd have to recoup energy; he flopped to his knees in the grass, and was unable to stop his body from collapsing in the direction of the pavement. He probably lost consciousness as he fell because he felt no pain when his face hit the concrete.

The hand swabbing his sore eyebrow and cheek brought him back into the land of the suffering. The stabbing pains were so severe that the Count struck out.

"Hey, easy does it, Bobby," said a voice. "They gave you enough to eat and take away . . . Let me clean you up a bit, then they'll X-ray you up to your ears."

Conde realized the voice wasn't his enlightened friend's and, imagining he must be in a place as mundane and nasty as a hospital he asked: "Did they knock one of my eyes out?"

"No, it's still there but in a mess."

"Who are you?"

"A nurse. The doctor gave you a painkiller and we're going to stitch you up now."

"With a needle?" asked the Count, appalled.

"Yes, of course, though you've got so many holes we could use a sewing machine . . . Up you get . . . now faint again, I'll start on the eyebrow . . ."

"Wait a minute . . . Let me weep a few tears first . . ."

"All right, but make it quick."

"Hey, by the way, you ever seen a big guy around here in an orange tunic?"

"Yes, he was round and about, but went off to the carnival. Come on, faint, then I can get on with it."

Five minutes or hours later the Count moved his eyelids and suspected he really was dead – definitively, unequivocally dead, as if someone had ignored all his sins and he was ascending to heaven, where an angelical voice said: "It's him, it's him."

When he opened his working eye, he could see, from his supine position, Tamara, Candito, Rabbit and Yoyi's faces: his blurred brain worked out that the voice he'd heard belonged to none of those archangels. He dropped his head to one side and found himself level with the face of Skinny Carlos, leaning forward in his wheel chair.

"Hey, brother, you got one hell of a pasting."

"You're kidding, Skinny, they didn't even take an eye out."

Mario Conde refused to report the incident. He thought it would be absurd, a sign of softness in the head, to start telling a policeman that some bad guys had kicked him to pulp because he'd poked his nose somewhere he wasn't invited. Besides, who could he blame for his drubbing apart from himself, his own naivety and stupidity? The unlikely names of Veneno and Michael Jordan were the ones that came to mind as possibly being behind the attack, but lack of proof and his conviction that both would have set up good alibis were grounds enough to see that making a statement would be futile. To cap it all, in the depths of his battered self he felt grateful: they were only telling him he was unwelcome in the barrio and bidding him farewell in their time-honoured manner.

The doctor insisted on keeping him under observation in hospital for a day, but when he discovered nothing was broken, that he'd only severe bruising, soreness and a couple of wounds they'd already stitched on his left eyebrow and behind his right ear, Conde asked to leave and swore an oath – which he conveniently faked by raising his fingers – that he'd inject himself with the prescribed antibiotics. Taking full advantage of his situation, he pretended to turn down Tamara's suggestion that she could put him up for a few days: why should she bother, he said, if it's nothing serious, but yielded tamely the first time she insisted.

When he finally saw himself in the mirror, Conde confronted a budding monster he only vaguely recognized. Although the swellings on his eyebrow and cheek had gone down thanks to an intake of anti-inflammatory pills and bags of ice, and he could half-open the eyelid, his eyeball was completely bloodshot and its vision mediated by an opaque film bent on changing his view of the world by painting it pink.

After he'd swallowed a couple of pills, suffered a sharp jab in the buttock and begun to reconcile himself with the world after drinking fresh coffee made by Tamara, Conde slipped into a warm bath and soaked there until it went cold. The peace and elegance, the feeling he was safe and the centre of attention of the woman he'd loved the most and longest, restored his sense of well-being, and he wondered if the whole of his life shouldn't be like that. However, some difficulty was always lurking ready to divert him from the peace he so desired, as if he were fated to hover between the edge and centre of a whirlpool of doubt.

Keen to make the most of a bad situation, his friends converted his convalescence into a party, rolling up at Tamara's at ten a.m. Candito and Rabbit had taken turns to push Skinny's wheelchair fifteen blocks, and when Yoyi arrived he lambasted them for not giving him a call: he'd have driven them all the way in his Chevrolet, listening to his birthday gift from the Count, that selection of hits by Credence Clearwater Revival.

Sheltering under the foliage of the flowering ceiba that dominated Tamara's patio, they drank cold lemonade out of militant solidarity with their battered friend, Conde, who reeled off possible reasons why he'd been chased so forcefully out of the old barrio of Atarés. Skirting round his flirtation with drugs and his encounter with the pale J.D., he announced he was going back the following day to find the elusive woman whose address he'd finally tracked down.

"You think they beat you up to stop you talking to her?" asked Candito, who, after more than ten years of Christian clean living, still maintained his streetwise knowledge from his time as an urban warrior in the most diverse fields of battle.

"No, I don't," the Count replied thoughtfully. "They can't know the African left me that lead. They drove me out so I wouldn't fuck up their trade. They're cooking up big deals with guys from abroad who move lots of cash and I bet they thought I was police."

"You reckon they'd dare take on the police?" wondered Carlos.

"Down there, man," interjected Yoyi, waving a finger at hidden depths under the soil, "they don't believe in anything or anybody. And the guys not from the barrio work like the mafia. But they

199

didn't do you over for being police, that's too dangerous. It was because you were being a nosey parker."

"My problem is I need to talk to that woman soon. The world is the way it is, independent of any specific thought you might formulate about it. What that woman says will decide if I'm on the wrong path or not. I've meditated long and hard and I think enlightenment may be just around the corner."

"You got a temperature?' asked Carlos, alarmed by Conde's florid language.

"Why the hell should she tell you something she probably doesn't want to tell anyone?" Rabbit's merciless logic brought the Count's desires back to the real world.

"Because if what I think is true," the Count went on, "Lotus Flower has lived in fear for the last forty years. And that's too long, right?"

"True enough. But she even changed her name . . ." Rabbit continued to doubt.

"And when do you say you're going?" Skinny Carlos sat back in his chair.

"Tomorrow," asserted the Count, his vehement tone sparking off pain and bewilderment.

"I'll go with you," said Candito, "and don't argue."

"What the hell, so will I," joined in Rabbit.

"How many pistols should I hire out?" asked Yoyi, enthused. "The rate's dropped recently . . ."

"No, we've got to go clean," rasped the Count,

"A couple of truncheons might come in handy," concluded Candito, before adding: "May Jesus My Lord and Saviour forgive me."

They left the Bel Air Chevrolet under the watchful eye of a vigilante on an hourly rate, opposite Fraternity Park, and, still limping, with one very sore eye and a bruised eyebrow covered in sticking plaster, the Count led his troops towards the Calzada de Monte and the barrio of Atarés. Candito and Pigeon, in loose fitting shirts, hid steel bars in their waistbands, which they'd use in self-defence if necessary, while Rabbit, in trembling tones, insisted on recounting the history of that eternally marginal barrio famous for its rabid inhabitants, and where it was always perilous to put a foot wrong.

When they were on the doorstep of 58, Factoría, Conde asked his friends to wait on the pavement and keep out of trouble. He apologized for the sewage flowing down the street opposite which infected the air with its stench. He overcame his lameness and walked through the door to an inner patio which opened out like a small square, where two women were trying to wash clothes white in concrete washtubs. Conde looked around for signs of danger, but imagined that at this time of the morning a necessary truce must rule after a night of non-stop hustle and bustle. Forcing a smile, he advanced on the washtubs where the women stopped wringing and turned to challenge the intruder. The Count thought his appearance could arouse curiosity rather than seem threatening. He broadened his smile as he greeted them, and asked which was the room where an elderly lady called Carmen lived. The women glanced instinctively at each other.

"No Carmen lives here," replied the bigger of the two, a black woman with arms like soft hams.

"Yes, a Carmen does live here," the Count insisted as a light flashed in his brain. "My friend Veneno gave me her address."

The women exchanged more glances, but said nothing, and the Count added: "I'm not a policeman, I just want to speak to her about a relative of mine we lost track of a long time ago."

"It's right at the back, at the end," said the stouter black woman, making it obvious how much she disliked giving information to a stranger.

Conde waved gratefully at them and headed to the back of the ruin, dodging wooden supports that, miraculously rather than from any feat of engineering, propped up the second-floor passageway, and poked his head round the open door of the last room. The room was four by six yards, littered with grimy, battered objects, the most noteworthy being a small, narrow bed, a flaking fridge from the fifties that coughed asthmatically, and an altar covered in various plaster images, as well as a wooden chair where, a thin, elderly, balding woman was dozing. Her skin was all cracked.

He tapped softly on the door and the elderly woman opened her eyes and looked up. She didn't move.

"Carmen?" he asked, bending in her direction, but not going through the door.

"Who are you?" The question surprised Conde who didn't have a good reply ready: a second-hand bookseller who'd found a photo and listened to a record?. . .

"It's quite a long story. Can I come in?"

The elderly woman looked him up and down and nodded him in. When he was inside, she pointed her chin to a small wooden bench. Conde saw that Carmen was sparing in her movements and the awkward way she was holding her left arm against her chest suggested she'd suffered some kind of paralysis. It pained him to see how life and time combined so cruelly to ravage a human being. Had that eyesore once been a beautiful, thrusting, depraved and hot-blooded woman, *the* sexy number in Havana because of rumbas she danced naked on stage. Or might it just be, he wondered, all a tremble, a false trail dreamt up by the African or one of his mates, to send him after an old woman who really was called Carmen, and had nothing to do with Elsa Contreras, alias Lotus Flower?

Conde sat on the bench and leant towards her.

"I apologize, I've probably got it all wrong . . . The person I'm hunting for was called Elsa Contreras . . . lots of people knew her as Lotus Flower."

"Why are you after her?"

Conde jumped in at the deep end.

"I was told she was the best friend of a singer. Violeta del Río."

"And who might you be?" the elderly woman asked again, not changing her expression, and the Count realized he'd no choice but to tell the truth.

As he'd run through who he was and why he was looking for Elsa Contreras, the Count began to see how ridiculous his story was: he was trying to erect an impossible structure without foundations or supports, that would collapse under its own weight. Even so, apart from Dionisio Ferrero's murder, he told all, including his father's silent infatuation, still not knowing if that elderly lady was the person he was after and without the slightest hope that, if she were Elsa Contreras, he had aroused her interest and could perhaps extract the missing links from her memory to bring together the disconnected parts of that incredible story that was lost in the past. The Count saw a first flicker of light when he related the beating he'd received and glimpsed a sign of life: the woman's cracked lips puckered into a smile.

"You're crazy," she said when she assumed he'd finished his tale. "You have to be crazy to get mixed up in a shitty barrio like this . . ."

"So you are?. . ."

"What was it you said about your father?"

"I think he once saw Violeta, probably heard her sing and fell in love. He'd listen to her record at night, by himself, in the dark. I think he even mentioned her name to me . . ."

"Violeta was like that," she said, slowly lifting her right arm to point to a ramshackle sideboard. "The first drawer. A cardboard box."

Conde obeyed and, under a mountain of pills encapsulated in plastic, phials, syringes and tubes of cream, he saw an eight by twelve-inch cardboard box.

"Take it out and look inside," she ordered.

Conde took the box out, rested it on the sideboard and lifted the lid. A sheet of stiff white paper filled the box. When Conde extracted the paper, he realized it was a sheet of photographic paper folded in half. Not looking at the elderly lady he unfolded the huge photo and beheld a woman in her twenties, as blonde as blonde could be, a supple, smiling beauty, saved from complete nudity by garlands of gorgeous lotus flowers draped over her pubes and the nipples of her prodigious breasts.

"You're now looking at Elsa Contreras when she was Havana's Lotus Flower," she said, adding, "Look this way: you're now looking at a half dead crone by the name of Carmen Argüelles."

16 February
Dear love:
Since I last wrote I have hardly made any headway in my search for a truth I need so badly for my own sake but I keep finding other truths to torment me.

Several days ago I went to see the wretched nosey-parker journalist your friends almost took a hand off. I found an alcoholized human wreck, in a state of permanent fear that he can only throw off by swigging hard liquor. The man refused to tell me anything, but thanks to him I did track down that bolerista *who once rowed with that woman, and we talked at length about what happened and, though she was a tart from the world of singers and cabaret girls, I would almost say she was genuine. As far as she was concerned, as she said at the outset, her problem with the deceased ended the day they had the row, because she realized she was on to a loser in that war when she knew who the powerful people backing her foe were. But she assured me she got satisfaction from the four things she did say to her hypocritical face about her role as the little innocent. She never went near her again and heard next to nothing about her until she found out about her death several weeks after it happened, on her return from the performances she gave in Mexico. We spoke at length and, when she felt like confiding more, she told me almost casually something I refuse to believe, that only you can deny or endorse. According to her, she backed off from that woman forever because, a few days after they rowed, you went to her house with the black chauffeur you employed towards the end, and told her to keep well away and not to speak to her ever again if she wanted to go on singing and eating. At that moment a friend of hers (as she described him) came out of her bedroom, heard your threats and started to protest, but the black chauffeur, without saying a word, took out a pistol, put it between his eyebrows and, almost immediately, brought the pistol down on his mouth and split his lips. Then, still according to her, you said she was lucky you had come on a peaceful footing, but that they might imagine what a second visit would be like if they decided to declare war or started to talk openly about the fact you'd paid them a visit . . . The singer burst into tears as soon as she'd finished telling that horrible story, and do you know what I told her? I said it was all lies, and left.*

Nonetheless, that woman seemed so sincere I am compelled to ask you: did something like that happen? Please tell me it didn't, and also please tell me that the disappearance of the poor chauffeur you used to conceal our secret wasn't also the result of actions I'd rather not imagine. Tell me, did you declare war on him when he was foolish enough to blackmail you?

I assume one often pays a very high price to find out a truth. While looking for one that still eludes me, I have come up against something else I would have preferred not to know and it showed me how much I was struggling against the current where you'd put your life after you went crazy over that woman, the cause of my unhappiness . . .

22 February

Dear love:

I was so saddened by my exchange with the singer that I felt I had to speak to your daughter about it and everything else I'd been thinking over recent months. We hadn't had a conversation of any significance for several weeks, only exchanges on everyday matters, because what with my obsession and increasingly depressed state of mind, and the new responsibilities she had taken on at work, there are days when we only see each other for a few moments, if at all, over breakfast or when she's swallowing a couple of mouthfuls of something at night.

To my surprise, your daughter seemed delighted to hear the story. She said she wasn't surprised, she wouldn't expect any other attitude from you, because you were always selfish, thought only about yourself and used those around you for your own ends: your parents, for their name and prestige, your wife for her money, me for my fidelity . . . On the other hand, you treated her and her brother like strangers despite them being of your blood, as much your children as your others, who you also used to get favours from your parents-in-law with their money and influences. And she added, as if wanting to drive me mad, given I was already a total wreck, that she'd been wondering for some time, and my story was confirmation you had eliminated or ordered that woman be eliminated because of something she asked you for, something you didn't want to give her or simply because her presence was inconvenient and didn't fit with your new life; she knew too many things that you preferred to bury, next to her body . . . Your daughter only shut up when I slapped her . . . But she'd already spat her poison out.

If I'd once suspected she might feel spitefully towards you, I now realize how much she hates you because of the way you denied her everything that belonged to her. It was very unpleasant to face that terrible truth, and I felt guilty that I had been so weak and told her about where she really came from. But you must realize I did so hoping she'd feel proud and confident, although in the end, as you see, I only generated more resentment. A resentment that makes her feel happy, because she possesses one more proof of your real character and, with that proof, the certainty you were the one who ordered that woman be silenced forever.

Do you know what is most painful, most cruel about this terrible revelation? That I now understand that even when I always loved you and dared defy all conventions, even gave you two children, I too was afraid of you and perhaps that's why I was never determined enough to rebel against the role and fate

205

you moulded for me, while you broke every promise you'd made over the years . . . And even now, I dare write all this only because I know this letter will never reach your hands. In fact, I would never dare to have sent it for two reasons you are well aware of: fear and love. I prefer to think out of love. Out of a love able to forgive everything.

Your Nena

Here you have me now, a human mess, living in this shitty slum, and still thinking life has been generous. Very generous. I've been whiplashed, like everyone else, at times viciously, but I've seen and enjoyed what others could never dream of, even if they lived two hundred years and didn't sleep a single night.

Look, when I celebrated my thirteenth birthday, I discovered something that would be my salvation: I had something special, and I told myself: I'm going to use this gift of nature to survive. Go on, take a second look at that photo, a good look . . . Can you feel it? That something's in my face, my hair, in my firm tits, which were like two apples when I was twelve, and above all down here, between my legs. When I was thirteen, my father died: he fell from a building where he was cleaning windows, and as he didn't belong to a union and we didn't have money to hire a lawyer, we didn't get a single peso in compensation. Not even funeral expenses. My mother, little sister and I lived in a tenement three blocks from here on Indio, and were left totally skint, were almost starving to death, really starving, had nothing to eat: that hunger forced me to stop being a young girl, like that, over night. When I went into the street, men stared at me and some said things, and I thought: If God's given me this body, the biggest sin I could commit would be to let it die, and let my mum and my sister die . . . I started to lay the Spaniard who owned the room where we lived so he didn't throw us out, and then it was the turn of the butcher, the owner of the corner store and the baker, and, as it seemed to work well, I went on to the tailor and the furrier. I really never saw or felt it was at all dirty or immoral, because when I did it I felt good: I liked giving men a good time, and thought it was wonderful when they gave me one too. So, as easy as pie and without guilty feelings or any shit like that, because as the wise man said, the one who seemed to know what he was talking about: the best thing about being a whore is that you work on your back in bed and in the worst scenario, if you don't earn much, at least you get something hot in your belly . . .

By the age of fifteen I knew all there was to know about men, what they need and what you must do to soften them up, what they like and sometimes don't dare ask for, and most important of all: I learned how to make them think they fuck better than anyone else and make them feel happy when they give you money and things for one little fuck . . . That's why I told myself, right, you can get more than your food and clothing out of this, you could turn professional and earn real money if you could get to people who pay for a good night between the sheets without protesting. I say this quite brazenly: the least of it was my fantastic body; what decided it was the fact I was more intelligent than most whores. I had a wild animal's natural intelligence, and realized there were two very dangerous things in this trade: one is to fall in love with a bastard who'll pimp you for all the money you've earned and the other is not to know your limitations, because you need to know that however well you look after yourself, by the age of thirty you'll be in decline, and what you don't get by that age you'll never get. Like most things in life. That was why I started to look for a way to be more than a common whore: I decided to speak to the impresarios who ran the Shanghai and told them I wanted to dance in their shows. The Shanghai had a bad reputation as a clip joint, people said, but the key thing was that every night guys with money went there, high society guys, some on a binge, others who liked to get their thrills looking at naked girls, and I felt I'd catch a good fish there if I worked on it. When the theatre people saw me dance naked, they saw I'd be a star and for a few pesos bought me a birth certificate in the name of Elsa Contreras, that said I was twenty-one, and not just sweet seventeen.

I was dancing within a fortnight and men went crazy: they packed out the theatre to see me, and I met Louis Mallet, a forty-year old Frenchman, the representative of Panama Pacific, a big shipping line in New Orleans, who also ran a business in Cuba importing wood from Honduras and Guatemala, in partnership with a Cuban, Alcides Montes de Oca. And my life changed, just as my name had changed. Louis and I started seeing each other and within the month he'd rented me a flat near the university, so we had a nice place together. Louis was a good man, affectionate even and never banned me from dancing at the Shanghai. He'd say: you're an artiste. As he spent three or four months in Cuba and the rest of the time in New Orleans or Guatemala, I used that time and worked extra, but only with people who paid over the odds, and I started to save money, wear expensive clothes, use classy perfumes and my customers got even classier.

But my life really changed in 1955 and I was able to give up the theatre and all that. Louis was in Havana around that time and told me to ask for a week off from the Shanghai, we were going to go to Varadero, because he wanted a rest and to introduce me to some friends who were going to make me a really profitable offer. When we reached Varadero we checked in at a beautiful sea-front hotel, a wooden building straight out of an American movie. During the day we swam on the beach, like a honeymoon couple, and swanned around in a convertible. That night we went for dinner in a big house on the banks of the canal, near the spot where they built the Hotel Kawama, soon after. Alcides Montes de Oca, Louis's partner, was there, who I'd seen a couple of times before, and a very elegant man with a clown's face who spoke softly although he never laughed, and turned out to be Meyer Lansky. When it was time to eat, another man, Joe Stasi came along. It was a really boring dinner, because Louis, Alcides, Stasi and Lansky spent the whole time talking about imports and exports, and as Lansky only drank a couple of glasses of Pernod and hated drunks, we hardly saw a drop of wine. Then, when they offered us cognac and coffee on the terrace, opposite the canal, Alcides Montes de Oca finally told me what they wanted me for. They were organizing a scheme to attract millions of American tourists to Cuba and these tourists required four essential items: good hotels, casinos, readily available high quality drugs and young, healthy, elegant, dissolute women. If I accepted, my responsibility would be to work with those women. They were planning special journeys to Havana for extremely wealthy people, celebrities, artists, journalists, and so on, and would treat them all so they felt they'd been to paradise, so they'd spread the good news about holidays in Havana. I had to create the kind of agency with only top-notch girls – none of your average, unsophisticated whores. I'd to choose the best and create a quality service. Sometimes these women wouldn't only go to bed with their men, they'd also have to accompany them in Havana and needed to know how to behave in a restaurant, cabaret, casino or even at the theatre. The women would be paid a fixed wage, a high wage, whether they had lots or little work, so they weren't soliciting all over the place. If I accepted, one of Stasi's men would set up the whole structure: he'd be a kind of accountant-administrator, working with hotels and casinos, and I'd look for the women and be responsible for training them, together with an etiquette expert who'd teach them to behave and dress well. Then I'd deal directly with the girls, be like a manager and get a three per cent cut of whatever the rich and famous lost gambling in casinos, which might be quite a lot . . . Initially, in the three or four months necessary to get the agency up and running, I'd be paid a salary of 500 pesos. 500 pesos! Do you know what 500 pesos meant back then! A small fortune.

I immediately dropped the dancing in the Shanghai and started on my new role. By the beginning of '56 the elite agency, as Bruno Arpaia dubbed it, was up and running. He was Stasi's man who was working alongside me. We recruited sixteen women, almost all from outside the brothel districts. I inspected cabarets and clubs in Havana and went on expeditions into the interior, as we described it, and to big cities like Cienfuegos, Camagüey and Matanzas. We selected girls to fit our business needs and taught them to eat, dress, speak softly, and I taught them how to behave with men and how they should let themselves be treated . . .

By the end of that year the agency worked so well we had to find more women. On one of our expeditions, I came across a girl who sang there three or four nights a week in a little cabaret in Cienfuegos, and apart from being one of the most beautiful women I'd ever seen, she had a special voice: I say it was a woman's voice because that was the only way to describe it. Her only drawbacks were the what she was wearing and her name, Catalina Basterrechea, although people called her Lina or Lina Beautiful Eyes, to get round that.

As soon as I met her I realized Lina was a Cinderella: singing was her life and she spent the whole time dreaming someone would appear and give her the opportunity to put her glass slippers on, show off her talent and become famous into the bargain. The usual old story! Only as far as she was concerned singing was a pleasure, not just a means to an end. So, though Lina wasn't a whore and had no such inclinations, she might be ready to do the necessary to attain her goal. I was delighted by the idea of signing her up, because the minute I saw her I knew I'd found a diamond in the mud and that with a little polishing she'd become the star of the agency, but after I'd talked to her for a while, I felt she had something different, something that moved me, and the fact is I was never usually one to be moved by stories of dead parents, lousy aunts and cousins that rape you at the age of ten, like the ones she told me. No . . . But I explained quite clearly what I was about and – I still don't quite know why – offered her a special deal: if she wanted, she could come with me to Havana and help me in some way with my business, without having to whore, and I'd use my contacts to find her someone to help her find a place where she could sing. And, of course, she packed her cheap little suitcase and left with me, and didn't say goodbye to the bastard of an aunt who'd made her life impossible . . . I've always thought that destiny meant for Lina and I to meet, for her life story to touch what remained of my heart, and for me to like whatever she sang. Lina and I were good friends from the start, and if I'd ever thought of suggesting she worked with my girls if she didn't make it as a singer, I quickly gave up on that and decided to protect and help her any way I could. Was it a kind of maternal feeling? As if I could see myself in her and wanted to give myself a second chance? You tell me . . . but that's how it turned out.

Within a month or month and a half of Lina being in Havana, Louis returned from New Orleans and told me we must go back to Varadero and meet Lansky, Alcides and two American entrepreneurs who were going to build hotels in there. I don't know why but I persuaded Louis it would be a good idea to take Lina, because I thought she'd sing for his friends and make dinner a little less boring . . . That was how Alcides Montes de Oca and Lina Beautiful Eyes met up: he was almost fifty and she was under twenty, but when the business talk ended and Lina started to sing, Alcides fell madly in love with the girl, her looks and her voice.

210

Alcides Montes de Oca was a character with some strange baggage, I should tell you. He came from a high society family and was very wealthy, even more so since he'd inherited the fortune belonging to his wife who'd just died. He liked talking politics and was very proud to be a grandson of a general in the Army of Liberation; he loathed Batista. According to him, Batista was the worst disaster that had ever hit this country, and I'm sure that at the time he supported the rebels, because many had belonged to the Orthodox Party which Alcides had been a member of when Batista struck with his coup d'état and suspended the elections the Orthodoxers were about to win. He was also a very cultured man who read a lot, and Louis told me he had books galore in his house. But at the same time he had a nose for business and although he didn't appear to own anything, because he didn't need to, he owned shares in all the big companies in Cuba. Through his business concerns he got on with Lansky like a house on fire, though this friendship was never reported in the newspapers, because everyone knew the Jew had been a drug-trafficker in the States, although here he only operated legal business and behaved, well, as I said, like a gentleman.

So Alcides and Lina became infatuated; they were crazy about each other, and, to please her, he got her a singing spot in the second show at the Las Vegas and quickly moved her from my place to a flat in Miramar, in a building that had just received its finishing touches. The only problem complicating their romance were Don Alcides's political aspirations and his social situation. He'd been widowed only recently and couldn't enter a formal relationship with a poor country-girl, who was thirty years his junior . . . If it had been nowadays! But in those days a scandal like that could have damaged Alcides's position considerably and so they decided to keep things quiet: he kept her, saw to all her wants, paid for the flat and gave her a car, although Louis appeared as the legal owner of everything in order to avoid nasty gossip.

The person responsible for looking after Lina's needs and expenses was Alcides's personal secretary, an awesome woman by the name of Nemesia Moré. She saw to all his commercial and political paperwork, as well as being something like the administrator of his household, but with more power, because since Alcides became a widower, Nemesia had assumed the role of lady of the house. She was in her forties, had retained her good figure, and had a real gift: she was always able to anticipate Alcides's thoughts and satisfy them before he'd even asked for anything. Consequently Alcides would say, half jokingly, half seriously, that the most important woman in his life was Nemesia Moré: he couldn't live without her.

In the meantime, Lina had started singing and the owner of the Las Vegas only imposed one condition before contracting her: a change of name. Just imagine a compère announcing: "And now ladies and gentlemen, the one and only Catalina Basterrrrechea!" After a moment's thought Alcides said: "Violeta del Río", as if he'd already got the name in his head, and so Catalina Basterrechea, Lina Beautiful Eyes died, and Violeta del Río the *bolerista* was born. She immediately got a big reputation and sang in the best places, even made the Parisién, by which time Havana knew her as the Lady of the Night, and she had countless men chasing after her to hear her sing and, naturally, trying to seduce her, because the country-girl had transformed herself into a spectacular woman, wearing clothes from New York, perfumes from France and with her hair styled by the best hairdressers in Havana . . . Was this the woman your father fell in love with? Poor man, how he must have suffered . . .

As far as I know, Lina saw life through Alcides's eyes, and the only thing she refused was classes from a singing teacher he'd insisted on hiring for her; she wanted to sing from her soul, and if someone taught her, she said, they'd damage the desire she'd had naturally from childhood and that had saved her from going crazy. And I think she was right. She needed a microphone, not classes. On stage she was a fantastic act, I'd never seen or heard anything like her – and I'd seen plenty in my lifetime – she turned everything into magic. Even today, after all these years, I shut my eyes and see her holding the microphone, throwing her hair back that fell like a mantle over her beautiful eyes, wetting her lips with the tip of her tongue, and I can hear her sing those songs that came straight from her soul . . . Poor girl . . .

Violeta was a happy woman, the happiest woman in the world while her dream lasted. It sounds like a radio soap, but that's how it was. And she was still happy when 1959 came and everything suddenly changed: for Lansky and Alcides, for Louis and me, and for the girls who worked for the agency. Because the country changed . . . The rebels won the war and Batista left Cuba, which was what everybody wanted. Although people only spoke about Revolution to begin with, some people were already mentioning the word communism and Lansky was the first to grasp what might happen: he immediately started to pack his bags. Louis also thought it would be better to be on the other side of the sea and he persuaded Alcides to take whatever he could out of Cuba and forget about politics now his moment had come and gone. Initially Alcides refused, but within a few months, deeply upset, he saw Louis and Lansky were right. Even so, when he decided to leave he did so thinking he'd be back in a few months, a few years at most, and only took the money he'd already taken out and what was most important to him: his children and his wife-to-be, Violeta del Río.

I wasn't very surprised when Violeta accepted Alcides's suggestion that she should stop singing and go the States. She was probably persuaded by Alcides's promise that they'd be able to marry and lead a normal life where nobody knew them. Or maybe he convinced her by saying she'd be able to take up singing later on. Or perhaps she agreed because she thought the most important thing was to safeguard her relationship with a man who idolized her and whom she loved deeply. Whatever the reason, Violeta announced she was retiring from the stage at the end of 1959 and Alcides began to prepare his departure from Cuba, trying to salvage what he could, although he lost an enormous amount of money when they started to take over sugar plantations and nationalize American companies in which he held shares.

Violeta and I saw lots of each other over those months. Lansky had returned to Cuba for the last time in March or April 1959, shut his business ventures down and returned to the States. Obviously, one of the ventures that died the death was the escort agency, so I was soon unemployed, with lots of time on my hands and money in the bank. Louis, for his part, promised he'd still come to Cuba whenever he could, but it was clear he couldn't take me to New Orleans because that's where his wife and children were, a life where I didn't fit. Anyway I wasn't too concerned by all that:

several girls wanted to carry on working with me and I told myself: this revolution may be a big deal, but if one line of business will never close, it's whoring. So, while this or that did or didn't happen, I had lots of time to decide what to do. You know, sometimes you do fucking stupid things, however clever you are . . .

Poor Violeta was desperate to leave. After she'd announced her retirement she was adrift here and just wanted out, but Alcides kept delaying his departure, waiting to see if something might change so he wouldn't be forced to leave and lose so much. Six or seven months went by, and everything suddenly got hectic when the government declared it was nationalizing American businesses in Cuba . . . The following day Violeta told me about their travel plans. They were off within a month, and now it was for real, because the next Sunday Alcides was intending a crucial step: he was going to take her home and introduce her formally to his children, who were now adolescents, and tell them of his decision to marry her.

Never for one moment did I think that that afternoon I was talking to my friend Catalina Basterrechea, Lina Beautiful Eyes for the last time . . . Apart from the political complications, which she didn't understand, there wasn't a cloud on her horizon; on the contrary, it was all light and promises of bliss. What fucking shit, right? I've wondered a thousand times why they didn't just say to hell with all this and leave Cuba two or three months earlier, happy, in love, with the best of their lives ahead of them . . .

I found out what happened the following Monday, when I went to Violeta's flat to see how she'd got on in what we'd dubbed her opening night in the big world of the Montes de Ocas. When I got there, I was surprised to see strange things going on and found myself face to face with Nemesia Moré, Alcides's secretary. She received me as if I were a total stranger and asked me to leave immediately. "Who the fuck do you think you are? This is my friend's house," I started to reply, and the bitch blurted out, as hard as nails: "Your friend's dead and you're not welcome here . . ." I was in a state of shock and barely managed to ask her what had happened. "She's committed suicide," she said, and told me: "Don't ring Mr Alcides, he's very upset and it would be best to leave him in peace."

As Alcides Montes de Oca was still Alcides Montes de Oca in Cuba, and had kept Lina's private life out of the public eye, there was only a brief mention of her suicide in a couple of newspapers and the whole matter was shelved. I was desperate to find out what had happened, but the people in the know sealed their lips. Eventually, thanks to a lad I knew who lived near my place and was in the police I did find out a bit more: Lina had used cyanide to commit suicide. But why? Why kill herself when she was at her happiest? Because she'd given up singing? That was impossible, it must have been hard, but she did so of her own free will. Because she had to leave Cuba? No, she wanted to leave, was leaving with her man and the promise of marriage . . . The only explanation was that something had gone wrong between her and Alcides. I couldn't imagine what that might be, if he was now preparing to take her on publicly as his new wife.

I was desperate and started following Alcides. I needed to speak to him, to know what he knew, and find out why Lina had dared do something so terrible. I called several times but he'd never come to the phone, I sent him messages via a couple of friends but he didn't reply and in the end I started trailing him. One day I saw him leave home, in his Chrysler, driven by his chauffeur and I followed him in my car as far as Old Havana where I saw him enter the Western Union offices and followed him in. When he saw me next to him, he barely seemed surprised, but looked grim. I thought for a moment that he was going to cry. He'd delivered a few messages, picked up others and we left. As he was opening his car door, he said: "Lina broke my heart. I was going to give her everything, why did she have to do that?"

Without a second glance, he got into his car, which turned the corner and disappeared from sight. It was the last time I saw Alcides Montes de Oca and the last time I tried to find out why the girl we all thought so happy ended it all, as if she were living out one of those boleros she so liked to sing.

A primitive jungle instinct urged the Count to ask the questions he'd been stifling as he went further into the tragedy of frustrated love recounted by that elderly woman. But when he saw the tears flooding the deep wrinkles on Carmen Argüelles's face, he held back, restrained by the sorrow brought by death: he decided to live with his doubts. Although the woman's confession rounded out a story that still lacked clinching detail, he finally had something firm in place and a first mystery he'd definitively cleared up. In effect, Violeta del Río had died more than forty years ago, as he already knew, but had done so under her real name of Catalina Basterrechea, and that circumstance helped by the last ripples from Don Alcides Montes de Oca's muscle, explained the strict oblivion into which her other ego, Violeta del Río the singer, had been relegated a few months before.

Mario Conde promised to be back in a few days and said goodbye to the old woman, who now seemed even more feeble and shrunken, as if that descent into her past had worn her out physically. He stopped on the doorstep, then went back inside. He put his hand in his pocket and took out a few notes: one hundred and forty pesos, all he was carrying on him. He placed them gently in her lap.

"It's not much, Carmen. Today's pesos, but it all helps," he said and, unable to contain himself, caressed the woman's sparse, dank hair.

His team of bodyguards on Factoría slouched like troops defeated by boredom and the stench. They sat on the jamb of a staircase, surrounded by a cemetery of peanut shells, cans of soft drink and even two abandoned newspapers, remnants of the strategies they adopted to resist attacks of hunger and the long wait.

"Fuck, man, how long did that old woman witter on for," protested Yoyi, and the Count imagined he was reckoning up the time invested in economic terms. "I suppose you know everything there is to know now?"

"What did she tell you, Conde, what did she tell you?" repeated Rabbit, and Conde promised to tell, but first wanted to rid himself of a thorn in his side.

"You lot coming with me into the barrio?" he asked, looking at his friends.

"Hey, Conde, what are you after now?" asked Rabbit, in the tone of someone already familiar with all the potential answers.

"Nothing really, just a walk across the barrio to show them I've not surrendered. Yoyi, do you agree with Juan that the guys in charge here are mafiosi? Well, they'll see killing is the only way they'll get rid of me. You coming?"

"Why the strongman tactics, Conde?" Rabbit smiled anxiously, displaying all his dentures. "You've never been the strongman type."

"Well, must say I do like the idea. Let's see if anyone wants a bundle and a round of grievous bodily harm from me," spoke up Yoyi, touching the side where he'd got his steel bar. "Fancy daring to lay a finger on this guy who is blood of —"

"Cut it out, Yoyi. I want to go because I've got a hunch . . ."

"Not another?" quipped Rabbit, hurrying to keep up with the crowd.

With his left eyebrow bandaged, a black eye and slight limp in one foot Conde strode off towards calle Esperanza. A group of evil-looking black and white youths on the next corner watched the strange retinue advance: their keen sense of self-preservation warned them of approaching danger and they scattered swiftly like insects, much to the relief of the invasion party.

Conde stopped his friends in front of the slum where he thought he'd been beaten up. They looked inside the building, down both sides of the street, and he looked for a cigarette and lit up, as if to say, here I am. But only two uniformed police, a few cyclists, and a hard-pressed taxi-cyclist came along the street and, along the pavement, a couple of tarts, including one the Count identified as the mulatta from his frustrated whoring episode.

"Let's go for a beer," he suggested without thinking, turning his back on the woman, who carried on, apparently not recognizing him with his new look.

"Conde, watch it," warned Rabbit.

"It's OK, man, the guys in this barrio are all dicks anyway . . ." shouted Yoyi and Candito smiled.

"Forget it, kid," said Red, "being born and living around here is a schooling you never had. You see how it's all ugly, filthy and stinks? Well, that's how people's hearts are and they do ugly, filthy, stinking things as if it's what comes naturally. God's the only power that can change them . . . But hurry up, the Count's turning into a hard man."

217

Conde got his bearings and pointed towards the next block, certain it was the one with Michael Jordan's alcohol shop. As he walked, he noticed something had changed in the barrio over the last two days, but couldn't pin down where that feeling, more atmospheric than physical, came from. When he peered into the lot, before going in, he discovered the transformations were more drastic than he'd imagined: the inside patio, where three days ago several men had been drinking, blasted by music, was now completely deserted, as if the crowded, illicit bar run by Michael Jordan's double had never existed. Conde worried about his sense of direction, perhaps he'd got the wrong place, and he looked for the African's building to make sure that this was where they'd drunk those beers.

"They've shifted the bar," he said, immediately suggesting an alternative. "Let's go to Veneno's chop shop."

They walked back two blocks, turned left in pursuit of Veneno's, and on their way Conde finally sussed out of one of the mutations suffered by the barrio: there were as many people as ever in the street, but music now only came from a few houses, unlike on previous occasions when he'd had to advance through a thick curtain of sound. As on his last visit to Veneno's, Conde clambered though the hole in the wall separating the ruined building from the street and, followed by his friends, headed over past the precarious canvas and zinc roofs where newly arrived pariahs resided. He went on, searching for the yard with the improvised restaurant tables, and behind the big entrance found a panorama of desolation similar to what he'd found on the lot which once housed the illicit bar.

"Something big's happened, Conde," was Candito's verdict when he saw his friend's amazement.

"They took fright after the beating they gave the Count. Perhaps they thought they'd killed him," ventured Pigeon.

"That's right, and as they thought he was police . . ." concluded Rabbit.

"No, they knew I wasn't in the force anymore, and that was why they did me over. Perhaps they thought they'd killed me," surmised the Count.

"They didn't think anything at all . . . If they'd wanted to clean you out of the way they'd have done it by now." Candito looked at the closed doors of the houses opening on to the patio. "There's something weird going on here. We'd better beat it."

"Yes, Red's right. Let's go. Look at the sky, it's going to rain."

"I wanted to see a guy I know," said the Count.

"Leave it," insisted Candito. "We're out of here."

"So what did that woman tell you, Conde?". Relieved by the prospect of leaving this barrio, Rabbit had recovered his perpetual curiosity.

"That Violeta del Río was really Catalina Basterrechea, that she had beautiful eyes and that singing love songs was what she most liked to do on this earth," said the Count, beginning to tell the whole story.

"So you mean when you were in the force, you didn't have computers?"

"Of course we did. A big brute of one . . . We called her Felicia. Hey, if I look old, it's because I've worn badly."

"Did you work with it?"

"No, I've always felt computers were a bit of a headfuck. I haven't a clue when it comes to all that technology, I'm not joking."

"But they're easy enough."

"I didn't think they were easy or difficult. We don't get on and I don't have a clue . . . How many computers does Headquarters have now?"

"Two . . . but one's broken."

"I bet it's more stupid than I am. What do you bet we find nothing at all?"

Sergeant Estévañez smiled and shook his head: this guy's a joker. His mind couldn't tolerate the image of a detective too thick to find a simple piece of data on a computer and be sure, in advance, whether it existed or not.

"What's the name?"

"Catalina Basterrechea," repeated the Count, agreeing with Lotus Flower that nobody could come on stage and sing a bolero after being introduced by such a mouthful.

The search was more arduous than the sergeant had imagined, and the Count felt happy when, after several attempts, the presumptuous cybernetic policeman was forced to use the phone and consult a specialist over locating certain files from the past.

Estévañez gave the machine new instructions, as it had refused to reply to his questions, and Conde went into the passage, and saw the tremendous downpour that had started outside. He rushed to a lavatory and, while urinating, realized he'd held on to it for too long. He sighed with relief as he felt himself unloading as powerfully as the summer clouds. Simultaneously a voice made him start.

"They say great friendships are forged in lavatories. Or that old ones have been patched up . . ."

Conde didn't turn round: he was conscientiously shaking his penis, flicking it as if it were of slightly higher calibre than the one he actually wielded.

"But I'm not going to introduce you . . ." he said, putting his member away.

Captain Palacios preferred a stall, rather than one of the urinals where the Count emptied his bladder. When he'd finished, he twisted round and was shocked to see his ex-colleague's bruised face.

"What the fuck's happened to you?"

"They almost killed me, but evil weevils never die. And if they die, they re-incarnate, as a friend told me who knows about such things. It's the risk you take prowling around when you're not a policeman."

"Well, they really had it in for you . . . Did you find anything?" asked the captain.

"A few things about the previous owner of the library and the girl who sang boleros. There are people who think she didn't commit suicide . . . But don't you worry, nothing that had anything to do with Dionisio. How about you?"

"I've hardly had time to do anything. This gets worse by the day. There's no trace of that bloody tall, lame black guy who was at the Ferreros' the day before Dionisio died. The people trading in old books don't know him . . ."

"I know," said the Count. "I suspect Dionisio and his sister were fibbing about the tall black guy, and after what's happened, Amalia doesn't know how to wriggle out of the lie."

"Do you reckon?" Manolo looked at the Count, intrigued by his suggestion. "Why would they want to do that?"

"The answer to what happened is in the Ferrero household, in the library, to be precise. The other day Dionisio or his sister said something to me about that library that I think holds the key to everything."

"And you still don't remember what?"

"I don't remember who said it or what was said, but it's buzzing around my head . . . For some reason I think it's also connected to the bolero singer."

"You still on that tack? . . . You know, Conde, my way's much simpler: Dionisio refused to do a deal over some of those books, the person with him got upset, they rowed and he lost his temper and killed him. When he saw what he'd done, he took six books, because, whatever you say, they must be some of the most valuable ones . . ."

"Very neat," said the Count, "and, best of all, neither Yoyi nor I fit that version. We didn't need to kill anyone or steal books that Dionisio could sell us at a bargain price . . ."

"And what if Yoyi tried to reach a deal and leave you out? There were books you didn't want to sell because they were so rare . . . You told me some manuscripts might be worth a fortune . . . And the person who entered the house was someone Dionisio was acquainted with. He even knew where to find his knife."

Conde looked at Manolo's vague expression, eyeing him as suspiciously as if he held the trump card.

"Yoyi may be many things but he's not a murderer."

"How can you be so sure? Yoyi is in business and crazy about money . . .'

"Yoyi is also my friend," concluded Conde and Manolo smiled: he knew what such a status meant in the ex-lieutenant's ethics. "Forget him and look elsewhere."

"I'm looking everywhere, but it's like being a magnet: you turn it round, and when you let go, things turn by themselves and join up again . . ."

'If you'd listened to me like you used to . . . Tell me, do you know why Dionisio left the corporation where he was working after he left the army?"

"More or less, though you can't get a straight answer from anyone. It seems Dionisio was too strict and didn't like the way he saw things being done there. You can imagine what. It seems he started getting difficult and they made his life impossible. He was the only one who had to leave."

"I'd imagined something of the sort. He was a man of rock-solid principles. He almost starved to death as a result."

"Conde, Conde!" Sergeant Estévañez's summons interrupted the Count's disquisition. "Oh, Captain, I didn't know . . ."

"What's the matter?" enquired Manolo.

"I found something odd: the case on that woman isn't open but it's not closed either . . ."

"This is looking good. But we'd better leave the toilets," the Count suggested, "otherwise they'll start suspecting I'm some policemen's favourite piece of ass . . ."

The evening rain cleared away the grey haze that had wreathed the city since midday, as if releasing it from an oppressive burden, capable of driving it back into its weary foundations. The newly washed sky recovered its summery cheerfulness and a cool breeze rustled through the trees, painted by the impressionist light of dusk.

Muscular and spare in spite of his age, the man rocked gently in his wooden chair. He was looking dreamily into the garden, and every twenty-five to thirty seconds lifted his cigar to his lips. His face was momentarily hidden in a cloud of languorous smoke that began the perfumed ascent from his mouth to paradise, where the spirits of well-made and even better smoked havanas lived on eternally.

The Count observed him from his car window and was struck by an unmistakable wave of nostalgia. Seeing him smoking in the peaceful solitude of his porch, relaxed, apparently content, was a spectacle he never dreamt he'd be privileged to enjoy. In the ten years he'd worked to orders from that robust, gifted leader, the then detective lieutenant Mario Conde had felt a special fondness, a rich blend of differences and affinities, grow for the man with the cigar who, quite unselfishly, had given him the benefit of his massive experience in the police, the keys to his uncorruptible ethics and the more elusive benefits of his trust and jealous friendship. Consequently, when an Internal Investigations team had used their unlimited police powers and policies to decree that the man's abilities were dwindling and decided to remove him from the force via the procedure of early retirement, the Count rushed into the void after him, in an act of blatant solidarity. He handed in his resignation, risked being suspected of acts of corruption, indolence and prevarication that had already cost several detectives their posts and even prison sentences and, by simple hierarchical fiat, had put an end to the mandate of the hitherto spotless Major Antonio Rangel.

"Is the chief you've got now better than the Boss?" the Count finally broke the silence, turning towards Manolo, seated behind the wheel.

"He was one in a million. Especially as far as you were concerned."

"True enough," replied the Count, opening the car door, ready to go to meet his past yet again.

When Rangel saw them approaching he stood up. At seventy he still retained his impressive chest, flat belly and brawny arms that he proudly nurtured and kept on display.

"I don't believe it," he said, smiling, a cigar between his lips.

Conde realized old age and separation from commander status had changed Rangel's attitudes when he came over preparing to give them a hug. Could that man of iron have gone soft?

"Your cigar smells great. Where did you get it?" enquired the Count.

"When my wife brings out the coffee I'll give you one . . . I've got two boxes of León Jimenes that have just arrived from Santo Domingo. You know, my friend Fredy Ginebra. And he sent a bottle of Brugal rum that's . . ."

"That's what good friends are for," commented the Count. 'What are your daughters are up to?"

A lightning flash of expectation lit up his former chief's eyes.

"They're planning to come over on holiday to see the New Year in. The one who married the Austrian is still living in Vienna, and giving Spanish classes. The one who went to Barcelona works for an insurance company . . . They're both doing well. But I can't stop worrying about them and my grand-children . . ."

"You got over your resentment then?" asked the Count. He remembered the Major's foul mood provoked by his daughters' decision to leave Cuba and lead their lives in a different hemisphere.

"I think so. I spend my time reckoning up how long it is since I last saw them . . . You know what the best of it is? My wife and I live on the money they keep sending us. The pension goes nowhere fast. Can you imagine me living on dollars I receive from my daughters?"

"Your daughters were always kind," the Count opined, unsure how to leave that minefield. "I'd have married either . . ."

Antonio Rangel gave him that peculiarly profound stare that still made the Count shake in his shoes.

"It might not have been such a bad idea. I'd have had to put up with you as a son-in-law, I wouldn't have the dollars that save my bacon now, but you'd have tied one of them to this bitch of a country . . . Why don't we change the subject?"

"Of course," agreed the Count. "Did you see what I brought you?" he said, pointing at Manolo.

"So you're a captain now," said Rangel, pointing at Manolo's stripes and trying to haul himself out of his well of sadness.

"He's turned out to be a bit of a bastard," the Count interjected.

"Don't take any notice, major, this guy's always coming out with shit," Manolo protested.

"Don't worry. I never did take any notice of him. But don't call me major . . . So what happened to you?" he asked, pointing at the Count's face, "you look like you've been hit by a train."

"You could say that."

"The eyepatch is most becoming. When did you last have a shave?"

"I won't answer that one. You're not my boss any more . . ."

"True enough. Can you tell me what the fuck I owe the pleasure of this visit to?"

While they drank the coffee poured by their ex-chief's wife and Conde lit a pale, silky smooth León Jimenes, Manolo gave Rangel the police version of the murder of Dionisio Ferrero's death and the reasons why Mario Conde was involved in the investigation, without letting on that the former policeman was still on the suspects' hot list.

"But the Count's gone off on another tack," concluded the captain.

"And I'm more certain than ever that something out of the ordinary happened forty-three years ago," the Count announced.

"Forty-three years ago?" Rangel enthused in policeman style, and puffed on his cheroot.

"Do remember you once talked to me about a lieutenant called Aragón?"

"Of course I do, he was my first boss. He was something special."

"Well Lieutenant Aragón left a case open forty-three years ago . . ."

"The case of the woman who used cyanide to kill herself?" asked Rangel, taken aback.

"How did you guess?" the Count was even more taken aback than his ex-boss.

"Because Aragón said it was the only one he never solved. After several months of investigations, his boss ordered him to call it a day. There was a lot of evidence pointing to suicide, but Aragón insisted something strange had happened and wanted to keep on the case . . ."

"Something really strange did happen," the Count agreed with Aragón.

"Go on then, tell me what happened, and see if I get it."

"Aragón followed orders and shelved the investigation, but had the forethought not to close the case," the Count went on. "That's why it took us so long to find the dossier, because we thought it must have been closed. They're looking out the rest of the paperwork, and the autopsy report, but in the précis we've got it says the woman died from a lethal intake of cyanide, although there were remains of antibiotics in her stomach . . . Aragón reckoned someone who's about to commit suicide doesn't bother taking antibiotics to cure a throat infection. He was sure it was murder, but had no way of proving it, and needed time to investigate . . . From what I've found

225

out, I agree the woman was murdered, perhaps because she was privy to some serious inside information. Just imagine, her lover and Meyer Lansky were as thick as thieves . . . So we came to see you. I wanted to set you thinking, you must remember something Aragón told you about that case . . ."

The ex-major put his cigar on the ashtray and looked into the garden. The Count knew Rangel's memory stored a huge amount of information, and his neurones must now be digging deep into memories of years of conversations with a prehistoric policeman whose infallibility was legendary.

"The woman was young and very beautiful. She was a singer . . ." said Rangel, returning the Count's glance. "And Aragón couldn't find any motives for suicide or murder for that matter. Those most under suspicion had no incriminating motives and there were fingerprints belonging to several people in the house, but all had watertight alibis . . . The deceased had everything ready to leave the country, even a visa in her passport, and was leaving with a man who'd been her lover for several years. Lansky's partner?"

"Uh-huh, that's him. You're on the right track," the Count encouraged him.

"Aragón told me a couple of things had surprised him: that the girl didn't seem to have any friends and that her lover left Cuba three weeks after her suicide. It also struck him as odd she put her own record on the turntable before committing suicide . . . Wait a minute, I remember what was most suspicious of all was that she diluted the cyanide in cough syrup . . . He reckoned if you're set on killing yourself, you swallow the poison, and don't bother diluting it in medicine."

"She was murdered. I've been sure of that for some time," declared the Count triumphantly.

"Aragón was sure, if he'd had more time, he'd have found more leads, but we're talking 1959, no, it was 1960 by then, when the acts of sabotage started and there weren't enough detectives to go round. That's why he was told to forget the singer and get on with other cases. Apart from that, there were no relatives or anyone demanding to know what really happened, and he had no suspects . . . But I don't understand why you're so keen connect that death with the murder of the man who was into books."

Conde smiled and took a drag on his cigar.

"Now I know they murdered her. First it was just a hunch . . ."

"I don't believe it, Conde, are you still banging on about your hunches?"

"Well what do you expect, Boss: when I really have a hunch . . . That woman's lover owned the library the Ferreros inherited."

"And he? —"

"He died in 1961," interjected Manolo, to show how crazy the Count was. "A car accident, in the United States."

"So?" rasped Rangel.

"So?" mimicked the Count. "Well, I'll continue with investigations, because I agree with Aragón: Violeta del Río didn't commit suicide and I'm sure that someone connected to that mystery murdered Dionisio Ferrero. What do you reckon? If they hadn't killed Dionisio, nobody else would have taken a blind bit of interest in Violeta del Río."

Rangel and Manolo looked at each other. They'd have liked to crack a joke, but experience urged caution: the Count's hunches usually had surprising links to reality. Old Rangel contemplated his cigar and smiled.

"Conde, it's ten years since I asked you this . . . and I won't die without getting a proper answer from you. Why the hell did a fellow like you join the police?"

Conde smoked his cigar, with a slightly sarcastic smile, prompted by cherished memories.

"Truly, truly, I didn't know why for a long time," he said, no longer smiling. "Although I sometimes liked what I was doing, I hardly ever felt happy as a policeman. Then I decided it was the fault of those bastards who do things and usually get away with it . . . But then, when I saw what was happening in the big, wide world, I think I imagined I'd sort it out a bit so it wasn't so fucked up, and I swallowed the story about police being able to do that. A romantic dream, right? I know I was swimming against the tide, but I don't regret what I did, although I'd never do it again. I'd not enlist again, even at gunpoint. Not even with a chief like you. I used to be agnostic, but I'm a total disbeliever now . . . Boss, I don't even believe in the four noble truths a friend of mine talks about . . . At most, in friendship, memories and a few books. It may sound cynical, but it's the truth. I don't like what I see every day and couldn't cope with it if I was in the force. I feel happier selling old books, wielding no power over others and being at ease with myself. At forty-eight I've learned that's important too. When I can, I enjoy the small pleasures in life, as faraway as I can possibly be from any whiff of power and the idea I have a right to think on behalf of other people and having to obey orders I sometimes didn't want to obey. You see? I'm much clearer about why I don't want to be a policeman than why I was one for ten years."

He abandoned his bed feeling as if he'd had another encounter with his friend J.D., though this time he didn't remember the essence of their dialogue: meditation and reincarnation. I expect, the bastard's into all that and doesn't want to write, he thought, while trying to get up as surreptitiously as his aches and pains would allow so as not to wake up Tamara. Back on his feet, he turned round and fleetingly observed the sleeping woman, her mouth slightly open, her nightdress rucked up, baring thighs as firm as ever as they climbed to the promising mound of her buttocks. Conde bent over, breathed in and filled his lungs with the smell of hot sheets and sweet saliva, ruffled hair and female vapours from that almost inert body and was surprised by the thought that he'd now crossed every frontier of self-preservation because he unreservedly loved a woman he felt to be his own, with whom he'd exchanged the most intimate secrets. He recalled the almost inaudible splash of Tamara's tongue in the well of her mouth and the seemingly pitiful purr she'd emit seconds before passing from wakefulness to sleep, and, when she lapsed definitively into unconsciousness, the way her body juddered and alarmed the Count. For her part, she was familiar with and suffered from the night-time snoring of a smoker with one nostril blocked from when a baseball hit him long ago, from the anxiety pursuing him in his deepest dreams, which, so she said, made him assume strange postures like sleeping face down, leaning on his elbows his forehead against the pillow, as if enduring a Muslim form of penitence. The quota of secrets they shared from years of passionate encounters encompassed knowledge of phobias and fears, of things admired and held in contempt, and the vital possession of the most subtle, efficient keys to release the springs of

229

sexual pleasure. The Count recalled how she liked his tongue to lick her clitoris in quick violent movements, letting his saliva run down to her vaginal and anal orifices, as the palms of his hands rubbed her erect nipples and he finally felt the tension in her belly, the changes in her breathing, the build up to the silent eruption of her orgasm. Then he felt his scrotum recede and a lascivious tingle run down his urethra, and pleasurably recalled the arts applied by Tamara to give him maximum enjoyment, licking his nipples, caressing his anal sphincter, revisiting his penis and testicles with her tongue and, opening her legs so that, when he knelt and penetrated her, he could eye her pink fleshy parts wet with saliva and tasty secretions, and watch his honourable member drill the hot insides of a body surrendering wholeheartedly to love and pleasure.

When the Count saw the hard on his imaginings had prompted, he wondered if the years hadn't transformed them into something more than two lovers: theirs was a well-established blend of knowledge and tolerance that, at some moment, they would have to accept was a definitive bond, but both liked to procrastinate, selfishly defending the last remains of a freedom reduced to the enjoyment of periods of solitude, a solitude that was too pleasurable because it was quickly ended by a short ride from one district of Havana to another, where they always found the life-saving sense of security, solidarity and belonging they gave each other.

When he entered her bathroom, after discarding the idea of masturbation which had been his goal, Conde stood in front of the mirror and told himself he was fed up of looking like a badly packaged mummy; he ripped the bandages from his eyebrow and the back of his ear. The sight of the three stitches on his bruised skin produced a slight queasiness and he looked away, horrified by his own scars.

After a coffee and his first cigarette of the day, he ran over a possible agenda: he decided he'd try to talk to Amalia Ferrero, now that Dionisio's funeral rites had been performed, and concluded he should go back to Elsa Contreras, the once famous Lotus Flower, now sheltering behind the name and terrifyingly real skin of the ravaged Carmen Argüelles.

Tamara took him by surprise as he was lighting his second cigarette, after a second cup of coffee.

"How do you feel?" she asked, lifting his chin to get a better view of the state of his injuries.

"Like shit, but ready for battle," he said. "The coffee's still hot."

She went to get the coffeepot and Conde, still with the morning hunger provoked by his musings, watched her well-endowed buttocks move under the flimsiest of nightdresses. Unable to hold back, he jettisoned his cigarette, went in hot pursuit, kissed her neck, and put his hands on her buttocks that he opened like the pages of a beautiful book.

"So you woke up with love on your mind?" she smiled.

"Seeing you makes me feel like love," he replied, rocking her gently against the small table.

"Can I drink my coffee?" she asked.

"Only if I can do other things afterwards . . ."

"You're ill."

"It's not catching. And we've been sleeping together for three days like brother and sister. I can't stand it any more. It's your fault I was about to jerk off and break my fast . . ."

"Mario, I've got to go to work."

"I'll give you a day's pay."

"Like a whore!"

Conde's memory flashed back. He glimpsed the mercenary mulatta's lascivious tongue, her pert nipples, and even heard her would-be temptress's voice. He felt his parts rapidly recede, like a timorous animal running into a cave.

"All right, off you go to work," he replied, picking up his cigarette that was still smoking and almost smoked out.

"What's the matter?" she asked, alarmed by his reaction.

"Nothing much really, I'm worried," he whispered and went off to get the telephone. He came back to the kitchen and, as if making his first ever confession, asked: "Haven't you ever seriously thought we should tie the knot?" and, seeing the startled look on Tamara's face, added: "Only joking, don't worry . . ." and left.

Still surprised by his question, Tamara looked ecstatic, almost not crediting what she'd heard and, telephone in hand, the Count smiled as he heard her say: "Is that what a knock on the head does for you?"

Yoyi Pigeon honked his Chevrolet's horn insistently and a pensive Count bid farewell to the concrete shapes by Tamara's house.

"What do you hope to get from the dead man's sister?" Yoyi asked, after shaking the Count's hand and shifting the gear lever.

"I'd like the truth, but I'll settle for any lead . . ."

"And the old dear in Atarés?"

"I want her to fill in the gaps. She didn't tell me a number of things. And I don't think it was out of fear. Too many years have gone by . . ."

"Are we going by ourselves? I've not come prepared. I've only got the chain and handcuffs . . ."

"Don't worry. I don't think they'll dare do it again. That's something I'd like to get to the bottom of . . . Anyway we'll take steel bars . . ."

When they were opposite Amalia Ferrero, Conde once again saw the exhausted, transparent woman he'd met several days ago. The food cure brought by the books seemed eaten away by grief and her sad eyes were hidden from sight by constant blinking. Her fingers were raw, about to bleed, and had suffered from a bout of frantic chewing.

"The police have told me to stop selling books until they finish their investigation," she said, when she saw her visitors, skipping any polite chitchat.

"We've come about something else. Can we talk for a few minutes?"

Amalia's lids started blinking again, uncontrollably, as she ushered them into the reception room. Conde inspected the closed mirrored doors of the library, and looked in vain for the glass ashtray. What the fuck had one of those two told him about that library? Which one was it? He tried to poke in his memory: the reply wasn't forthcoming.

"Amalia, I'm really sorry to bother you, but we need your help. The man who came to buy books still hasn't shown up, although we've found other things out and perhaps . . ."

"What other things?" the woman's eyes sparked.

"The singer I told you about, Violeta del Río, was really Catalina Basterrechea. She was Alcides Montes de Oca's lover."

"It's news to me . . . I didn't know. Didn't have the slightest . . ." she answered emphatically.

"It's strange you didn't know. She was going to leave Cuba with Alcides. And if you'd made your mind up, you'd have gone together."

"But I didn't know . . . I didn't want to leave . . ."

The Count decided it was time to apply a little pressure.

"Your Mummy knew. She knew everything . . . She sorted out all the red-tape to bury that woman when she committed suicide."

"Mummy did whatever Mr Alcides told her to do. I told you: she was his trusted help. But I didn't know . . ."

"There was a lot of doubt as to whether Catalina Basterrechea committed suicide or was murdered."

When he said that last word Conde knew he'd touched a sensitive spot. An almost imperceptible physical reaction rippled though her. She was on tenterhooks. Conde hesitated, although his instinct told him to stick the scalpel in and gouge out the dead tissue.

"I still think it odd that you were living in this house, so close to your mother and Alcides, and knew nothing about that tragedy. How old were you in 1960?"

"I don't know," stammered Amalia, who blinked frantically, put a finger to her mouth, and tried to restrain herself. "I was twenty. It was decades ago . . . and I was just a young girl."

"From what I gathered, you'd started working, joined the union, and accepted a post in a bank, a position in the Federation . . ."

"That's true enough, but I knew nothing about any Catalina, or what Mr Alcides did with his life. And what my mother once knew has gone with her madness . . . Satisfied? Why don't you go and leave me in peace? I feel very upset," her voice pleaded; she was close to collapse. "Dionisio was my brother, can't you understand? He was almost all I had left in this world . . . My nieces and nephews went. My mother's dying. Today or tomorrow . . . And that bloody hole of a library . . ."

A shaft of light rent the shadows in Conde's mind and lit up his memory. Amalia had struck a very personal note about the library which might just have opened a way to the truth.

"What's your problem with the library, Amalia? A few days ago you said something about the library rejecting you and you rejecting the library. Why did you say that?"

Amalia looked at the two men and blinked and blinked. Her voice sounded like an exhausted sigh.

233

"Will you leave me in peace?"

Conde nodded and accepted their conversation was at an end, convinced more than ever that that house, and in particular the coveted library of the Montes de Ocas, hid the secrets that couldn't be revealed, that Amalia perhaps thought had been swallowed by her mother's dementia and the occasionally merciful passage of time.

Yoyi insisted on being present at the conversation with Elsa Contreras – or would it be with Carmen Argüelles? – and the Count thought he had the right: after all, the police still reckoned he was a murder suspect in the present mess the ex-detective was intent on using the past to solve.

"You like the beautiful, expensive things in life, so I can tell you now: you're not about to see anything pleasant," said the Count as they drove into the barrio.

"Don't give me that shit, man, it's not as if the sight of an ugly old woman is anything out of the ordinary . . . You know what? I agree with you. The person who killed Dionisio didn't do it to steal. This isn't very charitable of me, but I think Amalia knows something, I'd swear to it."

The Count smiled, when they turned into Factoría.

"No need to swear . . . I'm going to ask a favour of you now: let me do the talking. Whatever bright thoughts you might have, keep your nose out of it, right?"

"You like being the boss?"

"Yeah, sometimes, man," replied the Count, when they peered into the yard and found that the place seemed to have recovered its usual rhythm. At the back, the two women from the day before were washing huge piles of clothes, and the Count assumed it was how they earned their living. The music people had chosen blared from doorways, in counterpoint, in open warfare, competing to burst unaccustomed eardrums. One doorstep was home to three men worshipping a bottle of rum on the dirty floor, while a young boy under the stairs was busy washing a pig with water stored in a petrol tank. A black woman, all dressed in parchment white, necklaces dangling from her neck, was smoking a big cigar on the balcony of the upstairs flat, behind a washing line of patched sheets and almost see-through towels. Next to her, a young mulatta, her curly hair fanning out like a peacock's tail, rubbed her eyes swollen by sleep and scratched under her breasts with mangy pleasure. All the gazes, including the pig's, followed the steps of these strangers, who, without a word of greeting for anyone, trooped to the back of the lot.

Carmen Argüelles sat in the same chair, in the same position as the previous day, but that morning she had company and Conde presumed this must be the niece who lived with her, as the elderly woman had mentioned. She was fat, coarse, with ballooning breasts and fifty tough years behind her, and was now busily arranging small packets in a bag on the bed.

Conde greeted them and apologized for interrupting; he then introduced his companion and asked Carmen if they could continue their chat.

"I said all I had to say yesterday."

"But there are other things —"

"What are you after?" blurted out the fat woman.

"This is my niece Matilde," Carmen confirmed, turning to speak to her. "Don't worry, you go, or you'll be late . . ." and she looked at her visitors. "She sells peanut nougat and this is the best time . . ."

Conde stayed silent, waiting for Matilde to reply, and glanced at Yoyi to tell him to keep quiet.

"All right then," Matilde finally said, putting the last packets in the bag and hanging it over her shoulder: "I'll be back soon."

When she left, Conde and Yoyi walked into the middle of the room and saw the smile on Carmen's face.

"I didn't say anything to Matilde about the money you gave me yesterday. If I tell her, it'll disappear like that. You know, there's never . . ."

"That money was for you," replied the Count, giving approval of Carmen's precaution and raising her hopes of another little sum at the end of today's conversation.

"What else do you want to know?" the elderly woman asked and Conde congratulated himself on the way he'd played it. "I told you all there is to know yesterday . . ."

"There are two or three things . . . Did you know the children of Nemesia, Alcides's secretary?"

"She had two, boy and girl, but I never saw them. They lived in Alcides's house and, obviously I never got an invite there."

"What was Alcides and Nemesia's relationship like?"

"I told you . . . She saw to his paperwork and the house, particularly after he was widowed. She was a highly intelligent woman, very cultured, but rather harsh on everybody, except Alcides, naturally . . ."

"And that's all?" the Count persisted.

"What else do you know then?" Carmen responded, somewhat taken aback.

"Nothing really," Conde admitted. "I don't know anything . . ."

The elderly woman hesitated for a moment, but only for a moment.

"Lina told me that Alcides was the father of Nemesia's son. They were very young when it happened. The family decided the best thing was to marry Nemesia Moré off to Alcides's chauffeur, so he'd have his surname. Then the daughter was born, but Alcides swore she wasn't his, although Lina didn't believe him. According to her, she was his spitting image. They paid the chauffeur a hundred pesos a month on top of his wage to keep his mouth shut. The strange thing is that the chauffeur disappeared one fine day, as if the earth had swallowed him up, and nothing was heard of him again . . ."

Conde weighed up Carmen's words and glanced at Yoyi.

"What do you reckon happened?"

"I can't imagine, you know, but it was strange, wasn't it?"

"People don't vanish like that, particularly when they have a job that pays double the rate . . . unless Lansky?. . ." exclaimed the Count, in a flash of inspiration.

"What about Lansky?"

"When did Lansky and Alcides become friends?"

"When Lansky started to come to Cuba in the early thirties. But they started doing business together later, during the war."

"What kind of business?"

"Alcides's family was very influential and he knew everybody. Lansky had money he wanted to invest. That was what it was about. When the world war started, Alcides made a fortune importing lard from the United States. Lansky used his connections over there so that Alcides had a monopoly . . . Luciano helped them. At the time he controlled the port of New York. Alcides paid Lansky back by introducing him to the people in charge over here. The politicians and so on . . ."

"And what was the line of business they were pursuing in 1958, when they met in Lina's flat? If Alcides didn't have the same clout under Batista and Lansky wasn't exactly popular in the United States . . ."

"I wouldn't know about —"

"Oh, yes, you would . . . It was fifty years ago, Carmen. They're all dead and can't get you now. I'm sure it was something important . . . They shattered a man's hand because they thought he was trying to find out what they were up to."

"The journalist?"

"That's right. What was it?"

"I don't know, but they were hatching something."

"As well as hotels and gambling?"

"Yes, as well."

"Drugs?"

The elderly woman shook her head vigorously.

"Carmen," said the Count, playing his last card, "it's probably why they killed your friend Violeta . . . They staged the suicide, but that fooled no one. Not even the police . . . Not even you . . . But Violeta was your friend and you kept your head down . . ."

The elderly woman looked down at her withered arm. "Is it her arm or her conscience that's giving her pain?" wondered Conde. When she looked up her expression had changed.

"No, Alcides wouldn't have let them. He was a son of a bitch, but he loved Violeta. Nobody killed her because of what she knew . . ."

"You sure Alcides wasn't involved in trafficking drugs?"

"Alcides wouldn't have got into that, and Lansky, who was boss of everything the mafia did here, got a percentage, but wasn't personally involved. Drugs were Santo Trafficante's preserve, the son; Lansky was intent on becoming a businessman, and wanted to live without the police on his back, like his friend Luciano, who had a taste of prison, was booted out of the United States and had to leave for Sicily, where his life was worth next to nothing. The Jew cultivated his image in Cuba as if it were sacred and avoided

237

anything that might tarnish it. Besides, with all the plans he had for building hotels and casinos that were going to make millions and millions, all above board, he couldn't take risks with anything dicey. But he let others get on with it and raked in his commission . . ."

"So what were they both hatching that was so secret? If all their business was above board . . ."

"I can't help you there, though it might have something to do with politics."

Conde glanced at Yoyi, as if looking for support. Such an idea fell outside all the scenarios they'd dreamt up so far: it lit up the void at the centre of that drama.

"Yes, that's possible . . . that's why they were acting so furtively. But what exactly?"

"They talked a lot about Batista, and never had a kind word for him. They thought he was going to fuck up. Alcides loathed him, and Lansky said he was a shark, a bottomless pit as far as money went, the country was slipping out of his hands and he was going to fuck up their big plans."

"Right, which is what he did," the Count thought aloud, adrift in a sea of ideas and possibilities.

"He was intent on winning the war and lost," commented Yoyi, unable to maintain his enforced silence any longer. "Lansky and Alcides had to leave and lost a fortune . . . In the end Batista messed it all up for them."

Conde looked at Yoyi, remembering he was like a tiger out on the street but that he tended to forget he'd been to university and that something must have rubbed off on the way.

"While we're at it, Carmen," said Conde, more gently. "Why did you change your name and disappear from the register of addresses?"

The elderly woman looked at the Count and then at Yoyi. She smiled mischievously.

"There are things best left forgotten . . . Did you realize I met your father?"

Surprised by this change of subject from Carmen, Conde tried to stop her predictable drift.

"My father's not the subject of this conversation," he tried to fob her off.

238

"Don't worry, there's nothing to get so upset about . . . Your father was always going to hear Violeta sing and started to knock it back, until he fell off his chair. I twice saw him being dragged out of the club. He was a coward and never had the courage to approach Violeta. I talked to him two or three times, I felt sorry for him. The poor wretch was like a lovesick puppy . . . He kept hovering around Violeta until someone told him if he wanted to keep walking on two legs he'd better not show up again when she was singing. I never saw him again after that . . ."

Conde felt each word score his skin, but decided it wasn't the moment to let himself be bowled over by discoveries he couldn't cope with.

"I'm sorry for my father's sake . . . But you've not told me why you changed your name . . ."

The elderly woman looked back at her withered arm.

'Louis Mallet never returned to Cuba. I decided not to leave in 1960, or in 1961 . . . and by the time I saw what was happening here, I was boxed in. My money was all gone and I had to go back to work, but was the wrong side of thirty-five and set up a brothel in Nuevitas, when that was still possible. It went pear-shaped in no time and I was put in a kind of school, to be reformed. They even taught me how to sew. I was still branded a whore though, so I made the best of my one chance to get rid of the label. I started to use my real name and lodged Carmen the seamstress here in Atarés, and let Elsa Contreras whore on a few more years, using her reputation as the Lotus Flower of old at the Shanghai in Havana. But being a whore at forty was shit. You had to fuck what came along, for next to nothing, because competition got really fierce: women were emancipated, just like men, and fucked for the fun of it, young girls started jumping into bed with anyone, anywhere, after all, we were all equal so had a right to equal pleasure, right? In the midst of this madness I met a man . . . a good man . . . and decided to bury Elsa Contreras for good and keep Lotus Flower in that drawer . . . By the way, the lad's not seen the photo," she went on, as if referring to someone else, who was dead and gone. "Go on, show it to him and leave today's money under the box, so Matilde doesn't see it when she comes back . . . That fat pile of shit scoffs the lot . . ."

Conde smiled, went to get the photo and handed it to Yoyi. He took a few notes from his pocket, put them in the drawer, but suddenly had a change of heart.

"What else?"

The elderly woman didn't seem to understand the question. Nor did Yoyi, who put the photo down.

"What do you mean 'what else'?" asked Elsa.

"You're still hiding a chunk of the truth. And it's an important chunk. I told you, it's from forty years back. And that's a long time to be frightened . . ."

Carmen watched Yoyi put the photo back in the box and hand it to the Count who put the possible reward back in his pocket before accepting it.

"The last time I saw Alcides he was getting into his car in front of the Western Union offices," said the old lady meekly, "he told me Violeta had broken his heart."

"I know," recalled the Count. "What I don't understand is why he said that. If Alcides wasn't involved in Violeta's death, he must have known better than anyone that she hadn't committed suicide. He must have suspected she'd been murdered. Why did he desert the scene like that? He must have said something else . . ."

The elderly woman glanced at her arm and went on, without looking up:

"Alcides told me not to poke my nose in where it wasn't wanted. Right then he couldn't put his children's future at risk and that's why he was going, but he would come back as soon as he could, because he had a few things to settle. And his chauffeur, that black Ortelio, would look after some of his lines of business one of which meant making sure nobody stirred up Lina's death or his secret meetings with Lansky. Everything should stay as dead and buried as Lina until he returned to dig things up. For my own good, he said, I should forget everything, and in particular shouldn't mention that conversation to the police . . . He said it in a way that still scares me. So I shut up and didn't poke around any more. He wasn't a man who requested something for the fun of it and then forgot about it. He wasn't ever like that . . ."

4 March

Dear love:

The voices pursuing me have forced me to do what my conscience refused to do. They told me to persevere in my pursuit of the final truth, not to prove my innocence, which you will never accept, but to demonstrate the truth about you, which is now challenged by your own daughter, and to find peace in the knowledge you didn't deal so foully with someone you said you loved. But the fact is I'm more and more frightened that finding that truth will be as terrible as living this life-sentence of oblivion and neglect, or possibly even far more painful than my present uncertainties.

I've spent days trying to track down that whore who danced naked, hoping she might give me some helpful information. But my efforts have been in vain. The places someone in her trade might go have been closed down by the government as part of their campaign to liquidate the past. I didn't find her in the flat your friend rented for her or at an address in Old Havana where she once said her younger sister lived.

So I took my courage into both hands and looked out the lieutenant who investigated her death and this time I was the one who asked the questions. He agreed to see me in his office, for half an hour, because he said he was overwhelmed by work, what with the plots and sabotaging everywhere, as a predictable reaction to the revolutionary decrees. Even so he was pleasant enough and listened to why I wanted to know more about that woman's fate. He also confided that he too had initially thought you were possibly behind her death. They knew all about you and your friendships with certain individuals he preferred merely to describe as dangerous. They also know that in your student days you belonged to the most violent gangs of pickets and showed yourself capable of anything. But, precisely because of your style, the way she died didn't seem to fit your character, and when he saw how you reacted to what happened he was soon convinced you weren't directly connected to the murder and that's why he let you go. Who did he suspect then? I asked, and I got a categorical answer, if she hadn't committed suicide, as people always assumed, her death must have been prepared and carried out by a woman, and he explained how the lack of violence and the opportunity offered by the bottle of cough syrup were very feminine touches, and had led him to think along those lines. His first suspect was the dancer, because of her record, but he discounted her after a couple of conversations. He admitted that more than once he'd thought (like you? you see?) I might have been the guilty party, because I was the only one known to

241

have access to the flat and because, when he found out about our relationship (how? I wonder), he thought I was the one with most reasons to want her dead. However, when he'd seen the consequences for me of what happened, he realized I too must have considered the outcome and he decided to discount me as a suspect, though he didn't eliminate me entirely. What then? I asked: I was left empty-handed, he replied, and despite himself he had had to accept orders from his superiors to drop the case and rule that suicide was the probable cause of her death, although he was still convinced it was murder and that the murderer, or rather the murderess, was an individual driven by horrific motivation he was unaware of, to want and then dare to consummate her desire for revenge.

As you can imagine, this conversation both soothed and upset me. To be almost sure that you are as innocent as am I brought a peace that soothed my tormented brain (the poor thing has continued hearing voices, even in the middle of the day) and showed me why you were so positive (like the policeman) that I was a possible guilty party. But if we discount the dancer, you and myself as the guilty ones: who does that leave? The idea now going round my mind is so horrific and my suspicion so great, that I prefer to shut my eyes, ears and mouth, if I put such a thought into words it would drive me crazy for good . . . besides, what proof do I have? None. A touch of hatred, a pinch of frustration, a slice of resentment can't be sufficient ingredients to transform someone who is so sweet and gentle, almost docile I'd say, into a murderess, intent on reversing destiny and capable of sacrificing a person to whom she'd never spoken a single word. Don't you agree? Tell me you don't believe that either, that it's impossible, that I'm mad or out of sorts to think something so brutal and unhinged, I beg you.

I will always love you, love you more, I need you so much at such a terrible time . . .

Your Nena

Mario Conde decided unilaterally, at a stroke, that his convalescence and relationship with antibiotics was over and asked Yoyi to stop by a market and get provisions for the indispensable celebration of this historic happening. The events of recent days, playing havoc with a routine he'd almost become used to, had frayed his nerves and set his brain to work at a dizzy speed. To calm such turmoil, Conde knew of no better cure than a good session of booze and chat.

The six bottles of rum, lined up on the iron and glass table, were a challenge. Skinny Carlos, who'd not been skinny for years, eyed them greedily, as if they were priceless jewels. The Count saw the bliss shining in his friend's eyes, and wondered again if he was doing the right thing by giving him the means to commit gradual suicide. But when he saw him enjoying his first swig, with physical and mental relish, he thought that helping him depart that ravaged body with which Carlos had no desire to co-exist was the hardest test his sense of friendship and life itself had to face: at the same time it was a supreme act of love and he would be the main loser. When Skinny wasn't around, where would Conde take his words, his thirst for rum, music and nostalgia?

"We have just one problem, Conde." Carlos moved his chair to where his pensive friend had seen him take his first swig. "By the time your money's gone, our taste buds will have developed bad habits. This rum is too good."

"True enough, you savage, but it's nothing to worry about," answered the Count. "You always get used to the worst. We know that too well, right? Don't worry, God will provide, as Candito told me and he's never let me down."

"Well, he's providing pretty well for the time being . . ."

"Where are Rabbit and Candito?" enquired Pigeon, now holding a full glass.

"They'll be here any minute," replied Carlos, draining a half glass in one gulp.

Evening had come suddenly, as was usual in the last weeks of the Caribbean summer, but the heat was just as intense. Nonetheless, in Carlos's backyard, under the trees and orchids that had just been watered, the temperature was tolerable.

"As we're celebrating, let's put some music on, hey, Conde?" Skinny enthused, pointing to the cassette recorder and the pile of tapes under the window.

"And listen to what?"

"The Beatles?"

"Chicago?"

"Formula V?"

"Los Pasos?"

"Credence?" asked Rabbit, the new arrival, bringing the curtain down on a routine Carlos and the Count sporadically rehearsed, proud and pleased to possess something that was unchanging and their very own, that nobody, not even time, hard knocks, frustrations, denials and absences, had been able to snatch from them. And death? Bugger death that fucking son of a bitch, Conde told himself, pointing an index finger at Carlos:

"Uh-huh, Credence . . ." immediately adding, as if put out: "But don't go telling me Tom Fogerty sings like a black dude . . ."

"I know, I know, he sings like God . . . What do I know . . ." smiled Yoyi, tired of nodding his head to the ball the others kept hitting to and fro. "You lot are incredible, you're not true, I swear by my mother . . . How often do you talk about the same old things?"

"So how's your investigation going, Conde?" enquired Rabbit, now holding his glass of rum and not pausing to address the young man's concerns.

"It's going nowhere fast. The truth's there, in front of my eyes, but I can't see it."

"What's the latest then?" asked Carlos.

"I'm sure Dionisio's death is connected to Violeta del Río's, and that she didn't commit suicide. But the only two people who can connect those deaths for me are Amalia Ferrero and her mother . . . The mother's been mad for over forty years and Amalia swears she knows nothing."

"And you believe her?" interjected Yoyi.

"No . . . And that's my problem. She's been hiding something from the beginning, or perhaps did so to protect Dionisio . . . Or her mother? Or the memory of Alcides Montes de Oca? It looks as if he was definitely her father . . . But how do I persuade her to tell all?"

Carlos, Yoyi and Rabbit looked at each other and reached the same conclusion. Yoyi took on the role of spokesman.

"Give her up to the police, for Christ's sake. Let them interrogate her like they interrogated us, they can try out all their subtle routines again: Sit there! Shut up! Hands by your sides! We're the ones asking the questions and you'd better cooperate! Look me in the eyes! Were you like that, Conde?"

He opted not to reply.

"Manolo's talked to her and got nothing out of her. But he reckons I exaggerate when I say Violeta's death is connected to Dionisio's. Although I did make him think a bit —"

"And what about Lansky and Montes de Oca? What's their role, man?" Yoyi filled his glass with ice and poured himself another shot.

"That's another part of the story. We may never find out what they were plotting but I've got a good idea —"

"Come on, out with it," urged Rabbit.

"They wanted to get rid of Batista. Business was going downhill fast and Alcides Montes de Oca couldn't stand him . . . He thought Batista was a disaster for the country. They were probably planning to kill him —"

"It sounds likely," agreed Rabbit. "If they'd got rid of him they'd have had room to manoeuvre and wouldn't have lost what they were setting up in town."

"But something did happen to prevent them from doing just that, if it was what they were intending," digressed the Count.

"Time had run out for them," said Rabbit. "The war ended too quickly, and it was too late."

"Maybe," the Count allowed.

"And the mysterious black guy?" Yoyi interrupted. "Why doesn't someone turn up to fit his description?"

Conde poured himself another rum. He looked into the bottom of his glass as if, down there, under layers of rum, an oracle existed that could give him answers and a blinding flash lit up his brain.

"Why didn't I think of that before? Fucking hell —"

"What?" asked Carlos.

"That black guy doesn't exist. He never existed. It was a charade to get more money out of us. Fuck —"

"So what about the fingerprints?" Rabbit's logic put in an appearance.

"They could be anyone's. An onion-seller in the street, the guy from the electricity . . . Anyone with a reason to go into the library —"

"Wait a minute, Conde," Carlos tried to bring a little common-sense into the conversation. "Were those prints put there to sidetrack the police or by chance?"

"By chance, obviously. Somebody went into the library for some reason or other, but not to buy books. Nobody in the trade knew that was the library Yoyi and I were mining, because we didn't tell anyone."

"So what about the books that went missing, man?" Yoyi continued.

"No books went missing. They moved those six from their shelf and put them somewhere else."

"So who moved them? It must have been Dionisio or Amalia."

"Then who the hell killed Dionisio?" Rabbit didn't seem very convinced by the Count's hypotheses.

"Someone killed him who had nothing to do with the book trade. They killed Dionisio for another reason, because of something in the library, whatever that might be."

"And you're saying it wasn't a book?" interjected Carlos.

"It looks that way," said the Count, lifting the palm of his hand level with his eyes. "It's all here but I can't see what goes where."

"It happens sometimes," said Candito, waving at his friends. "What you been up to, Red? You going to have a drink today?"

"No, not today."

"Christ watching over you?" Conde smiled, though he immediately realized he'd cracked a joke in bad taste.

"Yes, I've come from a wake," Candito leant back on the wrought iron chair and looked tired.

"Who died?" inquired Carlos.

"The brother of a member of my church. You knew him, Conde . . . it was Juan Serrano, alias Juan the African."

The Count put his glass on the ground and stared at his friend.

"What are you saying, Candito?"

"They found him yesterday. He'd been dead for two days. In an abandoned water tank in the yard of the Tallapiedra power station."

246

The pain was a dead weight, anchored behind his eyes, a dark sludge he couldn't erase, although he felt if he could put his hand inside his skull he'd grab it, wrench it out, and bring immediate relief. He'd given himself a double dose of analgesics and used up the entire contents of a pot of Chinese balm, but Conde predicted the headache wouldn't go away and decided to confront it like a man.

When he strode up calle Esperanza, looking for the sick heart of the old barrio of Atarés, he couldn't explain why he was there, or what he was after. As he walked along cracked pavements, skirting debris and petrified rubbish, he reflected that being born, living and dying in that place was one of the worst handouts that Lady Luck could send your way. Like one that brings you into the world in Burundi or Bombay or a Brazilian favela, rather than letting you see the light in Luxembourg or Brussels, where nothing happens and everything is usually clean, tidy and on time. Or in any other pleasant spot, faraway from that barrio where people were weaned on violence and historical frustration, grew up amid the most foul ugliness and daily moral degeneration, between Chaos and the blaring trumpets of the Apocalypse, all intent on atrophying a person's ability to make ethical choices and transforming him into an elemental being, fit only to fight and kill to survive.

The stench, the landscape of devastated buildings, the urban rivers of human detritus, the ever bigger bars behind which the locals imprisoned themselves, the aggressive reactions as the means to express needs accumulated over generations and centuries. All this gave those condemned to grim life sentences here without trial or reason, crammed in slums, a shit life that could end when cold thrusting knives broke the heart of a person who, in a coda to so much misery, was granted the putrid bottom of an abandoned water tank as his grave.

Conde penetrated further into the barrio, nervously stroking the steel bar wrapped in a plastic bag, driven by an irrational desire to find an individual to unleash his hatred on, and he realized once the emotion of that first moment had passed, that the unnatural silence reigning over those streets two days ago, he'd not known why, had gone. Life – if that's what it was – had returned to miserable normality in this circle of hell. After all, he was only one more dead man. Music again asserted its ownership of the air, vied with the cries of street-sellers; people huddled indolently on street corners, their looks as hazy as ever; women wilfully displayed mounds of flesh; bicycle-taxi drivers, come from the east of the country in search of a livelihood, sweated their wretched frustrations, pedalled against their ill-treated stomachs and battered backs. Oppression and despair had reclaimed the throne that had been momentarily displaced by pain and fear.

What codes had the African flaunted for his death to be decreed like that? Was it a debt of one, two or three thousand that decided that man's fate? Were they laws of a nascent mafia, geared up to impose respect via exemplary punishment on transgressors and painful warnings to nosey-parkers? Conde remembered how almost fifty years ago a different mafia had viciously punished a journalist for being curious and putting himself where he wasn't welcome, and how only four days ago, he himself had been lucky to escape with a beating and a couple of scars. But the poor African . . .

When Mario Conde reached callejón Alambique, in surprisingly good physical shape, he climbed to the third floor of that ramshackle building and walked, for the first time fearlessly, across the planks over the void. He passed by the door to what had been the African's home, now sealed by the police, and made his way to the roof terrace.

The dazzling 10 a.m. sun gleamed on the cracked, discoloured tiles and the Count knelt down by the air vent and put his arm in, up to and beyond his elbow. His pincer-like fingers extracted the plastic envelope he'd returned to its hidey hole with 700 pesos.

He put the envelope on the floor, plunged his arm back in until his armpit hurt and felt a synthetic surface that eluded his fingertips. Almost horizontal, he pushed his arm in further, his fingers pulling a slippery surface towards him, so it rolled on to the palm of his hand that finally locked on something round, hard and familiar.

Not worrying unduly about the painful way he rubbed the skin on his elbows and knuckles, he extracted his arm and hand that was clutching a baseball wrapped in several layers of cellophane. Sitting on the tiles he removed the wrapping and examined a capricious ball that, on the field of play, could rule the desires and needs of so many. The African's ball was quite ordinary, and very worn judging by its porous skin, frayed seams and soil stains that hadn't quite obscured the black lines of a signature inscribed on the leather. Conde wet a finger with his saliva and gently cleaned the area around the scrawl and read the name written in tiny, awkward letters: Ricardo Lazo. He remembered the catcher who played for the Industriales and died in an accident many years ago, who in his glory days had been distinguished by the elegant way he received hits and, most of all, caught foul-flys. Despite his death and the passage of time, he reflected, Ricardo Lazo was still important in someone's memory and he tried to imagine what that ball had meant to the man who'd just died for him to decide to hide it as his greatest treasure. How had he got hold of it? What great feats were suggested by that circumference that fitted a man's fingers so perfectly, a shape measured in dreams? His questions would remain unanswered, at least while the Count was on earth and the African in hell. But perhaps they'd meet there in eternity, and the Count would ask for his forgiveness, say how sorry he was not to have given him the three or four thousand pesos he needed, the price he'd put on his life, and would then ask him all about that poor, worn ball that had clearly enjoyed the priceless fulfilment of a solid, resonant encounter with a wooden bat.

Mario Conde's eyes clouded over and he realized he was crying. A feeling of frustration, rage and impotence released tears that kicks and blows to the head hadn't. He was crying over the African, and himself, over the errors of their ways, the old baseball and unknown people who'd played with it and shared the dead ex-jailbird's fate of living a wretched daily existence between the boundaries of the barrio, and who now tried to escape that larger prison down paths of violence. He was crying over the demise of so many dreams, hopes and historical responsibilities. He wiped his eyes vigorously on the back of his hand, gathered up the cellophane and put the ball back in place. He thought it ought to stay there until the tottering hulk collapsed, if not the whole rotten, fractured city. He tried to imagine someone, perhaps one of Juan the African's children finding it buried in the mountain of debris, on that spot where a guilty man now stood, guilty of sins of omission and lack of will, sins of indolence and stubbornness, a man called Mario Conde.

Dazed by his headache he pocketed the envelope with the money and walked to the edge of the terrace. He surveyed the vista, the barrio and its clothes lines of threadbare garments, rickety huts for breeding pigeons and pigs, shaky television aerials, improvized zinc roofs beneath which slept the taxi-cyclists from Oriente and, in the street, the bustle of individuals trapped in the quest for a way to improve on a fate framed by that decay.

The scream escaped from his entrails, spewed out like vomit and ran over death-stricken terraces, cracked walls, rocky stairs, doors bereft of paint but plagued with bolts and locks and stinking streets, splashing, leaping, spreading through the air, until it reached the boundaries of the barrio and of fear, and went on unchecked, beyond and further, perhaps even over the sea, to sail stubbornly to where sorrows and memories are buried.

"Bastards!" he shouted, in a hoarse voice, until he was out of breath, and then went on: "Bastards, I'm here," panting, his horizon again clouded by tears and his head about to explode and shatter.

He opened his eyes slowly, almost warily, and realized the kicking pains had gone. Whom should he thank for the miracle? God, who seemed to exist a little less each day? Buddha the Enlightened One, or the earthly inventor of analgesics? The darkness now reigning over his bedroom confirmed it was night-time and he reckoned the pile of painkillers he'd ingested had put him out for two or three hours.

He heard someone banging on his door and realized the first knocks were what had woken him. He shouted: "I'm coming!" from his bed before sitting up.

A groggy Count welcomed Manolo for the first time in many days, and he almost smiled when he saw the policeman's exhausted face.

"I heard you wanted to see me," said Captain Manuel Palacios and the Count nodded.

"Come in, I'll make some coffee." "How come you're asleep at this time of day?" Manuel asked, a touch envious.

"My head was throbbing," explained the Count after he'd put the coffee in the percolator and shut the coffeepot. "Today's been a strange one. What day is today?"

"Thursday. Why?" enquired Manolo, settling down on one of the kitchen chairs, his arms on the table, as the Count shrugged his shoulders, as if the day of the week were unimportant. "Not still furious with me?"

"I'm at odds with the world. I'm getting surer by the day that it's a fucking awful place . . . But as it's Thursday, I think I'll forgive you."

"Just as well," he swayed his head, expressing no other feeling, and added: "I feel like fucking death warmed up . . . So what can I do for you?"

"Tell me what you know about Dionisio's death."

"Nothing new, we've reached a dead end. What about you?"

"I've got an idea, but both of us need to work at it."

"Go on," replied Manolo, seemingly indifferent.

"Let's wait for the coffee."

Mario Conde put in the minimum dose of sugar he used to sweeten his coffee and poured out two cups. He drank his standing up, blowing hard, and lit a cigarette.

"Good, right?"

"Conde, what's up? You seem so, so, you know, limp . . ."

"Everything . . . But back to the business in hand. I'm sure Dionisio's sister knows something and doesn't want to let on. There was or is something in that library that can explain what happened."

"You still on that tack? OK, what do you suggest?"

"To check every bit of the library, force Amalia to let us talk to her mother, to see if she's really as mad as she says. And I want you to question her again, but not softly, softly like last time."

"Conde, she's a woman. She's over sixty. She's no juvenile delinquent. Did you know she belongs to the Party?"

"Start gently and then you'll see how far you need to push her. You're good at that. And you like doing it."

Manolo moved his empty cup over the top of the table, apparently wondering whether he should fall in with his old boss or not. When they worked together, Manolo obeyed the Count's orders almost blindly and things usually turned out well.

"I'm not sure, really —"

"Look, I'm practically sure of one thing: the tall black guy is a phantom; he never existed," he said and spelled out his theory to Manolo.

"But if they both did it to get more money," Manolo reflected, "I can't see how it connects with Dionisio's death."

"If the unidentified fingerprints belong, say, to the electrician, and the rest are mine, Yoyi's and Amalia's, and if neither Yoyi nor I killed Dionisio, who does that leave us?"

"You're kidding, Conde," reacted Manolo.

"Obviously, it could have been someone who was there and didn't touch anything."

"You're giving me the shakes," Manolo shifted nervously, picked up his empty cup and looked inside.

"Join the club. Amalia is the key to all this. Amalia and the library," said the Count while he went to get more coffee.

"It makes sense," agreed Manolo.

"What have you got on one Juan Serrano Ballester who turned up dead in Tallapiedra?"

Surprised by the sudden change of topic, Manolo suspended his cup in mid-air.

"Did you know him?"

"He was an informer of mine, years ago."

"Say your . . . We've got nothing so far. He was stabbed eight times."

"What's going on in that barrio, Manolo? It's got laws unto its own."

"It's common knowledge. Every two or three months we take a little dip and bring in ten whores, five pimps, three sellers of crack and marijuana and a number of traffickers."

"And?"

"In two months it's back to square one. Some go to jail, others come out; some close their businesses, others start up, new ones. It's never ending."

"So why do you think it's like that?"

Manolo finished his coffee, and took a cigarette from Conde's packet. He puffed the smoke towards the ceiling.

"It's the only way they know how to live. It's like an incurable disease: it can be treated but it won't go away."

"You know they're organized? That they function like a mafia and the real *capos* aren't even from the barrio? They're the people who handle the funds and have the power to order someone to be taken out."

"Yes, and I know it's very dangerous. It could end up getting very nasty."

"We're fucked, man."

"And the fact is there are more police than ever . . . But even so —"

"That illness, as you call it, can't be cured by police . . . Poor Juan."

Manolo looked at the Count and smiled faintly.

"There's something you don't want to tell me."

"And won't tell you," the other asserted, returning to his chair.

"You weren't involved with what happened to that guy, were you? Come to think of it, he was killed near where you turned up the worse for wear . . ."

"You going to accuse me of killing him as well?"

"No, because he was killed the day you came out of hospital. But I'm sure you're connected somehow . . ."

"All right, now tell me, what do we do with Amalia?"

Manolo stood up and placed a hand on the Count's shoulder.

"You're a bastard, Conde. You want me to confide in you but it's one-way traffic. Although I'll act on what you said. We'll inspect the library and question her . . . But it'll be tomorrow. I can't even think about it today, I've got three cases on the go and need a rest. Just like you. You look terrible. Anyone would think you were beaten into a pulp today."

13 March

Dear love:

I have been remembering your father a lot recently. I can see him sitting in this library where I now write to you, at his desk strewn with papers, but always ready to speak to me for a few minutes while he drank his freshly brewed coffee that I, personally, made and brought him. In my memory his image is that of the most kind and generous man I have ever known. On two, three, however many occasions, he told me how he liked to motivate his pupils at university and by making them read Oedipus Rex, *because he thought that Sophocles, five centuries before our era, had performed the miracle of writing a play about what he considered to be the perfect criminal investigation: that which finally accuses the investigator himself of a murder he never thought he'd committed.*

Although I read that tragedy several times at his insistence, for many years I forgot our conversations and for many months also ignored the voices of the demon (yes, I now know it's a demon) that lives in my brain, when it both tempted and warned me of the dangers of finding out a truth that could turn sour. Perhaps it was my mistake, despite my every desire, to believe that these voices referred to you, and I even began to think again that, somehow beyond what I'd been able to find out, you were to blame for what happened and that there was the terrible truth I might find if I kept scratching around. But what I've discovered today, entirely by accident, is a reason not only to gouge my eyes out but also to rip my belly open: the source of the seed of this real tragedy has been finally revealed to me beyond all doubt, in all its horrific magnitude. And I have learned, most terribly, that the fate of Oedipus is the fate of all humans who have sins hanging over them.

A totally innocent comment, made by our old vet (he came to examine our decrepit Linda, your favourite terrier, who, like me, has been sick with melancholy ever since you left) about the disappearance of two cyanide capsules from the packet he brought months ago to combat the invasion of rats we had had in the patio and garden. It might have seemed a chance loss, perhaps down to the vet's miscalculation, and might have sounded like a random remark, totally unrelated to the death of a person who, in almost everyone's eyes – our vet included – wasn't in the slightest linked to you. But cruel, persistent fate ensured that this scrap of information that could feed all my suspicions fell precisely into my hands and brought me face to face with a truth I had been seeking so insistently, never imagining I could be to blame for what happened by providing, I now know only too well, the arguments to inspire this crime.

254

I've wracked my brain for some thread of justification and I think I've found it in the reason that forced this tragedy to its fatal finale: and I can only blame love; love was to blame for everything. Our poor little girl always loved you silently, always hoped for the reward of a father and because of that love she rebelled and refused to give up what that woman was going to steal from her, from me, even from you . . . But such thoughts can't save me from the eternal condemnation brought by the knowledge I created a person able to resort to the most premeditated crime to save her rights and need for love, who never imagined that her action would kill that love and those rights, definitively . . .

My dear: such is the burden of grief within me that I find myself without the strength to continue writing these senseless letters. You will never receive them, firstly because you have no desire to, and secondly because I would be incapable of sending them, even more so, knowing what I know now, because I prefer you to continue to blame me and never find out this desperate truth. At any rate, as my eternal punishment, I will keep them as a testimony to my sins, my sorrows, and also to my love. A love that from this day on becomes impossible, but will always be yours.

Goodbye, my love. Now and forever.

Nena

The police tape slithered to the ground like a decapitated snake. When he pushed the glass doors and breathed in the faint scent of old paper, Mario Conde recalled the excitement he'd felt ten days ago, when he first stepped into that dream library. Only ten days ago? So many things had happened since then in his life, and in the lives – and even deaths – of the people connected to that place, that he now wondered if his presence hadn't been like that of a prince endowed with the power to end a paralysing spell that had been decreed for eternity. At least that library, the dazzling fossil left by the efforts of three generations of bibliophiles with enough money to purchase on any whim, had been profaned by his commercial interests and, with a final vengeful, agonic swipe of the tail, had taken with it the wrong-headed life of a man who perhaps never found out who he really was.

Perhaps the most unforgivable sin committed by Mario Conde had been to think that, those books, accumulated over a century and preserved with sickly zeal for another forty years, could change his precarious economic state and, at least, books permitting, spread riches and happiness among his nearest and dearest, who needed emergency rations of both as much as he did. Consequently, he now thought everything that had happened was the work of fate overriding his sins, his karma and his errors; a fate lurking between those silent volumes that had come back to life to demand justice that had been put off too long. The clearly predestined discovery of the press cutting reporting the surprise retirement of Violeta del Río had turned out to be merely the tip of the iceberg. The fragments of truth the Count dredged to the surface as a result of that forgotten newsprint had gradually given flesh and taste to a tragedy lost in the mists of yesterday, a drama whose mysterious cause had led to at least two more deaths.

Conde looked around and tried to resuscitate the hunch that had surprised him when he first came to the library of the Montes de Oca. But the hunch refused to surface. He studied the chaos he'd created in the centre and right-hand section of the precinct, in contrast to the rows of volumes still sleeping on the shelves on the left. He gently ran his fingers over the spines of the most valuable items and felt a tremor of thanks from those books for not having been turned into market fodder, despite the alarming amounts their beauty, antiquity and rarity augured, and his contact with the books finally convinced him the magic cipher to complete the truth equation was still in that room.

He looked at the well-ordered shelves and understood it must all have been a question of time. The six missing books hadn't been moved because of their quality or value, but because of where they were. The truth had been hidden in, on, above or below them and that insight brought a wave of frustration: whoever had taken the books had taken the truth, and no doubt the whole truth. But he had to be sure.

Using the wooden bench Dionisio Ferrero had provided them several days ago, he started to review the top shelves. To begin with, he took down a group of books – Enrique Serpa, Carlos Montenegro, Alejo Carpentier, Labrador Ruiz – and studied their ends looking for a possible change in thickness. He then looked between each of the volumes and, convinced there was nothing there, returned to the bench and examined the remaining volumes one by one, shifting them into the space vacated by the books he'd taken down.

When he was just about to finish the top section dedicated to Cuban authors, Conde heard Manolo calling out.

"Come on, she says she's ready."

When they'd got to the Ferrero household, Manolo had demanded Amalia let them check over the library again and talk to her mother. Curiously, on this occasion Amalia hadn't protested or repeated her warning about her mother being mad and, after blinking persistently, she'd asked for a few minutes to get her ready.

257

Manolo and Conde followed in the footsteps of Amalia through the portico of Tuscan marble columns and into a gloomy, big-windowed room, that, Conde supposed, might have been the house's large dining room, because he then entered a huge, dilapidated kitchen, with walls covered in colourful Portuguese tiles. The mansion was divided in two by a passageway lined with doors that led into equally enormous bedrooms and bathrooms. Amalia stopped by the third door on the right and, with the resignation of a woman whose strength had run out, unable to resist this act of violation, she pushed open the wooden and glass door etched with modernist arabesques.

Determined to find the endlessly postponed solution to that enigma, Conde strode into the room and almost screamed. A stark naked, living corpse of what had once been a human being lay on the imperial, dark wooden bed, its carved columns draped in tattered gauze. Overcoming his desire to make a run for it, Conde summoned all his strength and contemplated the skeleton supine on the mattress stripped of sheets. Only the slightest breathing movement in her collapsed diaphragm hinted at the remaining signs of life; the completely corpse-like skull, sunk in the pillow, seemed detached from the rest of the body, from which every fibre of muscle had vanished, as if devoured by a voracious scavenger. The inert arms and legs were dried up, brittle segments, and Conde was horrified to see the swollen, blackened opening of her sex, macerated by uric acids, and hanging folds of skin, which had been the preserve of the mount of Venus. Death tapped on every door surrounding that human waste, and its bitter scent hung on the air.

"Won't you ask her a question?" Conde sensed more than indignation in Amalia's voice: there was hatred, visceral hatred, a furious rage that could erupt in any direction. He was glad she'd reproached them, because it was the most dignified excuse to turn his gaze from that hideous spectacle.

"Why did you do this?" he gasped, moving towards the passage.

"You asked me to. There you have her . . . Isn't that what you wanted? Wasn't what I told you enough? Didn't you want this spectacle? Go on, ask her a question, go on . . ."

Conde felt Manolo tap his shoulders, telling him to step aside so he could leave that bedroom stalked by death.

"Amalia, I think we have to talk," said the police captain as the Count tried to take deep breaths.

"What else is there to talk about?" asked the woman intent on sustaining her aggressive tone and the Count thought that was preferable, because hatred made her more vulnerable.

"Lots. Let's go to the reception room."

The retinue retraced its steps, now led by the Count. He wanted to distance himself as fast as he could from that Goyesque tableau of his own making and, as they walked back to the reception room, he told Manolo he wanted to return to the library.

"But what do you think you'll find?" Amalia's voice was still deep and piercing, and the Count felt it was another woman speaking. "When will you let me be? When will you let us die in peace?"

"When we know who killed your brother," replied Manolo. "Or don't you want us to find out?"

"I don't know how you'll ever find out by prying around that accursed library and watching my mother die. I really don't —"

"Well I do," replied the Count, more convinced than ever of what he'd suspected, as he turned to Captain Manuel Palacios: "Leave the conversation with her till later. Get an ambulance and someone to keep an eye on Amalia. Then help me in the library."

Manolo reluctantly obeyed the Count. He'd been honing his talents as an interrogator and only wanted to talk to Amalia. After ringing for medical help and police reinforcements, he criticized the other man's decision as soon as they were back inside the library.

"Don't you worry, if something turns up it will be so conclusive you won't have to work her over . . . You take the bookcase down there. Check between the books, look at them individually, for whatever we might come across . . ."

Conde climbed back on the wooden bench and resumed his interrupted search. He kept moving the volumes, inspecting the edges and, occasionally, shook them by the covers. When he'd finished the top shelf, he went on to the next, and moved items to the space he'd cleared on the one above. In no state to consider the quality of the books he was handling, he made good headway on the second shelf and noticed his hands were sweating, disgustingly. He tried to control his anxiety and told himself to be more meticulous, at the same time instructing Manolo:

"Look carefully. We're close," and went back to his task, convinced his lost hunch was back in the fold, confirming that whatever had sparked it was still hidden there.

"Close to what, Conde?"

"To whatever it is we're looking for. Something that rejected Amalia —"

"And you don't have any idea what?"

"Not the slightest."

"Could it be a letter?"

"Possibly," answered the Count, concentrating on his search.

"And does it have to be signed?"

"Manolo, how do I know . . . A letter . . . It's my hunch, fucking hell," he whispered, wincing at the pain shooting through his left nipple.

19 March

My dearest and only love:

Six days ago, numb with grief, I said I would not write to you again and I bid farewell to you, not knowing what I was doing. My God! The punishment I then received for that act of pride which led me to tell your daughter several years ago about her true origins, had confirmed me in my belief that, if someone really was to blame for the death of the woman you loved so much, then I was that person. And I was blameworthy because, thinking I was opening the doors to love, I exposed the hatred and ambition of an individual who was not to blame for who she was or for not possessing what she began to imagine, egged on by me, was her right in natural law. Because it was I, and only I, who put the motive for the crime in her hands, as she screamed at me a few days ago when I told her what I'd found out.

But yesterday, when I received the terrible news, the devastating knowledge that your death will also weigh eternally on my soul descended on me, like a mountain. Knowing you as I do, I can see that you sought out this finale and the reasons driving you were the love you still felt for that poor woman and your frustration at not being able to come back and mete out the punishments that would relieve you of that grief.

I have discovered, far too late, that you were a much weaker man than I ever imagined or wanted to imagine. The extent of your capacity to feel love and suffer because of a woman shocked me and showed me how even someone like you can be left defenceless (as I always was) by the spell of true passion. And perhaps that forcefulness your daughter inherited pushed her to the extreme of committing a crime to reclaim what had been snatched from her.

Now I don't know what will become of me. The hope I might recover you some day, which waned but never disappeared, has vanished, taking with it any possibility of ensuring you knew your suspicions about my direct guilt were unfounded. Together with my incurable sorrow at the knowledge that you died thinking I killed that woman, I must now add my sorrow from the knowledge that I was really to blame for everything that happened. As if I'd not been punished enough for my crazy actions, now imagine what I suffer when I see your daughter, our daughter, and recognize her as the one directly responsible for these misfortunes . . . It is too much, my heart cannot stand it, because I know she is the person I have most loved in the world, after you, and that I can never forgive her. From now on I shall always see her as a murderer who killed not only that woman but, forgive her, Lord, her own father!

Dear love: these horrific discoveries have made me see how fragile are the worlds that seem to have the firmest, almost indestructible foundations. Your life, mine, the family you created have collapsed, ravaged from within by an insatiable scourge, just as the health of this house is beginning to give, with paint dissolved by rain and gardens invaded by weeds.

The voices from hell echoing in my brain have become more aggressive and, I know, they will rob me of my reason. The demon who speaks to me and pursues me through the day, has finally revealed his true intent, for he pushed me towards the abyss into which I am now falling . . . Thus, before reaching the bottom which I will never leave, I decided to write to you, confident you will receive this last letter, wherever you are, where I don't dare ask for your forgiveness (I don't want that, I shall wallow in my guilt, anticipating the fires of hell), but where I must reiterate that my greatest sin was to love you too dearly and expect something in exchange for my love. I beg you to forgive your daughter: do not blame her for my sins.

I am sure God will take you into his bosom. A man able to love so much deserves for his sins to be forgiven. Goodbye, my love. I love you more, now and forever . . .

Your Nena

"After years of chewing on humiliation, as if it were our natural diet, when it finally seemed that luck or divine justice were lining up on our side to enable us to enjoy what was ours through natural law and the rights of fidelity, that woman appeared. She came from nowhere, ready to take everything and, when I realized what would happen, it was already happening, irrevocably. I couldn't resign myself and that was why I did what I had to do. I wasn't going to allow her or anyone to take away what belonged to us, what I'd been waiting for every day of my life, with incredible patience, in a corner of this accursed house, where I was born with Montes de Oca blood yet could never become a Montes de Oca . . . That's why, even today, despite everything that's happened, I don't feel an atom of remorse and I say this with my conscience intact, because I'm not mad. If I found myself in the same situation today, I would do it again.

"From the moment I acquired the use of my reason, my mother taught me the great truth in my life: I wasn't the daughter of an illiterate chauffeur, my surname wasn't Ferrero, and my life would one day be different, because I was the daughter of Mr Alcides Montes de Oca, grand-daughter of Dr Tomás Montes de Oca and great-granddaughter of General Serafin Montes de Oca, one of this country's heroes who left his home and fortune to fight in two wars of independence and came back with one eye, one useless arm and eighteen sword and bullet scars on his body. And coming from that stock I had a right to the privileges that one day, Mummy swore, I would enjoy. But meanwhile I had to stay silent, and my pride flourished in the shadows. That was a secret we two would share, but not my brother Dionisio. Although he was equally the offspring of Mr Alcides, he lacked my patience, and was rebellious, like our great-grandfather the general, and possessed a mind best not made privy to that secret.

"Thanks to my origins, I had my opportunities in life, although I couldn't enjoy all the luxuries and considerations that were my right. I studied in a good private school, had a rich girl's food and clothes and in 1956 enrolled at the university to study business. But in fact they were only crumbs and from a young age I was forced to introduce myself as having no father, an object of charity within my own family.

"Luckily, Virgilio Ferrero, the chauffeur, disappeared from our lives when I was around seven, and Mummy thought that was the best thing that could ever have happened to us. Dionisio missed him a lot: he loved him like a father, because he'd never known any other, and over time decided he was no good because he'd abandoned us, no doubt to go after another woman. I never discovered what happened to him, but in hindsight I'm sure it was something quite nasty, because Mummy once talked about him as an ungrateful so-and-so who had bitten the hand that fed him . . . and Mr Alcides wasn't a man to allow his dogs to bite him.

"When Mr Alcides's wife died in 1956, Mummy and I hugged each other for joy: it's difficult to imagine someone's death being so welcome, but for us it was as if the only obstacle stopping us from enjoying what was rightfully ours had gone. From that day on Mummy waited for what should happen to happen: after twenty years of clandestine love, Mr Alcides would marry his Nena, as he always called Mummy. In all that time, apart from being his lover, she had seen to every detail of Mr Alcides's business and political life, and was more than his right hand: she was his two hands and often his eyes and ears. Moreover, he'd always encouraged Mummy in her expectations, and he never stopped visiting her room, even after his marriage. Until that woman appeared.

"Initially Mummy flew into a rage, and then tried to persuade herself that it was the fleeting passion of an almost fifty-year old man for a young woman of my age, that is, someone who could easily be his daughter. Women at that time were, as you know, much more patient, and Mummy said if she'd waited in the shadows for so many years, she wasn't going to go crazy because of an affair without a future that would disappear as easily as it had come. In fact, Mummy suffered terribly, it was insulting, worse, humiliating, although she had no choice but to wait. She wasn't in a position to demand anything of Mr Alcides: Dionisio and I were legally the children of Virgilio Ferrero, and Mummy was only an employee of the household, albeit the most trusted. And in her heart of hearts she was afraid: she knew that man would do anything to get what he'd set his sights on and that it wasn't advisable to cross him, as Virgilio Ferrero once had . . .

"Around that time Mummy began to suffer from her nerves. She wasn't sleeping well, took pills, had stomach problems, although she'd always been so strong and healthy. She started to lose her high spirits. If she'd once been a woman waiting, confident in her future, she now become desperate, jealous, and envious, an aggrieved woman watching the man she'd always loved, her life long dream slipping through her fingers.

"And I imagined that woman, the singer, in seventh heaven now she'd hit the jackpot . . . I saw her for the first time in 1958. I told Mummy a story about a friend of mine who was going to hold her engagement party in a cabaret and I needed money so I could give her a present the day of her party. I agreed with my friend that I'd invite her and her fiancé to come with me to the Parisién. It was the first and last time I ever went to a place like that. I still remember it as if it was yesterday, the plush seats, the coloured lights, the elegant men and women, the casino with roulette wheels, tables with dice and playing cards, waiters dressed in black suits with shiny lapels, hair sleekly combed, looking like film stars . . . We watched the first show, with Roberto Faz's orchestra and some dancing-girls, then it was the cabaret orchestra and finally, at about one o'clock, or later, that woman finally emerged and sang. The Lady of the Night, they said . . .

"It was then I understood why Mr Alcides had fallen in love with her. Any man could have fallen in love with her just by looking at her, her angelic face, her body like a Greek sculpture in a glittering tight-fitting costume and, above all, hearing her voice that was so strong and direct it almost didn't need music to get into your ears and compel you to continue hearing her. So I hated her even more: because she was more beautiful than I would ever be, and because people worshipped her. That night I realized that unless something big intervened, Mummy and I would never have our opportunity, because that woman was invincible . . .

"For the sake of appearances and above all to avoid falling out with his in-laws, who were filthy rich, he kept his love affair secret, but forced Mummy to be at the beck and call of that woman, as if she were already Mrs Montes de Oca. She lived in a flat in Miramar, bought by Mr Alcides, and Mummy had to go at least once a week, to ensure she had everything she needed and sign a few cheques to cover what she spent on clothes, perfumes, or whatever she fancied. That duty was more of a humiliation than a punishment, but Mr Alcides was so love-stricken he was unable to understand the pain he was inflicting on the person who loved him most.

264

"Mummy waited, prayed for something to happen, and something did, but that only complicated matters: the rebels won the war, Batista fled and the Revolution triumphed. Initially we both welcomed that victory as a blessing, because we'd lived for several years in a state of constant anxiety over Dionisio's well-being: when he was a youngster he'd joined the opposition to the dictatorship when he'd enrolled at the university, and the clandestine struggle here in Havana, which was bloodier and more dangerous than the war in the mountains. I remember how Mummy and I lived everyday in fear of receiving news that Dionisio had been found tortured and murdered on a street corner. When the Palace was attacked in 1957, we almost went crazy because Dionisio didn't show up for three days and we thought he must be one of the dead who were being talked about in the street but about whom the newspapers said nothing. But he was safe now and that made us happy, as did the knowledge that the horror of those years was past. Even Mr Alcides celebrated the rebels' victory but in particular the fall of the tyrant who'd done everything possible to ruin him, by refusing to allow him to participate in the lucrative business deals the government handed to its acolytes. In fact, Mr Alcides had power that escaped Batista's designs, because he did business with a group of men who had as much, if not more sway over important matters than Batista, because they supported him economically, sometimes more than the Americans.

"I remember seeing Meyer Lansky twice in this house. He was ugly and never laughed. Mummy told me Lansky and Mr Alcides were working on a big hotel and casino project, one that would make them multimillionaires in a few years . . . Their big problem was that they needed Batista in power in order to be the main stakeholders of the business venture, but politically clumsy Batista was about to throw everything overboard; it became clearer by the day that he would lose the war because no one wanted to fight for him. Then they started to plan how to get rid of him, before the rebels beat them to it. Their problem was that there was only one way: they would have to kill the tyrant. I don't know the details, nor did Mummy, and, if she did, she refused to tell me, but other influential men were involved in the intrigue apart from Lansky and Mr Alcides. The idea was to contract a professional, a man who'd come from outside to do the deed. He had to be a contract-killer who wouldn't ask questions and wasn't linked to any mafia families, because the immediate reaction of Batista's supporters was predictable – they were complete animals – and Mr Alcides, Lansky and their other partners couldn't appear to be responsible, at least not initially.

"A mistaken calculation undermined their plan: the Americans didn't give Batista the support he asked for, the English wouldn't sell him more planes and the army, with no desire to fight for a dictator, crumbled, so the war finished long before anyone thought it would. Mr Alcides was delighted, because he thought anything was preferable to living under Batista, but on this occasion the wiliest of the Montes de Ocas got it wrong. The first thing the revolutionary government clamped down on was the gambling and the prostitution industry, and Lansky and Mr Alcides's project ran out of steam in a few weeks.

"Lansky immediately understood that his moment had passed, and one fine day cleared off and never came back. Mr Alcides couldn't stand the idea of leaving: this was the country of the Montes de Ocas, and he clung to the hope that things could be saved legally. Everybody knew that tourism was the only feasible option for this country, and that without trade with American companies the island would grind to a halt; he hoped that when the storm was over everything would function as before. After all, any government needs money, and the investments they anticipated making were the best source of finance. Consequently, he waited the whole of 1959 without deciding to leave Cuba, although, anticipating what might happen, he started recovering money and putting it in American banks outside the country.

"Apart from our peace of mind now we knew Dionisio was safe and in the front line of the Revolution, the changes were a beacon of hope: Mummy thought Mr Alcides would have to re-think his life and that an individual like that woman would no longer suit his horizons. Yet again Mummy misjudged the pull of that relationship . . . The months passed, there was a tense atmosphere in the house, as if the war was still on, and when Mr Alcides realized it was more serious than he'd predicted, and there was talk of nationalizing US

266

companies, he decided to cut his losses, began to close down his surviving businesses and prepare to leave before it was too late. He also took a decision that killed all our hopes and meant those long, silent, waiting years had been in vain: he would marry that woman and take her with him, although if we wished, he said, right in front of me, sitting in this room, if we girls wanted – because he'd already discounted Dionisio – we could follow him. And although he didn't say so, it was clear that if we went in these circumstances Mummy would continue to be his secretary and I'd still be the chauffeur's daughter, living on a blend of charity and tradition in the shadow of the Montes de Ocas, although we no longer lived in their country.

"It was the most humiliating experience of my life, far worse than not being able to use my surname and it dashed all of Mummy's hopes. That was why she asked Mr Alcides for time to think it over on the pretext she didn't like the idea of leaving Dionisio behind. She couldn't bring herself to tell him the truth to his face . . . For her part, delighted to have finally landed a rich man all set on marrying her, that woman gave up singing and started to prepare for her departure from Cuba.

"All this happened at the beginning of 1960. I'd decided I wasn't going anywhere on those terms and was ready to take advantage of opportunities life was offering me irrespective of whether I was or wasn't a Montes de Oca. So I started to work in a bank, and festively enjoyed the entire process of nationalization, agrarian and urban reform, and particularly the currency change that ruined so many rich people and compelled many of them to leave Cuba. My hatred, frustration and side-lining turned to fervour and I felt my strength grow as I turned into an executioner of all the Montes de Ocas and those like them: men able to dictate people's lives, fortunes and even their names.

"Mummy was visibly languishing and seeing her like that was the most painful thing that could happen to me, more painful than the loss of all my past dreams. Nonetheless, I still expected her to react in some way: these were her rights, her life, her years of loyalty and sacrifice, and it was her love affair . . . But although she'd been so strong and ready for anything, she was incapable of forcing a solution, and that was when I decided to help.

267

"One day, when the Montes de Ocas and that woman had got everything ready for their departure, I decided to strike where it would hurt them most. As Mummy carried a key to the flat in Miramar, I made a copy. From then on I sought my opportunity and one afternoon when Mr Alcides must have taken that woman to see to some arrangements or other, I took myself to Miramar and entered her flat. My first surprise was to see how well she lived: compared to this house, it was a modest flat, but it was luxuriously furnished. It was a real blow below the belt when I went into the bedroom and found a stylish king-size double bed, where she and Mr Alcides no doubt wallowed, watching themselves fornicate like animals in a mirror they'd had hung from the ceiling. She had exquisite pieces in various jewel boxes that must have been worth a fortune. And the clothes: wardrobes full of expensive clothes, shoes of all the best makes, fur coats she'd never be able to wear in Cuba . . . She'd bought all that with money that belonged to Mummy, Dionisio and myself, and I'd never worn clothes like those and had only one adornment: a small gold chain and ring, a present from Mr Alcides on my fifteenth birthday.

"I'd decided that poison would be my means to get rid of that woman. We'd had a plague of rats in the patio and garden two months before. As my job was to see to some of the most unpleasant tasks in the house, I'd had to ring the vet and be with him when he prepared the extermination and get whatever he needed. Chatting to him I discovered he was going to prepare a few food pellets where he'd hide some cyanide pills. The vet used rubber gloves to handle the poison and covered his nose with a handkerchief. I didn't even have to ask: he began telling me about the characteristics of cyanide and how it worked in animal organisms and even told me the lethal dose for a human being was two of those 150 ml pills . . . As if something was already buzzing in my subconscious, when I brought the flour where he told me to mix in the pills he'd ground down, I stole two pills and put them in a safe place.

"Everything went in my favour that day and I didn't have to wrack my brains about how to get her to swallow the cyanide. She was already clearly taking various medicines, because there was a tube of antibiotics and a bottle of cough syrup on the kitchen table. Moreover, that guaranteed I didn't run the risk of putting the poison in a liquid Mr Alcides might drink.

"Then I went to the living room and took the record I'd seen when I arrived out of its sleeve. It was the one Mr Alcides had paid to record. I put it on the turntable and switched it on. When I heard her voice, I felt my legs shake. She was singing a song called *Be gone from me*, and I suddenly felt she was addressing me. So, without more ado, I took the precautions I'd learned from the vet, ground down the pills and dissolved them in the syrup. Then I cleaned up and left.

"The next day, the maid who cleaned that woman's flat rang Mummy to tell her the news: she'd been found her dead on the bathroom floor. The idea it was a suicide seemed the most logical, because there were no signs of violence or theft. However, although he didn't find any real leads, the policeman in charge of the investigation, was very suspicious and almost came down on the side of murder, despite the lack of evidence and suspects that closed off all the paths to the truth he sensed was there. The fingerprints found in the flat belonged to people who were the regular visitors and he couldn't be sure any of them had anything to do with that woman's death.

"A few days after the funeral, Mr Alcides rushed through the red tape needed in order to leave Cuba, although his attitude to Mummy didn't change. Rather it got worse. He was convinced that woman had not committed suicide and perhaps suspected my mother was to blame for her death. I'm certain he thought it such an unlikely thing for her to do and he didn't dare to mention it, but he didn't ask Mummy again if we'd leave with him, at the point when he most needed her . . . So the day of his departure came and I realized I'd made the most awful mistake: Mr Alcides was still in love with the dead woman and would never re-establish his old relationship with Mummy. Anyway, he asked her to stay in the house, saying he'd be back in a few months, a year at most, because the tension emerging between Cuba and the United States would be resolved one way or the other and almost everyone thought he knew which. It was then he told Mummy to look after his things, particularly the Sèvres vases and his library. Mummy pledged that when he returned, the porcelain and books would be in their proper place. As would she.

"My mother's dog-like behaviour made me completely lose my self-control. I had cleared the path for her and she put up no fight, not for herself, not for me. I decided to play my last card: if Mummy had no way out, perhaps I did. I wrote a letter to Mr Alcides where I told him everything my mother had confessed to me about their relationship, her suspicions about Virgilio Ferrero's disappearance, and told him that Mummy had confessed to me she'd prepared the cough syrup with the two cyanide pills in order to get rid of that woman. And I assured him that I'd tried to stop her, since for me his happiness was as valuable as my own, after all he was my father and I'd always loved him as such. Then I put the letter among the clothes Mr Alcides had packed in his suitcase and waited for my reward.

"Mr Alcides left and it was the last we heard of him: not a single letter or call. That silence filled my mother with despair and she became more and more distressed. She wasn't the same woman and shut herself away for days on end without talking to me, sometimes refused to eat, heard voices in the night and even started writing letters to Mr Alcides. They were long letters she sometimes wrote over several days and put in airmail envelopes, before starting another, not imagining that with every explanation she sank deeper into the swamp where I'd pushed her. She rarely left home, but as I was out almost all day working in the bank, I supposed she'd found someone to post her letters, perhaps the postman, because she used to wait for him every morning, hoping to get correspondence from Mr Alcides.

"That lasted several months. And I waited patiently, thinking my letter must have fulfilled its function because Mummy never received a reply. I felt she was increasingly tense and obsessed by that woman's death and Mr Alcides's forgiveness . . . until everything collapsed. The news of Mr Alcides's death in a traffic accident, drunk and driving along a road in the Keys in southern Florida, was the coup de grâce. The first sign something strange had happened was the fact Mr Alcides was drunk, because he never drank more than a couple of glasses of wine with a meal or a beer at a party. The other was the fact he was driving, when we all knew he didn't like to, which was why he always employed a chauffeur. What was he doing by himself, drunk and driving on a road in the Keys? It all pointed to premeditated death, to suicide, and Mummy realized that straight away, and, subsequently, two or three days after receiving the news, she told me she knew about that woman's death and accused me of being to blame for all her misfortunes . . .

"One night, about a week later, Dionisio rang me at the bank. He'd gone by chance to see Mummy and had found her dying in her bedroom. She'd cut her veins. Clotting prevented her from losing all her blood, but she'd lost a lot and her life was in danger. When I reached the hospital the doctors assured me she'd survive, but that she was suffering from severe shock. At the time I wanted her to die, for her suffering to be over and done with and, above all, for her never to look at me so reproachfully again. Mummy did recover, although she seemed to be in a state of lethargy . . . and she never spoke again. It's incredible, she remained silent for three or four years after that, until she completely lost her reason and started to live her previous life again, saying things that made no sense, talking about her correspondence with Mr Alcides, the children's schooling, the illness of her master's deceased wife, about cleaning the books so he wasn't thrown into a bad mood when he went to work in the library . . .

"That's the whole story. My story . . . Those letters Mummy wrote can never have reached their destination, which is what she wanted. But poor Dionisio ruined everything. Overwrought by the money we were earning through the sale of books, he invited home an old army colleague of his, who'd also been demobbed, because his friend, or so he said, knew a lot about books and had had dealings with a few foreigners. Dionisio wanted to show him the books this gentleman said were the most valuable, to ask his friend if he'd any idea who might be interested in them. He invented the story of the tall black dealer looking for books afterwards, to force you to hike up your offer and have an excuse if his friend found a buyer. He messed everything up when he decided to check through the whole library, looking for items you'd not touched and which seemed valuable, and that's when he found four of those damned letters. He read them, especially what must have been the last one, and then he came to my room, accused me of murder and causing Mummy's madness because I was a selfish megalomaniac because I thought I was a Montes de Oca. I told him it was a pack of lies, asked where'd he got all that from, and he showed me the

271

letters. 'Read them, for Christ's sake,' he said, throwing them in my face. When I read them, I felt the whole world I'd tried to shore up through oblivion and self- sacrifice, looking after Mummy for forty years, not marrying, not having children, not living my own life, was falling apart as a result of letters written by a woman on the verge of madness, who blamed herself for what happened because she'd incorporated me into her story of frustration, never imagining, poor thing, that I was the one who sealed her fate and pushed Mr Alcides over the precipice.

"Killing my brother was easy. I couldn't spend the rest of my life looking at those accusations in Dionisio's eyes and living with the threat he'd tell the police everything. Mummy's death is a matter of days, of hours even, but Dionisio's might have been a long time coming, his threat to inform on me might have been a spur of the moment thing, but it was also a real possibility. He was capable of doing such a thing and, worst of all, I wasn't strong enough to resist his hatred or the fear I might be accused and sentenced because I'd done my duty, first to save my mother, then to save myself and possess what was mine . . . I decided there and then and killed him with his own knife, then I looked around the bookcase, found five more letters and destroyed the lot. I buried the knife in the patio, rang the police and sat down to wait for Mummy's death and prepare my own.

"I'd never thought Mummy would have written a letter to Mr Alcides after he died . . . When I searched hard, I took five more letters out of the books, all written between the day Mr Alcides departed and the one Mummy wrote and sealed two days before he died. Who'd ever imagine she'd write a letter to a dead man and hide it on another bookshelf? The wretched, crazy, sad old . . .

"Now you can do whatever you want with me, it makes no odds. I suppose you are going to have me shot, aren't you?"

What will happen to you now? Where the fuck will you end up? Mario Conde caressed the book, sorrowfully contemplated the highly desirable remains of the library and felt his poverty weigh heavily on his heart, as he'd rarely felt it before. When he was a kid, with his first friends in the barrio – almost all now defeated by life, exile and, recently, even by death – Conde would sit under the tamarind trees in Grandfather Rufino's cockpit and play at being rich and buying the most coveted items: a pellet gun, a baseball glove, or a Niagara bike for the biggest dreamers. But the scant realities from which they could choose and lack of possibility they would ever own any of the riches they imagined finally gave them a frugal sense of their needs and pleasures, that, with time, some transformed into a kind of existential asceticism, while others tried to find a solution by crossing the water in search of the world of abundance they longed for. Conde would never forget saying goodbye to his close friend, Miguelito el Ñato, at the age of fourteen. The night before his departure for Miami, after getting the two old baseballs that were his due in his friend's distribution of goodies, they remembered the fantastic evening when Miguelito had found the perfect investment for his imaginary millions: "If I had money, lots of money," the boy'd said, "I'd buy myself a magic wand." Standing in the centre of that library he'd like to take with him, Mario Conde wondered if the best solution for his bookish greed might not have been to possess Miguelito el Ñato's magic wand: an ordinary bit of wood extracted from some Scottish woods, but endowed with the power to shift to his house, with a little flick of the wrist, each and every one of those books, with their burden of wisdom and beauty, the summation of two hundred years of literature and thought from that lopsided country where he'd been lucky to be born and had obstinately stayed on, against all the odds.

As the aftertaste of frustration settled in his mouth, Conde tried to recall the precise order in terms of a quest for perpetuity that had existed there for forty-three years, but it wouldn't gel in his mind. The disturbed shelves, the mountains of books classified according to their commercial value, the noteworthy absence of items they'd taken off to the market and the recent disarray provoked by his insistent hunch, had disrupted a structure that had seemed perfect when, in fact, its entrails hid painful secrets, ready to trigger greater upheavals than those the eye could easily encompass. Conde wondered if anything else extraordinary remained to be discovered in that sanctuary. To be quite sure he consulted his hunch thermometer and got a negative reading: no, there were only extraordinary, irreplaceable, disturbing books, beautiful books that were worth a fortune and books that enriched you when you read them, many books he wanted to take with him . . . but only books, no more mysteries or revelations.

He walked past the shelves and touched several of the volumes he would most like to possess, but soon abandoned an inventory that threatened to become endless. A magic wand. That was the solution. For everyone . . . Poor Amalia, poor Nemesia Moré, poor Catalina Basterrechea, poor Dionisio Ferrero, poor Alcides Montes de Oca, poor Juan the African, poor Silvano Quintero: dead, mad or mutilated. With the same magic wand Mario Conde would perhaps repair the tragic destiny they'd all been drawn into, removing them at a stroke from that story and giving them another life. But his assets as a bookseller didn't stretch to the purchase of that instrument of salvation and he had to accept the idea that, despite Rafael Giró's theories, the fact is that life can seem too much like a bolero and the only elegant way out is to give its joys and sorrows to a voice that can release it from its intrinsic burden of misfortune: a voice as warm as Violeta del Río's.

"Who's going to cut the cane now, man? Who the fuck's going to make a pile from those books? Go on, tell me . . ."

Conde blew twice before sipping his coffee. He liked drinking it like that, when it had just percolated, but lowering its temperature until it felt warm on his palate and ready to yield up its deep bitterness.

"It's really a pity. Amalia has no heirs. Dionisio's children left Cuba ten years ago, with all the raft-people . . . I expect the books will be confiscated and taken to the National Library."

"Every single fucking one?" Yoyi Pigeon's incredulity was like a kite taking off and trying to break free from its cord.

"Every single one," the Count acknowledged, almost smiling, his cigarette smoking on his lips, as he qualified his statement. "If only."

Skinny Carlos looked at him from his wheelchair.

"I think you're pleased really, if I'm not mistaken, you savage. Those books were driving you crazy, weren't they?"

274

"The books and lots more besides. I suddenly discovered I like the feeling I've got lots of money; Violeta del Río's ghost got inside my body and, when I was beaten up, I talked to Salinger. Then, when I was investigating other things, I discovered my father was a man who could get drunk and weep when he fell in love, but above all that he was a coward . . . and last of all I tried to turn into a magician and magic those books away. The sooner they take them wherever, the better . . ."

"You're mad, you're all mad," protested Yoyi. "Abnormal, I swear, incurably abnormal."

"And what'll happen to her?" Candito wiped the sweat from his brow. "May God forgive her . . ."

"I'm not sure . . . They took her mother to hospital. She was completely dehydrated and apparently there's no hope. Amalia had her tied up for five days and didn't give her food or water . . ."

"She's what you call hard," said Carlos. "One day without food and I'd fade away."

"But that woman's mad, isn't she?" Rabbit asked, leaning towards the Count.

"I think she is, and that's the problem," said the Count: "She has to be mad, but she doesn't look as if she is. She doesn't talk like a madwoman and does things fully aware of the consequences. She killed her brother without giving it too much thought and now wanted to kill her mother and kill herself. No, she can't be right in the head."

"A bloody bastard is what she is," Yoyi fulminated. "And those poor books . . ."

Conde shook his head, accepting it was his business partner who was the really incurable one, and tried to fill his lungs with the peace from that afternoon. The confession made by Amalia Ferrero, or Montes de Oca, as she'd have preferred always to be known, had swept him like a tidal wave to the boundaries of depression and that's why he preferred not to bind his state of mind to alcohol. Despite his efforts, he couldn't throw off the feeling of guilt that had been tormenting him from that morning, when he took responsibility for taking the lid off that regrettable story through his own presence. Drained by his own sorrow and the sorrow of others, he realized his recent experience was a macabre warning about his inability to patch up other people's lives and, in particular, his own.

"What did Manolo say when he saw your hunch was spot on and you put the solution in his hand?" Carlos felt pleased he'd asked the question and that his wording paid tribute to his friend's wit.

"He apologized again. He didn't have much choice. Although this time I wish I'd got it wrong, you know?"

"You wished what?" Yoyi smiled. "Hey, Conde, if it hadn't been for Amalia, that stiff would still be haunting you and me . . ."

"I don't mean that. I'd rather Amalia hadn't done any of this. She's been an unhappy wretch her whole life."

"Yes, that's the bloody conundrum in this story," Rabbit anxiously declared. "Who's the bad guy? Alcides because he fell in love? Violeta because she got in the way of Amalia and her mother quite unawares? The Ferreros' mother because she told her daughter who her father was? Amalia because she thought she had a right to be a Montes de Oca and wanted to rescue her mother's love or wanted to have what was hers? Dionisio because he always took a hard line with everything he felt to be improper and decided to inspect the books?. . ."

"You're right," agreed Carlos. "A story with no bad guys is tricky shit."

"I'm the bad guy," Yoyi then said, "well, not the bad guy, the asshole, because after that first time we visited the house together, Dionisio rang me at home . . ."

"He rang you?" the Count felt his curiosity rising to the bait.

"Yes," went on Pigeon, "after I gave him my number, he rang me to suggest the sale of the books you didn't want to buy . . . That's why he had the bit of paper with my telephone number in his pocket."

"So what happened?"

"I told him we'd have to wait, because I couldn't do anything behind your back in that library . . . That I'd try to persuade you, but that you were a champion asshole, and if you said no, then no it was."

"You did that?" Conde looked at him unable to hide his astonishment.

"I swear I did. I mean, I swear I did."

"You're a bit loopy too, Yoyi, don't you reckon?"

"The ways of the Lord are unfathomable," decreed Candito.

"Forget your bloody Lord, Candito . . . I'm catching it from you. Abnormal is what I am. Do you know how many thousands I could have made from just one item? And now they'll impound those books and you'll see: less than half will make it to the library."

"Do you reckon?" Rabbit shifted uncomfortably. His love of books, especially history books, could also reach irrational levels.

"Some always vanish en route," agreed the Count. "It's happened with other libraries . . ."

"That's not right. No, siree," declared Candito. "Look, if I weren't a Christian and bothered about sinning and, if I were you," he pointed at Conde and Yoyi, "I expect I'd get into that house and help myself to at least a couple of sacks of books. After all, you were going to buy them."

Yoyi's eyes drilled the Count's. The young man's mind must have been turning at supersonic speed, juggling with figures and considering final tallies.

"Don't start fantasizing, Yoyi," the Count warned.

"Hey, Conde, I think Red's right," interjected Carlos. "For a would-be saint the bastard still gets ideas . . ."

"And Manolo owes you one," Rabbit opined. "And one favour repays another . . . I'd do that if I were you and, while I was at it, I'd suggest looking out a few books for your friends, that is . . . for us."

"Don't fantasize, I said, for hell's sake. You won't persuade me," the Count asserted as he stood up and turned his back on his friends. He walked to the back of the patio, lit another cigarette and kicked a dead bottle of rum.

Yoyi was about to speak to him, to giving him more grief, but Carlos signalled to leave the Count to him, and smiled.

"Leave the savage alone, gentlemen," he shouted. "After all, what's in few poncy books —"

"Not one poncy book, Skinny," the Count protested, half turning round, "It's the best library I've ever seen or will ever see in my whole friggin' life."

"Come on, Conde, it's not so bad," Carlos continued, smiling at the others. His machinery of persuasion, oiled by the frequent use he put it to persuading the Count, was revving up.

He opened the book with the same relish he might have separated the legs of a woman vanquished by love, ready to meet ecstasy as he appropriated her secret perfumes and deepest shades of colour. He closed his eyes and breathed in: slightly darkened over the years, the paper oozed the breath of proud old age. Intoxicated by the aroma, he glanced at prints still displaying their original tints, and enjoyed the images of a powerful sugar mill at the height of the campaign and seemingly paradisiacal canebrakes that, like any duly manipulated and invented reality, concealed the daily inferno of men who were considered to be less than men, transported from afar to leave their sweat, blood and lives among the accursed sugar cane that contributed to increasing the wealth and national lack of proportion about which Rabbit had spoken. Perhaps, a hundred and fifty years ago, a man called Serafin Montes de Oca might have thought something similar when he felt that volume in his hands and, after enjoying its engravings and caressing its leather covers, he'd shut the book, ready to join in a war intent on changing the reality engraved within its pages.

Conde carefully placed the coveted copy that drove hunters after bibliographical jewels crazy on one of the shelves of his own bookcase, gently slotting it between the worn jacket of stories by his friend J.D. Salinger and the rough cover of the volumes of the Heredia's poetry he'd placed there a few minutes earlier, and felt envy rushing back. Would he ever act that way with a book he'd written himself, where he'd tell some of those would-be squalid and moving stories he'd begun and abandoned, buried and exhumed, that he'd wanted to write for years? How could he demand J.D. continue writing if he didn't dare to throw himself into an adventure he endlessly put off? What would happen to his past and memories if he didn't get them into black and white and save them from oblivion?

He moved away from his bookshelf as if in flight from an accusing lawyer and went into the kitchen to put the coffee on. He opened the patio door to the night and met the happy figure of Rubbish, wagging his tail, his eyes sparkling.

"What's up, mutty?" he hailed him and welcomed the animal's paws, desperate to be stroked, up on his own legs. "Hungry are we? There's still a bit left. But be warned," the Count opened his fridge and took out the last portion of leftovers set aside for the dog, "don't get used to this: any minute now we'll be poor again, so keep some energy back for what's in store, who knows how long this will last . . ."

Conde walked on as Rubbish jumped and barked, placed his food on the metal tray and stopped to watch him eat.

The smell of coffee lured him back to the kitchen. He put sugar in the jug and stirred the infusion before pouring it in the over-sized cup his body was demanding. He sat at his table and looked through the window at the clear, starry sky, the epilogue to summer. That dark, infinitely extending void was perhaps saying something in terms of his own life, although Conde didn't want to know what. His quota of physical and spiritual aches and pains had overflowed after the crazy experiences he'd recently gone through and he needed the soothing balm of oblivion. But his gaze betrayed him, and his eyes returned, as if drawn by a magnet, to the sky's impassive void set on enveloping him. He took two drags on his cigarette and crushed the butt.

"Have I no choice but to think? To stir up the shit in my head?" he asked the darkness as he stood up. "Well, let's do it in style: no gloves and bare knuckles . . ."

He walked into his living room and opened Carlos's old record player. There, on the turntable was Violeta del Río's single which he'd refused to listen to for several days, and he switched it on. The record began to turn slowly and Conde lifted the arm and placed it on the musical plaque. He switched off all the lights and flopped on the sofa, as his father had done more than forty years ago.

The entry of the piano knocked him backwards, but he tried to stay firm, ready for the blow he received on chest from Violeta del Río's live voice, and shuddered.

> You, who fill everything with joy and youth
> and see ghosts in the night's half light
> and hear the perfumed song of the blue.
> Be gone from me . . .

Mario Conde realized that categorical order had always been directed at him, had always been waiting for him. Perhaps his father had anticipated something like that – is a propensity to hunches hereditary? – and, assuming all the anguish that record aroused, had kept a copy for his son, knowing the moment would come when he too would have to listen to it and feel the emotions stirred by that woman's voice. What was beyond doubt, nevertheless, was that Catalina Basterrechea, young Lina Beautiful Eyes, had been telling the Count insistently to go away and let the dead and defeated sleep peacefully behind the mists of yesterday. But he'd insisted on finding out and had finally dug out the putrid mud, which hid only more and more putrefaction. That voice had been partly to blame, he tried to defend himself: that voice had pushed him on mercilessly, as if while demanding to be remote, it was also quietly asking not to be totally and irreversibly lost in oblivion. The voice was the most powerful testament to Violeta del Río, the girl who'd been on the verge of triumphing over the fate written on her forehead but who had committed the most terrible sin of infidelity when she'd dared sacrifice what she'd always wanted to be and do in life, to enjoy a possible happiness that perhaps had never been her right. Maybe it was self-betrayal that led to her death: if she'd refused to sacrifice her greatest pleasure and continued singing, time after time, those songs of frustrated loves, would she have given death the slip? Nobody could tell now, or ever hope to know, but the possibility that you could override the designs of fortune always alarmed the Count: he was certain that only fidelity to herself could have preserved Violeta del Río, only singing and more singing could have saved her from the hatred that ravaged so many lives.

When the song finished he turned the record over, ready to complete his descent, and now had no doubts: those two songs had been recorded for him.

You'll remember me
when the sun dies in the afternoon . . .

A knocking on the door interrupted his dialogue with death and destiny. He felt life was calling out to him, opened the door and met Tamara's smile.

"How long are you going to go on listening to that woman," she asked, and he was shaken by the way she described Violeta del Río: forty years dead, "that woman" still provoked resentment.

280

"That's it, finished," he said as he let her in, and went to switch off the record player. The turntable turned, expended its last burst of energy and stopped. Finally obeying an order he'd heeded too late, he broke the small record into two, four, then eight pieces and threw them into the record player, lowered the lid and shut the catches.

"Why did you do that?" asked Tamara, astonished.

"I should have done it before. But you know how slow I am, at almost anything."

'Well, that's not always a defect.'

"You're right. Come here, I've made coffee." They sat on the chairs and looked at each other over the table.

"So what brings you here?"

"Carlos rang. He said you were depressed and doing things he'd never imagined you'd get up to. And it's true. I've just seen one."

"I did nothing terrible. I broke an old record and buried a few dead . . . All I did before that was steal seven books – one for everyone in the gang."

"You're crazy, Mario. If they catch you . . ."

"I don't know if José Martí ever said it, but he should have: stealing books is not stealing. It was a present to myself . . ."

"So, you self-presented books to Yoyi, Candito, Rabbit, Carlos and self-presented one to yourself . . . That leaves two."

"One for Andrés: as he's a long way away, we chose the *Picturesque Album of the Island of Cuba*, with illustrations by Bernardo May. A copy was sold at auction a year ago for twelve thousand dollars. If he wants he can sell it, although I know he won't ever dream of such a thing . . . And the other is for you."

Conde put the smoking cigarette on the ashtray and went to the bookcase, and extracted two dark volumes of Heredia's poems, copies that, perhaps on some distant day, the poor poet in exile had himself held in his hands.

"This is yours," he said.

"I'm honoured! What is it?"

"Listen and tell me what you think," and he opened one volume at random, imagining any page would be compelling, and read, happy his eyes had settled on that verse:

But, what does my eager gaze seek in you
in a vain effort? Why don't I look?
around your huge cavern
at the palms ay! the wondrous palms,
that on the plains of my ardent country
spring from the sun to a smile, and grow
and sway to the breath from the ocean breezes,
under the purest sky?. . .

"Heredia. 'Niágara'," she said, her voice choked with emotion.

"The 1832 Toluca edition. The most valuable, the one Heredia set with his wife's help, the best . . . For you."

"You're crazy . . ." she started to protest, but when she looked into his eyes she realized it would be criminal to resist such an act of love. "Thank you," she said, taking the books and standing up to kiss him on the lips.

"I wasn't expecting so much in return," he said, stroking her hair, and looking into her eyes. "Don't ever leave me, I beg you."

And Mario Conde felt he was casting off his moorings and the energy keeping him on his feet was draining away. He thought: hell, I'm going to cry. He realized he was crying when Tamara caressed his face and he felt the slippery moisture a woman's fingers, his woman's, were sliding over.

"I'm here," she said. "And always will be. That's my prize and punishment . . ."

Grateful she was there and existed, he looked from her to the window, and saw a round moon break through the darkness and light up a sky that glowed, where Violeta del Río sang to God an impossible bolero with a happy ending. Forever and ever.

Mantilla
Summer 2003 – Autumn 2004

A Comment and Thanks

Havana Fever is a story that ambushed, shoved and pushed me into writing it. I hadn't planned to return to the character of Mario Conde so quickly, but the months I spent working hard to transform him into the protagonist of four possible films – that some day will be shot, God and finance willing – forced me to rescue him and write this novel, the central theme of which – the search for a forgotten singer of boleros from the fifties – had been buzzing in my head for some time. And as I know no one so stubborn or fit to embark on such a hunt, I decided to give the story over to the Count, that great lover of ghosts from the past.

In creating this book, as always, I've had to call on the knowledge and experience of several individuals. I would like to express my gratitude to Daniel Flores the book-seller for his indispensable help: he introduced me to the mysteries and tricks of his trade, guided me on the issue of the pricing of the rarest and most valuable books in Cuba's bibliography and even prepared an "ideal" library for me, with the books that in his informed opinion had to be there. I was also helped in my research by the kind Naty Revueltas who even lent me some treasures from her own library; my essential friend, Marta Armenteros, from the National Library; the efficient and rigorous Olga Vega, head of the Section of Rare and Valuable Books at the José Martí National Library who after many requests allowed me to view and caress the most precious jewels in the treasure under her stewardship; and Dr Carlos Suárez, who introduced me to the world of narcotics and poisons, and their uses and effects.

As always, the advice of my most loyal, self-sacrificing readers was decisive, as they struggled with different versions of the manuscript, above all the absolutely key Vivian Lechuga and kind Álex Fleites, Elena Zayas, Dalia Acosta, Helena Núñez, José María Rodríguez Coso and Lourdes Gómez. My particular gratitude, as always, to Beatriz de Moura, for her confidence and insightful reading. And

285

my apologies, because she had to put up with readings, depressions and doubts, to my loving wife (although I much prefer to say: to my loving woman) Lucía López Coll, my first reader, for whom I always write, with love and squalor.